PHANTOM TRACES

CLAIRE GEM

SOUL MATE PUBLISHING

New York

PHANTOM TRACES

CLAIRE GEM

Cover Design by Fiona Jayde

Published in the United States of America by
Soul Mate Publishing
P.O. Box 24
Macedon, New York, 14502

ISBN: 978-1-61935-975-8

ebook ISBN: 978-1-61935-712-9

www.SoulMatePublishing.com

I dedicate this book to

my beloved husband,

since unless he'd shown me

what happily ever after means,

I could never have written a true love story.

Acknowledgements

My deepest thanks to all my ROM-CRIT critique group allies who helped make this manuscript the best it could be–before the wonderful editors at SMP took over and made it perfect.

Chapter 1

Abigail Stryker heard all the rumors about the pipe-smoking, book-hurling ghost who chased off Harvey Library's last two librarians. She took the job anyway.

The first, Liz Carter, resigned down at city hall sporting a golf ball-sized lump on the side of her head. She suffered a whack from *War and Peace*, the unabridged copy. A few weeks later her successor, Norma Porter, abandoned her post on a chilly spring evening. A group of students from the community college were on their way in to work on term papers when they heard a scream. The door burst open, and Norma raced past them—almost through them—jowls and flaccid arms flapping as if the place was on fire.

Abby walked the block and a half from her apartment just before nine a.m. on her first morning as the Harvey's new head librarian. No one else was stirring in Caldwell, North Carolina. A beautiful April morning, the square was still hushed, sleepy under the hazy chill that habitually settled over the Blue Ridge foothills.

So this is small town life. Huh. A bit of a change from the busy college town where I grew up.

After what happened, she wasn't ready to be completely on her own, though she hated to admit it. Her Aunt Dianne just happened to have an empty efficiency over her shop on Main Street. Just up the street from the library.

Perfect.

So, Abby might have to deal with a restless spirit. He couldn't possibly be as unsettled as she was, so it really didn't matter. She needed a new start, and the Harvey Library seemed the perfect choice. Away from Boone, away from the memories, away from her parents and their "helpful" connections.

She suspected this ghost was nothing more than the fabrication of a town mourning Dana Laramy's retirement. After running the place for almost thirty years, she'd become as permanent a fixture as the old school bell mounted in the lobby. There were no reports of any abnormal activity until the day she left. After that, talk surfaced about closing the Harvey Library permanently.

Abby crossed the empty street at the corner near Murphy's diner and covered the remaining half-block with a bounce in her step. Okay, so she was a little nervous, but she decided to channel it into something more positive—excitement. After all, this was her new beginning.

The town's county commissioner, Dennis Ludwig, waited for her, but he was not alone. A thin, sharp-featured redhead in an expensive-looking suit stood by his side, one of her hips cocked. She looked at least a decade younger than the commissioner. As she drew closer, Abby noticed the woman's bright pink talons clutching his elbow.

"Commissioner Ludwig. So nice to see you again." Abby guessed Dennis was around sixty, tall and lanky under his tailored jacket.

His smile briefly lifted drooping, tired-looking features. With his pure white hair and matching eyebrows, Dennis made her think of a worn-out, poorly fed Santa Claus. She shook his hand firmly and beamed her most confident smile. Then she tipped her head toward his companion and raised her eyebrows in question. "Ma'am?"

"This is my wife, Leda."

Leda leaned in and shook Abby's hand with cadaver cold fingers. "Charmed, Ms. Stryker. Dennis told me a lot about you." She didn't smile.

Civil enough, but Abby didn't miss the curt look Leda slanted toward her husband as she uttered the practiced line.

He cleared his throat. "I'm glad you accepted this position, Abigail. We need new blood here in Caldwell to invigorate the old town." He glanced at his watch, then toward the front door and said, "I'll walk you in."

When he turned and took a step toward the library entrance, Leda didn't budge. Her grip caused a crinkle in the arm of his jacket.

"I'm not sure if Dennis told you, Ms. Stryker," she chirped, "but we have a lovely new library at the community college. I've worked hard to make it the area's cutting edge resource. In case you need any pointers." She flashed a crimson-rimmed smile before finally releasing his arm. "I'm off to a faculty meeting. I'll see you later, darling." She rose to peck his cheek, then turned on one spiked heel and clicked away toward the red sports car parked at the curb.

Not exactly Lancelot and Guinevere.

Dennis closed his eyes on a long breath and swiped a hand down over his face. He herded Abby toward the steps with an open arm. "Let's get you settled, Abigail."

"Please, call me Abby."

He nodded. "Monica Browning is due in anytime. She's been an integral part of our staff for a number of years now. She can fill you in on much more of the operations here than I possibly can."

They climbed the stone steps of the boxy, federal-style building. A peaked porch roof perched atop massive pillars, and she noticed how their once-white paint was now yellowed and peeling in spots. Still, the building held a regal air, solidly bound in red brick. Plentiful tall, multi-paned windows flanked the entrance, promising great natural light, at least in the front rooms. She waited as Dennis fumbled through a huge ring of keys and chose one, fitting it into the lock. As the door creaked open he reached into his breast pocket and handed another, single key to Abby.

"This opens the doors of the building," he said. "Front and back."

She folded the cool, metal shape into her palm, and then followed Dennis through a tiny foyer. On one side a curved, varnished wood counter defined the perimeter of the reception area. On the other, an open doorway revealed a small room with a central table set amid book-lined walls. A brass plaque on the jamb declared *Reference* in elegant black script.

He flipped on light switches in the short hallway. They snapped with the audible declaration of far-from-modern technology. Abby squinted above her, into the pale glow of yellowed fluorescent tubes suspended high over the book stacks.

First item on the list. Brighter lighting.

"We have a children's section upstairs, in the loft." He motioned toward the steps to the right. "And a private office on the other side." He pointed to a door at the head of another staircase on the left. "I believe it's been cleared of all of Ms. Porter's things by now. Would you like to take a look?"

Abby shook her head. "I should be fine with the common area," she said, a little distracted. Her gaze settled on the iron bell mounted beside the staircase. Although it wasn't large, it was fastened to a polished mahogany plaque and displayed in a place that demanded notice. "Where's the bell from?"

"That's a solid old piece of our heritage." Dennis lifted his chin, standing a bit taller. "It's from our first private school here in Caldwell. Established in 1847. Served the entire county for over twenty years."

Sensing his pride, she stepped closer and studied the bell with new interest. "Where is the original building? I'd love to see it."

Dennis crammed his hands in his pockets and shook his head. “Gone. The school closed in 1868, and the building burned to the ground several years later. All that remains is that bell.”

“What a shame.”

She’d known about Harvey Library way before she applied for the job. It had a history. Abby respected history. She’d been so intrigued when Commissioner Ludwig led her through the first time, just two weeks ago. A tingle from that initial excitement came back to her now. From the moment she stepped over the threshold, she felt the building’s energy. It oozed out from the shelves, invisibly electrifying the musty air. The place exuded an almost palpable *need.*

Heritage established its character, but it wasn’t the architecture or the history of the place that made her fall in love with the Harvey. It was the collection of texts. No matter how hard she tried, she couldn’t downplay her awe that first visit as she perused the small yet precious collection of antique volumes. Although Harvey Library was stuck plumb in the middle of navigable nowhere, there was no denying one fact—someone, at some time in the history of the tiny town, had a firm handle on the importance of fine, recognized literature.

Abby jolted from her reverie when Dennis cleared his throat. Blinking up at him she asked, “Will Ms. Porter be coming in for my orientation?”

“No,” he snapped, and she blinked again in surprise. Then in a calmer, more measured tone he continued, “No, Ms. Porter had some health issues. She was a nervous type. She won’t be back, I’m afraid.” He angled his body away from her as if to say *case closed.*

Hmm, I wonder what the real story is?

The old school bell wasn’t the only one in the building. A cluster of small, brass bells hung from the doorknob. Odd.

She didn't remember hearing them when she and Dennis came in. But now they jingled cheerfully as a tall woman wearing khaki slacks and a crisp, tailored white shirt entered and clicked the door shut behind her.

"Hi, Mr. Ludwig." The pretty blonde smiled at Dennis, then turned her gaze toward Abby. "You must be Ms. Stryker," she said, extending her hand.

"As I've told you, Monica," he began as though Monica had been standing there all along, "I'm counting on Ms. Stryker to be our new blood for the Harvey Library. I'm hoping you'll help her all you can toward that aim."

"Certainly, Commissioner."

Monica Browning was willowy—an attractive woman in her mid-forties, Abby guessed. She noticed how the woman's face lit up, how her eyes glittered when he spoke. When she turned to address Abby, her warm expression evaporated.

"Mr. Ludwig has told me so much about you. I'm looking forward to working together," she said in a tone as flat and cold as marble.

The line sounded so rehearsed. Abby's silent reply was, *Yeah, right.* She chose to keep her reaction to herself, concentrating instead on the question foremost in her mind.

"Okay, so what's the deal with this library? People are saying it's haunted." She kept her tone light. "That's why you haven't been able to keep the place staffed, isn't it?"

She caught the flash of eye contact that joined Dennis and Monica, blatantly dogging it with her own glare. It was as though she'd dropped the F-bomb. Monica lowered her head and clasped her hands behind her back. Dennis tipped up his chin, studying the hammered tin ceiling as if searching for his reply there.

Okay, so apparently I've hit a nerve.

Abby'd heard the talk from her aunt, who had lived in Caldwell for over twenty years and operated a business on the same street. Who did these people think they were fooling? She folded her arms over her chest, tapping one sneaker-clad foot silently on the worn carpet runner.

Patience, Abby.

She needed to remember she was the fresh out-of-grad school newbie. This *was* her first real job in her field. All the more reason she needed to know what she might be getting herself into.

The silence ensued a little too long.

"Exactly how many librarians have you had here in the months since Dana Laramy retired? Two? Three? What's wrong with this place?" she asked.

Dennis leveled his gaze on hers, holding it silently for another beat. "I'm sure your aunt has filled you in on the rumors," he rumbled.

"Rumors. Yeah. You mean the ghost stories? Aunt Dianne, of all people, doesn't take much stock in supernatural phenomena without investigating their feasibility. She wouldn't have repeated any rumors, I don't think, unless—"

"Well, this particular, um, phenomenon has allegedly run off our last two librarians."

"He's even got a name, doesn't he? So what does this 'Harry' do? Scramble words on the pages? Misfile titles on the shelves?" She flipped her hands in the air. "What? Flick the lights on and off?"

Monica said nothing as she wandered off toward the reception desk. She slipped behind the waist-high counter where she nonchalantly checked in a stack of returns. Abby stared after her, amazed.

Certainly not the helpful, friendly assistant Dennis had described. Wonder what else he misrepresented?

Abby turned back to him. "Why isn't everyone spooked by this ghost? Is it just nice little old ladies like Norma Porter? My aunt says Dana Laramy ran the place her whole life. No problems then, right? You said Monica's been here a long time. She doesn't seem freaked."

He cleared his throat again. A nervous habit, no doubt, but Abby found it irritating. And more infuriating yet, he now appeared to be stifling a smirk.

"No, Ms. Browning is not 'freaked,' as you put it," he scoffed. "She's been with us for almost ten years. She's smarter than to listen to any silly chatter about a ghost."

Monica looked up. Her eyebrows arched, forming two crescent moons beneath a golden, peaked hairline. When she spoke, her gaze dropped back to the pile of books. "That's right, Ms. Stryker. The last two librarians were both, well, much older than you and perhaps a bit superstitious." Her lips pressed into a thin line that quirked up on one side.

Staged. This entire conversation had been practiced and performed, for who knew how many others before her. She didn't buy a word of it. It was obvious she wouldn't be getting any straight answers from those two. At least not today.

Planting both hands on her hips, she scanned the space around her. The place didn't feel creepy. Not even mildly mysterious. What it felt was familiar. A library was where she grew up, literally. Most kids went to daycare. Not Abby.

Her parents, both professors at Appalachia State University, spent more time on campus than in their rambling Tudor-style home on the edge of Boone. The university's library housed both Mom and Dad's offices on the fourth floor. Since Abby was reading by age four, Mom came to think of the stacks as a handy, and essentially free, babysitter. Ever since she could remember, books had been Abby's best and, for the most part, only friends.

She was standing in a place she thought of as home. The Harvey was almost 150 years old. Scents of aged leather, woody paper, and dust hung on quiescent air. To Abby this was incense. All around her, thousands of words lie suspended on pages, patiently waiting for her perusal, her attention, her loving care. The place bore signs of neglect, yes, but essentially, the Harvey was no different from any other old library.

Then a little thrill of excitement balled in her chest. *Ah, but this one could be different. This one can be mine.*

"Well, I guess I'd better start getting acquainted with Harry," she blurted, "since he and I will be spending a lot of time together."

She slipped her bristly black sweater off her shoulders and reached to hang it on the wooden tree at the base of the stairs. As she turned, her fingers trailed along the rim of the old schoolhouse bell. The pitted metal surface felt unusually warm, and left her skin tingling like a lover's touch.

Her first day was turning out to be one of the longest of her life.

As she struggled to gain dexterity with the Harvey's software program and memorize the layout of the holdings, barely a half-dozen browsers drifted in and out. Abby couldn't believe how much slower the pace was. Here, an hour passed without a single soul venturing through the front door.

Many who did come in headed straight for the meeting room table, plucking the *Hickory Herald* or *Blue Ridge Country Magazine* off the rack on their way. Around one o'clock, a man in a dark suit wearing black-rimmed glasses over his dour expression carried his bulging briefcase into the reference room and parked behind a stack of papers for an hour and a half. Later, a few younger patrons wandered through the fiction stacks for a time before leaving, empty handed, looking disappointed.

It didn't help that Monica acted as though Abby were invisible. Neither of them took a lunch break, a fine point

Abby had failed to establish in advance with Dennis. It didn't matter, since she was so wound up she couldn't have eaten anyway.

When she asked Monica what time she usually ate lunch, she got a shrug and a simple reply: "I don't."

This was Monday, one of the two days the library stayed open late. Dennis had supplied Abby with Monica's schedule, so she was not surprised when, promptly at five o'clock and without preamble, Monica left. She slung her purse over one shoulder, draped her sweater over her arm, then headed for the front door. She hadn't said more than ten words to Abby all day.

Monica tossed a casual "G'night" over her shoulder as she clicked the door shut behind her.

"Hmm," Abby said, looking around her.

The library was completely empty, and had been for at least the past half hour. Although it was quiet enough even with Monica there, now the silence thickened. The clock on the wall above Abby's head ticked louder, as though declaring its existence. She wondered if Monday evenings were ever busy, and what on earth she should be doing until closing time—three long hours to kill. Sighing, she pulled a granola bar out of purse. Then she flipped open an older John Grisham hardcover and, crunching away on her oats-n-honey dinner, began to read.

She was diving into the story when the bells on the door jingled. A tall man in a brown tweed jacket made an exaggerated effort to close the door behind him quietly. He carried a stack of books under one arm. Meeting his gaze she smiled, holding a hand over her mouth and hurrying to finish chewing her last bite.

History professor, Jack Wood, wasn't concerned about an alleged ghost, but he did worry over losing his favorite hangout. He was certain the local old biddies conjured up this notion about an unhappy spirit.

Now, here was Head Librarian contestant number three standing behind the reception desk.

She glanced up as Jack came in. “Good evening,” she said. “Got some returns there?”

“Yes, ma’am.” He kept his voice low, glancing around to see if anyone was seated in the reading area.

“No worries. We’re the only ones here. So far anyway.”

He slid the stack of books out from under his arm and pushed them across the counter. “You must be our new librarian.” He extended his hand and flashed a smile. “Hi. I’m Jack Wood.”

Her eyes were dark, their almond shape exaggerated even more by the black, Cleopatra-style eyeliner.

She scanned him, unabashed and evaluating. When her gaze flashed to his hair, she blinked. All the while, her slight smile remained politely impassive. “Abby Stryker. Pleased to meet you.”

That seemed sincere enough.

She began passing the book’s barcodes under the scanner. “Pleased to *see* you, actually. It seems Monday nights can get pretty lonely.”

He nodded. “I know. But you can count on me being here. It’s my favorite night to come in and get some work done. Tonight,” he lifted his leather tote up for her to see, “I’m grading term papers.”

Abby cocked her head. “You’re a teacher, then.”

“Yes, ma’am. Humanities and History.”

The screech of the scanner interrupted them. The computer refused to recognize the last book in his pile of returns. Abby ran it under the glittering green beam again but the same annoying squawk resounded. She squinted at the label. “I don’t think this is one of ours,” she said, tiny furrows appearing between her eyebrows.

He took it from her hand. “Oh, that one must be from the college library.”

One of her eyebrows drifted up toward her hairline. “So . . . is it Professor Wood?”

“That’s right,” he replied. “I’m sorry. This one must have gotten into the wrong pile.” He tucked the book back under his arm and raked his fingers through his hair. Seemed a little warm tonight.

She slid her gaze away from him, and he detected a faint sigh. “I hear the college has quite a nice, new library.”

“It does. Big, modern. But it’s a wide-open floor plan, high ceilings. It’s . . . cold. Can get kind of noisy.” He waited until she looked up. “I’m more *that* kind of guy.” He pointed with a thumb over his shoulder toward the small, cozy reference room, then tugged at the collar of his shirt.

Yes, unusually warm tonight.

“How long have you taught there?” she asked, pushing back the longer swatch of her hair. Her style was odd with one side nearly skimming her chin, the other clipped close, almost as short as his own.

Light bounced off three tiny, silver balls edging her ear. Such a delicate, feminine ear. Like a gracefully curved pink shell.

When Abby tipped her head Jack realized she was waiting for a reply. “I’ve been with Caldwell’s college since they opened. I graduated from Duke, and taught a couple of years there, but I’m not really a fan of big cities.”

She was still staring at him, curiosity widening those exotic eyes, saying nothing. He slid the remaining book higher up under his arm and shifted from one foot to the other.

God, this is awkward.

He swallowed and twisted his shoulders. “I grew up in Blowing Rock. When they opened the college here, I was thrilled.” Lowering his gaze, he shrugged. “I love this place.

This library. There's stuff in here you can't find anywhere else. Like a treasure hunt, every time I come in."

Okay, idiot, quit babbling. She's probably being polite, waiting for you to go away and stop bothering her.

The front door opened, much to Jack's relief. Four preppy-clad students, three boys and a girl, came barreling in toting their tablets and backpacks.

Glancing over his shoulder at the group, he patted the counter in front of Abby. "I'll let you get back to work," he said, then turned and strode away a bit more quickly than he intended.

He slid out the bundle of freshman term papers and stacked them on his left, then laid the scoring sheets on his right. The library was the best place for him to grade these local history papers, since it was easy for him to check the annotations the students recorded for accuracy—or determine if their references even existed. He'd gotten halfway down the opening page of the first report when he realized he probably wasn't going to accomplish much tonight.

From his seat in the reference room, he had a full-on view of the reception desk where Abby was perched. Her dark, smoky eyes flashed back and forth between a computer screen and whatever paperwork was on the counter before her.

And he couldn't seem to keep his gaze off her.

Wow. She was the youngest one the commissioners ever hired. Edgy too. Her satiny hair oscillated around her face, the asymmetrical cut revealing an ear on one side, intermittently obscuring an eye on the other. An inky sheet of dark hair. From what he could see, her whole body was draped in black. A voluminous, scratchy-looking knitted creation covered her upper half in nondescript folds. She was a petite sprite, and the sweater was obviously designed for someone four times her size.

Abby Stryker was certainly a change in protocol for the Harvey Library. She didn't even look old enough to have earned the credentials. Yet he knew she had to be at least mid-twenties, because Dennis Ludwig wouldn't have hired anyone without a Master's degree. His high-browed wife would never have allowed it.

Young perhaps, but this Abby did seem to know what she was doing. When the awkwardly shy students approached her, she tactfully prodded for the information she needed to help them. Jack found something unexpectedly provocative about the contrast between her trendy, cutting-edge look and her mature, confident air.

And boy was she attractive. Her expression was sultry, almost sleepy looking. She rationed her smiles. When she did let one go, a sort of glow enveloped her.

Graceful and swift, she swept out from behind the counter. Her full, gauzy black skirt swished inches above her ankle, the hemline either chopped ragged or lacy—hard to tell from a distance. That's when Jack caught a glimpse of her footwear. Black and white Converse sneakers, topped with lace-trimmed, white ankle socks.

He grinned and shook his head. Charisma. If nothing else, this one was sure to inject some life into the place. Abby passed outside the reference room door and paused, cocking her head toward a question a female student was asking. A sparkle caught the light above the flare of Abby's left nostril. It was a tiny diamond stud he hadn't noticed before. He wondered absently if her tongue was pierced too.

Stop it. Stop it, right now. You're probably at least ten years older than she is. There might even be as many years between you and this Abby as there are between . . .

Between Dennis and Leda Ludwig. And no one had to remind Jack how that relationship was working out.

Chapter 2

The next morning, Jack guided his SUV smoothly into his customary spot in front of the college. He checked his watch. Eight fifty-seven a.m. More than a creature of habit, he was obsessed with arriving on time. Civilization might collapse if punctuality was abandoned or worse yet, ignored by large numbers of people. In some way, in the scope of his sleepy, rural world, he drew comfort from the knowledge that he, if no one else, was doing his part to maintain world order.

As he reached in to heave his briefcase out of the back seat, a bright red Mercedes coupe whipped in beside him. Never had he seen anyone able to extinguish an engine and leap out of an automobile—especially such a small, low-to-the-ground variety—with such agility as Leda Ludwig.

"Morning," he called as she slammed her door. He glanced up over his roof. Leda's slicked lips were pressed in a red slash beneath her over-sized designer shades.

"Leda, everything okay? Looks like some Highway 321 idiot incited your road rage this morning."

She snorted and lifted the rear hatch, snatching out her briefcase, an armful of books, and a pile of overstuffed manila folders. Using the case as a tray, she stacked the other items on top in a haphazard pile that threatened to avalanche at any minute.

"No road rage, Dr. Wood," she huffed. "Let's call it library rage."

"Ah," he answered with a knowing nod. "So you've met our newest librarian." He struggled to keep his voice light.

"Yup," she snapped. "Just wait till the sleepy town of Caldwell sees what my husband's netted to run the place this time." Her tone was liquid acid.

Jack knew better than to divulge the information, at least at this particular moment, that he already had. His stomach did a little lurch as he conjured Abby's image in his mind. Why had he reacted to her that way? She was definitely not what he considered his type. He was a natural girl type, wasn't he? The radical hair and heavy eye makeup—that kind of girl had never appealed to him before. Maybe it was the nose stud. Oh, now that surely must have stirred Leda's blood.

He followed Leda into the front office, fighting his urge to offer to help carry her load. She wasn't impressed by chivalry. Although raised a gentleman, he was also a quick study. In today's modern world, he'd learned chivalry may not be dead, but could prove deadly if not wielded wisely.

Nodding a greeting to Clara, Jack signed in at the front desk. Clara, with her cropped mousey brown hair, tailored blouses, and knife-pleated skirts served as Caldwell Community College's Receptionist from Hell. Timid and shy she was not. The college chose their office manager wisely. If anyone was capable of protecting the staff and faculty from undue interruption to their workday, it was Clara Bennington.

Leda clicked past Clara's desk, then twisted the key in her office door. Her load teetered precariously, yet Leda deftly lifted an elbow to flick the light switch without dropping so much as a single sheet of paper.

"Mornin' Clara. Coffee please," she barked over her shoulder.

Shifting her attention in Leda's direction, Clara slid the readers down off her nose and folded them atop the stack of papers in front of her. Silently she rose and turned on one sensibly heeled loafer toward the employee lounge. Her almost inaudible sigh did not escape his notice.

Shaking his head, Jack strode to the mail slots, slid out his meager stack of envelopes and neatly folded memos, then followed Clara into the lounge.

"Mornin', Dr. Wood," she greeted him without turning.

She must have invisible eyes in the back of her head. Like his mother claimed she had.

"Ms. Clara. How goes it this morning?" He snatched his favorite ceramic mug from the mismatched collection crowding the shelf above the coffeepot, the one hand-painted with a blue spruce hovering in a primitive winter landscape.

Clara fussed with creamer and sugar in the elegant, gilt-rimmed china one she poured for Leda. "It's goin'." She sighed, then turned to raise a weary smile in his direction. "Sounds like it might turn out to be interesting."

Jack answered with raised brows and noncommittal silence. He carried his mail and mug down the long corridor to the elevator, riding it alone to the third floor. Normally he preferred the stairs—another chance to squeak some aerobic exercise into his day. A full mug of coffee, though, could make a jaunt up the stairs dicey.

Checking his watch again, he figured he had nearly an hour before his first class, since his lecture was written, and his readings copied, collated, and stapled. Maybe he'd steal a few moments to thumb through that old book he picked up at the library before his students began floating in.

He'd been teaching at the college for over nine years now. He loved his job and loved living in Caldwell. The compact ranch he built on the outskirts of town was only three miles away. Close to work, yet with enough distance between he and parents and sisters, a thirty-minute drive up the mountain.

Jack often felt trapped in a hiccup of time. His passion was history, and he was constantly following some elusive path into the past, mostly through old books. A mountain man in the true sense of the word, he loved to fish and hike and grow his own vegetables. And, most of the time, he didn't mind living alone.

Sometimes though, he had to admit, it would be nice to have someone to share all that peacefulness with. The right someone. Maybe next time, his luck would change.

The book he picked up last night was old, like most comprising Harvey Library's meager, yet precious collection. As he laid the tome on his desk he wondered what it must have looked like when the leather binding was new. Now, dust blanketed the gilded lines that were chinked in places, flaked off almost completely in others.

He lifted the cover and thumbed through creamy pages, velvety with age. Even the book's essence evoked reverence: grassy, musty, with an odd twinge of scent he couldn't put a name to. But every museum he'd ever visited, every old box of books he'd dug in, all smelled the same.

As far as local history, the Harvey held some volumes that didn't exist anywhere else. When Jack found out Dana Laramy was retiring, he acknowledged the closing of the library was a distinct possibility. He made it his mission to enjoy as many of the venerable volumes as he possibly could.

There was no telling, if Leda Ludwig got her wish, how long it would be before the Harvey Library, with all its irreplaceable antique volumes, would disappear forever.

"Monica, if we're going to work together, you have to loosen up and talk to me."

Abby loved quiet. She was a librarian, right? But Monica's silent treatment from day one had her about ready to snap. An entire week had passed, and her icy distance had not improved. Even getting basic information from the woman was as painful as pulling a molar. Yet contrary to

Abby's first impression, she no longer believed Monica was just a pompous bitch.

Her interactions with the patrons, the children, the awkward teenagers, and especially the elderly impressed Abby. She believed many of Caldwell's seniors came into the library simply to visit with Monica. So her problem, Abby surmised, had to be with her. She couldn't tell if the attitude stemmed from resentment, suspicion, or plain dislike of her new boss.

When Abby came in that Monday, she cheerfully greeted Monica good morning and offered to make her a cup of the new herbal tea she brought in. Peppermint, one of her favorites, and her Aunt Dianne's bestseller. Monica, busying herself with the book list spread out on the desk, didn't respond. She acted as though Abby wasn't there.

Her behavior went beyond rude. *It's demeaning, infuriating. You've had a week to adjust to me. Time's up.*

Abby thudded both elbows on the counter, and her coworker jumped, glaring up at her. She leaned so close she could smell the strawberry scent from Monica's lip balm. "What is your problem, Monica? Am I invisible or are you just trying to pretend I am?"

At first Monica's eyes narrowed under her overly tweezed brows. She closed them as she spoke. She could be so damned condescending. "I'm simply trying to get along with you, Ms. Stryker. You're my new boss, and I don't want to make a bad impression."

Abby couldn't tell whether she was being honest or facetious. "Yeah well, silence is golden and all that. But this isn't Macy's or McDonald's or some other bustling, busy place of business where we can conveniently avoid each other for a full eight hour day."

Monica snorted, an unexpected and not particularly attractive noise coming from the likes of prim and proper

Ms. Browning. Still, to Abby's maddened frustration, she didn't say another word.

"All right." Abby stood and folded her arms, puffing herself up with as much authority as she could muster. "If you keep this up, I'm going to have to resort to extreme measures."

One of Monica's eyebrows arched at the implied threat and, keeping her focus determinedly down on her work, she responded with a soft, cynical, "Oh?"

Challenge accepted.

She waited since Monica seemed hell-bent on avoiding her gaze. A long silent moment stretched out, with neither she nor Monica moving or saying anything. Finally, curiosity got the best of the older woman. The moment she looked up, Abby cocked her head to one side, crossed her eyes, and stuck out her tongue.

Monica's scowl didn't last long. Abby caught the tiny twitch of humor trembling at one corner of the other woman's perfectly painted mouth.

"Com'on, Monica. I'm your boss, and I'm ten years younger than you. It's obvious that one of those facts doesn't make you too happy. Or maybe both. We're going to be spending a lot of time together in this place, even if you do only work part-time. Can't we start out being friends and work on the boss-employee thing later?"

For the first time since they'd met, she saw what she hoped was a genuine Monica Browning smile.

"A few more than that, I think," Monica quipped, jutting her chin.

Abby hunched her shoulders. "A few more what?"

"Years. I think there's more than ten years between you and me," Monica replied flatly.

"Dunno." She pushed back from the counter. "Can't tell. I'm twenty-six. How old are you?"

Monica's smile faded to an almost shy grin. "Thanks for

the compliment, but I'm old enough to be your mother," she mumbled.

Abby feigned shock with an exaggerated gasp, drawing back and slapping one palm to her chest. "Do tell," she gasped. "Wow, you're old." She rolled her eyes toward the ceiling. "I can't believe you haven't retired yet." Then she leveled her gaze at Monica, blinking fast like an innocent, small child.

Monica fidgeted in her chair, staring down at the scattered papers before her. "Okay, Abby. You've made your point. Can you blame me, though? I've had to get used to two new boss ladies in the past few months, and they were both classic, stuffy old lady librarians. That was easy. I worked with Dana for almost ten years." She cleared her throat. "You were, well, kind of a shock. You . . . well, you are going to take some getting used to."

Abby realized her Goth-fashion, her extreme makeup, and her numerous piercings put off some people at the start. Particularly conservative women like Monica. She chose, at least for the moment, to ignore the last part of Monica's comment.

"So what's the deal with that, anyway?" Abby rattled on. "The last two librarians didn't even last three months, right?"

Monica nodded, suppressing a smirk. "Norma Porter lasted only two weeks, five days."

Abby clasped her hands behind her back and paced slowly. "You know, I have to be honest. About this ghost. I've been wondering these past few days if it's you."

Monica shot her an indignant glare, but before she could say anything Abby held her hands up and shrugged. "You've been the constant, right? Maybe you're the one running off the head librarians and not any ghost at all."

"You go ahead and believe that," Monica snapped. "You

obviously haven't met Harry. When you do, come back and tell me there's no ghost."

"Oh-ho, so you do believe in our pal Harry."

Exasperated, Monica made a rumbling sound deep in her throat. "I didn't say that," she spat. "Things started getting . . . weird after Dana retired." She jerked to her feet and headed for the small rear office. "Where are those fancy tea bags you brought in, anyway?"

Abby had broken the ice. Over the next few days, the tension between them gradually dissipated, evaporating slowly like the wisps of early morning mist that blanketed the foothills each morning. Little by little, she sought to draw information out of Monica about the library's questionable recent history. The more she learned, the sharper her irritation spiked.

"So let me get this straight," she began, resting one hand on her hip. She and Monica stood near the arched rear windows behind the book stacks, where a cozy reading nook resided. "I've relocated, accepted my first real career position. I'm here high on the hopes of a stable job and secure future. From what you've told me, though, the future of this place is on pretty shaky ground."

Monica's back faced the windows, and she rocked, toe to heel and back, her hips swaying. "More than just shaky, I fear."

Abby wasn't sure if her rocking represented a nervous tic or an 'I told you so' taunt.

"The commissioner? He wants this place to stay, grow," Monica continued. "Become the cornerstone attraction for the trickling tourist trade we get here in Caldwell. Sort of a museum of local history. His wife? Not so much."

Abby rested against the shelves. "I kind of caught that drift from Leda when I first arrived," she said. "I didn't know before that day she was Commissioner Ludwig's wife. She's quite a bit younger than him, huh?"

"She is," Monica replied, studying her manicure. "Quite a bit. The whole town was in shock when Dennis came home from a political fundraiser with her on his arm. It's been, oh, I guess almost ten years now."

"So what does Mrs. Ludwig do for a living? She was dressed like a highbrow attorney or bank president the other morning and rattled on about some important meeting she was headed to." As she relaxed around Monica, her cynical side continued to squeak out in small, spontaneous bursts.

Monica giggled. "Yeah, she's pretty important, I guess. She's the dean."

"Oh, so that explains her quip about the college library. I couldn't understand why it was so important to her."

"Yup, ever since she landed that job last fall, it seems as though she traded in Dennis' leather collar and leash for a spiked choke chain."

"Oh my," Abby sputtered. "Poor Dennis."

"Yeah, poor Dennis." Monica wasn't laughing. She sounded sad. "He hasn't been the same since Leda's gained her own status." Her last word oozed with sarcasm.

Abby studied her coworker. There was more to this than Monica was letting on. "You act as though Dennis is pretty important to you."

"We both grew up here." Monica's reply was soft, almost more to herself than to Abby. "I've known Dennis all of my life." She fixed a stare at the worn carpet runner under their feet.

A long beat of silence passed, and before Abby could probe further the telephone echoed from the lobby.

Monica leapt toward her escape. "I'll get it," she snapped, turned, and trotted off.

For a few moments longer Abby gazed out the window as a pair of blue jays argued over position on the gnarled branch shading the rear of the building. Her eyes refocused, and she caught sight of her own reflection in the wavy, old glass. Her image was transparent, ghostlike. How depressing that this, her first real job in the field she loved, might end almost before it began. Sadder still that a historic facility like this would be shut down and the building re-envisioned. Or worse yet, razed.

She had come here prepared to take things slow, to allow the people in Caldwell to accept her, get used to her, before she initiated any radical changes to revive the library's reputation. That was the advice she'd gotten from Dianne.

Aunt Di ought to know. The elders of the community were ready to run her out of town the first few months after she opened Ancient Healings. And her aunt had grown up in Caldwell. With Abby being an outsider, Dianne advised that she proceed with caution. "Give them a chance to realize you aren't evil," she'd said, "that you don't cast spells and you won't corrupt the town's youth."

I may not have time.

Monica made it sound as though if Leda Ludwig got her way, the funding for the library could be cut off at any moment. Abby couldn't help but wonder why.

The new college library was funded by the state education stipends and student tuition. No competition, money-wise, at all. A private endowment fund kept the Harvey going, Monica said, without further explanation. She claimed she was unaware of the details. Abby suspected she knew more than she was letting on.

She sighed. If the library was going down, it will go down with her fighting.

It wasn't only for the library's sake. She didn't really have a choice. This move and new job was the fresh start she so desperately needed. She hoped that if she focused all her energy on preserving this precious piece of history, she could bury her own painful past and move on with her life.

There was no way she could have stayed in Boone. Too many memories haunted her there, especially after Cameron's sudden death. She should never have gotten involved with him—her thesis advisor. What had she been thinking? He was old enough to be her father, as well as being her dad's colleague and best friend. No, she had to start over in a place fifty miles south and 2000 feet down the mountain, where her guilty secret was easier to keep. A place she'd seldom even visited, since the family denounced her aunt's Wiccan ways all those years ago.

Abby turned from the window and headed back toward the lobby. As she rounded the end of the stacks a sound startled her.

Swish, thump.

She wheeled to find a book laying on the floor mere inches behind her. It landed on its spine, open on the carpet runner, its pages neatly parted as though someone had been sitting on the floor reading.

"Did I knock you off?" She stooped to scoop up the book and examined the spine carefully. It didn't bear any obvious injuries from the fall.

She scanned the shelves from left to right, scowling when she realized there didn't seem to be any empty spaces. The fallen book was Charlotte Bronte's Jane Eyre. The fiction stacks were, of course, alphabetized by author's last name, with hardcovers and paperbacks grouped in separate areas.

The shelves along the wall to Abby's left held the paperbacks, romances first, then mysteries. To her right were the F's, a few of the G's. Charlotte Bronte's book didn't even belong here, but back with the B's, all the way down the other end of the stack.

"Jane, you've obviously been misfiled," she addressed the book as though it were a lost child. She stroked the cover as she returned it to its proper slot. "I'd better check to make sure none of Charlotte's other works are lost up there too," she said as she patted it back into place.

On her way back to the reception desk, she performed a quick scan of the section in question.

Nothing else out of place. That was weird.

A chill jittered up her spine. The books were all neatly lined up and packed snug. Nothing else was misfiled, and there weren't any loose spaces between the books at all.

Chapter 3

"Why didn't you level with me, Aunt Di? Why?" Abby slammed the front door of Ancient Healings in mid-sentence, the breeze sending a displayed set of metal wind chimes clanging defiantly in her wake.

Dianne, from behind her desk, slowly raised her silvery eyes. "Honey, it's just a rumor. Nobody's actually seen any ghost. It's an old building. Old buildings creak and shift sometimes—"

"Not that," Abby snapped. "A ghost I can handle. Not Leda Ludwig. From what I hear, if she gets her way, there will be no Harvey Library. I feel like I've taken a job on the Titanic."

Dianne hesitated, her gaze flitting to one side, then back to Abby. "I swear, honey, I didn't realize how hell-bent Leda was on trashing the thing," she said in a breathy stream. She whisked around the glass display case and took two strides toward her. "I didn't. I knew she was pushing the college library. Fundraisers and all that. I never figured Dennis would let her go after the Harvey." She wrung her hands and shifted from one foot to the other. Her waist long hair swayed back and forth like a pewter pendulum. "How's it going, anyway? Getting along okay with Monica?"

Abby huffed and pressed two fingers to the base of her nose. "What have you got for a horrific headache?"

Fifteen minutes later the two sat in the tiny side room where Dianne's friend, Vera, did tarot card readings on Tuesdays. Dianne lifted an antique porcelain teapot to fill two matching cups with a steaming, golden brew. Abby sniffed the chamomile and lemon balm and automatically relaxed with a long sigh.

"Monica's okay. What's the deal with her and Dennis, anyway? Judging from how she ogles him, it seems there's more to that relationship than part-time employee to boss." Abby lifted the saucer and blew across the top of the cup. She sipped tentatively. "Mmm."

"Well, there isn't anything between them anymore," Dianne began. "Those two did have a thing a long time ago. Monica never did marry. I think she was hoping she could eventually stir Dennis' embers again."

"Then Leda came along," Abby added. "Monica told me. He met her at some political event?"

"It was a fundraiser for the college, at some swanky hotel down in Hickory. Dennis had just gotten the township to approve the building fund," Dianne said, drizzling honey into her tea. "Leda comes from money. I guess her family plunked down a big chunk."

Abby snorted. "So Miss Leda ended up with her very own college, complete with the county commissioner as mascot."

"Yup. There was quite a rumble around town last year when Leda got the dean's chair. I guess enough time had passed since her family's big donation that nobody could argue with the city council's choice," Dianne said.

Abby sighed and took another sip. "I think this is helping my head already," she murmured. She studied the little room. "You've got this done up real pretty." Then she glanced from her cup to the teapot to the rambling rose wallpaper. "How'd you do that? Get everything to match?"

Dianne's smile gleamed. "Magic, darling. You know how I can do. Just a little old fashioned magic."

Abby scoffed. "Will you be able to work some of that magic stuff on old Leda Ludwig?"

Her aunt's smile faded. She set her cup on the lace-covered table between them, meeting Abby's gaze. "Hey," she growled. "Don't you worry about Leda scooping that job out from under you. This town needs Harvey Library. It's part of our history. And if anybody has half a snowflake's chance in Tahiti of saving it, it's you. You are here for a reason, Abigail." She reached across and patted the back of her hand. "So whatchya got planned? What's your first project for the old place?"

Abby let out a long sigh. "I want to reinstate the children's story hour. I've printed up flyers and posted them everywhere I could think of. In fact . . ." She paused and pulled a folder out from her gigantic purse. "I've got some right here. Do you think you could put them near your register somewhere?"

Dianne took the folder and flipped it open, frowning. "A week from Saturday, huh? Timing may not be so great, Abs. The Spring Festival comes to town next week. It runs through Sunday."

"What's that?"

"It's like a county fair, mountain-style. Arts, crafts, some homespun quilts, with a Ferris wheel and cotton candy thrown in for the kids. I have Vera set up a booth with some of my jewelry and candles and stuff every year. Didn't it come to Boone too?"

"I've sort of been out of the loop as far as social events," Abby murmured.

Dianne nodded. "Well, the festival is real popular with the younger families. On Saturday, the place will be overrun with tiny people."

Groaning, Abby dropped her head into her hands. "Well, that figures. How was I supposed to know that?"

"I'm surprised Monica didn't mention it to you."

"Monica is just now starting to treat me like I'm not the ghost."

Dianne patted her shoulder. “It’ll work out, Abby. Even if this first event doesn’t go over well, you’ve got time. I’m telling you, no matter how hard Leda pushes to shut that place down, it’s not going to happen overnight. The library is a local icon. She can’t make a decision like that on her own.”

Abby rested her elbows on her knees. “I can’t tell you how much I appreciate your support, Di. And the apartment upstairs, incidentally, is the bomb. Thank you for that.” Tears blurred her vision. “I don’t know what I would have done if you hadn’t been here. I couldn’t stay in Boone after . . .”

Dianne squeezed her shoulder. “Oh, don’t you worry now. This is the beginning of an exciting new life for you. It’s all going to work out. I’ve lived here a long time. If there’s anything I can do to help you figure stuff out, just ask. If I don’t have the answer, I’m sure one of my friends does.”

“Okay, I’ve got one for you,” Abby said with a chuckle. “Is it a good sign or a bad one when the library’s resident ghost throws a copy of Jane Eyre at you?”

Thursday evening arrived and again, Abby was working alone. Monica was on her way out the door, one hand on the porcelain doorknob, her sweater draped over one arm.

“We usually don’t get much traffic until around seven. That’s when most of the college kids come in to dig around, working on their history papers. College library closes early on Thursdays.” She shifted from one foot to the other. “You gonna be all right?”

Abby’s gaze flashed to the ceiling. “Of course. I’ll be fine,” she sang out. “Alone is my specialty, remember? Besides, I’m going to get started going through that budget and see how much honey I can squeeze out of a stone.”

“Good luck with that,” Monica huffed, rolling her eyes. “G’night.”

Monica was right about the foot traffic. Between five and seven the only person who came through the door was Aunt Dianne. About six she slipped in carrying what looked like a tiny picnic basket. At least, it looked tiny against her aunt's generous form. Its cheerful red-checked covering clashed hideously with the glowing fuchsia of her flowing caftan.

"Whoa, that's quite the outfit." Blinking at the sight, Abby looked up from the papers strewn on the counter. "Where the heck are you going dressed like that?"

"Saturday is Beltane, my dear. First of May. Fertility Festival. The girls and I are getting together to make plans." Dianne swept her gaze down across her dress. "Don't you love it?" She twirled in place, the silky yards of cloth spinning out around her. "How 'bout my hair? This is how I'm going to wear it for the feast Saturday night."

Dianne's waist-long hair glowed with a youthful sheen incongruous with its color. Completely gray since she was Abby's age, almost twenty years ago, Dianne's hair was her pride. Tonight she plaited two sections from her crown with satin ribbon that matched her dress. As she spun, the colorful braids tangled with the thick charcoal-to-silver streaked waves flowing down her back.

"You certainly look . . . cheerful," Abby struggled, not wanting to insult her. "So Beltane is a happy holiday?"

Dianne's mouth gaped in mock horror. "Why of course it's a happy holiday. Abigail, I would think that with all that book reading you do, you would at least have learned something about your Aunt Di's calling." She sniffed. "Out of curiosity, if nothing else."

Switching gears, Abby pointed her pencil toward the basket. "So what'd you bring me?"

"It's no good for you to survive on granola bars and peppermint tea." Dianne lifted the edge of the checkered towel theatrically. "This is a wedge of the asparagus and

Swiss quiche Armand made for our dinner tonight. You do like asparagus, don't you?"

Abby's eyes narrowed. "Did Uncle Armpit know you'd be bringing some to me? Is it safe? Have you guys eaten any of it yet?" Her tone simmered with suspicion.

"Abigail Stryker, I will never for the life of me understand what you dislike about my dear Armand. You just don't know him very well, is all." She plopped the basket on the counter under Abby's nose. "Doesn't it smell wonderful?"

The warm aroma of salty cheese and buttery crust wafted up as Abby peeked into the basket. She may not be a fan of Armand Le Mon personally, but she had to admit, he sure was a fantastic cook. Trained in a fancy chef's school somewhere in the south of France, Armand had come back to his hometown in the Appalachians and opened the first upscale French restaurant the area had ever seen. At first, the locals were certain he'd be bankrupt in a month since there wasn't barbecue sauce in a single dish on the menu.

Just like Dianne's New Age shop, though, the tourists loved it, and the locals started straggling in out of sheer curiosity. Over the last two years since it opened, Le Petit Mon had became a favorite celebration destination for even the most countrified of the town's residents.

And the instant sparks between Dianne and Armand generated enough electricity to keep both businesses running without a single kilowatt from Blue Ridge Power.

"Well, I can't argue he can handle a quiche pan," Abby stated, lifting out the foil-wrapped dish. She smiled up at her aunt. "Thank you, Di. You even remembered a fork."

"No problem, sweetie. Now you go ahead and enjoy that before somebody comes in who might make you feel guilty enough to share it." Dianne folded the towel back into the basket and slid it onto her arm. "I'm due at Wisteria's house in ten minutes."

After Dianne departed, Abby forked up chunks of the fluffy egg dish as she looked around at what was quickly becoming her second home. Hell, first home. She certainly couldn't call the teensy studio above Ancient Healings anything but a temporary place to sleep. It had been so generous of Dianne and Armand to offer it, rent free, though, until she got on her feet.

It shouldn't take long, she hoped. Her salary, though meager in comparison with what she could have made working in one of the bigger cities, should add up fast without rent or utilities to pay. And she did feel a little better without the obligation of a lease, or the permanence of a mortgage hanging over her head. At least not until she figured out what was going to happen next in her life.

The longer she was there, the more the library's character spoke to her. Original hand-hewn beam ceilings soared two stories high in the front part of the building, over the entry, the checkout desk, and the large, open room where local groups held their monthly meetings. Wide, dark oak planks underfoot were cushioned in strategic places with area rugs and runners to keep the echo of footsteps to a minimum.

On the main floor, the rear of the building housed stacks of hardcover classics, nonfiction, and paperbacks. The reference room harbored dozens of huge, rare volumes, mostly on local history. Two sets of stairs rose from the lobby, one leading to the children's loft, carpeted in bright colors and decorated with colorful prints and posters. On the other side, the steps led to the private office. A plaque beside the old bell at the foot of the stairs read, "Harvey Library, dedicated 1868."

Although Dennis offered the private office to her the day she started, she hadn't ventured to check it out. She'd always preferred staying close to the action, and the small room behind the reception desk had been all the private space she really needed. Now her curiosity was stirred. After she scraped up the last flaky bits of crust of her dinner, she opened the cash drawer and fished out the key he gave her from its hiding spot under the tray.

The uncarpeted steps groaned quietly under Abby's feet. Once at the head of the stairs, she fit the key in the antiquated lock, jiggling until it slid home. The click as it released echoed against the tin ceiling, closer over her head here on this level. She fumbled for a light switch along the inner wall as the door sighed, swinging open freely as if improperly balanced, or of its own accord.

The room was small and sparely furnished. An antique roll top secretary flanked the far wall beside a tall, paned window, bare of treatments. Behind the door, a small oak desk wore only a faded, rose-colored blotter and a metal lamp. Built-in bookshelves lined the wall behind the desk, empty except for a light film of dust.

She skirted the edge of the desk and plopped into the leather armchair. This too, she guessed, was antique. Time and use had scarred the carved, wooden arms and slashed scattered cracks in the burgundy upholstery. She pulled at the brass handle of the pencil drawer and found it unlocked, sliding open easily. It was empty.

The curved roll top of the secretary was raised, and the small shelves underneath stared at her like dust-laden, empty eyes. From her vantage point, Abby could see a spider web netting two thirds of the opening with intricately woven, concentric gossamer rings. The web oscillated gently in the air flowing in from the open door. Dennis said the office "should be clear of Norma Porter's things" that first day. Yet it didn't seem as if anyone had inhabited this room for quite some time.

The air smelled of old books even though there wasn't a single volume in the room. She wondered what kind of books Dana Laramy, who ran the library for so many years, had filling those built-in shelves. Had they been personal treasures that now lived somewhere in Dana's retirement home, or had they found their way back into the collections downstairs?

The jingle of the front door's bells jolted Abby from her reverie, and she rose to go back downstairs. As she swept through between the desk and the window, a shape on the sill caught her eye. Long and narrow, the slim box nestled up close in one corner, nearly invisible though in plain sight. The color of the worn cover almost matched the mustard-hued paint on the sill and sash. Bending, she lifted the box with two fingers.

A tarnished brass clasp held the box closed. Its velvet covering was faded and balding in spots. It appeared to be an old jewelry case for a necklace or bracelet. She used her thumbnail to press on the closure, and it popped open easily. Inside, cradled on a bed of stained ivory silk, lay an intricately carved golden ink pen.

"Excuse me? Is anyone here?" The impatient words of an elderly woman echoed up the stairwell.

With a flustered sigh, Abby closed the dusty box and laid it on the desk's blotter. Turning, she snapped off the lights and pulled the door closed behind her.

Mrs. Hawkins, a mystery fan, took forever deciding between a John Grisham and a classic Sherlock Holmes. In the end, she took both. Abby waited until she was out the door before heading for the stairs again, anxious to get a closer look at the pen she found. Until the door swung open and Jack Wood's arrival stopped her in her tracks.

Mercy, that man had the most incredible eyes. Tonight their unusual color looked more green than gray against the beige tweed of his jacket. His ivory shirt was open at the throat, revealing a tuft of dark chest hair. Her heart rate kicked up a notch.

"Good evening, Ms. Stryker. Working late again?"

Unable to meet his gaze without the fluttering in her chest, she turned away. "Well, it looks like I'm going to be the only evening shift for a while." She tried to sound flippant. "Monica never liked working nights, and she's done more than her share these past few months, I guess."

"She seems like a nice woman," he said. "Does she have a family?"

"I don't think so," Abby replied thoughtfully. "She's a pretty private person. I'm just glad she was willing to come in on Saturday to cover for me while I read to the kids."

He cocked his head. "This Saturday?"

Abby strode back to the counter and pulled off one of the flyers she had stacked there. "No, next week. Harvey Library children's story hour, reborn." She swept the brochure toward him with a grin and a flourish.

His expression fell. "Abby, you do know about the Spring Festival, right?"

"Yes, yes," she snapped. "I've already been informed about my exquisitely poor timing. What can I say? I'm new here. If this one doesn't fly, there's always next month."

His concern had seemed so sincere it made Abby fidget, twisting her fingers together and taking a step back toward the stairway. "Hey, didn't you tell me you were a history expert?"

He scoffed. "Not an expert by any stretch. I do like research, and I teach local history. I've picked up a thing or two along the way."

Tipping her head toward the stairs, she motioned for him to follow. "I want your opinion on something."

She reached the office door and turned the porcelain handle she left unlocked when Mrs. Hawkins interrupted her. Jack followed close behind her, and she detected a musky scent she assumed was his cologne.

"You smell yummy," she said, then whirled and clamped a hand over her mouth. She hadn't meant to say it aloud.

"Sorry. But you do." Feeling the heat rise up her neck, she turned back to switch on the lights.

She reached for the velvet box on the desk and held it out toward him. "Look what I found."

He wasn't looking at the pen. His gaze wandered around the small, spare room, landing on the roll top desk. "Wow, now there's a beautiful antique." He strode forward and stroked the edge of the warm toned wood.

"Oh, be careful." She caught his hand inches from piercing the web. "Some spider spent a good long time weaving a lovely tapestry over that thing."

He shot her a look. "I'm not afraid of spiders. Nor am I allergic." Then slowly, his lips curled up at the edges. "Or is it the spider you're defending?"

She realized she was still holding his wrist, and he hadn't pulled away. His skin was warm, and the way he was smiling at her made her cheeks burn. She dipped her chin, embarrassed, and released him. "I don't believe in destroying art. Even if it is the handiwork of a lowly arachnid." She held up the tiny box. "I found this on the windowsill. How old do you think it is?"

He took the velvet case and flipped it open. "Nice," he mumbled, lifting the pen from its silken bed. "This isn't even a fountain pen." He turned it over, pointing to the hollow space under the nib. "No chamber to hold the ink. That didn't come around until the late 1800s, I think. No, this is called a dip pen." He held the pen between his fingers as if to write. "A single dip in the ink seldom lasted through more than a line or two of script. The user had to have an inkwell right beside them while he worked."

"Or she." Abby took the pen, rolling the decorative barrel over in her palm. "Seems like a lady's pen. It's so intricately engraved," she said, tracing a finger along the delicate pattern. "Do you think it's gold?"

Jack shrugged. “No telling. The fact it’s still here in an abandoned office says probably not. You can take it across the street to Martin Laramy’s place, though. He’d be able to tell you what it’s worth.”

She laid the pen back into its cradle, snapping the cover shut. “It doesn’t matter, since it’s not mine anyway. It’s library property. I think I’ll leave it up here, where it must think it belongs.” She slid the box onto the windowsill into the corner where she found it.

As she followed Jack back down the stairs she asked, “So what brings you in this evening? Grading more papers? Or research?”

“Research. I’m looking into the library’s history. I’m trying to figure out why all those crazy rumors started flying about this place right after Dana Laramy retired. Before that the Harvey was just our boring local library.”

“Laramy.” Abby paused near the reception desk, tilting her head. “Any relation to Laramy’s Antiques?”

“I think Dana is his aunt, though I’m not certain. Neither one is much for personal chit-chat. Weird family, the Laramys. One of these days I’ll have to take you over to meet old Martin. Now there’s a piece of work.” Jack chuckled.

At that moment, the lights in the building flickered, dropping dim and pale. They pulsed for a beat, then went completely out. It was still light outside, though the fading twilight cast the interior into near blackness.

“What the . . .” She looked around, wrapping her arms around herself and instinctively moving a step closer to Jack.

“Oh, that’s not unusual around here.” His voice was calm and reassuring. “Blue Ridge Power is infamous for testing transformers at the darnedest times of day.”

By the time he finished speaking, the lights began to glow, then steadily increased until they were fully illuminated. He grinned over at her. “At least it doesn’t last long.”

His killer smile shot a jitter through her middle again. She smiled back but found she couldn't hold his gaze long without feeling as if she had a fever coming on. She turned away.

"I'd better let you get to work," she mumbled, then scooted around the reception desk and into the back room.

Tea. I just need a cup of peppermint tea to get my mind back where it belongs.

As she stood in the small anteroom, she could feel Jack watching her from his seat across the way. She dunked the tea bag in the steaming water for way longer than necessary. As the pale green essence oozed into the water, all she could think of was how the hue almost matched the color of his eyes.

Chapter 4

During the next week, spring washed over the town like a balmy breeze. Abby's brief walk to work Saturday morning was pure delight. A carpet of fallen cherry and dogwood petals draped each tree's base on new grass, and their branches sprouted tiny, pale green leaves. Flower boxes all along the town square overflowed with purple and pink petunias. Her fears about her first story hour seemed to float away on the scents of freshly cut grass and newly fragrant blossoms.

She skipped up the library steps, key in hand, then pulled up short on the landing. Stepping back, she scrutinized the entryway. The stark stone façade seemed so sterile, so cold in contrast with the colorful new life springing up all around.

This place doesn't seem inviting at all. It needs something homey, to make people notice. The library needs a makeover.

Planters. Not window boxes or small pots. Something as grand and regal as the building itself. Urns. Huge, matching planter urns flanking the doors might coax the tired, lonely looking old building to smile. Making a mental note, she slid the key into the lock.

She'd posted her flyers all over town, from Murphy's Diner to Boswell's Drugstore to the post office. She stopped at the elementary school and handed a stack to the pinch-faced, curt receptionist, asking her to post them in all the classrooms.

Abby had little hope that this, her first official children's story hour, would be an overwhelming success. The weatherman predicted an unseasonably warm spring day. There hadn't been any kind of children's program at the library in at least three years. And she had been warned that everyone with a child old enough to listen to a story was also crazy about the Spring Festival.

In truth, she was terrified that not one single child would show.

Adding to her already unsettled state of mind, as she flicked on the light switches, she smelled smoke. She froze and sniffed the air. It was smoke, all right, but not the wood-burning kind. In fact, she found the scent faintly familiar. It took her a minute until her memory clicked. Her father smoked a pipe. This definitely smelled like tobacco smoke.

She turned on all the lights in the place and did a quick walk-through. Nothing seemed amiss. Even a building this old must have mandatory fire alarms. Obviously, the fumes weren't strong enough to have tripped them. As she made her way to the rear of the main stacks, the scent grew stronger.

When she got to the rear wall, Abby spotted the open window. Next to the reading chair nestled in the back corner, the window was raised several inches.

The aroma here was so pungent she could almost see wispy curls wafting in the air. Wide-eyed and crouched low, she slowly scanned the area, listening. The only sound was the twitter of the birds in the elm outside the window.

Oddly, she could almost identify what kind of tobacco it was. Maple? No, this was sweeter. Like the cherry blend her father stuffed in his pipe on special occasions and holidays.

Prickles rose on her arms, and a chill washed over her, yet the spring breeze leaking in under the sash was warm. This was the kind of chill that came from the inside out. She hugged herself.

Afraid to move, she called out, "Who's here?" The sound of her voice fell flat against the heavy insulation of paper and cloth bindings. "Is anyone there?" she called again. Nothing.

I should call the police. Confused and uneasy, she crept up and down the aisles, scanning the stacks. Not a book seemed out of place anywhere. She returned to the desk and checked the cash drawer. Nothing had been touched. There was no other evidence that anyone had been here since she locked up and left the evening before.

She lifted the telephone to call the police, then hesitated, recradling it. *What am I reporting? A break-in*? The door was securely locked when she arrived. She racked her brain, trying to remember if she or Monica opened the window yesterday and maybe forgot to shut it before they left.

Other than the open window, what other evidence did she have that anyone broke in? The odor of pipe smoke? Abby sniffed again. Now all she could detect was the slightly dusty, woody aroma of old books.

Could Dennis have stopped by after closing? He had the master key. If so, why? She could dial city hall, but maybe that wasn't too smart an idea. The last thing she needed was for her new boss to think of her as—what had Dennis called Norma Porter? A 'nervous type.' No, unless she had concrete evidence of a problem, he was the last person she should call.

Maybe one of the patrons had raised the window to enjoy the spring air as they perused a book yesterday. As for the scent of smoke, perhaps a gentleman had strolled by the open window puffing on his pipe right before she arrived.

Or perhaps, she imagined the scent entirely.

Abby drew her shoulders up around her ears and twisted her neck until a quiet pop sounded.

Must relax. She'd make herself a cup of tea and get to work.

The library was extra quiet today, and for the first time in her life she was actually uneasy there, all alone with the books. The hands on the wall clock barely moved, seemingly mired in thickened time. Only two patrons came in all morning. Both middle-aged women knew exactly what they were looking for and didn't need her help. Within minutes they plucked their romance paperbacks off the shelf and checked out.

"I thought you'd never get here," Abby huffed as Monica breezed in right at noon.

Monica checked the clock above her head and snapped, "Why, am I late?"

"No, you're not late. It's just been an agonizingly slow morning." Abby couldn't disguise her tiny sigh of relief.

Monica tilted her head. "And . . ."

"I'm beginning to imagine things about this so-called ghost. I found a window open this morning. It smelled like Harry was having himself a smoke on his pipe."

Monica's eyebrows rose.

"I could even tell what kind of tobacco it was," Abby went on. "I guess I should be glad he was considerate enough to crack open a window."

"Hmm." Monica whisked around behind the counter and stashed her purse. "I can't say it's the first time."

"You mean it's happened before? To you?"

Monica stopped, took a deep breath and seemed to consider Abby for a moment. In a patronizing voice she said, "Abby, this place has some idiosyncrasies you're just going to have to get used to."

Abby blinked, disbelieving. "Idiosyncrasies? Is that what you call them?"

The bells on the door interrupted them with a tiny, small jingle. Both women turned as the heavy oak door started to creak open, ever so slowly.

"It didn't latch when you came in," Abby said as she started toward the door. Monica stopped her, laying a hand on her arm.

"Wait a minute."

Around the edge of the door a balding, wrinkled head appeared first, then the rest of a hunched old man wearing baggy, faded overalls. Beside him shuffled a tiny woman, clutching his elbow with one gnarled hand and wielding a cane with the other.

"Good afternoon, Mr. and Mrs. Spivey. What brings you folks out on a Saturday?" Monica raised her voice to near-shouting level.

The couple took several long moments to make their way through the doorway in silence. It was as though the simple act of navigation took every bit of energy and concentration they had. Monica caught Abby's gaze and winked as they waited.

After the old man finally clicked the door shut, he turned to Monica. "Mornin', Miss Monica. Didn't expect to see you here today either."

His voice was cracked and quivery. He squinted through a pair of thick lenses bound over his ears with gold wire. Together, as one connected unit, the pair trundled toward the counter. "Finished that last Holmes book right quick," he said, then slid the book from under his arm and laid it on the counter. "'Twas a good one, too, eh Edna?" He patted his wife's hand.

Mr. Spivey craned forward, scrutinizing Abby. His eyes were huge and watery behind the smudged lenses. "This here our new librarian, eh?"

"Abby, I want you to meet Cory and Edna Spivey. They have been my regular weekly patrons ever since I started working here."

Edna's bent, rounded frame seemed even frailer under a droopy housedress made of white cotton so worn the faded lavender print was barely visible. Her pale blue gaze fixed on Monica, and her face brightened before her attention wandered to Abby.

Her smile faded to a grimace as her straggly eyebrows drew together. "Mighty young one this time. You graduate high school yet, young lady?"

Abby smiled. "Why yes, ma'am. Quite a few years back, actually." She came around the counter and extended her hand. "I'm Abigail Stryker. Pleased to meet you both."

Edna made no move to take her hand. She scanned Abby slowly, head to toe and back up again. "You in mournin', Abigail?" Her voice was tinny, like an antique car horn.

Abby's heart did a little tumble. She'd never thought of it that way. There was a time when she wore nothing but pastels. Now dark, somber colors were all she was comfortable in. She cleared her throat and struggled to smile before answering. "No ma'am. I simply like to wear black."

"You ain't one of those crazy devil worshippers, are ya?" Edna's lined face remained set in a scowl.

"No, ma'am." Abby chuckled and twisted her shoulders. She felt like a bug under a magnifying glass. She breathed a sigh of relief when the old man's gaze dropped to her feet and a grin spread across his face.

"Leastways, I see you appreciate comfort." Cory motioned toward Abby's sneakers, an amused twinkle lighting up his eyes. Then he squeezed his wife's arm. "Come on, Edna. Let's go pick us out a good story to fill up the hours this week."

As they shuffled toward the fiction stacks Abby turned toward Monica, wrinkling her nose and grinning.

"They're the cutest little pair," Monica whispered, shaking her head. "Edna can't see well enough to read anymore. Once a week they come in and pick out a book. Cory reads to her."

"Aw." Abby glanced back toward the couple.

"It's a good thing Edna can't see very well. If she'd noticed that diamond stud in your nose she'd have grilled you even harder."

Abby drew back and covered her piercing. "Maybe you'd better check out their book for them. I'll go make us some tea."

After the Spiveys left with their James Patterson hardcover, Abby came out of the back room with two steaming cups. "I appreciate you coming in today, Monica. I know you usually don't work Saturdays."

"No problem. I didn't have any other plans anyway."

Abby sipped gingerly, then set her cup on the counter. She plunked her elbows down and propped her chin on clasped hands. "Do you think anybody'll show?"

Monica stared down at what appeared to be a shiny, fresh manicure. "I can't say. Young families who live in Caldwell can't wait to get out of town. Ever since they opened the big mall in Hickory, they don't come in on the weekends as much. Then there's the festival. I'm so sorry I didn't remember to tell you until after you set the date."

Abby sighed and wandered toward the front windows. Main Street was quiet, especially so for a Saturday. She studied the storefront of Laramy's Antiques across the street. A heavy leather harness swayed from the eaves, emitting a soft squeak she imagined more than heard.

So sad. An outdated, worn-out, no-longer-useful piece of history hung out on public display. Is that what the library had become? Had the Harvey outlived its usefulness too?

A lump rose into her throat, which only served to make her mad. She hated getting all weepy. It was because she hated failure, and she had a feeling she was about to experience her first big one here at her new job. How much more pathetic could a situation get? A children's story hour and no children show?

"It's not only the ghost thing that's got you upset, is it?" Monica asked.

She had followed Abby to the window and stood behind her. Abby shook her head vigorously, unable to speak. Her throat ached with the effort to stay in control. This was her first chance to show she could accomplish something on her own. She couldn't show any signs of weakness. When Monica's hand rested on her shoulder, Abby's resolve faltered.

"No. I'm not afraid of any old spirit," she choked on a sob. "Hell, if anyone has a handle on the spirit world it's my Aunt Dianne. If I need any help on that front, I have all the resources I need."

"Then what's eating you, Abby? Has something happened with Leda?" Monica asked.

"No. I haven't seen that witch since my first day," Abby said. "It's just that everything I want for this place seems doomed."

"About today, I think that was bad timing. It's my fault, really. I should have paid closer attention to the flyers you were working on. How could you have known about the Spring Festival?" Monica squeezed Abby's shoulder. "I'm so sorry."

Monica walked back to the counter and snatched several tissues from the box at the end of the desk. She brought them to Abby, who sniffed and blew her nose, dabbing gingerly at what she was sure were black rivers of dissolved eyeliner streaming down her cheeks.

"I had such high hopes," she whined. "New job honeymoon glow. Now my first attempt to pump some blood back into this place is going to fall flat on its face. Doesn't look real good for me, does it?" She searched Monica's face.

Monica let out a long breath, looking down. "No, Abby, it doesn't. Not today, anyway. It's not the end of the world, though. It's one little glitch in the planning." A smile tugged at her lips. "You better hope nobody's little darlings do show up for story hour, my dear, or they'll be running back out the door screaming. You're not looking too good yourself at the moment. You could stand in for Frankenstein's bride right about now."

Abby dragged her purse into the tiny restroom and

repaired her drizzled makeup. What was going on with her? She hated this side of herself. It was the one facet of her former life she'd promised to banish. She hardly recognized her own reflection in the pitted oval mirror. She'd reinvented herself in the most radical ways she could think of. On the outside, anyway.

The fresh-faced, freckled bookworm now hid securely beneath layers of makeup. The waist long mane of hair was gone, chopped off and donated to Locks for Love. What was left hid its original warm chestnut hue beneath an inky black disguise. She'd suffered through the multiple piercings, all in one day.

When she moved to Caldwell, she wanted no one to recognize the person she used to be. Now was definitely not a good time for sweet, sentimental Abigail to reappear and drag her backward in time. She had to get tough and accomplish something on her own. Without her parents or a lover always taking care of her, paving the way for her successes.

Story hour was scheduled for two o'clock. Although the library had been slow all day, business ground to a halt shortly after one. Monica busied herself in silence, tackling the tedious job of re-alphabetizing romance paperbacks. Abby propped a hip against the counter, tapping a pencil on the desk calendar as she glowered at the wall clock.

At three minutes past two, she blurted, "Nobody's coming." Her words echoed in the silence. "Not a single, solitary child in the entire county wants to hear a story told by the gawky girl in black with a crooked haircut and dorky sneakers."

As if on cue, the bell on the front door jingled and burst open with such force both women jumped. In streamed a line of little kids. Two, three, five, seven . . .

Abby stared in disbelief as the children clambered through the entrance, clustering at the foot of the stairs leading to the children's loft. Ranging from hip-perched toddlers to roiling preschoolers, the youngsters rallied around a half dozen young mothers, who chattered among themselves and gently corralled the children into one cohesive group.

She didn't know any of these women. She was shocked, though, to recognize the last face coming through the door, neither child nor female. It was Jack Wood.

Grinning sheepishly at her, Jack made his way around the group of fifteen or so children to the reception desk. "Hello." His smile was so electric his whole face glowed. "I've brought you some patrons for story hour."

"What's this?" A tiny thrill washed over her. "Where . . . ?"

She glanced over toward Monica, who grinned and winked. "I guess you'll have a story hour after all."

Jack dipped his chin and locked gray-green eyes with Abby's. "My sister runs a daycare up on the Rock. Blowing Rock," he explained. "I happened to mention you reinstating the story hour." He shrugged and held up his hands. "Her kids and moms just couldn't be dissuaded."

Abby stared at him. His look of mischief was decidedly boyish.

A short, curvy redhead with glittering green eyes like Jack's stepped forward and extended her hand. "Hello Abby. I'm Elena, Jack's sister. We're so glad you're doing this." She squeezed Abby's hand and smiled. "I hope you don't mind." She motioned toward the raucous group of preschoolers. "Jack's timing, as usual, was spot on. He waltzed in yesterday and made his announcement right in the middle of snack time. On a Friday afternoon, no less."

She shrugged, mirroring his stance. Although Elena seemed some years younger, there was a definite sibling resemblance.

A little girl wearing a cap of tawny, kinky curls burst free from the group and surged forward, wrapping herself around Jack's leg. He lifted her onto his hip, glancing at Abby. "This is my niece, Lexi." He pressed a kiss on the child's rounded pink cheek. "Lexi, why don't you tell Miss Abby what your favorite story book is? In the whole wide world?"

She couldn't have been more than three, maybe four, Abby guessed. The child toyed one finger thoughtfully on her lower lip and stared at Jack with an expression Abby could only describe as awe.

Never turning from her uncle, Lexi mumbled in a tiny voice, "I reeeally love *The Very Hungry Caterpillar*."

A chorus of voices roared from the group. The enthusiastic "me too!"s were garbled amid shouted titles of other books Abby couldn't quite decipher.

She popped into action and grabbed a notepad. "We'll have time for more than one. We'll all get a turn to choose."

The children huddled around her, hushed with eyes wide.

"I'm taking requests," she said with an impish grin. "*The Very Hungry Caterpillar*. That's a popular title, Lexi. Now I want each of you to tell me your name, then the title of your favorite story book." She winked at Jack. "Your very favorite in the whole wide world."

Before the clamor recommenced she held her pencil up in the air. "First, let's all go upstairs and sit in a big, round circle. Then we'll take turns."

Abby waited as the children and their mothers filed up the stairs, feeling Jack's eyes on her.

"You're good with kids," he said, his voice a low rumble that struck her with an almost electric shock.

Shrugging, she looked away. "I have no idea how that happened. I've never been around them much." She shot him a glance over her shoulder. "Even when I was a kid."

"With some people it comes naturally." His voice was deep and soft, causing warmth to spread over her she wasn't quite sure how to handle.

She sensed him studying her, but fought the urge to meet

his gaze. Was her trembling from nerves about this new role she was about to play? Or from the musky scent of the undeniably attractive man standing close beside her?

Clutching the notepad to her chest like a shield she muttered, “I guess we’ll see about that,” before trotting up the steps on the heels of the last little boy.

She couldn’t ignore the small twinge of disappointment when she heard Jack close the door on his way out.

Abby’s planned story hour stretched into almost two, and she lost count of the number of books she read to the group of mostly mesmerized pixies. A few of the younger ones nodded off, sprawling across laps as their mothers remained transfixed to the pages of their own books, the latest romance or mystery. Just when she was sure her throat was about to dry up and crack like a desert creek bed, Monica crept up the steps with a cup in her hands.

“I’m afraid I have to be going, Abby,” she whispered with an apologetic wince, holding the mug forward like a peace offering.

Abby glanced at her watch. “Wow. I guess we got carried away.”

Amid disappointed groans, the children reluctantly clambered to their feet. She encouraged them to pick out a book to take home, and as they scattered through the low, colorful displays to choose, she sipped her tea and chatted with some of the moms. She was surprised to learn Caldwell’s library had once been a treasured local resource. Until quite recently, actually. The Harvey had been the only library within a navigable distance for residents of the Blue Ridge foothills.

“The mountains do change the way people travel in these parts,” Dahlia, mother of the toddler twins informed her. “Blowing Rock is less than twenty miles away, which doesn't seem too far. But since they started construction on the new mountain highway two years ago, the drive can take an hour or more." The young woman smiled, holding tightly onto the hands of her sons. "Blowing Rock's library doesn't have much for the kids," she said. "So it's definitely worth the drive. I'd love if we could plan on making the trip to Caldwell a regular routine."

Abby's heart swelled. This was exactly what she needed to hear. Maybe there was a chance to bring this place back to life after all.

One by one, the children crept down the winding staircase clutching books like precious puppies to their chests. Closing time had come and gone. She was in no hurry. One strawberry-blonde preschooler was still wandering through the upstairs stacks. She could hear her mother quietly urging the child to make a decision.

"Sarah, it's past closing time. The nice librarian wants to go outside and enjoy this beautiful day too."

When they finally descended the stairs and arrived in front of the checkout counter, Abby asked, "Did you find what you were looking for?"

The little girl reached up and slid three picture books onto the counter.

"She certainly did. Too much." Her mom chuckled. "As a matter of fact, I had a hard time convincing Sarah she could only take home three books today. At first she had so many gathered she couldn't even carry them."

Abby stood on tiptoes and peered over the counter. The child fixed her with strangely luminescent hazel eyes. "How old are you, Sarah?" she asked.

Sarah lowered her head, twisting her hands together and fidgeting one sneaker-clad toe along the rug's frayed edge as she whispered, "Four and a half."

"So I see you like to read," she said as she took the

library card from Sarah's mom and scanned it.

"I do," Sarah proclaimed, holding her gaze. After a pause, the child asked in a small voice, "Are you going have story hour every Saturday, Miss New Librarian?"

Abby's heart went to jelly. She came around the counter and crouched to address the child at eye level. "You can call me Miss Abby." She grasped one of Sarah's chubby hands and pumped it gently. "At least once a month, Miss Sarah. Maybe more. Can I count on you being here?"

Sarah's mom answered for her. "We'll plan on it. Ms. Stryker, I hope you'll stay on. We'd love if this library came back to life. There are a lot of people wishing for that."

Abby smiled into her warm gaze. "I'm going to give it my best shot."

After Sarah and her mom left, Abby stood alone in the library foyer and looked around. The late afternoon sun cast long golden bands across the common table in the meeting room, and light fell in broken swatches across the faded tapestry rug. Although the usual hush had reclaimed the rooms, the empty space somehow didn't feel quite as lonely. Even the musty air seemed lighter, freshened by all the sweet smelling little people who traipsed about all afternoon.

Story hour had been a success after all. Abby wondered if there was a chance the ghost of this place was on her side. There'd been no strange book dislodging, no windows sliding open, no scent of smoke wafting about since this morning.

Straightening her shoulders, she took a deep breath and spoke in a whisper. "Thank you for not scaring the children, Harry."

Her only answer was silence, and she surprised herself to realize she was actually disappointed.

Yet a niggling heaviness underscored her joy. As she

gathered her things and did a final walk-through, she replayed the events of the day. Yes, story hour had been a success after all. But why? It didn't take a genius to realize the credit didn't belong to Abby. Not because of her talent, her initiative, or her efforts. Story hour succeeded only because of outside influence. Again. From a man—an older man.

The truth of the matter extinguished her initial glee like an icy wave. Story hour only happened today because of Jack Wood.

Anguish knotted her stomach. This was exactly what she didn't want. All through her life, she had never achieved anything entirely her own. Sure, she graduated Summa Cum Laude from Appalachia State, but her parents were both influential members of the faculty. She'd achieved her graduate degree, true, but not without making other significant . . . connections. She'd grown up a part of the university community, for God's sake. There was no way she could fail.

Now Abby was twenty-six. She was ready for a life of her own making. This time, she wanted her accomplishments to belong to her and only her. The more she stewed on the situation, alone in the quiet of the fading afternoon light, the madder she got.

She didn't need anyone to take care of her. No more sugar daddies. She had sworn that oath the day she left her hometown. Jack Wood was older, possibly much older than she.

Okay, so he was hot. She couldn't deny she was attracted to him. What he did today, though, illustrated that he was also the kind of man who liked to protect women, as though they couldn't take care of themselves, or wouldn't survive a little disappointment. She wasn't going anywhere near that kind of relationship. Not ever again.

Her half-hour of ruminating left her irritable and filled with resentment, effectively overlaying her bruised confidence with a wing of thorny pride. She grabbed her bag and headed for the door. As she stepped outside and the lock clicked, a voice behind her made her jump.

"Fine afternoon for a drive in the mountains, Ms. Stryker."

She turned to see the object of her consternation resting on the fender of his SUV with his arms folded across his tweed jacket. This time the stuffy blazer topped a casual Henley shirt and fashionably faded, snugly fitting jeans.

A mischievous twinkle in Jack's eyes amplified an almost smug smirk. "Might I have the pleasure of escorting you on a regional tour of our lovely foothills?" He motioned with one hand toward his vehicle.

Abby bristled. "No, thank you. I think you've done quite enough for me today. I appreciate your intention, Dr. Wood. I have to say, though, your gesture came off as a bit patronizing. I mean, seriously—dragging in the entirety of your sister's daycare? A pre-packaged entourage?"

He stared at her, his jaw slack. "I only wanted to help spread the word about what you were doing here, Abby."

"Well, in the process, you made it painfully clear to me and everybody else that you had no confidence in my ability to pull this off on my own."

He raked a hand through his steely-laced curls. "That's not even close to the truth. I figured with the festival in town your story hour might be a bit thin this first time."

"Sure you did," she snipped, avoiding his gaze and stalking down the steps. She deliberately shifted her path to swing wide around him.

As she swished past, he snapped, "So how thin was it, exactly? How many takers did you have this afternoon that weren't part of, as you call it, my 'entourage'?"

The fact hit squarely in her pride. Of course, he was right. Not one child had shown up before, or after, Elena's group. So yes, he saved the day for her. A knight in shining armor come to rescue poor, pathetic Abigail. Taking care of the little woman who wasn't capable of managing her own life.

Her shoulders twitched, and she jerked to a halt, her back toward him. Fury overrode logic. She spun around and took one long step until she was only inches away from him, deliberately challenging his space.

Which might have been a mistake. This close, she could smell him, a musky scent that made her blood thrum a little faster in her veins. And she realized that instead of face to face, she was actually face to chest. She blinked, stunned as she studied the few dark hairs peeking out through the open placket of his shirt. For one fleeting second she forgot completely what she'd intended to say. Almost why she'd been so upset.

Center. He was attractive. Smelled fantastic too. So what?

She took a deep breath for courage.

I must remember this guy is also arrogant, domineering, and way older than me. And too freaking tall.

Abby threw her head back and glared up at him. "Okay, point taken. Without your kindly intervention this afternoon, Dr. Wood, not a single child would have shown up," she spat, hating to admit the truth.

A muscle in his jaw worked, and she could tell he was struggling not to laugh. He thought this was funny. Her throat tightened, but there was no way in hell she was going to cry in front of this man. She spun on her heel and stomped down the sidewalk.

"Now wait just one minute," he said, his voice softer as he caught her arm.

She wheeled around, jerking to free herself. "How dare you? Get your hands off me."

His hold, although gentle, was insistent. He wouldn't let go.

They stood there, frozen in an awkward, confusing

moment that made Abby's head spin. She was outraged, hurt, and indignant, yet it had more to do with her own private ghosts than what happened today. Deep down she knew she was acting irrationally, venting on a man who'd meant no harm.

Her attraction to him frightened her. It would be so easy to yield to him, to fold herself into his embrace. To fall right back into the same treacherous, vulnerable place she was a few years ago.

Jack was studying her face with concern, head tipped with his brows drawn together. "How could my trying to help you possibly have pissed you off like this, Abigail?" His sincere, puzzled tone undid her.

The tears welled, and she knew she had to shut down, close up, and fast. She had to protect the raw, still-unhealed parts inside her. There was only one way she could do that.

Attitude. She let the anger take hold, climbing over her weakness. She was shaking, her hands clenched. When she spoke, she sounded icy and foreign, even to her own ears.

"Look, I know you are the older, wiser, esteemed Professor Wood. A lot of people in this town respect you. You probably think I'm overenthusiastic and inexperienced. Trust me, I really do know what I'm doing. I don't need you, or anyone else for that matter, to take care of me."

She yanked her arm free and took off down the street. "Not anymore. Not ever again," she shouted. Her words echoed back to her from inside her own head.

Abby broke into a run, dodging dangerously between the stopped cars waiting for the light near the corner.

I need to get back to my room. Back to my cloistered solitude, where I'm safe and can't get hurt again.

As her trembling fingers fumbled with her apartment

keys, she realized a terrifying truth.

This was a small town, and Jack Wood wasn't going to go away. And with him around, no matter how she steeled herself, her resolutions were in peril. She feared she was slipping straight back into the spiraling uncertainty, a soft, emotional pit that once threatened to destroy her entire world.

Chapter 5

The tap on her door came two hours later. Abby lay sprawled on her bed, still wearing her work clothes, her face planted in the pillow. She'd dozed off that way, rubbing her damaged ego raw with waves of self-pity. Finally, she'd surrendered to an exhausted, dreamless sleep.

She wasn't sure how long she slept and not certain whether the pale glow leaking in around the window shade was dawn or twilight. At first she thought the rapping on the door had spilled out from a dissolving dream. Then it sounded again, crisp and insistent on the glass door at the foot of the stairs.

Strange. She hardly knew anybody in town but Aunt Di. If it was her aunt, she had a key. Why didn't she just come up?

The tapping repeated, every thirty seconds or so, echoing in the stairwell.

Dragging to her feet, Abby snapped on the lamp and glanced in the mirror. Smeared eyeliner had turned her eyes into two black-ringed holes. Her once crisply pressed white shirt wore an erratic pattern of creases. What used to be a trendy hairstyle now looked like a black bird's nest stuck on one side of her head. She groaned.

The knocking continued, annoyingly, in regular short bursts. She threw back the deadbolt on her door, pulling it open as far as the chain allowed, and peered down the stairwell.

He stood outside the storm door at the foot of the stairs. Waiting between knocks, Jack crammed his hand back into the pocket of his khaki slacks. He was shifting from one foot to another and glancing from side-to-side.

For a beat she was tempted to ease the door shut, fasten the deadbolt, and go back to her private pity party. Yet something inside her wavered—some part of her she knew was far too weak to begin with. She called out, "Just a minute!"

Darting into the bathroom, she rubbed away the dark smudges with a wet washcloth, re-rimming her eyes quickly with black pencil. She replaced her wrinkled Oxford with an oversized T-shirt imprinted with *Blessed Be*—a Christmas gift from Aunt Di she'd never worn. Several painful swipes with a plastic-tined brush tamed the bird's nest. Taking a deep breath, Abby threw open the door and slunk down the steps.

Jack moved back, wearing a meek smile over his tweed jacket as she pushed through the door. "Hey."

"Hey." She studied her bare feet. "Sorry," she blurted, while a little voice in her head whispered, *Sorry for what? Sorry for who?*

"It's okay, Abby," Jack murmured. "I guess I overstepped my bounds. I didn't mean to patronize, and shouldn't have interfered." He shifted closer. "I only meant to help."

Lifting her chin with a finger, he forced her eyes to meet his.

"I hardly know you, Abigail. It's your smile. I wanted to do something, anything, to insure I was going to see that beautiful smile of yours again."

She gazed up at him, unable to keep the curve from her lips. "I believe you meant well, Jack. I'm sorry I acted so irrational. I didn't mean to be a witch."

His eyes lingered on hers, and she couldn't ignore the naked sincerity in them. A lump clogged her throat. Squeezing her eyes shut, she turned her face away.

"Too late now for a scenic drive. It'll be dark soon,"

Jack said. "The festival buzzes until midnight or later. Let me take you there."

She absolutely shouldn't do this. The last thing she needed at this point in her life was to get involved with another man. Especially another *older* man. She'd been down this road before. A dead-ended, secret maze. She definitely needed a friend, though, since beside Aunt Di and Monica, Abby had none in this town. As long as she kept her intentions clear, what harm could it do?

"I could use a friend, Jack. Just a friend."

He smiled into her eyes, then glanced down at her bare feet. "Wanna get your sneaks?"

Abby ran upstairs and swapped her skirt for jeans. She slipped her black sweater on, leaving it open over the T-shirt. Fifteen minutes later she found herself seated in the passenger seat of Jack's car feeling like an awkward teenager on a first date.

"Are you sure you want to do this?" she asked as he pulled out onto the two lane highway headed south.

Jack chuckled. "Why not? The festival is kind of fun. It's not your usual carnival. They attract lots of artisans. Arts and crafts. Sort of a Renfest."

"I know," Abby said. "My Aunt Dianne has a booth there." She studied his chiseled jaw in the lights from the dash. Square, strong, and clean-shaven. Her heart did a little tumble. Memories flashed. "That's not what I mean," she continued in a small voice. "I mean, are you sure you want to be seen out in public with me?"

He shot her a quizzical look. "Why wouldn't I want to be seen with you?"

She blinked. *That's right. This isn't Cameron. This is Jack. We're just friends. There's nothing to be ashamed of.*

What was it that made him smell so good? His cologne or wood smoke? Whatever the scent was, it was earthy, masculine, and extremely appealing. A warm flush washed over her, temporarily offsetting the panic she tried so desperately to suppress.

Then she remembered one more possible complication. “Isn’t there a chance we’ll bump into lovely Leda down there? It’s at her college, right? She’s your boss, isn’t she? I don’t think she’s fond of me, or what I’m here to do.”

He hesitated, cocking his head before turning to look her way. “All true. But I doubt we’ll find Leda at a fun family activity like this. She’s more likely to be found sipping a glass of two hundred dollar a bottle wine down at Le Petit Mon.”

“My aunt’s husband owns that place.”

“Really? Your Aunt Dianne? Caldwell’s resident witch?” He shot her a wide-eyed look. “Do they serve eye of newt there?” Then he grinned.

“Very funny. Dianne is not a witch, not like what you’re thinking. Although I’ll admit Uncle Armpit is a bit strange.”

Jack burst out laughing. “Did you say Uncle Armpit?”

“Don’t ask. I’ll tell you the story sometime. He and I got off to a bad start, that’s all.”

“I’ve heard the food there is pretty good. We should have dinner one night.” Jack smiled. “I’d love to try it out with you.”

She fidgeted in her seat, saying nothing.

“What kind of stuff does your aunt sell in her shop?”

“Dried herbs, soaps, and candles. She has some Wiccan things, like crystals and wands. Some books.” She turned to face him. “Despite local rumor, she is not a wicked witch.”

“I was only kidding, Abby.” His lips pressed into a thin line. “People who grew up in the wilderness—sometimes they conjure up the strangest notions. Like your library ghost, for example.” He reached over and plucked one of her hands from the knotted ball in her lap. He squeezed her fingers, his brows drawing together. “What are you so nervous about?”

She pulled her hand free and turned to stare out into the darkness. “Harvey Library might be right where I belong,” she murmured, more to herself than to Jack. “I’ve got a few ghosts of my own.” She said the last so quietly she wasn’t surprised, only relieved, when he didn’t ask questions. Maybe he hadn’t heard her.

As they crested a rise in the highway, a growing glow hovered over the field in the distance. The crisply lighted corners of the massive, modern college building loomed in the foreground.

“Wow,” she said. She’d driven past the college before in the daytime, always too busy watching traffic on the busy highway it fronted to notice how impressive a complex it was.

He followed the winding drive past the cluster of buildings. Under the glow of security lights, she could make out the chain-linked perimeters of two athletic fields, abandoned in the darkness. A paved path flanked the fence, then on into an open field. The driveway turned first to gravel, then dirt, and then grass.

Jack parked in an empty spot along the field’s perimeter. He cut the engine, then the headlights. Off to her left, bright, multicolored spots outlined a small Ferris wheel and a string of white globes traced a row of low tents. She turned toward him when she sensed his stare.

“You okay?” he asked.

“Yeah,” Abby mumbled. Her heart thudded against her ribs, and a chill washed over her. Gooseflesh rose on her arms, and she slipped both hands under her sweater to rub them up and down.

He started to open his door, but she shot forward to touch his arm.

“Give me a minute, okay?” she asked, her voice wavering.

A flash of headlights behind them startled her, and the car parked a few spaces down. The sounds of doors slamming and muffled conversation drifted past them, causing her to slide down in her seat.

"What's the matter, Abby?" Jack asked as he took her hand.

She turned away and pressed herself against the door, squeezing her elbows to her sides. If she shrunk into the smallest possible space, she might become invisible. The tightening started in her throat, and she realized she hadn't brought her inhaler. Damn. She hadn't had a panic attack in almost three months. Now her breath came in short, rapid bursts, and her eyesight blurred, casting halos around the lights in the distance. The rush of memories filled her mind, hitting too close to the edges of an unhealed wound.

A panicked, familiar voice screamed inside her head—*You cannot, must not, be seen with this man.*

She just couldn't do this. Not yet. She knew this was all different from before, yet her psyche wouldn't let logic convince her.

"I'm sorry, Jack. I'm feeling awfully tired all of a sudden." She barely got the words out through her clenching throat. She sucked in a short breath. "And my asthma is kicking up. Fresh cut grass or something. I'm sorry you brought me all the way out here for nothing. Please, can you just take me home?" Her words tumbled out too fast, and panic leaked all over them no matter how hard she tried to contain it.

He paused, studying her face, his brows forcing little vertical creases into the space between them. He said nothing, didn't ask any questions or try to persuade her, only patted her knee and started the car.

Relief whooshed out of her as they entered the highway.

The twenty-minute drive back to Caldwell was silent except for a few times when he asked if she was okay. She kept her arms wrapped around herself and answered with silent nods.

His car had barely come to a stop at the curb when Abby yanked on the handle. As she scrambled out of the car she muttered, “I’m sorry, Jack.”

He made no move to follow her, and she was grateful. Gentleman as he was, he waited with the headlights on until she unlocked the door into her stairwell before leaving.

Panic subsided as soon as she was back in her room, alone. She was even more exhausted than before, embarrassed, and guilt-ridden. It wasn’t fair for her to play cat and mouse with Jack. He seemed like such a nice man. His intentions were most likely honorable. But the place inside her where a heart used to be was still cloaked in black and underneath its protective shroud, bloodied and raw. Tonight proved to her it was too soon for her to be alone with a man, even if only as a friend.

Abby sat on the edge of her bed, staring into the dark stillness of her lonely room. Did she even know how to socialize with a man? Under normal conditions?

Renewal. That was the key word in Abby’s mind early the next morning as she deftly navigated her tiny hybrid car up the twisting highway out of Caldwell. She loved the springtime.

Having grown up in the mountains, she knew how contagious the energy of renewal could be. The forests came alive with aromas and sounds and colors of rebirth. White jasmine and clematis blossoms peeked out from the undergrowth alongside the road. Their intoxicating aroma enveloped her, seeping in to surround her through the open windows.

In the Chamber of Commerce’s brochure, the mountain highway was described as scenic. Perhaps. Truth was, unless you had a chauffeur, this route was no joy ride. The highway between Caldwell and points north was challenging, even in the light of day. On the map, Route 321 looked so direct, so easy. Maps didn't show how the highway was stepped, repeatedly doubling back on itself to climb an impossibly steep grade. The journey defined a twisted exercise in vehicular navigation, even on the weekends when construction crews were absent.

As she concentrated on keeping her front wheels centered in the narrow space between the lines, she regretted not being able to take in the scenic views. No matter. She was on a mission. Yesterday, she made up her mind to dress up the entrance of her library. She remembered an artisan halfway up the mountain between Caldwell and the Rock who created lawn ornaments.

She'd seen urns there once—giant, flute-edged cauldrons of stone. They'd been displayed out by the road alongside the birdbaths, griffins, and gargoyles. She hoped the place was open for business on Sundays.

They would be perfect. She imagined lavish plantings of daffodils in spring, petunias through the summer, and hardy mums into the holiday season. There's no better way to breathe life back into the old building than by decorating the doorstep with brilliant, living blooms.

The artisan's yard appeared around one of many sharp curves in the road. The chain-linked property perched precariously on the flattened crest between two steep sections of highway. Abby pulled into the narrow graveled space along the fence. She was glad to see the gate was swung back and latched, hung with a hand-lettered sign. *Open.*

She wandered through, her huge purse hoisted over one shoulder, knowing exactly what she was looking for as she strode past the monstrous gargoyle sculptures squatting inside the gate without a second glance. A pebbled path wound toward a low-roofed structure where another hand-lettered sign swung, squeaking on rusted chains from the eave. Trinkets & Treasures. She avoided the touristy gift shop, turning right on the gravel around to the back of the building.

She followed the path into a magical garden of stone. Creatures of every imaginable shape and size posed silently along the gravel walkways, some lined up into what looked like stone choirs. A gnome with his perky pointed hat rested atop a huge section of oak trunk. Clusters of woodland creatures, rabbits, squirrels, foxes, and baby deer huddled in clusters as though they might warm their cold bodies into life if they drew close enough together.

Mythical creatures commanded their own corner. A winged fairy struck a graceful pose on a faux log. A wood sprite perched atop a mushroom, staring at something only she could see. Across the way, a clutch of grotesques hunkered down on scaly haunches.

Finally, she spotted them. Designed in varying shapes and sizes, the planters guarded the rear boundary in a sentinel row. She spotted the ones she wanted right away.

They were huge, rising waist-high on fluted pedestals molded into realistically rendered, clawed feet. A carved outer shell fanned open at the top with a scalloped edge. Abby could imagine colorful petals spilling over the rim. She knelt beside a matched pair, running her fingers over the smooth surface.

The sudden scratchy voice behind her made her heart leap. She jumped up and let out a small shriek.

"Oh, I'm terribly sorry, miss, I wuz sure ye'd hear my footsteps on this noisy old gravel."

The woman sounded rusty and ancient, an impression echoed by the leathery folds of her face. She squinted in the bright sunlight so Abby couldn't see if she even had eyes. Her hair, dyed a shocking pale pink and styled in a spiked crew cut, jarred Abby from any immediate assumptions.

"Oh that's all right," she managed with a nervous chuckle. "I was admiring your handiwork. You have some truly amazing sculptures here."

The woman cackled a dry laugh. "Nawt so much as a sculpture among 'em. Every one of 'em comes from a see-ment mold." The strange old woman stood taller, straightening her shoulders. "It's my son who does all these. Glad you like 'em." A proud grin fought to lift her wrinkles.

Abby smiled back, amused. "Well, you ought to be pretty proud," she said. "I was looking for a pair of urns to plant some flowers in. To decorate an entryway."

The woman nodded toward the urns beside her. "Well, I hope you got a right grand place to be puttin' urns that size a-front," she said. "Why, each of them urns weighs near as much as you do."

She giggled, shaking her head. "No, these aren't for me. They're for the entrance of the library down in Caldwell. I'm the new librarian there, and I want to dress up the place. Make it a little more inviting."

The woman's expression sobered. "The Harvey?" she asked, stitching her brows into even deeper creases. She leaned closer, dark eyes appearing from between slits to scrutinize Abby. After a moment she said, "Well, those sure would be about right for that size building. Tell me. I done heard that old library was set to close down. Thought it already had." She scratched her scalp through spiky, thin pink fronds.

"No," Abby replied brightly. "Not closed. And it won't be if I have any say in the matter." She waved a hand toward the urns. "How much are these?"

"Ninety-five dollars apiece," the woman replied. "If you want two, I'll do a hundred and a half for both." She turned her head to spat onto the gravel path, and it was then Abby noticed the slight bulge in the woman's right cheek.

Chewing tobacco. The woman's cheek was stuffed with chewing tobacco.

"Young lady?" she continued with brows fighting to inch upward into the folds. "How do you plan on movin' these things?"

Abby's shoulders sagged as reality hit her. She hadn't considered logistics. She doubted if even one of the urns would fit into the back of her tiny car. And if it did, how on earth would she ever get them up the library steps?

"Oh," she said quietly. "I guess I hadn't thought the plan through very well."

The pink-haired woman crossed her arms and considered her in silence. When Abby frowned and shifted to leave, the woman spoke.

"Young lady, I'll tell you what I'll do. Since this is for a good cause and all, and also because my son and me was planning on headin' down to the festival in Caldwell today anyway . . ."

She paused, and Abby waited in hopeful disbelief.

"Well, I'll have Jonathan load two of these planters right in the back of his dually, I will. We can drop 'em off on our way." She paused to spat another thin stream of amber fluid into the gravel. "Jonathan, he's a big strappin' boy. He'll have no problem settin' those urns right there on the library steps where you want 'em."

Abby stared at her in delighted shock. "That would be more than kind, Mrs.—"

"Miss Cornwell," the woman replied with a smile. With one gnarled hand, she covered Abby's with a swift, firm squeeze.

"I'm Abigail Stryker. Call me Abby, Miss Cornwell."

"I'll never remember that," the woman mumbled, shaking her head and looking down at the ground. She glanced up. "I'm sure you won't mind too much if'n I just call you Miss

Librarian." Then she flashed a wide, sincere grin, revealing a not-quite complete row of yellow stained teeth.

A few hours later, Abby stood in front of the library, waving goodbye to her new friends, a strange pair pulling away in a rust-flecked white Ford dually. Jonathan had refused the folded money she tried to press into his palm after he easily slid the urns into exactly the spots she wanted.

She plopped down on the top step and glanced from one side to the other. The planters flanked the library's front door in proud silence like two stone guards.

"There." She addressed the headless sentries. "Now we'll get you properly dressed.

Jack Wood's morning ritual had been set in stone for as long as he lived in Caldwell. Up before the sun's rays leaked through the leafy cavern where his woodland home hid, he donned his running gear. Three miles every morning, no matter the weather. The pounding of his footsteps, the whoosh of his own heartbeats in his ears aligned and meshed with the subtle sounds of the forest gearing up for a brand new day.

Sundays were his favorite. After his run and long hot shower, he loved the decadence of lounging on his back deck with a steaming mug of coffee. This first weekend in May, for some reason, seemed to pulsate with unseen promise.

A drive. Perhaps a drive along the Blue Ridge to take some snapshots of wildlife and foliage on that fancy new Nikon his parents gave him last Christmas. His favorite hiking trail, just off mile marker 251, had a picnic area tucked halfway along its two-mile length. The oasis overlooked one of the area's many hidden waterfalls.

Too bad he didn't have anyone to share that lovely hideaway with.

His mind drifted back to Abby as he slumped in his Adirondack chair watching a pair of baby rabbits search the perimeter of his garden fence for entry. He was sure asking his sister to bring her group of children down to story hour was an ingenious way to befriend the strange young woman. Abigail Stryker was a bit stranger than he imagined.

What he knew about her he learned from Leda, either by casual, indirect questioning or outright eavesdropping. Although Abby had only recently earned her degree, Jack wondered how Leda's husband managed to lure Abby here, to tiny Caldwell. Surely, one as young and ambitious as Abby was looking for a challenge bigger than the Harvey.

Jack thought back to a few days ago when he overheard Leda complaining to Clara about what she considered Dennis' "latest faux pas."

"I figured after the last one up and ran out on him, Dennis would surely listen to reason and close the place down. Until Dianne, the old witch, cornered him at the town hall meeting."

Leda's secretary, Clara, was older and wiser than her years gave her a right to be. A long silence yawned in their conversation before she casually asked, "I assume you're referring to the leader of our local Wiccan sector? The one who runs Ancient Healings?"

"Of course I am," Leda snapped. "I swear that woman really does have supernatural powers."

Although he couldn't see them from where he stood in the mailroom, he heard a fist slamming the counter.

"Turns out she has a darling little niece, newly graduated. Perky and raring to go with exactly the credentials Caldwell needs to bring the old library back to life." Her voice sizzled with sarcasm.

Of course his curiosity was piqued. Newcomers to Caldwell, at least those who intended to stay, didn't happen along all that often. And there weren't that many single, eligible women who might be looking for a relationship.

His solitary bachelor's life suited him—for now. Yet he knew in his heart he didn't want to be alone forever.

He came from a big, close country family. His sisters all married young and had their first children before they turned thirty. That hadn't happened for him, though he wanted it to. He thought once, in his last year at Duke, he'd found his soul mate. He'd fallen in love with a girl named Dawn. He'd been so smitten with her he'd actually looked up the meaning of her name.

First light. Daybreak.

It was a sign. He gave his heart and trust to a woman who ultimately chose her career over a future with him. She'd delivered that decision with a murderous blow. The harsh lesson he learned marred him and haunted him still. Now, twelve years later and some wiser, he was much more cautious.

Curiosity had stirred him to return several books early, right after Abby started her new job. He had anticipated a prim and proper, classic librarian, fresh out of school. Most likely the conservative, older-than-her-years type, if not downright classic-librarian-dowdy.

What he expected to find behind the library's reception desk that night, and what he found, were as far different as fire and water.

Of all the professions Jack might have labeled the petite brunette with, librarian wasn't even on the list. She looked too damned young. He did the math, knowing she'd completed a Master's degree. Twenty-five maybe? Twenty-six? She sure didn't look it, though she carried herself with a disconcerting assuredness.

Her dark, almond eyes were wise. Her trendy, extreme hairstyle shouted confidence. The piercings, though subtlety elegant, were another jolt—a downright enticing one. And all that black clothing. Her entire persona screamed Goth.

In retrospect he shouldn't have been surprised. When he found out Abby was Dianne Le Mon's niece, he should have figured she'd belong to that odd group of Earth-Mother types, the ones who drank herbal tea and bought crystals and candles at Ancient Healings.

He sighed, draining his second cup of dark Arabica. There was no denying it. He didn't exactly understand what it was about strange little Abigail Stryker that caused his blood pressure to rise. She was radically different from the type of women he usually was attracted to—the conservative, English teacher types whose most drastic fashion statement was a new pair of dangly earrings.

Maybe her unpredictability intrigued him. So far, she'd baffled him. He tried to help her with story hour, and she read him the riot act. Tried taking her out for a fun night at the festival, and she freaked out. A mystery. An enigma.

Probably as eccentric as her aunt.

Except he loved exploring the unexpected. Abby had cocky attitude and confidence to spare. The woman he'd given his heart to in college was the same way, and his first instinct was to steer clear of types who valued their ambitions over emotions.

But somehow, his gut told him Abby's bravado was a façade. He couldn't help feeling as though underneath all that trendy independence, a softer side lie hidden. Maybe one with a big old bruise on it.

Chapter 6

Precisely at ten a.m., Jack hopped into his CR-V and headed into town. Breakfast at Murphy's was another part of his Sunday tradition, where he sat at the counter and read through the *Hickory Daily Record* over another cup of coffee. He'd packed his new camera, and planned to grab a grinder-to-go from the sandwich shop before heading up the mountain.

Finally on the road, he sat waiting at the traffic light on Main. The last sight he expected to see was a damsel in distress. Abby's miniature vehicle was parked at the base of the library steps, the rear hatch raised. Her knees braced on the bumper, she wrestled with a bag of potting soil that appeared to outweigh her.

Jack pulled up to the curb behind her. She glanced over one shoulder, then rolled her eyes when he cut the engine. He stepped out, and before he even slammed the door she muttered, "So here's my local knight in shining armor come to poor Abby's rescue."

He froze in his tracks. "Look," he snapped. "You obviously don't need any help. Sorry to have interrupted you. I'll leave you to it." He turned and reopened his door.

When she made another sound, he paused. This time, it was an exasperated grumble. Yet still she had not turned to face him.

After a beat of silence, she shouted a curt remark over her shoulder. "In this particular situation, Professor Wood, I obviously do."

He thought her plea for help sounded more like a cougar's snarl. He stopped, turned, and strolled up behind her. The back of her car looked like a loaded floral delivery van.

"What on earth are you doing?" he asked through a chuckle.

She silently glared up at him, a long lock of black hair hanging over one eye. Sweat beaded the visible part of her brow. She had a smudge of dirt on her nose amid a sprinkling of freckles he hadn't noticed before. The sultry dark eyeliner that usually rimmed her eyes was missing, and without it, he hardly recognized her.

He laughed out loud at her sour glare. "Where are you going with all these flowers?"

Abby blew her hair out of her eyes and jerked her head toward the library entrance. "Civic beautification project."

He stared in amazement at the huge urns on the top step, then looked back and forth between them and the waif-like woman in front of him. "By God, how did you . . ." he began, but stopped himself. He probably better not ask. "They're absolutely gorgeous, Abby. Perfect." He smiled down at her. "I'm a pretty fair hand in the garden."

She narrowed her eyes, sweeping her gaze up and down the length of him. "You're out of uniform. No tweed today?"

"Never on Sundays," he said with a smirk. "Here, let me give you a hand."

An hour or so later Abby stood beside Jack on the sidewalk perusing the fruits of their labor. The urns had sprung to life. Perfectly. He hadn't exaggerated his talents. He knew quite a bit about plants and offered some tips she thought were especially useful. The arrangements turned out exactly as she imagined.

She'd chosen a yellow and cream palette, accented by varying hues of green. Buttery petunias nestled in among sunny bright marigolds. Tiny strands of variegated English ivy spilled over the fluted edges, swaying gently in the slightest whisper of breeze. In the center of each urn, she placed a tall, thin baby evergreen to shoot skyward out of the colorful blooms.

"I like the junipers, Abby," he said, studying the completed planters with his hands on his hips. "It's a unique touch."

"I wanted them to span the seasons," she said. "I figured the marigolds and ivy might make it a ways into the fall, and when they die off, I can decorate the little trees for Christmas."

"You celebrate Christmas?" he asked, scratching his jaw.

She bristled, scowling up at him. "Why exactly would you assume I don't celebrate Christmas?"

"I thought you and your aunt . . ." Jack shifted from one foot to the other. "I'm sorry, I don't know much about that religion. Wiccan, or whatever."

She squinted and took a step toward him, her elbows drawn back. "Let's get one thing straight, Professor. My Aunt Dianne is into Wicca. I am not. And it's not exactly a religion, anyway. Not to her way of thinking. It's a-a lifestyle. A respect for Mother Nature." She huffed and slapped the drying soil off her hands. "Di also celebrates Christmas, by the way," she added quietly.

He raised his eyebrows and said nothing. After a beat he cleared his throat. "Hey, I'll gather up all the empty pots. Is there a broom in the library?"

"Why? Do you want to see how I ride on it?" The response burst from her before she had a chance to stop it.

Oh my god, I'm such a bitch.

She slapped a muddy hand over her mouth, sputtering on a mouthful of dust. Embarrassed, she broke into a fit of giggles. "I'm sorry, Jack. Bad joke."

She was relieved to see he was laughing with her.

Her chest swelled with joy. The urns were precisely what she wanted. She trotted up the steps, digging the key out of her pocket.

As she fiddled with the lock, a long, large car purred up the street, slowing when it reached the library. She turned as a shiny Lincoln town car stopped. The deeply tinted passenger window whirred down. Aunt Dianne's pewter mane glistened in the sunlight as she waved.

"Oh, Abby, what a wonderful tribute to Beltane!" she shouted, so loud the words echoed down the entire length of Main Street.

Abby cringed. She could see her uncle behind the wheel, waving.

"I'm proud of you, girl!" Dianne said, giving her the thumbs up as the car pulled away.

After they disappeared around the corner, Abby glanced at Jack sheepishly. "Beltane," she repeated. "Wiccan spring festival of fertility." Then she shrugged. "I'll go grab my broom and fly right back out," she chanted.

He shook his head, still chuckling. "All righty then."

When she returned, he was loading all the trash into an empty box he had in the back of his car. Abby swept the spilled soil off the library entry before returning the broom to its closet.

After she relocked the front door and came sauntering down the steps, Jack asked, "How about some lunch? It's a beautiful day for a picnic."

She blinked. A picnic sounded . . . reasonably private.

"A picnic, where?"

"There are some picturesque spots on the mountain. Quiet. I know you don't like crowds."

Considering, she sighed, looking off down the street. What could it hurt? She was a big girl. It wasn't as if she should be afraid to go off in the woods with him. He had a stellar reputation in this town, and had been nothing but a gentleman to her so far.

Friends. She would make it clear a platonic relationship was all she was interested in. In a private setting, with a friend, particularly a male one, she might be able to work her way through this . . . transition.

She blinked up at him and tipped her head to one side. Holding her grimy arms out in front of her, she said, “I think a shower is in order first.”

“I’ll run by and drop this stuff off at the recycling center,” he said. “I’ll clean up and be back in, what, about an hour?”

She studied his impish grin. Standing there in the brilliant noonday sun, he didn’t look like a stuffy professor. More like an impulsive teenager. The sharp lines of his jaw were softened by casual stubble. His white polo, still remarkably unsoiled considering the job they just tackled, enhanced an athletic, broad-shouldered frame. The shirttails had somehow remained tucked neatly into the waistband of crisp jeans that hugged him quite enticingly. Yet she couldn’t ignore that the chocolate tousled curls on his crown were still, unmistakably, laced with gray.

Friends, she reminded herself. That’s all she was ready for. Yet she couldn’t help wondering . . .

“How old are you?” she blurted, another sentence firing from brain to tongue without her intent. Warmth rose up her neck, and she stammered, “I mean, I’m not exactly jail bait, but I also don’t want people thinking I’m another Leda Ludwig.”

Realizing she was getting herself in deeper by the minute, she clamped both grimy hands over her face and moaned. “I’m sorry. I’m a bookworm, remember? I’m not very good at this stuff.”

When she peeked out from between her fingers he was grinning down at her with a mischievous gleam in his eyes.

"Neither am I," he said. "And don't worry. I don't think I'm quite old enough to be your father."

An hour later, Abby was waiting in the rocker on the porch of Ancient Healings when Jack drove up. She'd showered, changed into a gauzy black frock, and grabbed a wide-brimmed straw hat. She also had taken the extra five minutes for makeup. He got out and followed her around to the passenger side.

"A gentleman." She nodded approvingly as he opened the door. "You *must* be old." She smiled up at him from under the brim of her hat.

He slid behind the wheel and looked over at her. His smile evaporated. "You covered them up again," he whined.

"Covered what?" She cocked her head.

"Your freckles. How do you do that? Just make them disappear at will?"

"Yup. Magic. Poof! Freckles, be gone! A little spell my auntie taught me."

She could tell he wasn't sure if he should laugh. He played it safe with a simple "Ah" and a nod.

They started up the winding highway into the mountains, and she asked, "Where are we going, Professor Wood?"

"Well, I was originally planning a hike on the Appalachian Trail and a picnic near the waterfall. But I don't think your pretty dress would survive the brushy trails and hanging branches."

Her heart sank. "Why didn't you say something, Jack? You said picnic. I was thinking manicured grounds, pavilions, and picnic tables. I could have worn jeans and hiking boots."

"No, this is even better. Have you ever eaten at the Lookout?"

She shook her head.

"Well, you're in for a treat."

The Blue Ridge Parkway was winding and wooded, twisting onto the mountain's ridge in a place where heavy forest gave way to wide open sky. The car crested a hill, and a vista spread out before her on both sides. On the left, rolling pastures sloped steeply skyward, dotted with black and white cows. To her right, the entire lay of the eastern foothills spread below in a picturesque panorama.

She exclaimed, "Oh, how beautiful!"

He pointed down into the valley. "That's our own little burg of Caldwell."

"I can't remember ever seeing it from this angle," she said.

"It's a pretty spot."

The sign ahead read Scenic Lookout, and he pulled off and parked.

"We're here." He got out, came around, and opened her door.

Then he clicked a button on his key fob, and she heard the squeak as the rear gate of the car floated up. He came back to where she sat on the edge of her seat, her sneaker-clad feet kicking back and forth.

He held out a huge backpack with an assortment of zippered compartments over its surface. "Lunch," he declared with a grin. Out of a pouch on the side protruded the tapered, green glass neck of what looked like a bottle of wine.

"It's plaid." She laughed. "A plaid backpack. How come not tweed? Don't they make them in tweed?"

He shot her a wry look. "I told you, Abby, no tweed on Sundays." He offered his hand.

Off to one side of the parking area, a straggly hawthorn tree grew out from under the side of a monstrous rock formation. Gripping her hand, he led her around to the other side of the rise. There was no picnic table, but he had obviously come prepared.

He unzipped one of the compartments and drew out an olive green blanket, which he ceremoniously snapped into the wind and laid under the shady side of the tree. The spot was hidden from the parking lot and boasted a gorgeous view of the foothills below. He straightened and motioned with one hand toward the blanket as he bowed.

"Your table, madam," he droned in a bad British accent, and she giggled.

She fought with the breeze to contain her gauzy skirt and dropped to the blanket, tucking the hem under her. Her hat almost escaped twice. She finally snatched it off in and plopped it down near the blanket's edge, placing a stone on the brim to secure it.

In the meantime he was busy setting out their feast. He produced several containers, all looking suspiciously like takeout boxes from Murphy's. He uncovered one filled with a mound of fried chicken that smelled heavenly. Another held golden biscuits, and a third brimmed with an assortment of marinated veggies.

He frowned. "It's chicken. You eat chicken, don't you? I guess I forgot to ask."

She donned her most mischievous grin. "I prefer little children in my cauldron," she cackled. "But fried chicken will do in a pinch."

Jack shook his head, laughing as he plucked two bottles of water out of yet another pocket. Their sides dripped with condensation, so he tugged a heavy cloth napkin out of another and wrapped it around the sweating bottle before offering it to her.

When he spent several minutes digging furiously in the bottom of the sack, she asked, "What did you forget?"

"Uh oh," he muttered. He glanced up sheepishly. "I forgot the cups for the wine."

"No problem. Out of the bottle's fine."

They sat under the twisted old hemlock tree in the afternoon sun, munching on fried chicken and picking at the chilled veggies with greasy fingers. Abby took a deep breath and looked around her. This was so pleasant, so easy. A perfect way to spend a beautiful Sunday afternoon. With a friend.

"Jack, this is wonderful. A really great idea. And I truly do appreciate your help this morning. That giant bag of soil looked a lot smaller when you picked it up."

"How did you get those urns up on the top step, anyway? And don't say magic."

"No, not magic. I had some help from the Cornwells, the folks who own the place where I bought them."

He stopped chewing. "Up on the north ridge? That pink-haired lady and her Bigfoot son?"

She shot him a disapproving scowl. "They're nice people, Jack. They went out of their way to help me."

He swallowed and took a pull from his water. "You know, Miss Cornwell has the same rumored reputation as your aunt. As a witch, I mean."

"Huh. Well, I'll admit, she and Jonathan are a strange pair. They seem friendly enough, though." Abby thought this was as good a time as any to address the witch rumors. "So, tell me what the locals *really* think of my Aunt Di. And, by association, of me." She spoke between licking bits of chicken breading off her fingers.

"Well, oddly enough, mountain folk suspect anybody who looks or acts different of being somehow devious. Which is funny because some of the mountain people I grew up around are weirder than anybody I've ever met."

"Tell me about where you grew up. Blowing Rock. There's some Indian legend about the place, isn't there?"

He nodded. "The rock formations there cause the wind to blow in strange patterns. Sometimes it blows straight up the cliff face. Even snow swirls upward. The legend is that an Indian brave who tossed himself off the cliff was blown back up to his lover after she prayed to the Great Spirit for mercy."

She raised her brows. "Funny. I grew up not twenty miles away from the place. You'd think I'd know that.

"I'm surprised your parents never took you there as a kid. It's a pretty neat natural oddity."

"My parents are natural oddities in their own right," she said, rolling her eyes. "Until I started school I really believed we *lived* in the university library and our house was just someplace we went to sleep."

He chuckled, wiping the grease off his fingers with a napkin and sweeping crumbs off his shirt. "The Rock's become little more than a tourist stop. Gift shop, postcards. You know, there's still a lot of superstition alive in this part of the world."

"Do you think it's strictly superstition, or legend? My aunt is really into all the legends, the rituals our ancestors lived by. The Wiccan festivals, for example. A lot of it is based on Celtic folklore. She loves that stuff."

"You and I know it's based on legend, but some people from around here think Wicca means witch. Like, Elphaba. Wicked Witch of the West. When Dianne's shop opened, the locals were ready to replay the Salem witch trials. After about a month, when they realized nobody disappeared, died, or was struck blind, curiosity got the better of them." He paused for a drink of water. "It didn't hurt, of course, that she grew up here in the mountains. She wasn't an outsider. They figured out pretty quick she had some neat stuff in her place, lots of herbal teas and scented candles they couldn't buy in Wal-Mart."

"To be precise," Abby said, studying the container of chicken and choosing a drumstick, "those who actively practice Wicca *are* called witches. Unfortunately, that label has gotten a bit of a bad rap."

"Hell yeah," he retorted, and she laughed with him. "I try to stay open-minded about this kind of stuff. I'm not exactly the religious type anyway."

"Me neither. And Aunt Di, well, she's more of a tree-hugger than a witch. She likes all the cool festivals, the candles, and crystals. She's really more of a naturalist, into the healing properties of Mother Earth. She's big into herbal medicine. Di was raised in a Methodist household, same as me. Her Christmas tree goes up the day after Thanksgiving, no matter what." Abby pointed to the bottle of wine sticking out of the backpack. "Are we drinking that or is it just for decoration?"

"Oh, sorry," Jack said, grabbing for the bottle. "Nothing extravagant. Just a twist cap. Which is okay since I also forgot a wine key as well as the cups. If we had to break the neck off on a rock, sipping around jagged glass might get a little tricky." He removed the cap and offered the bottle to her first.

She wiped her mouth with the napkin before tipping the bottle back, sipping gingerly at first. "Mmm," she said. "Not bad for cheap stuff." Then she took another swig and handed it back to Jack.

"Cheers," he said as he placed the bottle to his lips and took a long draw.

As he drank, Abby said, "No need to be concerned about my herpes infection. I'm in remission."

He sputtered and inhaled part of his mouthful, the rest spraying out across the grass beside him.

"Only kidding!" she shrieked, jumping up onto her knees. "Are you okay? Oh my god, I'm so sorry. I was only joking." She thumped Jack's back as he coughed and choked.

She felt terrible, but once sure he was okay, she couldn't hold back a fit of giggles. She handed him her napkin, and he dabbed at his mouth and his eyes where his own tears of laughter had begun to spill.

"You," he said when he could finally again speak, "are a hoot." His eyes met hers and their smiles lingered. A long, still beat pulsated between them. "And you are absolutely, unmistakably beautiful."

Kneeling beside him, she looked deep into those amazing eyes and a familiar longing stirred in her core. He wasn't just looking at her. His gaze seeped into her, through her. A wave of heat flushed her cheeks. For a split second, the sensation was exhilarating, enticing, almost irresistible.

Then, memories flooded back, shattering the moment. The warmth washed to cold sweat. Her chest clutched, and her throat tightened. She brought a hand to her forehead.

"Hey, are you okay?" Jack extended a hand.

It was no use. The walls were already closing in. The last thing she wanted was for him to touch her. She turned away and wrapped her arms around herself, suddenly chilled.

"I'm fine. Just a bit . . . tired all of a sudden. I did a lot today. Too much fresh air, maybe."

Jack could see the change in her, hear it in her voice. Abby's ravenous appetite vanished. When he offered another swallow of the wine, she said, "I'd better not. I'm working early tomorrow. Thank you, though, Jack. This has been a truly nice afternoon."

Suddenly the other Abby was back. The librarian with an attitude. "Here," she said, struggling to her feet, "let me help you pack this up."

They spoke little on the ride down the mountain. Each time he tried to draw her out, she answered in soft, single word replies. He was downright confused. He kept going over the afternoon in his mind, trying to figure out what he said or did to offend her.

That was his problem with women. He always did something, yet had no clue what word or gesture flipped that switch. He was an honest, straightforward man. All he'd done was tell her she was beautiful. Was that so bad? He hadn't tried to kiss her. Hell, he hadn't even touched her.

He stopped at the curb in front of Ancient Healings, and Abby turned toward him wearing a forced, feeble smile. She refused to meet his eyes.

"I enjoyed today, Jack. And I appreciate your help with the plantings. Thank you."

Before he could even think of what to say, she opened the door, stepped out, and was gone.

Chapter 7

As Abby unlocked the library door on Monday morning, the colorful urns flanking the entrance made her smile. What a day to be working alone, when she had no one to share her glee. She wondered what Harry thought of her decorating the entrance. Did ghosts notice this sort of thing? She found herself subconsciously sniffing the air for pipe smoke. There wasn't a trace she could detect.

When she snapped on the light switches, she caught sight of something she wasn't sure was real. Back in the reading corner by the window, a bright splash of color drew her gaze. Abby dropped her purse and books on the counter and walked between the stacks. There on the floor, in the middle of the aisle between the end of fiction and the start of nonfiction, sat a bud vase. It held a small, wonderfully colorful arrangement of fresh flowers.

She remembered seeing the green glass flute sitting dusty and neglected on the top shelf of the reception office. Some leftover remnant of a birthday or thank you token sent to a previous librarian, probably Dana Laramy. Now, sparkling as though brand new, it posed proudly in the center of the carpet runner. In it, a stalk of cream petunias, a lone yellow marigold, and a single spray of variegated English ivy sparkled with morning dew. These, she realized, were from the flowers she planted in the urns the day before.

For a long moment she stared at the vase, hands on her hips, before stooping to pick it up. There was no doubt in her mind this time. She was not alone here. This gesture, without question, came from Harry.

Her tears were happy ones, and she didn't even feel foolish or embarrassed as she spoke into the empty room. "I'm going to assume this means you're pleased. I'm glad." She smiled.

She swiped her cheek as she carried the vase to the front and placed it on the end of the counter. The black smudge on the back of her hand had her chuckling. "Harry, you devil. I melt into a muddy pool when I cry. But thank you."

A few hours later Monica burst through the door, right on time. Abby could tell by the bounce in her step she was in an exceptionally cheery mood. Maybe she'd noticed the planters after all.

"Hey, the flowers look great, Abby," she chirped as she slid behind the counter, tucking her purse underneath. She touched the end of the ivy twirling down the side of the bud vase. "Ooh, pretty. Left over from the urns?"

Abby shook her head. "Nope. They're from my secret admirer."

Monica's mouth formed a silent "O". "Jack Wood?"

"Nope. I guess I should say, my ghostly admirer."

Monica shot her a quizzical glance but never got a chance to question further since the door opened and their busy spell began. Two middle-aged women who perused the romance stacks with every-other-day frequency came in to inquire about the newest releases from Robyn Carr and Kristan Higgins. Which, Abby was relieved to report, they had in stock.

A young man, a lawyer or PA, came in toting a briefcase shortly after. He had papers and books spread all over the table in the reference room. A younger woman, a college student, Abby surmised, was bent over books on MLA formatting at one end of the meeting room table. Just when it appeared they'd reached a lull in the action, the phone rang. Monica took the call.

Abby looked up from her computer screen and smiled. Already it seemed as though the simple act of fancying up the library's street presence had brought, if nothing else, a stroke of good luck.

When Monica hung up the phone, Abby pointed to her monitor. "Look at this." She'd spent her free time that morning designing flyers to advertise two of her newest ideas: a book club and a writer's group. "I thought we'd put a box up here on the counter and ask for suggestions. For titles for our first book club meeting. I'll ask Jack if the creative writing teacher down at the college would be willing to come in and help start up a critique group. What do you think?"

She was so wrapped up in her own enthusiasm it took several moments for her to realize Monica hadn't responded. Abby pushed back in her chair and turned to face her. The other woman wore a cat-who-ate-the-canary look. "What's up with you? You look like you've either got one big secret or won the lottery."

Monica wrestled a chair close behind hers, the news bubbling out in excited whispers. "You're right on both counts," she began. "Sort of. And it doesn't have to be a secret anymore." She lifted her left hand, and the flash of sunlight glinting off the hefty diamond on her finger almost blinded Abby.

Who was struck speechless. Monica had never mentioned a boyfriend, hadn't even acted vaguely interested in discussing men at all. There was a brief time when Abby wondered if she might be gay.

After a confounding beat of silence, she stuttered, "Uh, wow. I mean, it's gorgeous, Monica. Congratulations. How? Who?"

Monica leaned in conspiratorially. Her gaze swept the lobby as she whispered, "I couldn't say anything until the divorce was final. Friday was the day. Davin is officially free." The tears shining in her eyes reflected pure joy.

"We've been working together over a month. You never said a word."

"Davin Roth is my personal attorney," she began in hushed tones. "He handled my grandmother's estate when she passed ten years ago. That's how we met. It was one of those unplanned, inexplicable happenings. The attraction between us was instant and irresistible."

Abby raised her brows and blew out a breath. "Whew. Okay. He was married, huh?"

I guess my situation with Cameron could have been much worse.

Monica nodded. "Married to his law partner. And their son was only twelve years old. Davin didn't want to break up the family until Damon was at least out of school."

"Wait, wait. You mean you've been his mistress all this time?"

A pained expression crossed Monica's face. "It sounds sleazy and horrible, but it wasn't like that. His marriage was over long before we met. He and Amy lived together, more as roommates than spouses. Separate bedrooms. They accomplished what most would consider impossible. They stayed together in an amenable relationship for their son, at least until he was old enough to understand. Their marriage was more of a business relationship than a love story." Her words tumbled out like an avalanche.

How difficult, Abby wondered, had it been for Monica to carry this secret around for so long? "How long have you been seeing Davin? I mean, *seeing* him. That way."

Monica arched one eyebrow, looking down at her fidgeting hands as she confessed. "Over eight years. I'm so glad it's finally over, and we can begin the kind of life we could have been sharing so many years ago. At least now, we'll have every minute of every day to spend together."

Abby cocked her head. "How so? Is he giving up the practice?"

She nodded. "He's retiring next month. He's done extremely well, invested wisely and gotten lucky. It's been a long, lonely trek, and now finally I'll have him all to myself."

Abby knew Monica lived alone in the house she inherited from her grandmother, a block or so from the library. She always wondered how Monica made ends meet on a part-time librarian's salary. She assumed Grandma left Monica more than just the quaint Victorian on Ash Street. But now everything became clear. Davin had been funding Monica's lifestyle all along. Abby had thought, from what Aunt Di told her, she was pining away for Dennis Ludwig. All the while she had a secret lover—and not Dennis.

"Wow. I'm so happy for you," she said as she hugged her coworker. "Davin is retiring, though. What does that mean for your job here?"

Monica's smile faded. "That's what I have to tell you, Abby. Davin wants to do lots of traveling, take me all over the country. Abroad even. It means my time here at the library is going to end."

Wow. Double whammy. First the shock of learning about Monica's secret life. Now the realization that Abby's only help for all the new library programs was about to disappear.

"Whew." She raised her brows and swiped one hand down over her face. "This is way too much to hit me with on a Monday morning, Monica."

Abby's gaze returned to the computer screen, and she stared at the flyer she'd spent the past two hours enthusiastically designing. Her shoulders sagged. In addition to Saturday story hours, she wanted, by the first of June, to begin a book club to meet one evening a month. Near the bottom of the flyer a "Coming Soon" blurb mentioned the writer's critique group.

There was no way, even if she worked eighty hours a week, she could handle all this by herself. She'd already planned on asking the board for one more part-time library aide in addition to Monica to handle all the new programs. Now, instead of looking for one, she would need at least two.

Unfortunately, she was also aware her ability to do anything when it came to staffing hinged on the approval of the town council. A council, she reminded herself, whose chairwoman just happened to be Leda Ludwig.

"Looks like your sprite decided on floral arrangements for her funeral home."

Leda's words hit Dennis like daggers of icy cynicism. He concentrated on his driving as they passed the library, his arm draped atop the wheel, trying not to react. "Leda, let it be. She's young. Don't you remember what it was like to be enthusiastic about a new project?"

Oh, boy. Not the right thing to say, he realized seconds after the words escaped his lips. Leda's entire body stiffened as she hopped around in her seat, straining against the seat belt like a guard dog against its harness. Her eyes glittered with rage.

"Don't I remember? Don't I remember?"

She was shouting, and he squinted and braced himself for the onslaught.

"It hasn't been all that long, Commissioner Dear, since I was the enthusiastic young thing you were standing behind!" She turned her back toward him with a *hrumph* and growled to the window. "Behind, in front of, underneath, on top of—"

"Leda!" he snapped. "Enough already. I'm well aware you'd like nothing better than for the Harvey to become a fond memory. Could you please consider, for one minute, how I might feel about that?"

The silence that ensued was frighteningly pregnant, like the eye of a storm, or the pause between the sparking sizzle of a fuse and the—

"Why are you so insistent on keeping that old crypt operating?" Leda shouted, her hands flailing. "It's nothing, Dennis. It's a has-been. It's ancient history."

He sighed and closed his eyes as they sat waiting for the traffic light to change. Then he spoke as calmly as his frazzled will would allow. "Leda, history has importance. Compared to you, I'm ancient history. Don't I have at least some semblance of importance left in your eyes?"

She continued as though he hadn't heard a word. "Did you realize," she hissed, "that your diamond-pierced little witch has put in a request for yet another part-time employee? Two now! Seems she wants to start up all kinds of cozy community events. A book club, a writing group, movie night."

Leda swore under her breath and smacked the dashboard with the flat of her palm. "She's not getting it. Any of it. It's all got to be voted on." She snickered. "As long as I'm around, there's no way any of that stuff is going to get funded."

He kept his attention on the road, trying hard to keep his blood pressure from blowing off the charts. "Leda, you had a chance to run the place yourself, but—"

"No matter how much money was involved, that surely wasn't going to happen," she shrieked, the pitch stinging his ears. "I'm telling you, Dennis, this better not go much further. I won't stand for it. I've worked my ass off to build up Caldwell Community College, as well as sunk a good chunk of my family's cash into its foundation."

A long stretch of silence made him hope her tirade was over. She'd been having a lot of them lately. No luck.

Seconds later, her tantrum continued in a murmured snarl. "This is all big brother Martin's fault. He'll do anything he can to prevent that end of Main Street from becoming a ghost town. To keep his sorry little flea market business alive."

She wasn't speaking to him anymore, but from the corner of his eye Dennis cringed at how fury contorted Leda's features.

What's happened to her? Where was the sweet, adoring young woman who dazzled him with her beauty and brains, who made him feel like a virile stud when she came to his bed? It wasn't so long ago. She'd made him proud the day she became his wife. Back then, she was the inspiration that kept him young. Lately, she'd spun out of control, serving only to make him feel older.

He glanced toward her again. The hunger for power was consuming her. Too much of anything is no good. *Compulsive, obsessive ambition has made you ugly, Leda. Hateful and ugly, inside and out.*

Abby closed the library at five and headed straight for Ancient Healings, hoping to be there before Dianne locked up for the day. She prayed her dear auntie would have some words of wisdom as to what her next step should be. Maybe even a little magic. With Monica leaving, that's what it would take to keep her new job from killing her.

As Abby walked up to the door she was disappointed to hear voices inside. She needed a few minutes alone with Aunt Di and some sage words. So she settled down in the rocker on the front porch and waited, watching the traffic build on Main Street for this, the busiest hour of the day. In a small town like Caldwell, more than three cars lined up for the light constituted rush hour.

She didn't wait long. Minutes later the screen door squeaked opened and out whisked Leda Ludwig.

Abby froze and hoped Leda would hurry down the steps and on to her shiny red sports car without seeing her. She cursed herself for not noticing the coupe parked at the curb when she crossed the street. It certainly was flashy enough.

Why hadn't she spotted it? Luck was definitely not playing on her team that afternoon.

Leda swirled around to close the door and glanced up, straight into her eyes. "Well, good afternoon, Ms. Stryker. I guess I shouldn't be surprised to find you here," she sneered. "And how are things going down at the old book barn?"

Abby stood, facing Leda at her own level. "The old book barn happens to be a functioning library, Mrs. Ludwig. Actually, it's doing extremely well. Lots of new happenings, now and in the works." Fueled by defiance, she tipped up her chin.

"Is that a fact?" Leda sniffed, then chuckled. "I guess you're pretty much going to be running the place all by yourself after this month." She paused, theatrically, resting a fist on one cocked hip. "I hope you realize you're not paid by the hour. Your salary stays the same whether you work forty hours or a hundred."

Leda's smugness poked Abby in the pride. She could feel the anger and frustration welling up into her throat and hoped she could keep it together. Drawing in a deep, measured breath, she mustered up her sweetest smile.

"I'm glad I bumped into you today, Mrs. Ludwig, as I need some information. Who is it I contact to add an agenda item to the town council meeting next month?"

The twisted grin crossing Leda's face transformed her face into a sinister clown. "An agenda item, huh? Well, that would be Mrs. Terrell, down at city hall. She's town clerk. Gracie is happy to add agenda items. Whatever items she feels are worth the council's time, that is," she said with a cocky twist of her head.

"If more than one person requests an agenda item, Gracie must add it to the schedule. That's a fact." Dianne's voice boomed from inside the door, causing Leda to flinch. "So I guess we'll both be seeing you at the next town meeting." The flash of her white smile glowed through the screen.

Abby could almost feel sparks of irritation radiating off Leda. She flashed a glare from Abby to Dianne and back as she snarled, "In the meantime, I wish you both a joyous Litha celebration next week. I hear your book club is scheduled for that night."

"It is," Abby replied. "We're discussing *Madame Bovary*, Mrs. Ludwig. You might want to join us. I'm certain that's a title you're familiar with." She suppressed a smirk.

Leda snorted, the insinuation apparently floating right past her. "I'm not one much for reading, Abigail. I don't waste time dreaming about what I want to achieve. I get up off my butt and go after it."

Dianne didn't miss a beat. "Speaking of your butt, Leda, do let me know if that almond goat's milk soap helps that nasty rash you're suffering with."

Leda drew in a sharp breath, her eyes owling in her direction.

Di just grinned and purred, "Blessed be."

Leda huffed, spun on one needle-thin heel, then headed for her car, the pink plastic bag holding her purchases swinging from her wrist.

When the car screeched away from the curb, Dianne pushed open the screen and stood on the porch facing Abby, hands on wide hips. "That bitch is malignant. What is it with her? She's as venomous as any henbane potion I've ever concocted. And they call *me* the witch!"

Abby sighed and pinched the bridge of her nose. "If it were up to Leda Ludwig, Auntie, my career will be downgraded to scooping ice cream at Murphy's by the next full moon."

Dianne pulled another rocker from the end of the porch up next to Abby and plopped into it. "Tell me, child. What's going on?"

Abby's anger followed its usual course, rising to a crescendo, then plummeting her into despair. Despite every ounce of fortitude she tried to call into her corner, tears sprung to her eyes and wouldn't stop. Within minutes she found herself pressed against Dianne's amply cushioned bosom, as Abby's sobs rumbled out unhindered.

"There, there, Abigail. It can't be that bad. Tell me what's happening. What's got you so upended tonight?"

Finally Abby pulled it together and sat back, hiccupping and swiping futilely at her cheeks with the linen hanky Di handed her. Smeared black stains were evident, not only on the hanky, but on the stretchy green silk of the delicate blouse embracing Dianne's chest. The sight pushed Abby into a compulsive fit of laughter.

"Oh Aunt Di, I've ruined your blouse," she sputtered, pointing to the dark streaks.

Her aunt glanced down, tugging the fabric out so her cleavage nearly spilled over the upper edge. "Ah! Finally. An excuse to go shopping." She smiled, and Abby wasn't sure if it was sympathy or empathy in those clear gray eyes.

"You're the best, Aunt Di," she mumbled, now clenching one corner of the hanky in her teeth. "What am I going to do? Leda-bitch has about got me checkmated."

"What's happened?"

Between intermittent hiccups and nose-blowings, she explained Monica's shocking announcement and the fact Abby would be the only one rowing frantically to keep the library afloat as of two weeks from this coming Monday.

"Don't worry, dear. There's a town council meeting Friday after next," Dianne declared, brightly and as though the news was the answer to all of Abby's woes.

She knew it was not. Silence hung in the air between them for the next few minutes, as the evening traffic began to thin and reality settled like lead dust over the porch of Ancient Healings.

"What am I going to do, Auntie?"

Dianne settled her arm around Abby's shoulder and moved her close. Just when she expected her aunt to conjure some words of miraculous comfort, Di let out a deep sigh.

"I don't know yet. Reality bites sometimes, sweetie."

Armand was serving duck a la orange, accompanied by generous portions of potatoes a la crème and fingerling carrots. Dianne figured these were probably leftover portions he prepared for a less-than-full-house weekend crowd at Le Petit Mon. It didn't matter. She loved duck, and made sure Armand knew it.

She reclined lazily against the upholstered wingchair, sipping Chateau St. Michel from a frosted flute. Between her and Armand's antique ladder back, the small round café table was draped in the finest white linen of any five star restaurant.

Their French-style chalet disguised its European influence well. From the winding blacktop road passing yards in front of the cabin, no one would ever dream that stepping through the front door of their classic cottage could transport them thousands of miles and, perhaps, hundreds of years back into another era, another dimension. The Le Mons had transformed their foothills hideaway into a cleverly camouflaged time machine.

"The duck is marvelous, Armand," she hummed through her second mouthful, washing it down with the last of her wine.

He rose immediately with the linen-wrapped bottle to refill her glass as she asked, "So tell me, darling. What are we going to do about this situation with my dear niece?"

Armand was a short, broad, balding man with a nose much like the beak of an aging cockatiel. He wore a stained white chef's apron around his middle, one he seemed to virtually live in. Sweat beaded on his pleated brow. He drained his own wine glass, wiping his mouth first and the edge of his glass with his napkin before answering.

"Dianne, my dear, we were well aware of what innocent Abigail was coming up against when she took on this position. The antiquated civic commodity for which she labors in defense is rather, well, feeble. Limited in potential." He used a three-tined fork to spear his crispy, seared duck carcass while cracking it in half with a sharp steak knife. "Wouldn't you say, darling?"

She lifted her chin. "I don't," she proclaimed, "detect any glimmer of defeatist in your attitude, do I, Armand?"

"No, no, no, of course not, my sweet," he croaked, his mouthful of dinner competing with the sincerity of his tone. "But what can we do? What is it you would like me to do to help Abby?" He shrugged, waving his fork in a small circle in the air.

She settled back in her cushioned seat, her glass balanced between steepled fingers. "I believe what we need is a fundraiser. A fine, French dinner to incite interest in the revival of the Harvey Library. The endowment fund was sufficient to keep it afloat until now, but times are changing. Abby wants to bring the Harvey up-to-date, expand. That's all going to cost more than the meager stipend set back in the 1800s."

She sipped, savoring the wine as her mind buzzed with a plan. "The library is, after all, our little burg's only historic literary contribution. What we need is an evening of fine cuisine, good wine, and general community cheer. All to benefit a perfectly worthy, and of course, fully tax-deductible cause."

The man across the table had stopped chewing, his fork poised halfway between mouth and plate.

"Le Petit Mon is doing very, very well. Could probably use a little tax break for next year. Don't you agree, Armand?"

Chapter 8

On Wednesdays the library closed early, giving Abby a much needed few hours off. By the end of the month Monica would be gone, so Abby needed to do whatever marketing she could as quickly as possible. Perhaps, if she could raise enough community interest, she'd draw the support she needed at the town council meeting. Maybe she could stir enough enthusiasm to override the vote Leda was already counting as a win.

Right at 3 p.m., Abby gathered the flyers for her book club and slid them into her oversized bag. She did a final walk-through, a practice she started right after Harry left the window open that night. Although it wouldn't stop him from raising it again after she left, she slept better knowing she'd at least done her part to secure the building. Since the morning he left her flowers, there'd been no evidence of him.

Maybe even Harry had given up on the library.

The lights were off, windows locked, and all the reference materials properly re-shelved. She paused at the door, key in hand. Looking back into the dimmed interior, for a brief moment she imagined the faint aroma of pipe smoke. Her chest clutched with despair.

"If you're there . . . if you can hear me. I'm trying, Harry. There are some small bookstores up Wilkesbury way. I'm taking these up there in the hope we can inspire more interest."

Her only answer was silence. She locked the door behind her, shaking her head at her own foolish ranting.

The afternoon was sunny and breezy, although still a bit cooler than she had counted on. A shiver ran through her, and she pulled her bulky cable knit up closer around her as she slid behind the wheel.

Good thing I went with those tights under my skirt.

Wilkesbury was only about ten miles north, but at a considerably higher elevation than Caldwell. In the mountains, as evening crept closer, the temperature would drop all that much faster.

On impulse, she visited the drive-through at McDonald's and ordered a vanilla milkshake. Usually a health food fanatic, this was her one sinful pleasure. A decadent, fattening indulgence she put into her body every once in a while simply because it made her feel good.

The frozen treat was still as difficult to enjoy as when she was ten. Sucking it up through a straw was nearly impossible, at least until the ice cream began to thaw. As she drove up Hwy. 18 headed northeast, she swore in between futile attempts to pull the frozen mass of sugar and fat into her mouth, her more enthusiastic efforts threatening to implode her head.

She'd gotten just clear of the last traffic light when she remembered the back road Dianne told her about. Abby checked the time on her dash. What the hell. She'd called ahead. One bookstore didn't close until five, and the other stayed open until seven. An adventure through the foothills sounded intriguing. A change of scenery might even give her a fresh perspective.

Without a map and no GPS, she wasn't sure where the road she was looking for intersected the winding, two-lane highway. Slowing each time a road jutted off to the left, she soon realized the three, maybe more, cars behind her were getting tired of the dance. Up ahead, she located a wide place in the shoulder and left the road so they could go by. As she sat waiting for them to pass, she spotted the green and white placard marked "Greensville Hwy" just ahead. Exactly what she was looking for.

As she made the turn she slowed and swerved, giving wide berth to the jogger headed toward her. She'd gone a hundred yards or so before the image that flashed across her brain found a matching file. Screeching to a stop, she glanced in her rearview to find the jogger had done the same thing. He was standing in the middle of the narrow country road, staring after her with his hands on his hips.

Abby threw the car into reverse and whirred part of the way back, then gave up trying to steer straight.

I hate backing up. Never any good at it. Everything's ass backward.

Once on the shoulder, she killed the engine. By the time she threw open her door, Jack was standing outside peering in.

"Are you lost, pretty lady?" he asked, still panting.

He stood in a wide-legged stance, his compression shorts and sleeveless tee hugging his frame without mercy. Perspiration trickled down the curly tendrils hanging over his brow. Although she obviously recognized Jack, she was shocked to see him in this state of relative undress.

Her cheeks grew warm. "What are you doing? Where's the tweed?" she said through a chuckle.

Wow. That stuffy old professor stuffed his shorts pretty well.

She was so flustered she couldn't hold his gaze.

He'd been staring at her as though she were insane. Now he threw both hands up in the air and blurted, "What does it look like I'm doing? Duh?" His gaze drifted past her. The McDonald's cup was still perched in her console. "Seriously? I'm sweating my ass off, and you just came from Mickey D's?"

A washcloth appeared in his hand, presumably out of the back of his shorts, and he wiped his face. "So answer me. Are you lost or what?"

"Not lost." She shook her head. "I was on my way to Wilkesbury. To the bookstores there. Dianne told me about this scenic back road and—"

"Oh." He raised a hand. "Did you plan on getting to Wilkesbury *today*? Did Dianne tell you how long it takes to get to there on the twisty, turny, up-and-down the mountain road?"

"No, she didn't," she said quietly. "Not the best route, I'm guessing?"

"No. Not the best route. You might get there by midnight if you drive like Mario Andretti. Provided you don't get lost."

"What are you doing here, anyway?" she asked. "I mean, I see you're running, but . . ."

"I live here. Right around that corner." He gestured to a path leading from the pavement a little ways ahead. There was no road sign.

"The corner," she repeated, mockingly. All she could see was a dirt lane intersecting a grassy, sloping meadow.

"Yes, the corner." He sounded exasperated. "I've got a beautiful place back there. I had it built last year. Wanna come see?"

Ten minutes later Abby was pulling her car into the gravel driveway of what looked like Hansel and Gretel's last known whereabouts. The cottage was so perfect, it looked surreal. The steeply pitched roof shaded a wide rocking chair porch. A symmetrical row of multicolored pansies lined the curving sidewalk to the front steps. Plunked smack dab into a semicircular clearing in the heavy pine forest, the oasis was almost invisible, even from the unpaved lane meandering past it.

She climbed out, tugging her sweater tighter around her shoulders. With the sun blotted out by the heavy woods, daylight waned earlier. The forested rise behind the house to the west had already cast the hollow into near-twilight. A shiver quaked her shoulders.

"It gets chilly here at night pretty quick," he said. "Com'on in. I'll make you a cup of hot tea."

Abby pushed through the screened door and found herself tucked into a country hideaway. The wide, dark plank flooring grounded the open floor plan. Kitchen, dining, and living areas shared the same space under a soaring cathedral ceiling. A fireplace, flanked by twin loveseats, was clothed in fieldstone from hearth to ceiling, rising nearly twenty feet above her head.

"This is amazing," she whispered.

Jack hustled to the black ceramic range and grabbed a porcelain teapot. He paused before filling it over the stainless steel sink. "Would you prefer a glass of wine?" he asked. "I have an open bottle of merlot."

She hesitated. Wine sounded really nice, but she'd be driving . . .

Before she could answer he said, "Whenever a woman hesitates, it means yes." He slid two stemmed glasses off the rack hanging above the island cook top. "Please, sit down." He motioned to the burgundy corduroy loveseats.

She sank into the corner of one as he pulled out the stoppered green bottle and poured the wine.

"I'm sure you will understand," he said as he handed her a glass, "that I will be taking ten to hose off before joining you. But let's sample this stuff first." Raising his glass he tipped it to hers. As he bent to set it back on the table, he glanced down. "Hey, you're out of uniform too, I see. Where's the sneaks? I thought the Converse were the only shoes you owned."

She grinned and lifted one of her feminine bow-topped flats. "Figured I'd get taken more seriously pitching my wares if I dressed like a grown-up."

They clinked glasses, and Abby sipped the rich, dark wine. It warmed her from the first swallow. Or was it the glow from the mischievous glint in his amazing eyes? His riveting gaze made her blood pressure hitch up a notch. The moment stood still, hanging in the long, slanting rays of dappled light that fought their way through the multi-paned windows.

He straightened and cleared his throat, turning toward the hallway. “Excuse me for ten? I have satellite. What do you like to watch?”

She melted into the comfort of the cozy loveseat and took another sip. “I’m not one much for TV,” she replied. “Go on. Do what you gotta do. I’m fine here with my wine.”

When he disappeared into the short hall, she crossed her legs and snuggled in. What an entirely enchanting place. So *not* what she expected from the tweed-coated professor. More like a woodsman’s hideaway. Somebody who chopped the wood for his own fireplace. Fished for trout in a stream somewhere nearby. Certainly not the home of a stuffy history professor who looked old enough . . .

Old enough for what? She’d already broached that subject with him and hadn’t gotten a straight answer. She was aware hair color didn’t always define a person’s age. Look at her aunt.

He’d been jogging, and from the way his body looked in spandex, he wasn’t ready for assisted living. Why was she still so hung up on that?

Let’s not go there.

In no time at all he reappeared, attired in pressed jeans and a pale green cotton polo. Was it possible for someone to have a garment custom-dyed to match their eyes? That disconcerting thought, along with the freshly bathed scent of him enhanced by some musky cologne, overrode every logical process in Abby’s brain.

Jack reclaimed his wineglass and sat beside her. "So," he began, "what's in Wilkesbury that's intriguing enough to make you want to scout the entire wilderness of the Blue Ridge to get there?" He rested one arm casually across the couch behind her.

She swallowed, took a breath, and drained her glass. "Bookstores," she replied. "What else would draw a librarian? Bookstores."

"In Wilkesbury?" He raised an eyebrow as he took her glass and headed to the kitchen. "There's no Barnes & Noble in Wilkesbury, if that's what you're looking for. Hickory, I think, is the nearest from here."

"No, not a big chain. I have flyers for a book club. And writing group," she said. "I figured the wider net I cast, the better chance I'll have of support once I get to city hall."

"Ah, that makes sense," he replied. "How about some cheese and crackers to go with that wine? I've got some nice smoked gouda."

"I hadn't planned on this," she said, shifting in her seat. She fidgeted, yet she didn't feel nearly as out of place as she thought she should. "I do have to get to those bookstores before they close today, Jack. Time isn't exactly on my side."

"You are absolutely right. I'll drive you." He paused, one brow cocked. "If you don't mind, that is."

He insisted they take his vehicle and also suggested that if they were to make the one bookstore that closed at five, they take the main road.

"You must have banker's hours," she teased as they wove along the country highway toward Wilkesbury.

"You're one to talk," he countered. "Barely four in the afternoon and you're off for a jaunt through the foothills."

He hit her with one of those smiles again, the ones that had an unraveling effect on everything south of her chin.

"It's my only afternoon off," she protested, though a feeble attempt now tempered with wine and a healthy dose of unexpected relaxation. “Those tiny, privately owned bookstores aren’t open on Sundays.”

“I’m just joshin’ ya,” he growled and grinned. Then his expression grew serious. “You’re really determined to make this a go, aren’t you?”

“Damn straight I am,” she replied.

What other choice did she have? Fight like hell for this or start surfing Careers.com. What she started at the old library had to bloom and quickly.

“So fill me in on this ghost,” she said. “You know, Harry.”

For a long moment Jack drove in silence, his eyes straight ahead on the road. Then he said quietly, “I’m not really a believer in the whole paranormal thing.”

“The hell you’re not,” she said. “Do you think I don’t notice the books you check out? The ones you’ve been digging through in the reference room?” She shot him a knowing look. “I know damn well you’ve been researching the history of that old building. Why the sudden interest?”

He shrugged. “I’m a history buff. Isn’t that explanation enough?”

She narrowed her eyes. “What have you found out, Professor Wood, about our pipe-smoking, book-flinging resident ghost, the one everyone in town calls Harry?” Abby hopped around in her seat to face him fully. “Spill your guts, dude.”

He chuckled, flashing her another of those blasted grins that made her middle melt. “I can’t vouch for any supernatural entities,” he began, “but I have been researching the history of the old building.”

“Duh,” she retorted, rolling her eyes. “Not many people realize how much their librarian knows about them. They carry their deepest secrets around in broad daylight. Then they stack it all on the counter, right under my nose.”

He shot her a sidelong glance. “Okay, here’s what I’ve been able to find out so far. The structure was originally built in 1883 by a man named Elijah Harvey. He was a Bostonian businessman, a banker headed out west. During his short stay in the newly formed Caldwell township, he fell in love. Twice. Once with the Blue Ridge foothills and again with the local harness maker’s daughter.”

She tipped her head. “Jack, we’re talking almost a hundred and fifty years ago. They didn’t exactly have gossip rags then. How could you possibly find that information?”

He rested his arm across the top of the steering wheel. “It read something like this. Official marriage record, this 21st day of September, in the year of our Lord 1882. Elijah Harvey, bound in wedlock this day to the beloved only daughter of Jasper and Edna Laramy.”

He turned to face her, locking his gaze on hers. “Their daughter was Caldwell’s schoolteacher. Her name was Isabelle. Unfortunately, other than official birth, death, and marriage records, I found nothing more.”

June 16, 1881

My Dear Mr. Laramy,

I must say it was my unexpected pleasure to make your acquaintance during my visit to your lovely city last spring. Your hospitality echoed the pure spirit of Caldwell, a community whose memory kept me going during these long weeks of travel. Crossing this great country has proven a challenging feat, even considering the advantages my resources allow. I am pleased to announce my business dealings here are complete. Lady Fortune has smiled upon me, and many treasures will follow me back East. I will commence my return journey within a fortnight.

I am writing to ask permission to see your daughter again. My accommodations are already arranged in Caldwell with my cousin and our mutual friend, Cyrus Bland. It is my understanding that Isabelle's teaching duties during August will be suspended for the midsummer harvest. If you would be so kind as to grant your permission, I would like to call upon you and your family again during my stay.

I extend this request, Mr. Laramy, in utmost sincerity. Although I realize a number of years separate me from your lovely daughter, I believe as her husband, I could make her extremely happy. I am in good health and possess ample financial means. My intentions are honorable. If your daughter consents to our union, I shall provide for her a fine home, financial security, and the fruition of her dreams—a great house filled with books. Lord willing, I will also provide the children she so desperately longs for.

I have no intention of taking her away from her family. We will make our home in Caldwell where Isabelle can continue teaching if she so desires. I fully intend to build her the library she expressed the need for in your community. I can promise your daughter would want for nothing, and no one on God's green Earth would worship her more than myself.

Barring bad weather, plague, pestilence, and outlaws, I intend, with God's grace, to return to Caldwell in or around mid-August. I beg your permission to call upon you and your lovely wife, and of course Isabelle, at that time.

Sincerely,
Elijah J. Harvey

Chapter 9

Touring the bookstores in Wilkesbury took less than an hour, all told. Jack waited in the car, watching through the glass fronts as Abby politely perused their new releases and schmoozed with the owners before distributing her flyers. Each time she returned to the car, she seemed a bit less enthusiastic.

"Isn't anybody interested in a book club? No wannabe writers here in the foothills?" he asked.

"As soon as they hear it's at the Harvey, they give me this funny look, shrug, and say 'just leave the flyers on the counter over there'," she moaned.

When she slunk back to his car the last time her shoulders drooped, and the usual bounce in her step was gone.

As she slid into the passenger seat, he said, "Okay, work day's over. Now, what would you like for dinner?"

She answered with a half-hearted shrug. "I'm not sure I'm even hungry, Jack," she muttered.

"Hungry. Jack. Hungry Jack. Does that mean pancakes? Do you feel like breakfast for dinner?" he snapped back. He didn't have much hope it would revive her. Somehow, it did.

A slow smile crept across her face. Followed by a dubiously curious one.

"So now you perform magic too? Where in the bustling metropolis of Wilkesbury, North Carolina is Magic Jack going to find us some Hungry Jacks for dinner? Edible and not floating in last week's fryer grease, that is?" She added with a quick scowl, "I'm not a fan of Huddle House."

It was only another ten miles or so to the interstate where Jack knew there was a Cracker Barrel. Hot biscuits, fluffy pancakes, and the thickest bacon you could imagine sinking your teeth into. Traffic was light, and before he could explain where they were going, they were there.

He was amazed at the appetite on a slight woman who looked as if she weighed no more than a hundred pounds. She ordered what the menu called Uncle Hershel's Favorite, which seemed to include one of everything on the menu, plus fried apples. As he laced his pancakes with maple syrup, Abby split a biscuit and scooped up sausage gravy with it, like dip with a giant chip.

"Whoa, now you're a girl who knows how to eat a biscuit." He chuckled.

She glared at him, chewing.

"I guess you were hungry after all."

Scrunching her nose at him, she continued eating as though she hadn't had a meal in days.

When she finally slowed, Abby settled back in her chair and studied the antique trinkets and prints lining the walls of the restaurant. "I wonder where they get all this stuff," she commented absently, breaking the last biscuit in half and drizzling honey over the fluffy insides.

"Antique stores, I'm sure," he said. "Auctions, maybe."

Her gaze wandered the wall displays as she munched on her biscuit. "The antique store across the street from the library. It's got to be the same family, right? As Isabelle Laramy?"

"Most likely. It would be an awful coincidence if there weren't some kind of blood tie. But have you ever tried talking to old man Laramy?" Jack asked. "I don't think he'd be willing to sit down and chat with anyone about ancestry. He's the oddest character."

"He still displays a set of harness now and then," she mumbled. "Hangs it out front from pieces of twisted old wire. Sometimes I can almost imagine a flea-bitten old nag walking up into it as it hangs there."

She fell silent for a long moment, then turned to Jack with wide eyes. "You don't suppose that's an original antique harness, do you? One his family made all those years ago?"

"I can't imagine him selling family heirlooms," he answered, then quickly reconsidered. "You can't ever tell with old Martin Laramy, though. Some say he sold his sister to the county."

"Ha! I'm sure that's a deal that went down in the record books."

"Ah, but actually? It did. I guess I never mentioned it. Guess who Martin Laramy's sister is?"

She pushed her plate aside, then leaned her chin on her hand, fluttering her eyelashes mockingly. "Why who, dear sir? Do tell."

Jack snatched the last half-slice of bacon off her plate. "Martin's baby sister's name is Leda."

"You don't mean our Leda, do you? Leda-bitch Ludwig?"

"Leda-bitch Ludwig, now Dean Ludwig, used to be Leda Laramy. You'd never guess she and Martin are from the same universe, let alone siblings," he said.

Her mouth gaped. "I can't believe it. Dianne told me she came from money. Laramy's place looks like an old tinker's wagon. Where's the family money from?"

"From a shrewd banker, an investor in Raleigh-Durham. Leda's father."

"Wait, wait, I'm confused. I understand that's how Leda came into money, growing up in a banker's family. But to look at Laramy's place you'd think he was penniless, selling bits of junk here and there just to stay alive." She shook her head wildly, as if trying to encourage the facts to fall into some kind of sensible order. "And Dana was their aunt. So why is Leda suddenly so hell bent on closing the library?"

He rested back in his chair and folded his hands across his full middle. “That’s what I’ve been trying to find out. Apparently there’s some sort of secret power struggle going on between Martin and Leda, and my guess it has to do with money. Where the library falls into this mess, I’m not sure. And why so much weird stuff started happening after Dana retired, I don’t know either. That’s what I’ve been digging around trying to find out.”

He gazed out the window where globes set on iron posts cast pools of golden light along the sidewalk. Then he shook his head. “I’d hate to see such a valuable piece of our town’s history go down. And Leda seems determined to make that happen.”

They left the restaurant and drove back to Caldwell, and Abby peered out at a brilliantly perfect full moon rising out of the east. The cool light cast an eerie glow over the rolling pastures along the highway, where irregular white splotches transformed herds of dairy cows into abstract paintings. By the time they turned back into his driveway, the sky glittered with stars. The wind had died, leaving the air still and cool.

Jack shut off the lights, and she blinked, temporarily blinded. “My God, it’s so dark here. Not a street lamp in sight.”

He didn’t move to open his door right away, waiting with her in the blackness. “Once you get away from the city lights, Abby, you’d be amazed at what you begin to see.”

After her eyes adjusted, they got out, and when the glow of the car’s interior lights faded, Abby’s senses came to life in a magical way. Points of light winked overhead through the chinks in the leafy forest roof. The air smelled piney as a cool damp blanket descended, wrapping her in peaceful comfort. The night was full of sounds, chirping and buzzing with the voices of a million insects, pulsating out of the woods all around her.

She hesitated to move forward, unsure of her footing on the graveled, sloped drive. She heard Jack's footsteps crunch, then his arm encircled her shoulders.

"This is my favorite part of living out here," he said. "I've always loved the forest. There's something almost sacred about it."

She hugged herself and stifled a shiver. "Funny," she said. "I grew up smack dab in the middle of the Blue Ridge Mountains, yet I was never more than a hundred yards away from a streetlight."

"Boone, you said?"

"Yes. Boone may be classic Appalachia, but it's still primarily a college town."

He drew her closer and breathed into her ear, "Shh. Look. Over there. Beyond the garden."

She blinked again and made out shadowy shapes in the small semicircle of clearing beyond Jack's house. Fireflies twinkled in a symphony of sparks against the inkiness of the woods beyond. Squinting, she sensed more than saw the whitewashed bench flanked by the brilliant pink azalea bushes she remembered seeing earlier. Without light, the blooms faded to warm gray.

"Do you see them? She had twins this spring. You can still make out their spots."

Abby opened her eyes wider, groping for every fragment of light she could gather. The spots came into view when they moved, hovering ghostlike several feet off the ground. Her mind gradually deciphered silhouettes around the glowing dapples. Three intermittent flutters of white became tails.

The doe had frozen in place, scrutinizing them from her camouflaged corner. Her two fawns, young and still benign to fear, milled about her, their flag tails flipping. One pawed the grass at the edge of the stone patio. The other stretched its neck to nibble an azalea bloom.

"Oh, they must be beautiful," she whispered. "I wish I could see them better."

"It comes in time," he replied. "I throw apples out there for them. After dark, I sit on the back deck with all the lights off and wait for them."

"You don't hunt, do you? I mean, shoot those pretty things?"

"Not a chance. My dad does. My uncle too. I never could get past those limpid eyes."

Another shiver quaked her, more from thrill than chill this time.

He tightened his grip around her. "Come on in. I'll start a fire."

"I can't. I should be getting back. I'm working early tomorrow."

"Oh come on," he urged gently. "A cup of hot apple cider will warm you all the way back to town."

Once inside, she snuggled back into the corner of the loveseat as he broke twigs and crumpled paper into the hearth. Within minutes three small logs were flickering, casting dancing shadows across the shiny plank floor. While the fire snapped and began sharing its warmth with the room, Jack disappeared behind her into the kitchen. After a minute he reappeared carrying two mugs steaming the air with an unmistakable aroma of freshly baked apple pie.

"Mmm," she hummed and closed her eyes as she held the mug under her chin. "This smells wonderful." Abby sighed and sipped, realizing she hadn't been this relaxed in a long time. "I'm glad Aunt Di suggested I look for that back road to Wilkesbury. If she hadn't, I wouldn't have run into you this afternoon."

"I'm glad too. I'm also glad for that storm early this morning."

She cocked her head. "Huh?"

"I usually do my three miles at sunrise. This morning it was pouring rain when I got up. I don't mind the rain, but the thunder convinced me to reschedule. Lightning is the only reason why you caught me running in broad daylight."

"You run three miles every day?" she asked, impressed. "Marathon runner? Iron man competitor?"

He laughed and set his cup on the rough-hewn top of the coffee table. "If I was, three miles would only be the warm up. Nope. Just want to keep the old bod in good shape. It's the only way to stay young." He slapped his flat middle. "I don't look too bad for a gray-haired old codger, do I?"

She smiled as she studied him. Silver streaks liberally laced his cap of chocolate curls, almost as though he paid to have them put there. Along the sides, where the hair was shorn close, the silver proved genuine. The sharp angles of his face were strangely appealing, especially contrasted against the soft, sage color of his eyes. She couldn't remember ever noticing eyes quite that shade. Their youthful glint made him seem ageless.

"I should know better than to judge a person's age by the color of their hair," she said. "My aunt's only forty-six, and she started going gray when she was nineteen. I always wondered what causes that. I'd like to blame it on her hooking up with Uncle Armpit. But that liaison didn't happen until a few years ago."

"Uncle Armpit." He burst out a laugh. "You've called him that before. How'd he earn that prestigious title?"

"A funny story for another time." She shook her head, stood, and stretched out her hand with a smile. "I've got to be getting home, Jack. Thanks for the cider, and the fire. And the drive. And for Uncle Hershel's Favorite. Thank you for an unexpectedly wonderful evening."

He grasped her proffered hand, but didn't let her go, instead lifting her fingers to his lips. "So aren't you going to ask me again?"

For the moment, she was confused.

"How old I am? You keep tiptoeing around the issue, Abby. It does seem to bother you."

She looked away and started for the door. "I'm sorry, it does. I do have my reasons."

"I know, another story for another time," he answered, following her.

He walked her out to her car, and as she opened the door he touched her shoulders. Slowly, he pulled her back against him. He was warm and solid, and before her brain could prevent her body from reacting, she relaxed, molding to him.

So easy, so comfortable. She laid her head back into the crook of his neck. He smelled exotic and yet somehow homey, wild, and woodsy. His breath was hot and cinnamony on her brow. His lips brushed her ear, sending shock waves through her she wasn't quite prepared for.

"Thirty-eight," he whispered. "Older, yes, but not quite old enough to be your father." He placed a chaste kiss on her temple before gently pushing her away. "G'night."

The next week flew by, and the number of calls she got asking about the book club encouraged Abby. Some had already read the book she selected, and others asked if she had any copies to lend. For future meetings, of course, the members would have an entire month to read the selection. How *does* one start a book club for the first time? Pick a classic, one you can assume many have already read, and go with it? Her plan appeared to have been spot on in selecting a popular title. By the day of the meeting, she'd taken calls from a dozen confirmed attendees.

As she opened that morning she reminded herself that by the end of June, Monica would be gone. Only a few weeks left. She needed to make full use of her help while she could.

"Good morning. Are you feeling ambitious today?" she asked as she stowed her purse.

Monica yawned. "Not particularly. Probably boredom. What's up?"

"Well, you know tonight's my first book club meeting. I thought if we went through the stacks and culled some titles that don't get checked out much anymore, maybe I'd set up a mini-book sale tonight. We can hold a big sale later on, but I've got about a dozen people coming. No time like the present to get started, right?"

Monica shrugged. "I'm game."

"We'll start with the paperbacks." Abby gnawed on the end of her pencil. "Take out anything that's older than, say, ten years. Anything with a dust cover that isn't frayed from fond handling."

"Okay." Monica nodded. She flopped down in the chair behind the desk and yawned again. "I think, though, that's going to leave us with a bunch of open spaces on the shelves. Especially in the fiction stacks."

"That's all right. We'll fill them in. We'll have some money from the book sale. Not to mention the fundraiser Aunt Di and Uncle Armpit have scheduled. I couldn't believe it when she told me."

Monica chuckled. "Did you say Uncle Armpit?"

"Yeah. Don't ask." She stifled a smirk.

"Tell me about this fundraiser. Whose idea was that, anyway?"

"Aunt Di, of course. I can't imagine Uncle A willingly donating a single cheese puff without banking the proceeds."

"It's so nice of them to do this, though. Do you think it's gonna stop old Leda-bitch from shutting you down at the town meeting?" Monica steepled her fingers, tapping them together.

Abby bit down on the wood of the pencil until it yielded with an audible crack. "I can only hope so."

They spent the remainder of the afternoon stacking timeworn texts in a corner near the front desk. Classics, she decided, would stay. It didn't matter whether a copy of Mary Shelley's *Frankenstein* was five years old or fifty. Those titles still got checked out on a regular basis. Whenever there was doubt, she sent Monica to the records. Like an overstuffed closet of clothes, if it hadn't been 'worn' in a year or two, the volume lost its occupancy rights.

After a sluggish start, her enthusiasm infected Monica, and before long the two of them were so engrossed in their task patrons actually resorted to using the call bell on the reception desk when they were ready to check out. Each time the clang echoed, the two girls looked at each other and giggled.

"I never thought this was actually going to be fun," Monica said. "It's like a treasure hunt. Look at these old titles. I'll bet some of them are collector's items."

Abby considered that. "You're probably right. Maybe if we have two copies, we should pull the older original and leave the reprint on the shelf."

"And do what with the first edition? Sell it?"

"No!" Abby slapped a hand to her chest. "God, no. That would be like selling a child."

"Okay, mommy dearest, then what are we going to do with them?"

Abby narrowed her eyes as she thought. "We'll set up a shelf in the reference room for first editions. People can come in and look at them, read them in-house. Not check them out. What do you think?"

Monica rolled her eyes. "You are a weird one with books, Abby." She shook her head. "Still, it's a good idea. No sense letting somebody waltz out of here with a valuable first edition and posting it on eBay."

By the time Monica grabbed her purse and headed out the door, Abby was surrounded by stacks of books that could easily have filled the bed of a pickup truck.

"Book sale," she muttered as she navigated around the pile, waist high and four towers deep. "We should be able to accumulate at least enough tonight to buy a few copies of the current *New York Times* bestsellers."

A jolt of anticipation thrilled her. She pulled the book order list from under the counter and retrieved a brand new pencil from the desk drawer.

That's when the power went out, plunging the old building into darkness. The computer screens went black, and the gigantic old air conditioning unit rumbled to a halt, whistling feebly outside the rear windows. Fortunately, it was still daylight—half past four by Abby's watch.

For a few moments she wasn't sure what to do. She glanced toward the front door, half expecting someone to walk in and announce there was a citywide power outage. She listened for sirens out in the streets. Maybe somebody hit a pole? She heard nothing.

Then she looked toward the rear stacks, wondering if this might be a Harry caper. Perching her hands on her hips, she stalked to the back corner. No pipe smoke. The window was closed and latched.

"Harry, if this is some kind of joke," she called out, "your timing's not ideal. I've got book club tonight."

Silence hung like an invisible blanket. Growling, she unlatched the window and threw it open. The traffic light at Main Street and Vine flashed from green to yellow to red. No power outage down that way.

She waited five minutes, then fifteen. Checking her watch, she picked up the phone only to find it was dead too. Digging under the counter for her purse, she pulled out her cell and dialed Ancient Healings.

"Aunt Di?" She was relieved to hear Dianne's voice, as the hush and early gloaming of the library's interior had begun to creep up her spine. "Did you guys lose power?"

For a moment there was silence on the other end. "Lose power? What are you talking about, dear girl?"

"Electricity. We lost it. I mean, the library did. I'm sitting here in the dark."

Another beat of silence, then Dianne called for Armand. "There's not been any storms. Maybe a breaker tripped. I'll send Armand."

Ten minutes later Uncle Armand crept sheepishly through the front door, a quizzical expression twisting his already odd features into an even more clown-like façade. Abby met him in the foyer.

"No one else on the street has lost power, Abigail," he said in his melodic French accent.

"What do you mean, Armand? It's not like I forgot to pay the bill," she replied. As the words rolled off her tongue, she locked eyes with her confused uncle. "Today's the twenty-first, isn't it?" she asked.

"Yes, *ma cherie*. Happy Litha, by the way."

Of course. What a perfectly spiteful joke. Especially from someone who had the influence to pull a few strings. Someone who wanted nothing more than for the first book club meeting to fail.

Abby sat on the front steps with her cell phone pressed to one ear, getting more wound up by the minute. The call to Blue Ridge Power was futile. The operator on the other end could provide no details as to what caused the outage. She reminded Abby that she was not, after all, the designated payer on the account.

Next she dialed city hall and asked for Dennis. After five minutes on hold, she was transferred and disconnected. She redialed and went through the same routine, twice. Finally, when she was about ready to jump into her car and head over to the county offices in person, Dennis Ludwig came on the line.

"Commissioner? Abby Stryker. Got a little problem down here."

He coughed and waited a beat before asking, "What sort of problem, Ms. Stryker?"

"The sort that gets dark pretty fast once the sun goes down."

"Excuse me?" He sounded genuinely confused.

"The power's been shut off, Commissioner. My library is sitting here with no power."

He cleared his throat and muttered, "Just a minute, Abby."

She couldn't make out his next words, obviously muffled with a hand over the mouthpiece. When he came back on the line his tone was forced, phony. Like he was hiding something. "I'm having my secretary check with the local power company, Ms. Stryker. Any thunder up your way?"

"Not a single rumble, Commissioner. That's about to change real quick unless I get some answers."

"I'll look into it, Abigail. In the meantime, it's, what? Almost five o'clock anyway. Why don't you just lock up and take the rest of the afternoon off?"

Her laugh crackled with irritation she couldn't conceal. "I'd love to do that, Commissioner. Only problem is I've got a book club meeting in about an hour."

"Oh, Abby, I'm sorry. I had no idea. Let me make a few calls and see if I can get someone down there."

When she clicked off, she moaned and covered her face.

Armand was sitting beside her, waiting silently. After a moment he asked, "Is there anything more I can do for you, Abigail? I'm due down at Le Petit Mon for dinner hour."

She blew out a tortured sigh. Without looking up she moaned, "No, thank you, Armand. There's nothing more you can do here."

Chapter 10

Jack's summer class ended early. He figured he would stop by and check his mail on the way out. As he rumbled down the stairs crazed laughter echoed from the front office. It took him a minute before he recognized the distorted voice as Leda's.

"Clara, I only wish I could be there to see the look on the little witch's face," she cackled. "Let's see if she can conjure any of her black magic to light the place up."

When he reached the end of the hallway Jack stopped, staring at the two women facing each other over the counter. As Clara's eyes slanted his way, her cheeks flushed and her lips pressed into a line.

Leda turned toward him wearing a sinister smile. "Oh Jack! What good timing," she exclaimed.

Loud. Way too loud. For a moment he thought she was drunk.

"I figure you'll probably get a first-hand account of the news, seeing as you and our new librarian have become," she made air quotes, "rather chummy."

"Whoa. Stop it right there, Leda. My personal life is none of your business. I don't know what's got you so wickedly giddy, but I'm starting to worry you might be having a stroke. Are you okay? What's going on?"

Her grin widened. "I've never been better, Professor Wood. I've taken the first step to burying old rubbish in this town." She stretched out her arms and took a bow.

He squinted at her, wondering what the hell she was

talking about. Then he spoke slowly, as though to a child. "What are you talking about?"

Leda's clown smile faded as she folded her arms across her chest. She glared at him, shaking her head and making a tsk-ing sound. "You and my Dennis. You're both the same. History lovers. Preserve the past. Stuff the old corpse and prop it in a corner."

He blinked and looked to Clara for an explanation. She was pressing two fingers to the bridge of her nose and saying nothing. When another laugh burst out of Leda, Clara jumped.

"New and fresh," Leda shouted. "That's where the future's at, Jack. But why am I lecturing you? Ha. I don't need to tell you new and fresh is better. From what I hear, you're already sampling the town's newest stock."

Unsure of what was going on, he stared at her in shocked silence. Leda acted like a lunatic, and her comments indicated it had something to do with Abby. He brushed past her and pushed through the doors.

When he pulled up in front of the library he spotted Abby perched on the top step, chattering into her cell and waving her free hand in the air. He took the steps two at a time and stood looking down at her as she ended the call.

When she looked up, tears swam in her eyes. "She's gonna do me in, Jack. She's gonna win this one."

He dropped next to her and wrapped his arm around her. Her sobs broke as she buried her face against his shoulder.

"That bitch is crazy as a loon," he mumbled against her hair. "What did she do?"

Between sobs she explained. "Shut our power off. She did this on purpose. Perfectly timed. Tonight's my first book club meeting. I'm sure she thought it fitting since it's also another Wiccan holiday, Litha."

"Litha." Jack shook his head. "She's sick, Abby. I'm really beginning to believe she's mentally ill." He held her in silence for a beat, thinking. "Wait, isn't Litha summer solstice? That means today is the longest day of the year. It'll stay light here until at least eight-thirty, maybe nine. What time is your book club?"

She sniffled, swiping the smudged makeup from beneath her eyes. "Six-thirty. Less than an hour from now." She hiccupped. "What am I gonna do? Even if there's enough light, it's hotter than hell out here. And will be very shortly inside."

"Did you open all the windows? There's a breeze."

"Not yet."

"Did you get hold of anybody? The power company?"

"I finally got a call through to Dennis 'pussy-whipped' Ludwig. He said he'd make some calls. But you know how it works in this small town. I called Blue Ridge Power again but all the field technicians quit at five. They probably won't send somebody out here until the morning. Not unless it's life and death."

Jack's jaw ached from the tension, the sheer effort to contain the fury bubbling up in his chest. A car pulled up behind his and parked. "Maybe that's someone from the power company now," he said.

Abby stared in that direction. "No, that's Mamie."

The woman who stepped out of the car was dressed casually in khaki shorts and a sleeveless tank. Her short-cropped hair was salt-and-pepper gray. She appeared like somebody's mother, maybe grandmother, headed out for a day at the mall, except for the book clutched to her chest. As she mounted the steps she said, "I'm a little early, Abby, but I'm so excited! It's been forever since we had a book club here in town."

Mamie Greer was one of Abby's newest patrons. She had been the first to sign up for book club and was delighted with her choice for their first read.

She started up the steps, chattering excitedly. “It’s been ages since I read this book. Saw the movie umpteen years ago when it came out. I’d forgotten how much—” Mamie froze two steps below where Abby sat. “What’s wrong? What’s happened?”

Abby heaved a huge sigh, then swiped some more at the smudges ringing her eyes. “We have no power, Mamie. No lights and no air conditioning. The electricity has been shut off.”

Mamie tipped her head. “What do you mean, shut off?”

Abby shrugged, winding her arm underneath Jack’s as she scooted closer to his side. “I can’t say for sure why or how. Or who’s responsible, for that matter.” She chuckled darkly. “Although I do have a suspicion.”

The older woman struck a cocky pose—head tilted, chin tipped up, a hand on one hip. Then she blurted, “What the fuck?”

Abby rocked back as Jack stiffened.

“Go Mamie!” She chuckled. “But what the hell do we do now? I’m expecting a bunch of people.”

Mamie slid the book up under one arm. “We roll with it, girl.” She held out her hand and pulled Abby to her feet. “We simply fucking roll with it.”

Over the next forty-five minutes Jack helped Abby open all the windows in the building. Mamie disappeared for fifteen minutes and returned with a Styrofoam cooler filled with ice, bottled water, and cans of soda.

While she was gone, Jack turned to Abby and asked, “Who, might I ask, is that golden-tongued beauty?”

She couldn’t suppress her smile. “Mamie, believe it or not, is a retired elementary school teacher.”

His eyes widened. “You’re kidding, right? I went to school here, and I certainly don’t remember her.”

“Not here. Hickory. Mamie influenced the town’s

innocent young minds for the past twenty-five years, until just last month. Said she spent enough of her life censoring her language. Biting her tongue, as she put it. I guess when she decided to shed the mantle of schoolmarm she pulled out all the stops."

He lifted a hand to his forehead, laughing. "Well, I'm so glad she at least waited until her retirement party to let the dogs out."

The Harvey Library's first book club in almost three years met by candlelight. Abby was thrilled—fourteen people showed, not counting her and Jack. Dianne came down from Ancient Healings toting half a dozen scented herbal candles, which she lit and spread down the length of the long meeting room table. Although she couldn't stay, she made a formal announcement to all, promising free coffee and dessert for everyone afterward at Le Petit Mon.

The scheduled ninety-minute discussion of *Madame Bovary* had barely gotten underway when strangeness commenced. First, the overhead lighting in the room pulsed with a faint glow. Once, twice, three times. On the fourth they flickered on to full strength.

Abby jumped up and said, "Well, maybe they're turning the power back on tonight after all." After a few minutes she leaned over to whisper to Jack, "I didn't hear the air conditioner kick on, did you?"

He shook his head and said, "Maybe it has to be reset. I'll go check."

In a few minutes he returned, caught her eye, and shrugged. She excused herself from the discussion and ducked behind the reception desk. He followed.

"The computer is still dead. So is the phone." She glanced at Jack who shrugged again.

"Is there an emergency generator? Maybe it only runs

certain things." He sniffed the air. "I do smell something. Smoke? Great. What next? Is Leda going to set the place on fire?"

Abby sniffed too, then smiled. "No worries. It's the emergency power kicking on."

"I thought you said there was no emergency generator."

"Well, actually, there is. Just not the usual kind. We call him Harry." She winked as she turned back toward her group.

Although the air conditioner remained silently inoperable, the room cooled as if the unit hummed at full capacity. The candles lined up along the center of the table fluttered as though disturbed by the chilled air flowing down from the vents. And the conversation about the controversial classic novel whirred into a lively discussion.

She checked her watch at ten past eight. The group had gone forty minutes beyond scheduled time. She smiled at Jack, who sat on her right squeezing her hand intermittently throughout the discussion.

Jack could almost see a halo of joy surrounding Abby. She was so in her element. If ever there was a lover of the written word, it was Abigail Stryker. She listened with earnest interest to each comment made by the participants, offering alternate viewpoints and asking if anyone shared the same opinion. She obviously had done her homework, plucking questions from a script in front of her whenever the conversation lagged.

When he glanced up at the wall clock, he couldn't believe how fast the time had passed. He smiled to himself and remained silent, reluctant to break her spell.

After glancing at her watch a second time, she rapped her knuckles on the table. "Unfortunately, we're out of time, folks. I can't tell you how wonderful this has been. Oh, and don't forget to pick out a new read from our book sale over there." She pointed to the stacks of books she and Monica had piled in the corner. "Hardcovers are a dollar, paperbacks twenty-five cents."

Her glow could have lit the entire room without candles, without the long last rays of evening sun slanting through the window. Without any electric power at all.

"I want to thank you all for coming, for believing in me, for supporting our library. And for suffering through the untimely, unforeseen inconveniences," she said.

Mamie spoke. "Abigail, I want to be the first to congratulate you for bringing our dying literary resource back to life." A light cheer resonated around the table. "You are an inspiration, our heroine, and our hope."

Jack could tell Abby was fighting back tears. He stood and folded her into his arms. Everyone rose with him, sounding a round of applause.

As the last book club attendee filed out, he looked up. Over the meeting table, the lights began to fade, as though someone turned down a dimmer switch. He followed Abby through the building as she snapped light switches on and off, picked up the phone, and pressed the power button on the library's computer. Everything was still stone cold dead. No power, anywhere.

He didn't question her further about the strange power source. In truth, he was almost afraid to. "How much did you earn from the book sale?"

She frowned. "Only about twenty bucks. It's a start. I can at least buy one new hardcover to add to the holdings."

Moments later, they descended the front steps. "Are you going for coffee and dessert at Le Petit Mon?" he asked.

Abby tried to stifle a yawn but failed, hiding behind her hand. "No, I'm whipped. I need a hot shower that lasts about an hour. Then I'm gonna snuggle up in bed with the book we chose for next month's meeting."

Jack held her gaze, imagining what it might be like to

join her for that shower, to snuggle with her in bed. Clearing his throat, he asked, "Why don't you come by my place for a while? I'll drive you home whenever you want." But he already knew what her answer would be.

She sighed. "Another time, Jack. Thank you, though, and thank you for your support tonight." She hugged him around his middle and rested her head against his shoulder.

He smoothed her hair. The silky tresses almost reached her shoulder now on one side. "It's getting longer. Letting it grow?"

"No, just haven't had time to get up to my hairdresser in Boone."

As she pulled away he placed a hand on each of her shoulders and planted a soft kiss on her forehead. "When you do go, make sure the chair is level before the stylist picks up those snips." He flipped the longer side. "She got it a little crooked last time."

She grinned and turned to walk the half-block to her apartment.

He fell into step beside her. "I'll walk you. How do you know if you have power there?"

"Good question. I don't. But it would have taken a pretty determined effort to turn off power to my apartment and not affect the store downstairs," she replied. "I called Aunt Di right after the lights went out. She had power."

He waited on the curb until Abby climbed the stairs and flicked the lights on in her apartment. She came to the window and waved at him before lowering the shade.

Later, Jack sat up half the night researching the library's history, as he'd been doing for the past several weeks. He was more determined now than ever to unravel the mystery. A logical man, he'd never believed in ghosts. Not until today. But there didn't seem to be any reasonable explanation for what happened. Abby wasn't a kook. And she certainly believed in Harry.

Over the past week, he'd exhausted all of the hard copy resources he could find in the Caldwell and Hickory libraries. He'd even taken a trip to the tiny one in Wilkesbury. Although he always left the Internet as a last resort, he carried his laptop upstairs to his loft bedroom.

The last thing he needed was to open his homepage and be accosted by a pop-up message box. Not again.

Hey there, big guy. You haven't exactly been climbing over my invitations for friendship on Facebook. I found your account on LinkedIn too. Are you avoiding me, or am I falling helplessly into your spam folder?

Dawn. Or Killer Dawn, as he'd come to think of her. The last woman on this earth he wanted to connect with again, even electronically. She'd been virtually stalking him these past few weeks. He couldn't figure out how she found him or why. There must be dozens, maybe hundreds of Jack Woods on Facebook and LinkedIn. How had she figured out which one he was, and why was she actually paying LinkedIn's fee to send her message to somebody who hadn't accepted her friendship?

He swallowed, then blew out a sigh of relief. A wonder of modern technology was the power, with the click of one button, to make somebody disappear. With a satisfying little thrill, he clicked the X on the corner of the message. There. Done. Gone.

Then he went straight to his favorite search engine to continue his research. He followed a lot of links, some dead-ends. A few of the major historical sites had short blurbs on the Harvey, or a brief mention that Elijah founded the library. One site displayed an old photograph of the building with a horse-drawn carriage parked along the unpaved street dated 1885.

Directly beneath the photo was another faded image. A

wooden structure with a battered tin porch roof displayed a hand-painted sign hanging crooked from the front: Harnessmaker, Jasper Laramy.

Maybe he was going about this the wrong way. Instead of Elijah Harvey, maybe he needed to track down Isabelle Laramy.

Jack typed the name in the search engine. A long list of links loaded, everything from telephone directory listings to Facebook pages.

Not going to be hanging around on social media, at least not tonight.

He kept scrolling through the list of Google search results. Jack was surprised at how many hits he got on the name Laramy. After scanning three pages, he was ready to give up when one title caught his eye. The web address ended in .org. A good sign. He clicked, and the page loaded. He couldn't believe what he'd stumbled upon.

"Antebellum North Carolina," he read. "*Occupations in the 1880s—Census of free North Carolinians.*"

A census, and in the time period he was looking for. He bookmarked the site quickly, afraid it would disappear, then turned to jot the web address on the notepad on his nightstand. When he reached over to grab his water bottle, his alarm clock's red numerals scolded: 2:04 a.m.

"I'm afraid my hunt to find you will have to continue in the morning, Mrs. Harvey. G'night."

Even after his laptop closed down and the room went dark, Jack's mind didn't settle. He wondered about the strange happenings in the library earlier. How the lights came on and how cool air flowed from the vents even though the air conditioner remained silently dead.

And the mysterious smoke. Abby mentioned her "ghost" smoked a pipe. Could there truly be more to the legend of Caldwell's library ghost then just local superstition? Had Elijah Harvey smoked a pipe? And if his spirit did linger there in the old building, why had he only started making his presence known after Dana Laramy retired?

Jack finally drifted off with his mind buzzing with too much stimuli, too many images tangling. Of muddy, pot-holed dirt streets gridding the early, newly settled town of Caldwell. Of grimy stone masons working on a bold, new brick building across the street from a rickety harness maker's shanty. Of a hefty man in a pinstriped suit smoking a pipe as he helped a petite woman up into a horse-drawn carriage.

She was garbed in Antebellum finery and wielding a parasol. In his dream, as the woman turned her face toward him, it was Abby with her quirky, crooked dark hair. When she stepped up into the carriage, black-and-white Converse sneakers peeked out from under the bustled skirts.

The next morning as Abby opened the library, she wondered whether she'd be working in the dark. She clenched her teeth as she toggled the switches. They sounded their characteristic snap and light flooded the room. She listened and could hear the hum of the air conditioner behind the building already toiling against the promise of a steamy summer day. Her computer booted up in normal time, defaulting to the "Welcome to Caldwell Municipal Library" homepage. Power must have been restored sometime during the night.

Either that or Harry had gotten a good night's rest and had taken over completely.

When Monica came in, Abby was standing, hands on hips, staring at the still massive piles of books they'd weeded from the shelves.

"Hey," Monica said, "how'd book club go?"

Abby mumbled, "Great. No thanks to our friends at Blue Ridge Power."

"What happened? Was there a storm here?" Monica

asked. “I was down in Hickory at Davin’s place. No bad weather there.”

She rubbed her forehead. “Not from Mother Nature. From a tornado named Leda.”

Monica froze, her eyes wide while Abby filled her in on the previous night’s events.

“That bitch,” Monica growled. “She’s gotten completely out of control. What did Dennis say?”

“I don’t think Dennis knows how to handle his lovely wife any more than the rest of us do,” she retorted. “If I wasn’t so pissed, I’d actually feel sorry for him.”

“The council meeting is next Friday, isn’t it?” Monica asked, almost apologetically. “I’m so sorry I’ve put you in this position, Abby. Leaving like this. But Davin and I’ve waited so long.”

“It would have come to a head sooner or later anyway, Monica. Leda wants this place shut down. I’m sure she’d be glad to help me get a job slinging burgers down at Murphy’s.” She scanned the room, lifting a hand to knead the tension out of her neck. “Unless I get some support, she might just get her way.”

Monica picked up a pencil and slid it back and forth between her fingers. “Abby, what Leda’s trying to do may not be entirely legal.”

“What does it matter? Her husband’s the County Commissioner. The original endowment fund may have been plenty to fund the library a hundred and fifty years ago. Not anymore.”

“Davin is an attorney, and he isn’t on Caldwell’s payroll,” Monica said. “Do you want us to come to the meeting? If Leda’s bending any state or local laws, Davin can at least tell you and put you in contact with someone who might be able to help.”

“I don’t know if it will help, but that would be great.

If nothing else, the moral support will get me through the ordeal."

Their conversation was interrupted by the first of what developed into a steady stream of patrons over the next several hours. Abby was busy looking up a title on gardening for Mrs. Bernard when another woman strolled up to the desk.

"Be with you in a minute," Abby said without looking up.

"Take your time. I'm in no hurry."

She was shocked to hear Aunt Di's voice. Abby hurried to scribble the call number on a scrap of paper before handing it to Mrs. Bernard.

Once the patron headed off toward the stacks, Dianne rested an elbow on the counter and said, "Abby, I want to talk to you about the fundraiser. Details. Dates and menus and things. Your uncle and I want to help."

"That's so sweet of you. Both of you." She sighed and pressed her forehead into her hand. "After next Friday night, though, there may be no library to raise funds for."

"Don't you worry about that," Dianne replied smugly. "The vote's going to go just fine."

"What makes you so sure? Are you gonna cast a spell on Leda and make her sleep through the whole thing?" Abby quipped. "That's all I need. There are still a lot of folks in town who'd probably like to burn both of us at the stake."

A sly grin twisted Dianne's lips. "No spells. I promise." She patted the back of Abby's hand. "Trust me."

Chapter 11

Even before his run on Saturday morning, Jack spent the dawn's breaking hours on the banks of the stream near his house. The fishing gods were on his side. An hour or so later he headed home with two perfect, fat trout in the basket slung over his shoulder.

He'd called Abby the day before and offered to cook her dinner, and he was thrilled when she'd said yes.

Weekend hours usually zipped by too quickly, but today time slowed to an unbearable crawl. Finally, a few minutes before five, he slipped through the library's door and clicked it shut as quietly as the knob's chain of bells would allow.

Abby stared out the front window in a trance, her arms folded across her chest. He stood for a moment watching the golden light of late afternoon wash over her.

The silk of her hair caught the rays, reflecting them to iridescence. Warm tones shone through the inky strands, with mahogany and gold glinting through the coolness of the blue-black. Like a dragonfly's wing, the hues pulsed and faded with the light.

"Hey," he called softly. "You okay?"

She looked back over her shoulder, then dipped her head and chuckled. "Yeah, I'm fine. It's been slow the past hour. I was just looking over at Laramy's and wondering."

"Wondering what?" He came to her side and wrapped his arm around her shoulders.

"It seems so unfair that history slips past us and into oblivion. Only bits and pieces get recorded." She sighed and met his gaze.

Melancholy filled her dark rimmed eyes, and his heart clenched.

"So much of life," she continued, "the little moments, they slip away like water in a stream. We're left on the bank, never sure what happened between the people who walked in this very space all those years ago."

"That's why I love history so much," he said, resting his cheek against her brow. "Why are you so sad? Has something else happened? I realize you have plenty of reason to be upset already."

Taking a deep breath, her body rose and fell against him. "Not really. I don't understand why this crazy dream of mine—to save this place, all it stands for—is cursed. Who this spirit is and why he's trapped here. What happened all those years ago that's keeping him from moving on. I wonder if it's the ghost of Elijah Harvey." She searched his eyes. "You don't even believe there's a haunting, do you?"

A month ago he'd have laughed at anyone who believed in ghosts. And no matter what the townspeople thought of Dianne and Abby's Wiccan ties, he knew this young woman was too smart to believe in brew ha-ha. Or in anything that wasn't absolutely good.

Now she's even got me believing in magic.

He traced a finger across her cheek and tucked a strand of her hair behind her ear. "I know you wouldn't feel so passionately about the spirit of this old library if you didn't believe in your heart he was real. And after book club night, Harry or Elijah or whatever the spirit calls himself, made a believer out of me too. Mostly because I believe in you."

She buried her face against his neck. "Thank you, Jack.

Squeezing her shoulders, he said, "Come on. Dinner's waiting."

He drove while she told him about Monica's offer to come to the council meeting. He heard the worry in Abby's voice. His gut twisted at the sound of her anxious anticipation.

"Monica feels guilty, like she's responsible for all this. I keep telling her the showdown would have come to pass no matter if she left or not," Abby said, gazing out the window as they wove along the winding road out of town.

"What do you think Leda will do at the council meeting?" he asked gently.

She heaved a huge sigh. "I think she'll make a motion to the board to limit subsequent funding for additional employees. She's sure I'll work the place alone as long as I can. Fifty hours a week until I drop. I think it's gotten personal now. Rather than simply shut us down, she wants blood. What Leda wants from me is surrender."

He made a growling sound in his throat, trying with all his might to contain the rage building inside. "That's just like her."

When they arrived at his cabin, the heat of the day cooled under the cover of the pines. He poured them both a glass of blush wine in his kitchen, smirking as he held up the bottle.

"No twist cap tonight. I don't usually drink the pink, frilly stuff," he began, "but this pairs well with fish. At least that's what they tell me."

Lifting her glass, she said, "*They* are usually right, aren't they? What are we toasting, anyway?"

He held his glass in mid-air and rolled his gaze toward the ceiling. "To classics. Timeless classics. In books, buildings, and beauty. Classics should never go out of style." Clinking glasses with hers, he sipped before adding, "And to good fishing in June."

She raised an eyebrow. "What does good fishing have to do with classics?"

"Dinner. It has to do with dinner and totally." He set his glass on the countertop and turned to retrieve the marinating fish out of the fridge. "If the fishing gods had not been generous today, we would have nothing to go with our Chantilly potatoes. Except green beans. And pink wine."

He turned to find her shocked expression priceless and completely adorable.

"I'm not sure which to be more curious about," she said. "The fish or the potatoes . . . wait, did you say *Chantilly*? I'm surprised you even know what they are."

Abby sat on a stool at Jack's kitchen island as he prepared dinner. There was something incredibly sexy about watching a man work in the kitchen. Especially this man, who was such a paradox in so many ways. Highly educated, conservative, and even a little stuffy. He wore tweed, for God's sake. Yet his hands were callused from yard work, weeding the garden, and chopping wood for his fireplace.

His fit and toned body disputed his silver-streaked mop of curls. A history buff that fished for his own—as well as her—dinner, then cooked it up in his own kitchen? She was part amazed, part amused. Another, much bigger part, was charmed to her soul.

I'm going to have to monitor my feelings very, very carefully.

Dinner was amazing—tender, delicately seasoned trout filets on a bed of sautéed onions and mushrooms, clothed in a remoulade dressed with almonds. Jack lit candles in the center of a small round table of rough-hewn wood. Had he crafted it himself?

And the potatoes? Yes, they were genuine Chantilly. Abby might never have known except she'd sampled Uncle Armand's rendition. She and Jack ate from pewter plates using flatware bearing hand-carved bone handles. So classically masculine.

It's almost as though I've imagined him into reality. A strange, stress-born fantasy.

When the meal was through she rose to collect the plates, but he stopped her.

"I can do all of this tomorrow. Finals are over, and my summer schedule is light to the point of boring." He refilled her glass and motioned toward the glass doors leading to the back deck. "Com'on. Let's see if the deer family will visit us tonight."

"Where's your wine?"

He stepped so close she could feel the heat of his body, touching his finger to the end of her nose. "I have to drive you home, remember?" He held her gaze for a long moment, tracing his fingertip lightly around the diamond stud piercing. "This real?"

She nodded. "A present to myself when I decided to change my image. Done the same day I chopped off all my hair, dyed it black, and bought an industrial-sized tube of black eyeliner." As she turned toward the door she mumbled, "You should have seen the looks on my parents' faces."

"I can well imagine. I can't wait to hear the rest of that story," he said as he followed her outside.

They sat blanketed in the delicious privacy of darkness on his back deck. Points of starlight pierced an inky sky. Jack came out the door prepared for the forest's chill. Together they snuggled on the Adirondack loveseat under a fluffy blanket, lost in the wonder of the night's sounds.

"It's so quiet here, yet so not," she whispered. "I mean, at first, it's as though I've gone deaf. No street noise, no hum of the TV or air conditioner from the guy next door. Yet once I stop and listen, I pick up on a special kind of symphony."

"That's one of the things I love about living out here," he replied. "There's so much you can't see beyond the glare of the street lamps or hear over the roar of teenagers peeling out of the college parking lot."

She chuckled. "It wasn't so long ago I was one of those speed demon teenagers."

"You? No way. You were the girl struggling with a satchel of books weighing more than you across the parking lot to tumble into a sensible station wagon."

"Station wagon! What is that? Oh, Professor Jack, you are surely showing your age."

His eyes met hers then, burning with intensity softened by something else. Something a bit more scary. No man had ever looked at her that way before.

Gently, he brushed his lips over hers, on the tip of her nose, across her cheek. His warm breath in her ear sent shudders through her as she breathed in his musky scent. Her heart raced faster, stirring a warm buzz in her center she hadn't experienced in far too long.

Oh, I'm in really big trouble.

As though he could read her mind, he eased back, framing her face in his hands. "I can feel it, Abby. Every time I try to get near you. You don't pull away, yet something is in the way. As if I'm plucking at a scab and causing you pain."

Tears sprung to her eyes, though her reaction angered her. She had to get past this or she would live the rest of her life alone. She didn't want to be alone, she vowed. "No, I'm fine. This is wonderful, Jack. You . . . are wonderful."

But he was right. She wanted him, but fear tinged her exhilaration. Something more than lust filled those sage green eyes, an emotion she didn't understand. His gaze probed her clear through to her soul. Her heart clenched protectively.

"There's something, Abby. I've come to know you well enough to sense when that wall goes up. Whatever put it there, I'm not pushing past it. Not until I'm sure you want me to." His voice was thick with emotion. "I couldn't."

She'd never confided in anyone about what happened. Yet she knew until she moved beyond her past, her life would remain frozen, barren, on hold. She'd come to think of Jack as a trusted friend. Something inside clicked open as she made her decision. She must tell him.

"I had a lover. In college," she began, pulling away and hugging herself. "He's dead, and it's probably because of me. He may as well have died in my arms."

It was torment, trying to put words to strangled emotions she'd struggled to contain for so long. She couldn't hold his gaze while she spoke.

"I was twenty-three and beginning my graduate program. Cameron Bennett was assigned as my academic mentor," she said. "I wasn't surprised. In fact, I'm sure my parents arranged for him to be my mentor. He was my father's best friend."

Jack cleared his throat, and she studied his face, wondering. She pushed on. "Our affair was this huge, ugly secret. Nobody knew. We always met at his place, a cute little chalet up on Grandfather Mountain." She let out dark laugh. "How incredibly fitting."

"Why fitting?" Jack asked.

"Because when Cameron and I started sleeping together, I was a student, and he was faculty. I was twenty-three—he was forty-eight. Over twice my age." She hung her head. "Cameron was old enough to be my father. Plenty old enough."

Jack's arm tightened around her shoulders. He waited a full minute, then three, maybe four. Finally, he asked, "How long did you . . . where you with him?"

She stared out into the inky blackness. If she tried to maintain eye contact, she'd never be able to finish her confession. "Almost two years. I was about halfway through my graduate program. I was well into developing my thesis when . . ." She faltered, fighting the huge lump in her throat.

His hand stroked her back, and she was so glad he didn't rush her. He was amazing. No pressure, no judgmental questions. Drawing in a deep breath for courage, she continued. "It was Saturday, our favorite day. We spent Friday nights at his place. In the morning, he'd cook me a big, country breakfast." The memory stirred a smile. "He used to make fun of how I ate biscuits, like you did the other night," she said, flashing a glance toward him. "We ate on his deck or, when it was cold, in front of the huge windows overlooking the valley."

What must he think of her? A woman who jumps into the sack with her father's best friend?

"Did you make plans with him? I mean, long term. Or was this just a—"

"An affair," she snapped. "That's all it ever was. That's all either of us wanted." She shifted in her seat to face him. "Jack, I grew up with parents who were nothing more than academic colleagues. I never saw them show any affection toward each other. None. I wonder sometimes how I was even conceived."

He blinked, and his brows rose, then drew together. "Were they affectionate toward you?"

"I was an inconvenience. In lieu of preschool, my mother stuck me in the library outside her office. Instead of driving me to friends' birthday parties on the weekends, she let me pick out a new book at the local bookstore. My best friends were Nancy Drew and Amelia Bedelia." Abby barked out a laugh. "When Cameron brushed his fingers across my cheek that first day in his office, I was so starved for affection I melted into his arms without a second thought."

After a long pause, Jack asked, "What happened to him?"

Drawing in a deep breath, she released it in stutters. "It was December. Outside the windows, fat snowflakes drifted down like in Charlie Brown's Christmas. Cameron insisted on having me once more before I left. Afterward, I crept out of bed and got dressed, not wanting to wake him. That's the last time I saw him."

She pushed down the lump of pain rising into her throat, making it hard to continue. "My parents were hosting the faculty Christmas party that night. Cameron never showed up."

A shuddering sob escaped her. Jack drew her to him and held her close, rocking her as he combed his fingers through the short crop of hair at her nape.

"I couldn't even go to the funeral. If I did, I wouldn't be able to hide my feelings. They would have figured out what had been going on between us. I lied. I told my parents I had a terrible migraine and couldn't possibly go." Her next words came out garbled, muffled against his chest. "I never even got to say goodbye."

Such a relief to let it go. For the past year, she'd only had her pillow to console her, cold and alone in her room. Although Aunt Dianne knew there'd been "someone," she didn't know any of the details. Abby knew how highbrow the faculty community was, how important her parents' reputation was in a small college community like Boone. A scandal like this would ruin them both.

If he were still alive, Cameron would have lost his tenured position in a heartbeat. Even though he'd been divorced for years, it was strictly against policy for a faculty member to mess around with a student. If anyone found out about the affair, even now, her parents might suffer cruel judgment by their ultra-conservative jury of peers.

After her shuddering subsided, Jack spoke quietly. "What happened to him, Abby? An accident?"

"No. That's the worst part. Maybe I wouldn't be so screwed up in the head if he died on the slippery roads that night." She pushed away from him, sitting up straight and pulling the blanket up higher around her. "He died of a heart attack. Massive coronary. His son found him the next morning, right where I'd left him. The autopsy estimated he'd been dead about twenty-four hours. He must have died within minutes after . . ."

She looked over at Jack, searching his eyes for something, but what? Judgment? Forgiveness? Understanding? Her emotions were all jumbled, raw and confused. Would he think less of her? And why shouldn't he? She'd been eaten up with guilt and shame for so long, hiding a monstrous secret that was eating her alive.

His expression remained unreadable, causing an icy chill to clutch her chest, yet his voice was gentle as he said, "He was pretty young for a heart attack, Abby. He must have had a heart condition."

"No. Cameron never said a thing about problems with his heart. Daddy said they called what happened to Cameron a 'widow maker.' It's insidious, a condition that exists silently in a surprisingly large percentage of otherwise healthy men. The killer strikes without warning."

"That wasn't your fault."

A tiny spark of relief kindled in her chest. He sounded like he just might be on her side.

She slid out from under the blanket and rose to pace on the patio. "Maybe not. Cameron never did take very good care of himself. He was a bookworm, a classic academic. The most exercise he got was walking from his office to the parking lot. He never spent one day of his life in a gym."

She stopped, sniffled, swiping at her eyes. "He seemed strong, virile. But I had no way to know if he was . . . normal. He was my first. I . . ." She drew in a shuddering breath. "He said I excited him more than any woman had in his entire life."

Abby turned to Jack with brimming eyes. "I've always blamed myself for what happened to him."

He sat forward on the bench with his elbows on his knees. "No, Abby. Sure, you may have turned him on, got him more worked up than ever before, but you didn't put that blockage in his artery. You didn't cause him to neglect his body all those years before he even met you."

She sank onto the bench beside him, and they sat for long time in silence. Abby struggled with memories inside her own head, looking for some way to justify laying the whole tragic experience to rest.

Finally she turned and said, "So you see, I have this fear of relationships with older men. With men in general, for that matter." She sniffed. "Since the last one dropped dead on me. Cameron was my first. The only man I'd ever been with—that way. I'm also not sure how to act with a man out in public. That's why I freaked out that night you took me to the festival. It was ingrained in me that whenever Cameron and I were together, no one could know we were . . . together," she squeaked out the last words in a small, strained voice.

His arm came around her shoulders and he held her. "Shh. I understand. It's okay."

The night closed in, holding them in a cushioned suspension of time and space. Abby felt drained and numb, and as she dropped her head onto his shoulder she wondered if Jack might be the right man. Like Cameron, he was settled in his solitary, bachelor's life. Unlike when she was with Cameron, there would be no shame if she took him as a lover.

She couldn't give Jack more than that. She'd never learned how.

"I'd better get you home," he said, kissing her forehead as he swept aside her curtain of hair.

"Okay," she replied, wondering why he hadn't said more and worrying about his real opinion of her now. Wondering if Jack was the kind of man who could give her the affection she craved, but not ask for more.

May 23, 1883

Dearest Elijah,

I await daily, dearest, for word from you in the big city of the East. Nearly a month has passed since you left, and still I have no word from you. Though I endeavor to avoid playing the role of meddlesome wife, I cannot help worrying if your passage has been safe. I'm aware your business fills your days and nights, but please, Elijah, pen me just two lines to let me know all is well.

On a brighter note, the library continues to enjoy the local embrace. I've begun a reading group for those wanting to improve their skills. On Wednesday evenings, I invite the locals in for poetry recitals, readings I choose from the wonderful selection you so generously purchased for me. The library is the greatest gift, my love. I only hope I can, in return, provide you with the heir for which you so desperately yearn.

Yet that is impossible unless you come home to me! I anticipate your estimated return before the summer solstice. I hope and pray nothing has occurred to derail that plan.

In the meantime, know that I am well, as are Mama and Pa. My days are busy, but I end each longing for your embrace. I am praying for your safe return to me. With all my heart, I am

Filled with Eternal Love,
Isabelle

Chapter 12

It was nearly ten by the time they pulled onto Main Street, and Jack snugged his SUV up to the curb in front of Abby's apartment. As he did, she emitted a shocked squeak. A half a block up the street, light spilled from every window of the library.

"Is Monica working tonight?" he asked.

"Hell, no. She never works Saturdays. Only that one time for me, the day of the first story hour," she retorted. Then her brows arched. "I wonder if it's the ghost lighting up the place."

Jack drove down the block to park in front of the building. Her feet hit the pavement before he'd even thrown it into park. He scrambled out after her, taking the steps two at a time to catch up.

The front door was unlocked, and she walked in, Jack close behind her. She'd gotten as far as the reception desk when he heard voices coming from behind the book stacks. Not ghostly voices. These were scarier than any ghost he ever imagined.

Leda Ludwig strode around the end of the H to E stack, flippantly throwing one end of a Hermes silk scarf over her shoulder as she chattered away to some unseen companion.

God, Leda's finally lost it. She's in here dressed to the nines and giving a guided tour to an imaginary companion.

But seconds later a man in grubby Dickies work clothes appeared behind her, a yellow steno pad in one hand, pencil poised in the other.

"What the holy hell," Abby yelled, "do you think you're doing?"

She stopped halfway between reception and the shelves. From behind her Jack couldn't see her expression, but he recognized a battle stance when he saw one. Her feet were spread wide and her hands fisted on her hips.

When Leda halted, the man behind her almost plowed her down. Her eyes registered shock, then something akin to fear. She recovered quickly, mirroring Abby's pose, and stepped forward until she was only an arm's distance away. Then her slicked lips twisted into a satanic smile.

"Why here she is, Marshall," Leda said, far too loud and tainted with a slight, demeaning singsong. "Marshall Glover, I'd like you to meet Abigail Stryker. She's our librarian. As of right this minute, anyway."

The short, rough-shaven man stepped around Leda and extended a grimy hand. His eyebrows looked like dusty caterpillars. "How'ya do, ma'am? I run the local auction house down Hickory way."

Abby didn't budge, maintaining her battle stance. A flash of alarm crossed the man's face. Every man knows the "oh shit, a cat fight" look. Marshall retrieved his hand, then shifted from one foot to the other, his gaze flashing anywhere except in the vicinity of either woman.

When Abby spoke, acid laced her words. "Good evening, Mrs. Ludwig. What, may I ask, brings you to my library so late on a Saturday night?"

Leda's laugh was mocking, almost hysterical. "Your library. *Your* library?" she shrieked. "Since when does the newly installed resident witch consider this her library?"

Jack stood close enough behind Abby to see her shoulders trembling.

"Since your husband hired me as such," she snarled. "Now, tell me. What are you doing here?"

Leda flipped her hand toward Marshall. "I thought tonight would be a good time to have Marshall take a look at the merchandise. A good time to determine whether there's anything here worth salvaging or if we should have the whole lot hauled away in a dumpster. He's going to be the one liquidating the contents of the property. After next Friday, that is."

Jack said, "How can you be so sure things are going to go your way at the town meeting, Leda?"

The silence that hung for one moment stretched into two before Leda exploded. "My way! My way!" Even though it was Jack who'd spoken, she whirled on Abby, poking a finger at her chest. "My way is the only way it can be, little witch."

Marshall fidgeted, his fingers tugging at the collar of his shirt. "Mebbe I should come back another time, Mrs. Ludwig," he grumbled before whisking around her and hastening toward the front door.

She made no move to stop him.

Jack stepped forward the minute she reached for Abby, ready to move between them. It took every ounce of his self-control to keep from slapping the bitch, and he dug his fingernails into the palms of his hands. Both women stayed planted in their tracks, like positively charged magnets, glaring at each other in ominous silence. For a long, frantic heartbeat, time itself stood still out of pure fear.

It was then his eye caught the movement on the uppermost shelf above Leda's head. At first, he thought he was seeing things. Maybe it was an errant shadow, a trick of the light. His gaze flashed back toward the movement once, twice—then, there was no denying it.

A book was moving, all by itself—inching out from the stack on the top shelf above her head.

She burst into another tirade, obscenities and accusations spewing her fury like a person gone mad. Abby remained silent and still, her arms folded across her chest. Her eyes were fixed on Leda, so she didn't see the book coming to life.

Jack glanced up again and watched in disbelief as the book wiggled like an excited puppy, inching its way out from the tight fit of its companions. At the last minute he lurched forward and raised his hand, trying to warn her.

"Leda, watch out!" he called, seconds too late.

As though compelled by the moment he spoke, the book made a final rush. In the split second that followed the heavy, cellophane-bound text came plunging down. It didn't simply fall. The heavy tome seemed to have been thrust out by some propellant, some unseen mitigating force.

It landed flat on the top of her head, then bounced off her shoulder on its journey to the floor. The impact shocked her, and she stumbled to one side, then the other, clutching both hands to her crown.

For a brief moment he was afraid she'd go down. He lunged to break her fall, succeeding at only catching her wrist. His touch sparked another explosion of fury as she staggered upright.

"Get your hands off me, you devil!" she screeched as she tore her wrist free. Then she whirled on Abby. "You little bitch! You satanic, evil whore!" Tears welled into Leda's eyes, and her voice cracked. "Your black magic isn't welcome here, devil's whore! You will be cast out. I will make sure of it or die trying."

She stormed past Abby and out the front door. Anguish twisted Abby's features. He reached out and drew her into his arms. She melted against him, trembling.

"What the hell?" she said a bit unsteadily.

"That was really weird," he mumbled against her ear. "You didn't do that, did you?"

She pushed back with both hands flat on his chest. The

ferocity in her eyes was a little unnerving. "Are you kidding me? Are you freaking kidding me?"

He gathered her back to him, smoothing her hair as he struggled to calm her. "Yes, I'm kidding. What do you think that was all about? Leda's screech can make people tremble, but I didn't think it could actually dislodge books from a shelf."

Abby pulled away and swiped under her eyes as she bent to pick up the fallen book. Her unexpected laughter made him wonder if she might be going into shock.

"Hey look, Jack." She held the book out, almost proudly. *Witch* by Barbara Michaels. "I wonder what our ghost was trying to say. Is he on our side or Leda's?"

"The book bopped Leda on the head, honey. Not you."

Abby looked up into his eyes. "You don't really think I'm a witch, Jack? Do you?"

He held her close. "No, baby, no, I don't believe you're a witch. You've got some pretty amazing powers over me. But I believe the only witch in this town just waltzed out that door with a bump on her hard head."

Armand had listened to Dianne's chatter on the phone nonstop for the past three days. He knew her well enough to know that once she set her mind to a task, she was like a rabid bulldog. It was obvious she had no intention of stopping now.

"Hey, Nonni. How are you? Yeah, Litha was lovely. How's your summer been going?"

He sat across from his wife at their kitchen table, trying to concentrate on his morning paper. Alas, his efforts were in vain.

"No, nothing yet. Gonna be starting those plans real soon. Hey, listen Nonni, I need a favor."

He mentally rolled his eyes as Dianne went into her rehearsed sales pitch, the one he'd listened to at least a hundred times over the last week.

"So if you can make it down here to the town meeting tomorrow night, I promise you will be helping out one of our own. My own. My beloved niece, Abby."

As she hung up the phone she caught his glare. She locked on it, and challenged it.

"What?" she barked.

He folded his paper and set it beside his cup. "Dianne, darling, I know you believe this is a good cause. I do too. But you're going up against city hall this time. Literally. Do you think that's good for business? For either of us?"

Her eyes narrowed. "Armand, don't you believe what I am doing is the right thing? We're talking right and wrong here, not what's right or wrong for business."

He stared into his cup, silent for a moment. He loved this strong-willed, big-hearted woman fiercely, yet had learned to pick his battles with her. Finally, he sighed, and then spoke softly. "Yes, it is the right thing, *ma cherie*. However, sometimes the right thing is not the wise thing."

Dianne huffed and settled back in her chair. She lifted her cup to her lips and sipped. Her shoulders sagged. "My love, if this is something you are truly opposed to, I will not act. Blood is thicker than water. But love is the thickest serum of all." Her voice was gentle.

A long moment passed. This too was what he loved about his Dianne. She worshipped him, her faithfulness the only thing he'd ever seen overrule her stubborn will. He spoke from his heart.

"*Ma cherie*, if you feel this strongly about what you are doing, I am with you. Blessed be."

Jack had no summer classes on Thursday, and on this particular one, he was glad. He rose early, ran his three miles, showered, and shaved. He sat at his computer, notes by his side, and proceeded with his exploration of the life history of Isabelle Laramy. Ancestry.com was a wonderful thing.

Official records were all he could access, but it was enough. He learned that Isabelle was born in 1862 in Caldwell, only daughter of harness maker Jasper Laramy and his wife Edna. According to the 1880 census, Isabelle was listed as daughter, aged 18, living with her parents, her occupation as schoolmistress. Two years later a marriage record changed her name to Mrs. Elijah Harvey. In 1892, Isabelle Harvey died.

Jack did the math in his head. Hmm. If the dates were correct, Isabelle was only 30 years old when she died. Childbirth? Or some ravaging illness? He doubted he would ever find evidence to confirm either as fact. There were no children of record. The important date, in his mind, was the year of her birth.

If Isabelle had been born in 1862, she would have been 20 when Harvey took her as his wife. Records on Elijah Harvey set his birth date in 1827 in Boston.

Jack dropped back in his chair, reached down and lifted his cup, sipping the long-cold coffee.

If these dates told the true tale, Isabelle Laramy married a man thirty-five years her elder. Abby's words echoed in Jack's head.

A man old enough to be my father. Plenty old enough.

Caldwell's town council meetings were usually held in the meeting room of city hall, a space big enough to contain the ten council members, a stenographer, and the handful of residents who traditionally attended. Dennis Ludwig stood on the front steps of the building, enjoying a brief respite between his daytime duties and the long night still ahead of him.

He hated these monthly fiascos. He'd always dreaded them, a tedious formality until Leda claimed the dean's chair and taken a seat on the council a few months back. Since then, town council night had become, for him, a night of public humiliation.

Her ambition had been one of the many facets of the complex, fascinating woman he'd fallen in love with ten years ago. She was in her mid-thirties then, an Economics professor at the state university in Greenville.

That night at the fundraiser, he never forgot how she sidled up to him, balancing a sparkling Cosmopolitan in one carefully manicured hand. It amazed him how she could undulate her voluptuous body atop needle-thin heels without sloshing a single drop over the edge of her martini glass. He'd wondered why this incredibly attractive woman, obviously quite a bit younger than he, made a beeline to his side and never left all evening.

They spent a passionate night in his posh suite at the Marriott, and he'd felt as if he was sixteen again. She'd materialized out of one of his most exciting fantasies. They were lovers from that night on and exchanged vows at the county clerk's office three months later. The man of her dreams, she had called him. Age didn't matter. She convinced him they were made for each other.

Ten years later, he was no longer so sure. Another kind of woman was skulking beneath his smart, bold, and business-savvy sex kitten. More and more, Dennis questioned Leda's motivations in marrying him. He hadn't discovered until last year—last year!—that strange Martin Laramy, who ran the antique shop across from the library was her brother, and that she hated him. Things didn't go as she planned when their father passed away several years back, and since then, she had gone on a rampage to close the Harvey Library.

Dennis' worst fears were apparently becoming reality. Perhaps all Leda wanted from him all along was political power. His power.

She levied his connections well, earning the position of dean, then running for speaker of the city council. Since attaining those powerful positions, she got drunk on her own ambition. The Harvey endowment fund, she said, should transfer to the "nearest public library facility available": her college library.

He stood with one shoulder propped against the entry's pillar, arms crossed, absorbed in his own thoughts. Mesmerized, he stared at the caution light on Corona and Main blinking on and off, the sequence hypnotizing him. The trickle of people climbing the steps grew steadier, but he only noticed peripherally. He was jolted from his trance when a frail, older woman with cropped pink hair came trotting up the steps toward him. A massive young man with a shaved head and a bulldog's face followed close behind.

The woman's creased features crinkled further when she met Dennis' gaze.

"Well, hello there, Commissioner Ludwig," she said brightly. "Lovely evening, ain't it?"

He blinked in surprise as he squeezed the woman's weatherworn hand, then found his own dwarfed by the huge, leathery paw of her companion. "Evenin', Mrs. Cornwell. Good to see you too, Jonathan. What brings you folks here to town tonight?"

The woman's poised creases fell to their original state as she corrected, "That's *Miss* Cornwell, Commissioner. Of course you know why we came to town tonight. Our library's on the agenda, ain't it?"

He squirmed within a starched collar and tie that suddenly seemed way too snug. "Why yes, it is. I didn't think you and Jonathan were patrons of the library." He raised an eyebrow.

"Not only patrons, but staunch supporters," Miss Cromwell retorted. "Why, how do you think those pretty pots got from our yard to the library steps? Did ya think our dear Abby levitated 'em with some sort of magic?"

Her silent, steady stare stirred Dennis' heart to a gallop. Behind her, a line was forming rapidly on the steps.

"Come on, Mama. Wanna get a decent seat," Jonathan murmured, which broke the spell and set the old woman into action. As she whisked past Dennis, she winked.

His gaze flashed over the growing crowd, and his pulse skyrocketed. There had to be at least two dozen people gathering at the hall's entrance, with more climbing out of a line of parked cars and pickup trucks that trailed up and down Main Street as far as he could see. He turned and fought his way through the throng now spilling outside from a clogged foyer, ducking into a side hallway. There was a rear entrance to the town council's usual, modest-sized meeting room.

Leda was sitting at the head table poring over a stack of papers. So far, she was the only one of the council members to have arrived.

"Leda." His voice was tense, and he struggled for breath, as though he'd been running.

She glared up at him over her tortoiseshell Coach glasses, the ones with frames that cost almost as much as his new set of Titleist golf irons. The spectacles he knew were merely a prop, since they were fitted with plain glass. Her eyesight was perfect. Designer glasses, she insisted, made her appear more academically inclined.

They'd become part of her uniform when she began her quest for the dean's position. Leda wore the damned things to any event she considered important. Tonight, she had informed Dennis repeatedly over the past weeks, would be one of those significant affairs.

"Leda, we've got a problem."

"What?" she barked, clearly annoyed.

"There's a crowd outside. Thirty people, maybe fifty. More coming."

"For what?" One thinly tweezed eyebrow lifted into an inverted V.

He slammed both hands down on the table and loomed over her, causing her to jump back. "For the meeting, Leda. They're here for the council meeting."

She scowled at him, then snatched off her glasses and stared past him. "That's impossible. We never have more than half a dozen here other than the board."

Dennis started shaking his head, his chest tight with anger and in an odd way, pity. His wife had obviously become so engrossed in her own agenda she couldn't imagine anyone might disagree with her. God knows, he'd given up trying years ago.

"Leda, the Cornwells are here."

Her eyes widened then, a look of shock and fear passing over her face. Yet just as quickly, the panic disappeared. He couldn't believe what he was seeing happening right before his eyes. It was as though there were two Ledas—the one he married, and the one who'd been gradually emerging from a darker side of her personality. The woman he'd once loved, the smart and sensible one, had panicked and disappeared. The other, evil twin now stepped forward to take control.

She cleared her throat and slid her designer frames back onto the bridge of her nose, taking an extra second to adjust them, making sure they sat perfectly straight.

"Well, we certainly can't hold the meeting in here then, can we?" She sounded calm and cool, dispassionate. "Have Melissa go out and announce we're moving the meeting to the high school auditorium," she commanded.

When she arrived at city hall and discovered the meeting had been moved, Abby figured it was another ploy by Leda to upset the apple cart and set everyone off balance.

Secretary Melissa Daniels stood sentinel on the city hall steps, funneling the crowd toward Caldwell High School auditorium.

Abby arrived on Jack's arm, following Monica and the distinguished-looking Davin Garmond. Davin was a ravishingly handsome man who reminded Abby of a young Warren Beatty in his best Armani suit. Monica clung to his arm as if she'd never let go, floating about three inches off the ground. She looked ten years younger, her features softer, more radiant. Monica's hero. Funny what finding love like that does for a woman.

The place was packed. As Abby scanned the filled auditorium from the rear entrance, she was, for a moment, confused. Surely she must be in the wrong place. There were too many people.

Two long banquet tables had been set up on the stage. The ten members of the board flanked three sides on metal folding chairs, facing the audience. Tension sparked in the air like static electricity—insidious and unpredictable.

When she spotted Leda, surrounded by the other board members at the table, Abby turned to Jack and whispered, "What's going on?"

Before he could answer Dianne walked up the aisle toward them, taking her by the elbow. "We have seats for you down front, Abby. For all four of you."

She'd barely settled in her seat before the crack of the gavel rang out, its wooden block rattling the flimsy banquet table.

"I officially call this meeting of the Caldwell Town Council to order."

Dennis looked pale, and his voice sounded strained. Beads of sweat on his forehead shimmered in the bright stage lights, though the room was more than sufficiently cooled. Leda sat to his left, the court stenographer on his right, her furious fingers flying over a laptop keyboard. A huge, antique-looking microphone sat on the table in front of him, the thick black cord trailing over the table's edge.

The minutes from the previous meeting were read and approved. Then, one by one, new business items were introduced. Printouts of the agenda had been stacked on a table outside the door, and Abby squinted down at her copy in the dim light to see where the library issue was on the list. Of course, it was last.

Proposals on everything from new seats for the swings down at the city park playground to appropriation for additional flower boxes on Main Street were raised, discussed, and voted on. The meeting droned on for what seemed like an eternity, and she couldn't help but wonder which item brought out such a huge crowd. Surely, the tax hike. Or the zoning ordinance, maybe. Something serious enough to rally the entire community.

Yet as each item ticked off, not one person left the room. She leaned toward Dianne and whispered, "Why so many people tonight? What's the big issue?"

Her aunt smiled and kissed her on the cheek. "You have more friends, dear Abby, than you know." Her aunt glanced past her to Jack, who squeezed Abby's hand.

Stunned, confused, and a little numb, she sat and waited as each item was addressed and dismissed. Craning her head around, she tried to see if there was anyone she knew. She picked out the familiar face of a library patron here and there, scattered through the crowd. Still, most of these people were complete strangers.

Finally, the last item on the list was up. Dennis read from the agenda as it was written:

"Item Number 17: New librarian Abigail Stryker files a request to renew funding for the single, part-time position of library aide. Prior aide, Monica Browning, has resigned effective June 30. Funding has been conditionally extended for the past two fiscal years for Ms. Browning, since she had attained tenure as a city employee. Renewal of funding for the position to continue requires a vote."

Almost before he uttered the last word, Leda's hand flew into the air. "I would like to make a motion, Commissioner. I move this decision be indefinitely tabled."

He turned in his chair to face her. "On what grounds?"

Clearing her throat, she adjusted her glasses. Then she spoke into the microphone. "On the grounds that our library has deteriorated significantly. Like many other antiquated public facilities, reassessment of its need in this community is far overdue. There is also evidence of lack of community interest in the limited capacity of the old Harvey Library."

Her words caused a rise from the audience, escalating like the rumble of an oncoming train. Dennis rested his forehead on his palm for a moment, then turned to stare at his wife. Although he spoke low and close to her ear, he'd obviously forgotten about the microphone. It proved an unfailing witness.

"Do you honestly think you're going to get away with this?" His tone was sharp, icy.

Leda's chin jutted forward, and she ignored him, turning her gaze instead out over the crowded auditorium.

She spoke in a loud and authoritative tone. "We have a new, modern, and progressive library facility at the Caldwell Community College. There is no reason to waste funds on a commodity that has outgrown its usefulness. I move to close the Harvey Library immediately and transfer the endowment funds to a viable, useful public commodity—the new college library."

The thunder from the audience escalated to a roar, and several people leapt to their feet, shouting and shaking fists. Dennis rapped the gavel repeatedly on its mount, unheard for several moments. Finally, Abby could hear him over the din.

"Order! Order!" He paled even further, his face slicked with sweat.

When he rose to his feet, the crowd settled and quieted. Abby was glad to see the respect people still obviously had for Commissioner Ludwig. Even under the most trying of circumstances. Even though it was obvious his own wife had no respect for him at all.

"Mrs. Ludwig's motion as stated is a complete change of policy."

The tremor in his voice made Abby's stomach churn.

"Changes in policy must be posted for public consideration for the mandatory thirty-day period. No proposal can be voted on until this step is taken. We have only one, valid issue concerning the public library eligible for vote tonight. We will proceed according to *Robert's Rules*. We will vote on Ms. Stryker's request to renew funding for the position of library aide."

Murmurs of agreement fluttered through the crowd, then a hush fell over the auditorium. Time seemed to hover and freeze for what seemed like minutes—until Leda Ludwig came undone.

A guttural scream sliced through the silence carrying rage of a flavor Abby had never imagined. Leda jumped to her feet, wheeled around and crouched over her still-seated husband with her hands clenched. Dennis shrank back. As the echoes reverberated out of the recesses of the stage, she trembled violently, quaking all over as though she was possessed or experiencing a seizure. Abby held her breath and lifted her hand to her mouth.

In the next moment Leda's head dropped back, and she crumpled. Her form disappeared behind the table in a clatter of chairs, a heavy thud sounding as her body hit the stage floor.

They waited a little ways up the sidewalk, Abby tucked in close to Jack's side. The paramedics spoke with Dennis before closing the ambulance doors. As the vehicle pulled away in silence, lights flashing, he made his way through the onlookers toward them.

"They think she'll be all right." His voice was raspy and unsteady. "She's conscious, just dazed and confused. They're calling it a neurological incident. They'll need to run tests." He swiped a hand down his face, then hung his head. "I'm sorry, Abby. I don't know what else to say. I should never have brought you into this."

She laid a hand on his shoulder. "Are you okay? You don't look well at all," she said. "Don't you think the medics should check you out too?"

"I'm fine, just fine, Abby."

He didn't look fine. He looked tired and drained, a decade older than the day she first met him. Dennis Ludwig wore the look of a man who had given up.

Chapter 13

When Abby opened the library at nine the following morning, the weather reflected her sense of impending doom. Storm clouds rolled in overnight, and a menacing blanket of dark gray overhead grumbled low in the distance. A single raindrop splashed her cheek on a gust of wind as she unlocked the door.

Inside, the Harvey was peaceful, serene, and seemingly unaware of its tenuous future. Abby, however, felt as if she wore leaden shoulder pads. As she closed the door behind her she looked around and drew in a deep breath. The clanging of the bells on the door echoed into silence.

"I guess I'm it for now," she called out into the empty space. "I'll hang in as long as I can, Elijah. I hope you'll give me some strength. I'll need it."

The waiting was not over. Although she had been certain the outcome of last night's council meeting would give her an answer, for better or worse, again Leda Ludwig had tipped the scales in her favor. This time, quite theatrically.

After she passed out on the stage, everyone had milled about in limbo until the ambulance arrived. Of course, the meeting was adjourned. The board postponed the vote, and all matters relating to the Harvey Library were tabled for next meeting. Monica's last day was next Saturday. After that, if the library were to remain open, Abby would be running it by herself.

Still perplexed at the huge crowd who turned out, she picked up the phone and dialed Ancient Healings.

"Hey, Abby. Girl, how are you this morning?" Dianne's voice was warm with concern.

"I'm okay, Di, just a little confused. Who were all those people there last night?"

Her aunt's chuckle rumbled into her ear. "I told you, dear Abby, you have a ton of admirers you don't even know exist."

"Most of those people were strangers to me. They were your friends, weren't they?"

"Yes, some of the folks from our group came out—"

"You mean your coven, right?

Dianne cleared her throat. "We have a network in this part of the world, dear. Living out in the boonies like we do, we have to. We stick together, stand up for each other. Camaraderie. They were my friends, acquaintances. Part of the network I've developed over the years."

"Di, you promised your support, but you also promised no witchcraft. You didn't cast one of those mumbo jumbo spells of yours, did you?" Suspicion had haunted Abby all night, wondering what really caused Leda's collapse. "Please tell me you didn't have anything to do with Leda's episode."

"Now Abigail," she retorted, "you should know me better than that. I don't waste my energy on such foolishness. You surely realize, if my hand had been in it, Leda wouldn't still be upright and functional."

"So she's okay?"

"From what I hear, they kept her overnight for observation. She's supposed to be discharged this morning."

Abby whooshed out a breath.

When she hung up the phone she couldn't help but wonder if Dianne's network would be willing to travel to Caldwell again next month, since numbers were definitely what Abby needed if and when a vote was taken.

Gazing out the front window, she folded her arms, thinking. Chances were good before next month's meeting, her fortitude might give out. After Saturday, she was looking at a sixty-hour workweek—maybe more depending on how late book club meetings lasted. No matter how badly she wanted this to work, she might as well face reality.

Yet the alternative wasn't much more appealing. If she gave up and the Harvey closed, her future loomed before her as a huge void. She dreaded having to start the job search thing again. She was a librarian, a market not usually bursting with open positions. Most in her field retained their jobs until they retired. Like Dana Laramy. And the only other library within commuting distance was the one at the college.

Leda's college. Yeah right. She could imagine the glee on Leda's face to find Abby's application in her mailbox.

If she wanted to stay in her chosen career, a new job meant relocating. A whole different city to get used to. The hunt for a place to live and moving her stuff, again. Moving away from Aunt Di seemed impossible to consider right now. And going back to Boone was out of the question. Not with all the memories and all the secrets still hovering like a plague over her life there.

Then there was Jack.

He was older, but there weren't nearly as many years between them as she and Cameron. There would be no shame if she and Jack became lovers, as she wasn't his student. He was settled in his single lifestyle and loved the same things she did. Like Cameron, he made her feel alive, beautiful, and cherished. And Jack seemed content with his life, teaching by day and enjoying a quiet, conservative existence in his woodland home.

Another nerdy professor might just be the perfect choice for her.

But was taking up with him really safe? She recalled now, with no small trepidation, the gleam in his eye the day he led all those little kids in for story hour. The Pied Piper in a tweed coat. Jack adored his niece. Was he dreaming of a family of his own?

The thought caused a clutching in her chest. Long term commitment like that scared the hell out of her. She wasn't cut out for that role.

Yet suddenly, she missed him terribly. She wanted to hear his voice.

As she passed the front room's meeting table, her gaze landed on the single hefty hardcover lying before the head seat, lined up with the table's edge. She cocked her head, flipping back through her memories of yesterday. Yes, she'd been distracted at closing time with the impending meeting on her mind. But she always did a final walk-through. Always checked to make sure all the lights were out, all the books were re-shelved.

She picked up the book and ran her finger down the spine. Hemingway's *For Whom the Bell Tolls*. She must have been on her way to replace the book and laid it down halfway through the process of locking up.

Hmm. This whole Leda affair must be shifting the foundation of her routine.

Still clutching the Hemingway, she dialed Jack. When he answered he sounded gruff. Abby said, "Good morning. Don't tell me I woke you."

His warm chuckle brought his image into her mind. How his smile softened the sharp angles of his face and made his green eyes glow. She wondered if he'd shaven yet or if peppered stubble shadowed his jaw. Was he dressed? Or lounging in some pair of sexy plaid flannel sleep pants? An electric buzz warmed her center.

"Not hardly," he replied. "I've done my three miles, spent an hour weeding the tomatoes, and mowed the backyard already." His tone was soft as he continued, "How are you doing this morning? Any news on Leda?"

"Aunt Di says she's being discharged this morning. I'm okay too. Jack, have you had time for any more research on the Harveys?"

She could hear the clink of spoon against ceramic and imagined Jack in his kitchen, pouring himself a cup of coffee or tea. The thought of that warm, happy place caused a tingle to flow through her. She loved being there with him and longed to be there right now.

"Some. There isn't much beyond official records. Birth, marriage, death certificates. I found a Federal Census from 1880."

"Really? I didn't realize they started those that early, especially in little towns like this. Anything useful?"

"I found out that Isabelle was still a Laramy in 1880, living with her parents. Her occupation is listed as teacher."

"That's all consistent with what we knew already, right?"

"Yes, it is. I was also able to find her birth date and the date of her marriage," he said. "By 1882, Isabelle was a Harvey. She was only twenty years old."

"Not exactly a spinster," Abby remarked, a bit surprised.

"Pretty common back then. It was all about survival," he said. "Parents wanted their younguns away from their dinner table as soon as possible. Apparently, that wasn't the case with the Laramys. They had a solid business in town, crafting harness that gained them a well-respected reputation. Isabelle taught at the private school and so earned some sort of stipend herself. There didn't seem to be any reason for them to push her out of the nest early."

"Harvey was a pretty big catch for her, though, wasn't he?" she asked.

"I'd say. Big-city Boston businessman with money and status to spare. And May-September marriages were also quite accepted back then, especially in rural areas." He chuckled before adding, "In their case, it was more of a March-November."

She cocked her head, then sandwiched the phone between her ear and shoulder as she logged into the library's computer system and pulled up the checkout record on the waylaid Hemingway book. It still lay on the counter in front of her. "What do you mean?"

"Miss Isabelle Laramy may not have yet acquired spinster status at the tender age of twenty, but do you know how old her husband-to-be was on their wedding day?"

"How old?"

Distracted, she continued to study the checkout record on the book she now held in her free hand.

Jack cleared his throat. "Harvey was born in 1827."

"So?"

"Abby, Harvey was fifty-five years old when he married Isabelle. There were thirty-five years between them."

She blinked. "Wow," she whispered. "Worse than Cameron and me."

"Ironically, unlike your situation, it appears old man Harvey wasn't the first one to pass. Isabelle was only thirty when she died."

"Of what?"

"No record of it. Don't know if we'll ever find that out. Harvey outlived her. Elijah Harvey didn't pass until ten years after his young bride, in 1902."

"Over seventy," she muttered.

"Have you ever gone over to talk to Martin Laramy about his family? Maybe there are some ancestry records somewhere. Maybe, if we can find out more about Isabelle's family, some of this might start to make sense."

"I haven't. I'm a little afraid to go over there alone. Aunt Di says he's weird. You told me the same thing, remember?" She paused. "Will you go with me?"

She agreed to lock up a few minutes before five and go with Jack to talk to Laramy. After ending the call, she returned her attention to the checkout record on *For Whom the Bell Tolls*.

The computer record indicated the book hadn't been checked out in months. The last return date was before Abby ever started working there.

Jack arrived a few minutes before five and found Abby doing her final walk-through. He stood in the lobby watching her weave up and down the aisles, her fingers trailing over the spines, pausing to adjust any volume that didn't line up perfectly.

God, she was as anal as him.

When she made for the meeting room a second time he said, "You've already checked there. You were coming out when I got here."

She shook her head. "I know, but I left a book lying out on the meeting table last night and have no recollection of how it got there." She looked up and caught his gaze. "This whole business with Leda is telling on my sanity now, I guess."

"I helped you lock up last night, Abby. I don't remember anything out of place."

"It didn't hurt to check one more time," she said as she flicked the lights off.

"Maybe the book is what your ghost is reading," Jack quipped as he slipped an arm around her shoulders, and they headed out the door.

A shiver ran through her. "Well if that's the case," she said, "I certainly hope he's not trying to tell me something."

"What do you mean?"

"*For Whom the Bell Tolls*." Her mouth flattened into a thin, grim line. "I hope it's not me for whom the bell tolls. Not just yet, anyway."

Instead of an antique store, Martin Laramy's shop looked more like an indoor junkyard. Jack held the door open for Abby, then followed her along a narrow, twisting path through haphazard piles of dusty paraphernalia. Their destination was the lighted glass display case at the rear of the room.

The air smelled of mildew and moisture. Although short fluorescent tubes glowed from a high ceiling, they were too far away, too yellowed with dust and age, and far too weak to shed much light on the indistinguishable piles of junk below.

About halfway on their trek, she stopped so suddenly, he almost plowed right over her. Glancing down, he identified the problem. He squatted and with two fingers, detached the hem of her skirt from the spiny hub of a bicycle wheel before they could move on.

The display case held a similar disorganized clutter of items, only smaller in scale. Although the brightest spot in the place, even this light was dim. It filtered through a thick layer of dust streaked with greasy smears, a preserved fingerprint or two, and several brownish rings from beverage containers. An antique, black steel cash register consumed one-third of the counter's right side.

There didn't appear to be anyone minding the store. Jack mashed the bell perched beside the register. It vibrated against the glass with a buzz that made his teeth ache. Behind the counter, a dirty, pink window drape cloaked a doorway into some sort of back room. After a moment, the curtain swished aside revealing, he presumed, Martin Laramy.

He was younger than Jack expected. He looked to be in his late forties, early fifties at best. Although his receding hairline gave him a more brainy appearance than he might have earned, the rest of his hair was dark, shoulder-length, and shaggy. He needed a shave, badly, as well as a shower, which Jack detected with distaste when Martin propped an elbow on the counter.

"What can I help you with?" Laramy's diction was almost incoherent as he slurred one word into the other and spewed them out as fast as an auctioneer.

The thick lenses of his oversized, black-framed glasses exaggerated eyes that were pale gray, bloodshot, and watery. If not for the crisp white shirt fastened with a smart, Tartan plaid bowtie, Martin Laramy could double for any bum lurking in a back street of a big city.

"I'm Jack Wood." He extended his hand, cringing when the man covered his with lukewarm, limp fingers that hadn't been washed in a while.

"Good to meet you," Laramy returned, then glanced over at Abby.

"This is Abigail Stryker, our new librarian," Jack said.

"Yeah, I've heard about you," Laramy responded, though Jack could not detect any judgment, good or bad, from his tone.

He cleared his throat. "We're here to see if you could tell us any more about the history of the old library. This shop, your family's business," he motioned to the space around them, "has been here a long time."

Laramy crossed his arms to lean on the filthy glass and glared up at them. "Now why would you think I'd know anything about that?" he snapped. "I'm forty-four. That library opened sometime in the mid-1800s."

"Because, Mr. Laramy, your family has owned this building since then," Abby interjected, "and you're probably aware the library was built for one of your ancestors. Elijah Harvey commissioned the structure and built it for his wife, Isabelle Laramy."

Laramy's face twisted into a smirk, and he started shaking his head as he looked away. "Don't know a thing about that place," he muttered. "Not a goddamned thing."

Abby fidgeted from one foot to the other. This may have been a waste of time after all. Yet Laramy seemed uncomfortable too. As though he knew more than he was letting on.

"Mr. Laramy, we mean no harm. We're simply interested in genealogy, researching some local lore," Jack began. "I teach history at the college. Is there nothing at all you can tell us about Isabelle? Where we might find out something about her?"

Laramy kept his head down, avoiding his gaze. He didn't speak for a moment, but his head continued to oscillate. Finally, he said, "I inherited this heap from my great uncle Jasper. Uncle J, well, you know, he didn't have much knowledge about antiques. Not like me."

"Oh?" Abby asked. "You know antiques?"

Laramy snorted and looked up, challenging her with critical eyes. "Worked for Sotheby's on Broadway for fifteen years. Damn straight I do."

With the show of attitude Jack laid his arm across Abby's shoulders. He proceeded evenly, "Perhaps you can tell us if you have anything here in the store that might have come from the library."

"Your ancestors were harness makers," Abby offered. "I see you hang a harness out front from time to time. Is it one your ancestors made?"

Laramy scoffed again and pushed off the counter. He rested back against the wall, crossing his legs at the ankle and folding his arms. "I haven't got the slightest idea," he shot back. "Found it all twisted up in the back room covered with mold and horseshit."

He coughed then, a loose, wheezy sound that made Jack's stomach lurch. Laramy pulled a filthy handkerchief out of his back pocket and spit into it. Abby turned her head away.

"I'm sorry we wasted your time," Jack said, taking hold of Abby's shoulders and turning her toward the door.

"Look, uh, I do have one piece that might be linked with the library, though I got no proof of it." Laramy suddenly seemed as if he didn't want to let a live customer get away.

He slid open the back of the glass case and plunged his fingers into a disheveled pile of tangled jewelry. His fingers twisted around in the mayhem for a beat before resurfacing with a piece of tarnished metal clutched between them.

"This," he said, holding the oversized skeleton key above the counter, "was supposed to have come from the Harvey. That's what Uncle J told me when I was a kid." He chuckled, loose congestion rattling around in his chest. "We tried it one night—me and a friend from up on the mountain. I used to stay summers here with Dad when I was in my teens. Anyway, me and Leroy snuck over there one night and tried the key in the front door, but it didn't fit. We tried the back too, even the cellar door. Didn't fit anything. But Dad insisted it came from the Harvey. Original." He paused, then muttered, "It's probable the locks have been changed a dozen times since it was built."

Jack took the key, turning it over in his palm. "This for sale?"

Laramy winked. "Everything in here's for sale for the right price."

"How much?"

"How much you willing to give?" Laramy countered.

He locked eyes with Laramy and held them for long minute. Then without glancing away, Jack snapped the key back down onto the glass. "I don't want it that bad," he said quietly. "It doesn't fit anything I know of anyway."

"Twenty bucks," he barked as Jack again steered Abby away from the counter.

Jack hesitated but kept his back to Laramy. "I've got a ten-dollar bill. No more."

Abby waited until the door clicked shut behind them before turning on Jack with a perplexed scowl. "Now why would you go and do a thing like that?" she asked. "You wasted ten bucks on a useless skeleton key that guy probably found in an old estate sale somewhere back in New York."

Jack fingered the piece of metal stuck down in the front pocket of his khakis. "I don't know, Abigail. I figured it might be the key to something. Something, somewhere, at some time neither of us has discovered just yet." He smiled down at her. "Besides, it was only ten bucks. A lot less than I'm going to spend on our dinner tonight at Le Petit Mon."

She stopped short on the sidewalk, forcing him to an abrupt halt. "Oh no," she began. "I'm not going to Uncle Armpit's for dinner."

He clamped her hand between his own. "Yes, you are. We are. It was awfully nice for Dianne to rally all her friends on your behalf last night."

She closed her eyes and huffed. Jack was right. Dianne was her biggest advocate, and her solid rock of support. Had been for the past crazy few years, years when she couldn't feel safe talking to anybody else. She couldn't deny Armand was an incredible cook, and Le Petit Mon was certainly the nicest place in all of Caldwell to have dinner.

When she opened her eyes, Jack's penetrating green gaze melted one little frozen part of her soul. She was becoming extremely fond of this man.

Before her mind could form another coherent thought, her mouth was saying, "Okay."

Chapter 14

Abby stood beside Jack, studying the inside of Le Petit Mon's elaborately carved front door. Armand commissioned the piece custom-made by a local artisan, complete with an intricately patterned leaded glass panel. She remembered how excited Aunt Dianne had been, describing the purchase when the restaurant first opened.

"Reservations for two. Wood," Jack said to the tight-lipped maître d', a short, roundish man in a dark suit.

The headwaiter led them to a tiny table, secluded from the already cozy interior by a carved, wooden screen. Armand had insisted on these as well. Panels of wood, painted or etched, or shirred fabric sheltered all four of the corner tables to provide a sense of privacy for intimate gatherings.

The waiter appeared, a white cloth draped over his arm. He snapped open starched napkins to lay them across their laps, first Abby's, then Jack's. He handed them heavy leather-bound menus before asking for their drink order.

Jack didn't skip a beat. "We'll share a bottle of Chene Bleu Rose. On ice, please."

When the waiter scurried away, Jack turned to her and said, "I figured we'd start with that. You seemed to like it we had last week at my house."

She sat in silence, gazing around at the room she'd never been in before. She should be familiar with this place and was embarrassed she was not.

"What's wrong?" He chuckled. "You really have never been here, have you?"

She wiggled deeper into the cushioned leather seat.

"Aunt Di told me all about this place. I was working on my thesis and hardly ever left Boone. She's been bugging me to come in since it opened."

The screen sheltering their corner made the spot feel private yet still allowed a view of most of the room. Elegant oil paintings graced the walls in wide, gilt frames. The candle sheathed in crystal at their table cast a flickering pattern across the flocked wallpaper. When she realized there was music playing, soft and unobtrusive, at first she thought she was imagining it.

The waiter returned with a stone ice bucket on a stand. He wielded the wine key, then poured a splash of the pink liquid into Jack's glass, offering it for him to sample. Stifling a smirk, he lifted the glass, swirled it, and sniffed before taking a sip. He nodded to the waiter, who then half-filled both glasses and asked if they wished to order hors d'ouevres.

She peeked over the top of her menu, shrugging, relieved when Jack read her cue.

"Bring us the baked brie, and an order of the escargot please."

As the waiter left she leaned toward Jack, swallowing hard. "Isn't that something you use for fish bait?" she whispered.

"Have you ever tried them?" he countered. As she shook her head he reached across to cover her hand with his. "You act, Miss Stryker, as though you've never eaten in a fine-dining restaurant before."

She lowered her chin. "I haven't. Not much, anyway," she mumbled. "You shouldn't be too surprised by that. Not now. I've told you what my social life was like for the last few years."

He blinked, and she saw realization in his eyes. "You couldn't go out much with him, could you?"

She shook her head.

Jack continued, "So that's why you were all dressed

up that day I offered to take you to lunch. And seemed disappointed where we picnicked out in the middle of nowhere." Sadness laced his words. "I'm sorry, Abby. I had no idea."

"I know you didn't," she said. "Of course you didn't. I was so excited that day because it would be the first time in a long time—hell, maybe ever—I'd be going out on a date in public. After what happened the night before, my embarrassing panic attack when you tried to take me to the festival, well, I figured it was my chance to try again. To be the brave new girl." She poked her nose in the air, then giggled at the memory. "We ended up hidden behind a tree on top of a mountain. In the wilderness. I doubt even the squirrels knew we were there."

Jack took her other hand and squeezed them both, his gaze so intense her cheeks burned. He didn't simply *look* into her eyes. He found a way to climb into them. She'd never experienced the sensation before, as if the man truly wanted to explore what lie underneath the surface.

Cameron's eyes often swept her body, but avoided engaging with her own.

The way Jack looked at her made her center clench, her heart rate speed up. Exhilaration touched her in a deep, hidden place inside she wasn't used to acknowledging. She blinked, and felt the sting of tears.

Oh no, not now.

He seemed to read her expression, his brows furrowing. "What's wrong? You're here with me, in this lovely restaurant, a respectable, public place. You have nothing to be ashamed of and nothing to hide anymore. It's all different with me, Abby. Everything about our relationship will be different. I promise."

Different, yes. But how? *How much different do I really want it to be?*

Her next blink sent a fat tear trickling down her cheek, one she knew carried with it a dose of her godforsaken eyeliner. She dabbed at the corner of her eye with a smile. "I'm so glad Armand decided on black for the linen napkins instead of white."

She took a deep breath and shifted her attention to the menu. "Oh, my. I don't believe I can read any of this."

"Here." Jack laid his own menu crossways on the table so they could both see it. He scanned the list, pronouncing each entrée in perfect, eloquent French first, then translating.

"I didn't know you spoke French." She stared at him in amazement.

"I don't, really. Just took enough of it in high school to read a menu. Enough to impress the girls." He grinned and winked. "Works, huh?"

She decided on coq au vin, a wonderful chicken dish flavored with wine, while he chose the heartier steak au poivre. When the escargot appetizer arrived, she scrutinized the circular dish cradling dark, gelatinous blobs floating in steamy, shiny . . . something. The something, she had to admit, did smell divine.

In the end she consented to dip an edge of crusty French bread into the buttery garlic sauce, nibbling on one bite and trying to ignore where the sauce came from. She left Jack to enjoy what looked to her like slimy dark slugs.

They ate and drank wine and laughed for the finest two hours of Abby's life. He had a way of making her feel like a pampered princess, yet at the same time, a treasured peer. By the time the plates were cleared away she was feeling dreamy and relaxed, somewhat like a slug herself. The rich French cuisine, washed down with what might actually be her third glass of wine, had her eyelids feeling heavy. When the waiter rolled a dessert cart up beside their table, she pressed a hand across her middle. "Oh, Jack I don't think I could eat another bite."

He smiled into her eyes, and her insides went all warm and fluttery. Full, yet somehow still hungry. Now how is that possible?

"How about we order something to go and take it back to my place?"

Dennis Ludwig brought Leda home from the hospital that morning, leaving with more questions than answers. The doctors ran neurological tests, CT scans, and all sorts of blood work. They ended up calling her episode a classic panic attack. They prescribed some anti-depressants and advised she take a few days away from the office to regroup.

Knowing his wife would never pass up an opportunity for special treatment, Dennis was not surprised when she demanded a weekend shopping trip. He begrudgingly made a reservation at the posh Marriott down in Hickory where they first met. He also made one at her favorite upscale steakhouse on the south side of town.

They hadn't discussed the events of the council meeting at all. The elephant in the room, he kept thinking.

As they drove down US 321 in late afternoon traffic, Leda chattered on about the sale advertised at Coach. The fact the weather promised to be clear and warm, with no storms predicted. She tiptoed into sensitive territory when she suggested they stop by Barnes & Noble to check out what was on display for new releases.

"It never hurts to keep on top of what's hot and selling right now," she said. "I like to know in advance what books are best for me to order in for the college stacks."

"The college stacks," he repeated.

She turned and glared at him. "Yes, the college stacks. That's all I'm concerned about, Dennis." A shrill laugh burst from her, then as quickly, her expression fell serious. "Why would you think I'd be concerned about anything else?"

She was prodding him, looking for a fight. He struggled to remember what the doctors recommended.

"A few days of quiet acquiescence. No matter what problems you two might be having, it would be best for Mrs. Ludwig, right now, if you shielded her from further upset. I realize it might be difficult, Mr. Ludwig. Try to be patient."

Dennis' patience had about run out. He'd been shielding Mrs. Ludwig from 'further upset' for as long as he could remember. The first year or so after they'd gotten together was pure bliss. Gradually Leda became more demanding, less patient, more explosive. He kept reminding himself how lucky he'd been to land a younger woman, especially one so attractive, so educated, and from a wealthy family.

But it didn't take long before the repeated emotional abuse had his heart developing a protective callous. She made it obvious, at least from where he stood, that she could care less about him as a person. As her husband. As a man with ambitions, feelings, and a sense of pride. All Leda Ludwig cared about was her social standing, her career, and her own rapidly inflating ego. And his political influence, his only asset she appreciated.

Sometimes he wished he could walk away. One of the manacles of political position was just that—a set of manacles. In the small town where they lived, walking away from Leda would start a scandal, one his career, and his personal life, might never recover from.

He would be sixty this year. He never considered himself a handsome man but hoped he had that distinguished thing going for him. Of course, he could end his marriage to Leda and try to start over. Anything was possible. The problem was he loved her. In spite of the way she treated him sometimes, he still cared and hoped this wave of obsessive ambition might be a manifestation of her mid-life crisis. Maybe it would pass. Maybe the new drugs the doctors prescribed would help bring back his old, sweet Leda.

They sat over shrimp cocktail at the Limousine Steak Eatery, tucked away in their favorite side room off the bar. She hadn't shut up all afternoon. The only respite he had was the hour and a half she spent drooling over ridiculously expensive Coach purses—until she got into a snipping contest with a not-quite-attentive-enough salesclerk. She'd left the store declaring there wasn't anything there she liked better than her money. He wasn't sure whether to be annoyed or relieved.

"This shrimp seems rubbery to me tonight. Doesn't it, Dennis?" Leda exaggerated her chewing to demonstrate her perception of the shrimp's consistency.

"Tastes fine to me," he rumbled, snagging another tail and dunking it in the cocktail sauce.

She plopped her half-eaten shrimp down on her plate and motioned for the waiter. "Dear, this shrimp has the consistency of a Goodyear tire. Do you have a fresh batch in the kitchen or should we order something else?"

The waiter glanced from Leda to Dennis with a perplexed, quasi-apologetic expression.

Dennis pushed the plate toward the edge of the table and muttered, "Just bring her something else. Crab cakes or something."

By the time dinner plates were removed and coffee brought out, he was exhausted. She had complained about every single element of the meal, the temperature in the room, the volume and genre of the music playing overhead, the raucous laughter of the woman at the next table. Her steak was overdone, the lobster was dry, the melted butter was cold. How could melted butter be cold and still liquid? Her asparagus were stringy and tough. When the waiter set two cups of steaming coffee down in front of them, Dennis made a silent bet Leda would claim the coffee was too hot.

Then the elephant in the room lumbered over to join them.

"So listen, dear, we need to discuss this library issue,"

Leda began, tearing open the third packet of sugar to dump into coffee she'd already chilled to room temperature with half the contents of the creamer pot.

Ah, here it comes. Too bad my tolerance tank is dry.

He crossed his arms and leaned on the table toward her. "Leda, can I ask again why you are so hell-bent on shutting down the Harvey?" He kept his voice low but was not entirely succeeding at keeping the anger from simmering through.

She huffed and rolled her eyes. "Dennis, you never do hear a word I say, do you?"

Swiping his hand down over his face, he drew in a deep breath, counting in his head. *One, two, three, four . . .* "Humor me. Tell me one more time. I obviously still don't understand."

"Well," she declared, "you are aware my family has been instrumental in founding the Caldwell Community College."

"How could I forget?" he said, causing her eyes to narrow.

She did not hesitate long. "Daddy has applied for university status with the accreditation commission. Of course, one of the requirements is to have at least one Master's level course. As you probably realize, with our faculty, offering these courses will be no problem." Laying down the spoon she'd been clinking around in her cup for what seemed like ten minutes, she lifted the cup and sipped before wrinkling her nose. "Coffee tastes nasty."

Again, she motioned for the waiter and asked if she could please have Earl Gray instead.

"Our problem, Dennis, is that the college library is too small."

"The college library is four times the size of the Harvey. Not to mention the Harvey is a perfectly functional facility. It's only a few miles up the road from the college. Many students actually drive through Caldwell on their way to classes," Dennis said. "Why can't we kill two birds here?

Instead of appropriating huge sums of taxpayer money to expand the college library, why can't we pump up the Harvey? For what you want to spend on a bigger, better building, we could buy hundreds of new volumes to enhance the Harvey's holdings. Put in some computer terminals."

He'd made this argument a dozen times before. Still, her eyes registered no sign of comprehension. "Besides, it's part of the town's history. Doesn't historical preservation mean anything at all to you?"

"Dennis, every single taxpayer dollar that goes into keeping that old haunted building in operation could be instead going to the college. There's still a huge Laramy trust fund assigned to that place. One of the stipulations in that fund—as you well know—is if the Harvey should no longer continue to operate, the trust money would transfer to the nearest library facility in Caldwell County."

She blotted her mouth with the corner of her napkin and dropped it in to her lap with a flourish. "That would be the mine!" The squeal in her voice elevated to a pitch that caused heads to turn from several of the adjoining tables.

"You're embarrassing yourself, Leda. You need to leave it alone for tonight," Dennis growled, hunching over his coffee. He could actually feel the tension drawing his features down, making him feel ten years older.

"Honey, don't be like that," she chirped. "We've got to face this. Now I'm willing to forgive you for the little scene at the council meeting the other night. I mean, I realize you thought you were playing your role as commissioner, and that's fine and all, but—"

"Leda, leave it alone. I don't want to discuss this with you right now." Not with his patience dipping into the negative numbers. He didn't want to be pushed into saying things he'd regret, especially in a public place.

"Dennis, you know I'm right about this."

When he lifted his gaze, he couldn't believe his eyes.

There they were. Those damned four hundred dollar, completely useless Coach glasses. He hadn't seen her slip them out of her purse, or wherever the hell she kept them. Between her breasts, perhaps? They had appeared and were perched on the bridge of her nose—the protective goggles she donned whenever she was going into battle.

He pushed away from the table, causing coffee to slosh over the edges of their cups. He threw his napkin down on the table and in the same motion, signaled for the waiter whose gaze darted in their direction the moment Dennis stood.

"I'm leaving you the car," he spat icily, throwing his fob down on the table, "and you already have credit cards as well as complete access to every damned cent with my name on it. Have a wonderful weekend. I'm going home."

He peeled out several large bills and squashed them into the shocked waiter's hand as he whisked past him. When he reached the lobby Dennis barked a command to the headwaiter.

"Call me a taxi. I'm headed back to Caldwell."

Chapter 15

Abby argued that it was foolish for Jack to drive her all the way to his cabin just for dessert, then have to drive her back into town.

"I have to work tomorrow, Jack. And it's Monica's last day. Last story hour, for a while anyway." They were standing on the sidewalk next to his car. "I'd invite you up to my place, but it's barely bigger than a closet."

He unlocked the passenger door. "Nonsense. I've downed enough caffeine to keep me wide-awake until dawn. We'll go back to my cabin, I'll make you some tea, and we'll enjoy Uncle Armpit's special crème brulee. Maybe the deer family will be visiting my back lawn again." He regarded her with a warm, friendly twinkle in his eyes. "Don't worry, Abby. I don't intend to take advantage of you."

When they reached his cabin, she waited on the swinging bench on Jack's back patio while he fussed in the kitchen. In a few moments he appeared with a small tray holding two steaming cups and the crusty pudding they'd brought home. Two spoons protruded from the custard like slender silver wings. He lit the citronella candle on the patio table, and the flame cast a soft glow on his face as he sat down beside her.

"Won't the candlelight scare off the deer?" she asked.

"Might. But it's a bug repellent. What I'm hoping is that it scares off the mosquitoes," he replied. "I'd forgotten we're in that part of the summer when those nasty little buzzers seep out of the woods in small clouds."

She wasn't sure if it were the heavy meal, the way-too-much wine she'd ingested, or the fact she had a rough couple of days. Snuggled there in the corner of Jack's padded bench, she could doze off any second. The warmth of his body next to hers felt right somehow.

Through the cloud of steam rising off her mug, his candlelit profile was misty. When he slid the pudding off the spoon into his mouth with a deft little flick of his tongue, Abby's insides clenched like a hot vise. When he scooped out another hunk and offered it to her, she opened her mouth like an obedient little bird.

"Hmm," she replied, nodding as she licked a flake of the custard's sugary coating from the edge of her mouth. "I'm getting very, very comfortable with you. And so fond of the time we spend together."

"I'm glad to hear that. I feel the same way."

He set his cup and bowl on the table and scooted a bit closer. Gently, he plucked her mug from her hands and set it down too. With one finger, he lifted her chin.

"I'm older than you, Abby. I can't change that. But not by that much. Some might say I'm in the prime of my life, and I do try to take good care of myself. I can't promise I won't be a victim of statistics, get cancer or hit by a bus one morning on my daily run, but I do plan on being around for a long, long time." His gaze burned into hers with a sincerity that made her heart race. "I would love to think I could spend that time like this, with you."

He lowered his mouth, covering her lips with soft warmth that made her flush all over. Heat rose from low in her belly until it radiated throughout her entire body. Gentle at first, he worshipped her mouth with an almost reverent chasteness. Her lips were first to part, almost of their own volition, inviting him in. He answered her invitation.

She savored the traces of sugar on his tongue. He smelled of wood smoke and musk. It was the scent of the man, his unique flavor that made Abby stir deep inside with longing and desire. When he finally broke the kiss, her body ached in places she'd thought had died. Or, perhaps, had never truly come to life.

"I'd best get you home," he whispered, brushing his lips across her cheek, her temple.

He tucked one long swatch of hair behind her ear. She leaned into his hand, closing her eyes but saying nothing. His fingers traced around her ear, trailing down onto her neck. A shudder rippled through her.

"Are you cold?" he asked.

She kept her eyes closed, drifting deeper into a moment she thought surely was a lovely dream. "Nuh-uh," she purred, shaking her head. "Far from it. A wee bit ticklish, perhaps."

Jack growled deep in his throat. "Well, you ought not to have told me that. I might take advantage of that tidbit of trivia sometime."

She opened her eyes and tumbled into the depths of those sage green eyes. Her heart thudded in her chest, and her breath came faster. He bent his head and captured her mouth again, more demanding now as he sensed her surrender. As his fingers slid up the back of her neck and combed into her hair at the oh-so-sensitive spot at the base of her neck, a wave of passion washed over her, leaving her weak and wanting.

That's when the sliding glass door behind them slid open, and they snapped apart as though a bolt of lightning struck the patio.

"Oops. Uh oh. Sorry. Guess we should have called." Jack's sister Elena peeked around through the opening wearing an apologetic and embarrassed grimace.

He cleared his throat and sat back, running his hand through his hair. "No, no, it's fine. I was just getting ready to take Abby home."

His voice was a tad too loud, she noticed.

He jumped to his feet and gathered the cups and dessert bowl onto the tray. "Can I get you guys some coffee? Tea?"

Elena slid the door open wide and two little girls spilled out onto the patio. "I came down to see a movie with the girls. Would you believe it? The only place running the flick they wanted to see was clear down here. Thought I'd stop by and see if you wanted to come with us for some ice cream at Murphy's."

Lexi turned her face up to gaze reverently at her uncle as she wrapped herself around his leg. "We saw *Brave*," she exclaimed, her face beaming as she laid her cheek against him. Then she pulled back and rubbed the side of her face as though he'd poked her. "Ouch, Uncle Jack. What's that hard thing in your pocket?"

Uh-oh. Abby held her breath as she glanced from the child's face to Elena's, whose eyes had gone wide. Jack shifted away from the child, patting down the side of his trousers but avoiding any more central region. Then he broke out in wide grin. He reached into his pocket and fished out the skeleton key.

"I'm sorry, Lexi. I forgot I still had this in here," he said, holding the oversized chunk of metal high.

Abby let out a whoosh of relief.

Elena plucked the key out of his hand. "Where'd you get this old thing?"

He twisted his shoulders and let out a deep breath of his own. "Abby and I stopped into Laramy's this afternoon to see if we could find out anything more about the library's early history."

"Why so interested in that subject all of a sudden?" Elena asked, turning the key over in her hand.

He shrugged. "Just a history buff. You know how I am, sis."

She cocked her head and stared at her brother quizzically for a moment. "What on earth could Laramy tell you about the library's history? Didn't he just move here, like, six months ago?"

"Jack's been doing some research," Abby said. "We discovered that Elijah Harvey, who founded the library, built it for his wife. Her name was Isabelle Laramy. The same family has apparently owned the building across from the library for hundreds of years."

"Hmm." Elena handed the key back to Jack. "I thought Martin was from New York City."

"That's what my aunt told me too," Abby said. "Apparently, he's a descendant. I guess he inherited the antique shop from his uncle when he passed away."

"We assumed since the building remained in the family all this time, he could tell us more about Harvey's wife," Jack said.

"Why?" Elena asked.

"You know Jack," Abby said. "He's like a bloodhound when it comes to research. Once he gets on a trail . . ."

Lexi and the other girl had wandered out beyond the glow of the candle's flame. The two were giggling and snatching at fireflies, tiny winks of light drifting elusively out of their reach.

"Well, do you want to go for ice cream or not?" Elena repeated, looking at her watch. "I don't want to keep these girls out too late."

He shrugged. "We just had a huge meal and some dessert, but I could go for a cup of coffee. How about you, Abby? I have to drive you back into town anyway."

Murphy's was a classic old-time diner with round, red vinyl padded stools lined up along a stainless steel counter and a half-dozen booths set along the front wall. Down one end of the shop, huge five-gallon cylinders of ice cream bins held court, brilliantly lit under a slanted, glass front case. Abby followed Elena in choosing a booth while Jack accompanied the two girls up to the ice cream display to make their choices.

"He's so good with the kids," Elena said. "Lexi absolutely adores him."

"Is the other little girl yours as well?" Abby asked.

"No, that's Lexi's best friend, Delia. They live two houses down from ours, and those two have been BFF's since they both ended up on the same set of monkey bars down at the park. About a year ago."

"So Lexi is your only child?" Abby asked.

"No. My son, Edward Jr., is at home with his daddy tonight. Little Eddie's only eight months old. Not nearly old enough to appreciate a trip to the movies yet." She rolled her eyes as she smiled at Abby. "All in good time." She sighed.

The girls made their choices and headed back to scramble into the booth. Lexi started to climb in next to Abby, then stopped and stared at her with giant, liquid eyes.

"Is it okay if I sit on this side with you and Uncle Jack?" she asked, her voice soft and trembly.

Abby smiled and reached for the child. "Of course it is. I'm honored you want to sit with me." She helped Lexi up onto the booth, then wrapped one arm around her. Ducking her head close to the child's ear, she asked, "So what kind of ice cream did you choose?"

Lexi gazed up at her with trusting eyes. "Mint chocolate chip," she declared. "It's my favoritist in the whole wide world." Then, wrinkling her nose, she whispered, "Even though it's green."

The waitress brought out heaping cones of ice cream for the two fidgety girls, then went back for the coffees.

"I'll bring back some more napkins," she said, eyeing Lexi and Delia. "I think you might be needing them."

As the adults dressed their coffee, the children attacked their cones with determined concentration.

"So," Jack began, addressing Elena, "are you bringing the girls down for story hour tomorrow?"

"I am. Is it true what I'm hearing that it will be the last one for a while? At least until they can get Abby some help?"

Abby stared down into the clouds of cream swirling in her cup, nodding. "I wish it could be different. I can't see how I can tend the library desk and devote my attention to story hour upstairs if I'm the only one in the building."

"Is there a rule that says you can't have volunteers?" Elena asked.

She glanced over at Jack, then back at Elena. "I-I'm not sure, but—"

"Well, that's a question I'll be raising with the commissioner's office on Monday morning. There's no reason why someone can't help you out for an hour or two on Saturday afternoons."

Jack asked, "Do you think any of your moms might be willing to volunteer for a few hours?"

"I'm absolutely sure of it. I'll be first on the list." Elena turned to Abby. "How long do you think it will take to show me the basics of the computer system?"

"No time at all. As a matter of fact, Monica will still be working this Saturday. She can show you how it all works while I'm reading to the children." She paused, glancing at Jack. "I wonder if Dennis will have a problem with me taking on a few volunteers."

He shook his head. "I don't think Dennis is the one you have to worry about."

Elena sat back, a look of decided determination on her face. "I don't have to wait until Monday. I'll give Commissioner Ludwig a call first thing tomorrow morning. I have his home number," she bragged, sitting up a little straighter. Then she qualified, "My best friend is the secretary down at city hall."

Lexi and Delia, on each side of the booth, were losing the battle with their ice cream cones. Watching from behind the counter, their waitress came to the rescue with empty bowls and spoons just as the top scoop of Lexi's green mint-chip ice cream slithered off the cone. It tumbled into the bowl with a splat. Lexi looked up at Abby with owl eyes.

"Wow, that was close," she whispered with a slight lisp.

Abby smiled down at her and handed her the spoon. "You're lucky our fearless Murphy's server here has lots of experience with little girls and ice cream cones."

Elena shifted around toward Jack. "Let me have another look at that weird old key you bought."

He pulled it out of the breast pocket of his jacket and handed it to his sister.

"What's it to?" she asked.

"Probably nothing. Laramy said his uncle gave it to him when he was a kid. He said it came from the old library, but Martin and his buddies tried it in every lock of the place with no luck."

"I'm not surprised. I'm sure the locks on the library have been changed at least once in the past hundred years. And this key looks even older than that." She held the key up under the glow of the wall-mounted lamp at her end of the booth.

"I haven't had time to research it yet. We were somewhat disappointed Laramy couldn't tell us any more about his own family history," Jack said.

Elena raised a brow. "I don't know why you should be so surprised at that. Laramy is a bit," she slanted a look at the children, "different. So tell me again. I realize you're the obsessive history professor, but why are you suddenly so interested in the wife of the man who built the library? Like, hundreds of years ago?"

Abby glanced over at Jack, then down at Lexi and Delia.

He cleared his throat. "I'd rather not go into it here, now," he said, nodding toward the girls.

Oblivious, they were scraping the last bits of their ice cream from the bottom of their bowls.

"Oh, you're researching that rumor," Elena said. Her face lit up with a slow smile of realization. "You? I didn't think you believed in stuff like that," she said with a chuckle. Then she turned to Abby. "Has anything . . . happened since you've been working there?"

She shook her head in nervous jerks and said, "I think we have two little girls here with sticky faces and fingers. How about we go check out the washing facilities of Murphy's ladies' room?"

Jack waited until the door to the ladies' room drifted closed behind Abby and the children. Then he turned to Elena. "Look, I'm not saying I believe there's a ghost. But there's no denying some strange things have been happening over there. Abby's no squirrel. I don't think she's making this stuff up."

"Like what?"

"Nothing earth-shattering. A window found mysteriously open. Smoke floating around, like from a pipe or cigar. Books dropping off the shelves for no reason. One even whacked old Leda Ludwig on the head. I was there. I witnessed it."

Elena giggled. "Seriously? Must be a pretty cool ghost. What makes you think he has anything to do with one of Laramy's ancestors?"

"I don't. It's just a hunch. The library founder built the thing for his wife, who was a Laramy. There were thirty-five years between them, yet she died ten years before he did. Elijah Harvey is buried in the family plot back in Boston, and no spouse is buried with him. I checked the records."

"Thirty-five years? Wow, and I felt funny about marrying Eddie, a big five years older than me."

"It was pretty common back then. The choices for hooking up were definitely scarcer. Especially out here in the wilderness. A century ago, they didn't have Match.com." He slanted her a look.

She rested her chin on her hand, her brow furrowed. "She's not buried with him, huh? And they stayed married? Till the end?"

Jack nodded. "No divorce records. Only death dates, and I guess Elijah moved back home to Boston after his wife's death, or his family shipped him home for burial. Because by then, his wife had been dead for ten years."

"That's ironic, isn't it? She was so much younger than him yet he outlived her." Elena shook her head. "If your Isabelle isn't buried beside her husband, my bet she's in the Laramy family plot. That's right here in Caldwell."

He slammed his cup down on the tabletop so hard the coffee sloshed over the lip. "You have got to be kidding me."

The next day was Monica's last on the job. Abby wasn't expecting her until eleven. She climbed the stairs to the children's loft to pick out choices for the day's story hour. After sifting through the meager collection, she pulled a dozen from which she would allow the children to choose. She knew full well she would end up reading them all anyway. Especially today.

When she came downstairs she spotted a book lying on the windowsill above the radiator. In the reading corner, near the same window she repeatedly found open whenever pipe smoke hung in the air. She strode back, picked up the book, then stopped to sniff, but smelled nothing. The window remained closed and locked. The only thing out of place was the book, lying at an angle and within reach of anyone choosing to sit in the wing chair.

Abby sat and pulled the book into her lap. *The Bell Jar* by Sylvia Plath.

"Mmm. Are you trying to tell me something, Elijah? Are you telling me I'm headed down a dark, dead-ended path?" She fanned the pages, comforted by the aroma of old paper and ink. "Or are you partaking of some somber reading material on this, the day that may constitute the beginning of the end?"

She smelled the pipe smoke then, infusing gradually into the air around her. The aroma stirred memories, much like a long familiar melody. She remembered the pungent aroma of her father's pipe creeping up the stairs and slithering under her door as she lay on her bed, reading or studying. A wave of loneliness, oddly combined with comfort, washed over her.

As she sat there, staring at the cover of the book, her own memories tangled with ones not truly hers. What had Elijah Harvey been like, and his young wife Isabelle? From the facts Jack discovered, combined with Abby's active imagination, she recreated the couple in her mind. Imagined scenes flickered in pale, translucent images, like the stuttered frames in an old silent movie. She guessed this had been Elijah's place to enjoy his pipe. Maybe he'd sat in this very spot. In some ethereal sense, he still did.

Why? What kept Elijah's spirit here in this place?

She rose to re-shelve the book, and as she slid the text back into its rightful spot on the shelf another thump sounded. Ducking her head around the end of the stack, she spotted a book on the floor. Not even in the same row, but a row or two below.

Odd. She couldn't have dislodged it from this distance. The stacks are sturdy and strong.

She retrieved *The Bell Messenger*, by Robert Cornuke. Shaking her head with a grin, Abby spoke.

"Elijah, I don't know if you're trying to comfort me with your presence, or keep me amused with your antics. Keep it up, old fella. It gets kind of lonely in here sometimes." She tucked the book up under her arm and headed for the reception desk.

It was then she remembered the old key Jack gave her when they parted last evening. She'd slipped it into her purse, promising she'd try it in all the library doors, even though Laramy swore it fit nothing.

When she got to the desk, she plopped down the book and grabbed for her purse, digging the tarnished brass key out of her bag and carrying it to the entrance. Tugging back the heavy door, she threw the lock from inside, then holding the door open, tried the key. The end didn't even fit into the opening.

She closed the door and walked to the rear exit—the emergency door, which was seldom opened. Unbolting the deadlock, she pulled on the door and repeated the test. Again, the giant old key was too big for the smaller, more modern lockset.

She stood with her hands on her hips in the middle of the lobby, her eyes scanning the room. There was an office upstairs she never used, but the key to that door was smaller. Walking behind the counter, she scanned the built-in drawers and found only one top drawer with a keyhole. The key was far too big to fit into the notched opening. She examined all the desks and cabinets in the back office, finding none of them fitted with locks.

That's when another thump sounded in the main room. She peeked out of the doorway and spied yet another book lying on the floor.

Chuckling now and shaking her head, she went back to retrieve the book. This time it lay closed, front cover up. The original 1848 handwritten poem had been re-published many times, and this particular copy featured a close-up image of a rolled parchment letter, freshly sealed with a wax imprint.

The Bells, a classic poetry collection by Edgar Allan Poe.

"So you enjoy poetry too, I see," she said. "I've not read this particular Poe. I hear it's as haunting as his other works."

She still had the book clutched to her chest when Monica came in through the front door.

"Hey, what's happening?" She glanced around. "Typical ghost town Saturday morning, huh?" she asked.

Laughing out loud, Abby replied, "More a ghost town than you could imagine," as she slipped the Poe back into its spot in the stacks.

About twenty minutes before two, Elena came through the front door followed by a couple of the other mothers from her daycare who brought their children to story hour.

"Abby, Jeannie here can take turns with me volunteering at the checkout desk on Saturdays. Laura has to work at her job some weekends, but she's willing to help whenever she can too."

Abby smiled as she came around the counter to give Elena a hug. "How can I ever thank you for this, Elena?" She stepped back, looking over at the other two women. "All of you. I don't know what to say." Emotion clutched at Abby's throat, and her eyes went misty.

Watching her, Monica said, "Oh, don't go getting teary-eyed on us, Abby. You'll end up turning into Rocky Raccoon again."

The women all chuckled.

Monica motioned for them to come behind the counter. "Come back here, ladies, and I'll give you the trusty, condensed training session for Harvey book checkouts."

Later, Abby and Monica, both down on hands and knees, were cleaning up the last of the tornado scene in the loft after the children's story hour.

"You insisted you didn't want a going away party or anything like that, Monica. At least let me take you out for a drink after we close."

"I can't, Abby," Monica replied. "Davin and I are actually leaving tomorrow morning, believe it or not. I've got to finish packing."

She and Davin were flying to Vegas to get married, then spending two weeks driving down the coast of California.

Abby grasped Monica's wrist. "Okay, well promise me this, then. When you two get back, we'll go out for a celebration dinner. The four of us. Promise?"

A sly smile crept across Monica's face. "Things are going well with Jack then, huh?"

Abby smiled and busied herself with alphabetizing the colorful assortment of Dr. Seuss she had gathered. "Jack is a very nice man," she said quietly. "I'm not sure we're much more than friends, but I do enjoy his company. A lot."

As they rose to their feet Monica drew Abby in for a hug. "I'm glad for you, Abby. Jack is a great guy. I've known him a long time. I think he's good for you."

"We're going hiking tomorrow," Abby said as they descended the curved staircase.

"Oh yeah? Where?"

"Tanawha Trail, I think he said?" She hesitated on the name, unsure if she'd pronounced the Indian word correctly.

"I hear that's beautiful," Monica said. "Make sure you wear good hiking shoes." She glanced down at Abby's customary footgear, the black and white Converse sneakers. "If you wear those things you'll end up twisting an ankle for sure."

Chapter 16

Abby couldn't believe how excited she was. Although she'd never been one much for hiking, she did so love the beauty of the mountains where she grew up, especially in spring. She'd never gotten an opportunity to experience them much, other than gazing through a university library window or from the back deck of Cameron's chalet. Always the virtual participant. The book nerd, the geeky 4.0 student who didn't participate in outdoor sports and never took an interest in attending any activity other than perusing shelves.

Today's excursion would be a first for her and not only in a physical sense. As she dug through her tiny closet and bureau deciding what she should wear, she tried to ignore the tense knot of tension in her chest. It was silly to be afraid of hiking in the mountains, especially on a well-marked trail and with an experienced hiker. So why did she feel a little like a stray kitten hiding behind a garbage pail?

There would be no crowds, like at the festival, to trigger a panic attack. Jack and Abby could well spend the entire afternoon on the trail accompanied only by the occasional startled squirrel, an aggravated cardinal or bluebird.

What frightened her was how easy she felt with him, to talk and laugh with him. And how much more, every day, she found him drifting in and out of her thoughts. At the most unexpected times. At work, at home, in the shower, for god's sakes. Waking up and stretching in her bed with the early fingers of dawn creeping around the window shade. Late at night when at last she turned out the light to find her bed feeling so cold, so empty.

Her relationship with Cameron hadn't been like that. Sure, she looked forward to seeing him on the weekends, when he lavished her with attention, and ravished her body. But weekends had been enough. Cameron hadn't stirred her heart the way Jack did.

And that was terrifying.

It didn't take an extensive online search for appropriate hiking gear to discover she didn't own anything even vaguely similar to the attire recommended. And tomorrow's weather forecast called for steamy temperatures.

In the end she dug an old pair of lightweight, rip-stop khakis out of the back of her closet. She remembered Jack's warning about thorny underbrush they might encounter along the path. A silk tank would keep her cool. True, the silk might not survive the journey, but the blouse had a snag or two around the waist anyway from when she'd been too impatient yanking off a belt. Heeding Monica's warning about footgear, she lugged out the pair of sturdy, sensible Reeboks her mother had given her for Christmas last year.

Early the next morning, Abby ran next door to Boswell's drug store five minutes past eight and picked up sunscreen and bug spray. By ten, her muscles wound as tightly as a toddler's on Christmas morning, she was dressed and waiting for Jack on the front porch of Ancient Healings.

As always, he was right on time. He stepped up onto the sidewalk and called, "Good morning. Ms. Stryker, right? You must be my tour duty for the day." He perched both hands on his hips and scrutinized her from head to toe.

"You appear properly attired for the journey. I am your humble guide," he paused, motioning to himself theatrically, before continuing, "and have packed sufficient rations for the journey." He walked around to the passenger side and opened the door, sweeping his hand in an exaggerated invitation. "Entre, *sil vois plait*, madam." Then he bowed.

Abby giggled and climbed in. "You've been flashing that French around quite a bit," she said, eying him with a cocked brow. "Trying to impress me again?"

His shoulders drooped. "You mean I haven't succeeded in completely sweeping you off your feet yet?" He frowned. "Guess I'll have to work a little harder."

A warm blush rose into her cheeks. Such a paradox, this man. Such spontaneity and playfulness so at odds with the stereotype she'd imprinted on her mind, the one that shouted, "Jack Wood is a slightly younger model of Cameron Bennett."

Shaking off her objecting internal thoughts, she settled into her seat, determined to put the past behind her and enjoy this day.

The drive took them through the lush Yadkin River Valley, then up into the mountains. The day was gloriously summer, flowers blooming alongside the winding roadway in wildly colorful patches. He left the windows open, and the light flashed off the silver in his hair as the wind ruffled his curls. Occasionally she caught of whiff of his clean, piney scent. Or was it coming from the forest lining the road?

No matter. The scent was having the same effect on her, warming her insides to jelly.

The highway wound its way up through the foothills and soon passed the sign welcoming them to Blowing Rock.

"You grew up here, right?" she asked.

He nodded. "My whole family still lives here."

"Is Elena your only sibling?"

"No, I actually have three sisters. Connie teaches at the Blowing Rock elementary school, and Rene is a nurse."

"The only brother, huh?"

"And the oldest," he added, slanting a glance toward her with a smirk. "I had a somewhat interesting childhood. With markedly limited access to a bathroom."

They passed through Blowing Rock and were soon approaching Boone.

"This is where you grew up, right?"

"No, actually," she said with a head tilt, "I grew up on the campus of Appalachia State University." She shot him a mock-serious look. "If I didn't know better, I'd think I was actually born on the fourth floor of the library. My parents are the most obsessive, stuffy professors you could possibly imagine."

He reached over and patted the back of her hand. "Even stuffier than me?"

"I'm beginning to realize that you, Professor Wood, just look stuffy."

What scares me is how appealing you are underneath that persona.

As they drove through the center of town, familiar names of the shops and taverns drifted by. Places she'd seldom seen other than through a car window, like now.

When he turned the car onto the road leading to Grandfather Mountain, he asked, "Does it bother you to come up here?"

She shook her head. "We never came to town. Cameron's cabin is tucked away on the south side of the mountain." She let out a dark, sad chuckle. "The only view I ever had here was the one from his back deck."

Or of his bedroom ceiling.

"Well, be prepared. Today I'm taking you for a walk on the wild side." That caused her to arch an eyebrow, and Jack flashed her one of his disarming smiles. Then he shrugged. "How wild do you think a middle-aged college prof can get?"

They traveled up the Blue Ridge Parkway for a few miles, then took an exit onto a winding, two lane road.

"How far is it?" she asked, as the forest gradually grew thicker and even more densely shrouded in pine.

"Not far. Just a mile or two off the pavement."

He turned onto a dirt road marked with a carved wooden sign—*Tanawha Trail*— and an arrow. Abby was certain they'd arrived. They had not.

They continued to follow what constituted little more than a rutted path that stretched past several private campgrounds, dotted with tiny, old-fashioned aluminum trailers. Some were apparently semi-permanent fixtures. A few had small lean-to porches built off the side, while others had entire wooden rooms added on.

"Do people actually live here? Year round?" she asked, wrinkling her nose at the shabbiness of the grayed, faded plywood additions.

He shook his head. "Summer folks, is all. There's no way anyone could last through a winter in one of those things. Some late season fishermen come up for a week or two around Thanksgiving."

The unpaved road was pitted and dusty, and after her third sneeze, Jack rolled the windows up and turned on the air conditioning. The road narrowed even further and twisted along the edge of a rocky mountain face. A rushing river peeked through the trees on the other side. The chalky lime rock soon took on a hardened appearance.

When the dust cleared, he opened the windows again. The road was barely a path now, and she wondered if they happened along another vehicle traveling in the opposite direction, how they could safely pass without scraping up against rocks or low pine branches.

"How did you ever find this place?" she asked. "And don't say 'on my way to the grocery store.'"

He grinned. "I love to hike. All the hiking trails in these parts, believe it or not, are well documented. The parks division maintains them, and there's a map for each trail outlining where it goes and how long it is. They're even rated by difficulty level."

"And what's the difficulty level of the Tanawha?"

"Don't worry, there are several paths to choose from. I think we should start on one of the easier ones—especially since we're lugging picnic gear."

The parking area at the trail entrance was abandoned except for one other vehicle, which Abby found surprising for a weekend. "Not a popular hiking trail?"

"Apparently not on an upcoming fourth of July holiday," he replied. As he killed the engine he turned toward her. "Do you think you'll be okay toting a light backpack? I couldn't fit everything into one."

She scowled at first, but then pulled both fists up to her ears, flexing her biceps. "Me strong like bull," she growled, and he burst into laughter.

It took several minutes to unload and strap on backpacks. Jack slipped a map out of his chest pocket and spread it out on the tailgate. "This is where we are right now." He pointed to a red teardrop marking the spot. "And here's where we'll end up, and have lunch."

"And where's this?" Abby laid her finger on the small "R" symbol alongside the parking lot.

"Oh. Facilities, you mean?" He nodded past her.

The opaque white porta-potty stood between the woods and the gravel lot.

She raised her eyebrows and shrugged. "Beats behind a bush." As she turned to head in that direction she was snagged from behind.

"Let's unstrap the backpack first. I'd hate to have you drop our lunch down the hole. Or worse yet, fall in with it." He grinned as he unclipped the shoulder harness.

She screwed her face up and stuck out her tongue at him before heading off toward the john.

Once on their way, the trail proved to be a wee bit more difficult than the brochure's description claimed. Steep, winding walkways delineated with flat rocks wove their way up and around each rise. Abby couldn't tell how quickly they were climbing as the path wound back and forth across the steeper face in a zigzag of terraced steps. The thick forest cover shielded any lateral view.

A perfect time of year for this sort of adventure. Even though the forecast called for temps in the low nineties, the cool dampness of the mossy banks provided natural air conditioning. The leafy ceiling allowed only occasional flashes of sunshine to dapple through. Jack was obviously an experienced hiker. He followed behind her going up the grade, then passed along in front of her going down, as if he were afraid gravity might snatch her away at any minute. In especially steep places, she sensed him latch a finger through the strap on her backpack.

"Don't worry, scoutmaster. I'm not going to tumble down into the valley with your lunch," she muttered.

"You're actually pretty sure-footed," he replied. "Are you sure you haven't done anything like this before?"

She shook her head. "Naw. Just born part billy goat."

"Certainly not the billy," he said, and when she glanced back over her shoulder, his gaze wandered up and down her body.

That warm flush again. Only much, much lower.

An hour had passed when they paused in an exceptionally shady hollow. A small stream ran under the path, and an immense fallen log wedged between boulders formed a natural bridge. She took a long draw out of the water bottle he offered as she rested against the rock wall on the high side. The slate surface felt cool and smelled earthy. Her gaze followed the path of the trickling stream to its source, gurgling out from a crevice in the stone several feet above where they stood.

"Look at that." She pointed. "The water leaks right out of the mountain. Is that a spring?"

"Probably not. I'd guess it's water trickling down from higher elevations and filtering through the rocks." Cupping a hand under the flow, he said, "Probably cleaner than what we're drinking out of these," and raised his water.

"This is incredible," she whispered, holding her cool bottle to her cheek as she caught her breath. "I'm assuming you've done this trail before?"

He snapped a bandanna out of his back pocket and wiped his brow. "A time or two. But always alone. It's kinda neat to have company. I get to see it through two sets of eyes this time."

"Ooh, look," she breathed, gazing past him toward a bright patch of color suspended from the rocky wall they rested against.

Several feet above his head, a cluster of thick, dark green leaves sprung from a crevice between the huge boulders. At the center sprouted three spikes of purple and white flowers so perfect, and so exotic, they looked artificial.

Jack bent one of the spikes in Abby's direction. "Native orchids."

Standing on her tiptoes, she examined the flowers more closely. Triple lobed, pale purple hoods topped larger, lower petals of pure white. "They don't even look real. They're breathtaking."

He released the flower before squeezing her shoulder. "I'd love to pick a spike for you, but the flora in these parts are mostly protected. Besides, it would wither and die before we could get it back home."

"No. No, don't spoil it." She smiled, staring up at the colorful cluster. "I can see why people believe there's magic in the woods. Like fairies and green men. There truly is magic here."

Their faces were only inches apart, and Abby could smell Jack's scent over the woods' natural fragrance. He was looking into her eyes in that way he had that made her feel as though he could see clear through to her soul. His eyes mirrored the greenness all around him. The flutter in her chest, and the warm buzz low in her belly sent a tingle running down her back. Her breath quickened, and she had to look away.

Although the brochure claimed the hike was a two to three hour trek round trip, it took them almost two hours to reach their destination on the forested mountain. At what seemed the highest point, the trail jogged off to one side, further up through a relatively young patch of trees that were set apart at such uniform distances, she wondered if they had been planted by the forestry division.

The last part of the path scrunched down into a packed narrow dirt footpath. She found herself carefully placing one foot in front of the other to avoid slipping into the layers of moist leaves on the steep, downgrade side. Several times Jack gripped her upper arm when her footing seemed unsure. Soon she could hear the rush of water nearby.

"Listen." She stopped and turned around. "A river?"

"More than a river." He grinned. Then he grasped her shoulders and turned her away from him. His words warmed her neck as he pointed over her shoulder. "Look. Through those trees there."

She squinted and ducked to peek between the leafy branches. In the distance, a clearing aglow with brilliant sunlight came into view. An oasis in the jungle. He took her hand, hers feeling small and cool wrapped in its strong warmth. He led her along the rest of the path to where it ended on the top of the steep ridge. The rush of water was so loud she could barely hear his words.

Moving closer, he murmured into her ear. "This is one of the smaller sections of the Linville Falls." His breath caused another ripple of shock waves to skitter down her spine.

Together they scrambled down the side of the mountain, in places literally on hands and knees, using rocks and trees to steady their descent. It was worth the trip. Ahead, a wall of water cascaded in a foamy white tumble into a clear pool below. They reached the bottom breathless, where a huge flat stone formation formed a ledge hovering inches above the swirling pool beneath the falls.

Abby stooped to trail a hand in the water then snatched it back. “My God, it’s freezing!”

Jack laughed, then flashed a quick frown. “So I guess skinny dipping is out of the question.”

“Uh, yeah!” she shouted back.

They sat together on the ledge for several minutes admiring the thirty-foot wall of water plunge into its basin. Close by his side, she hugged her knees when an occasional shiver ran through her. Even though the early afternoon sun basked the area unobstructed here, the air was chilly. Scooting closer, she tucked herself into the warmth of Jack’s body.

Along the edge of the waterfall, a halo of mist created a rainbow that flickered and faded. The crystal clear water in the pool beneath her feet was alive with small fish flitting about under the surface. Their iridescent scales reflected the sun’s rays with similar rainbow flashes.

“What kind of fish are they?”

“Some are brook trout. They’re so colorful,” he replied. “It’s as though they were made to reflect the beauty of the world around them.”

“But you catch them. You kill them and fry them up for supper,” she challenged.

“I do,” he admitted. His lips set in a grim line, then he glanced over at her, searching her eyes. “That’s the extent of my savagery, I assure you. My father always wanted me to hunt with him. He brags about bagging a deer every year.” Jack turned his gaze back toward the waterfall. “I can’t do it. I don’t like the taste of wild game. And I can’t kill something I don’t intend to eat.”

They sat in silence for another few minutes, until her shivering continued in uninterrupted quakes.

"You're cold," he said. "Come on. We'll hike back up onto the trail and find a warm spot to eat lunch."

The strenuous climb back up the steep grade left her winded and no longer at all chilled. The path they'd come off earlier continued around a bend, hugging the contour of the mountain. A few hundred yards or so in the distance spread a secluded meadow.

The grasses grew tall in the fertile basin around the stream that wove its way through the center. He led her down a dirt path to the stream's edge, a place where the dense pine forest crept almost to the banks. The ground here was flat and dry, padded with pine needles, their pungent scent rising into the sun as it warmed them.

He stopped and said, "How about right here?"

The man knew how to picnic, with this spread even more impressive than last time. He unpacked an amazing variety of supplies out of the two backpacks they'd been carrying. When it was all spread out on the gingham cloth he snagged out of a side pocket, she couldn't believe her eyes. Slim ice packs sandwiching sliced cheese and cold meat had been stowed underneath a linen-wrapped loaf of crusty French bread. Tiny plastic vials held olives and pickle slices, and from the bottom of the satchel he'd carried, he withdrew a half-sized bottle of wine.

She eyed the bottle and said, "Uh-oh. Hope you remembered a wine key this time. This one's not a twist-cap."

Holding up one finger, he withdrew what looked like an oversized pocketknife from his belt. With the flick of his thumb, a metal spiral shot out and glinted in the sun.

She laughed. "I'm going to have to start calling you Mountain Man."

They ate and laughed and talked in a lazy, comfortable way Abby had never experienced with a man. They not only chatted, they had real conversations. She felt she could tell him anything, from the way she despised Leda to her pity for Dennis. They talked of the library and discussed the best way to convince the town board to continue the funding. They even debated the most recent top ten listings on the *New York Times* Bestsellers list.

"I wasn't crazy about that one," Abby replied when Jack asked her opinion of the latest, greatest new series. "But I tend more toward the literary stuff."

"Most of the American public doesn't appear to give a hoot about literary principle," he replied. "And keep in mind, the hot selling books are the ones people are going to be looking for in the library."

Begrudgingly, she had to agree. "I'm hoping, eventually, to update the library's holdings. I see too many new patrons drift in and back out again empty handed."

She asked him about how his Local History class was received.

"Most of these youngsters can't conceive that the world began more than twenty years ago. Unfortunately, they also don't realize it will survive beyond the end of their freshman year." He shook his head. "Literature and history. The two areas from which we can learn so much about the now and the future. It's a shame our younger generation can't see that."

He took her hand and kissed it, like an old-fashioned gentleman. He had a way of making her feel his equal and a pampered princess all at once. With Cameron, she'd only ever been a treasured pet.

"So why do you think Elijah Harvey still hangs around in the library?" she asked as she gathered up the containers and stacked them for repacking. "If Isabelle was as fond of the place as it would seem, why isn't she there too?"

Jack's gaze flashed to hers, one brow raised. "How do you know she isn't?"

"She isn't there," she replied without hesitation. "I get the distinct feeling there is a presence, a spirit there. But it's a male entity. For one thing, there's the pipe smoke."

"You've lived in the Blue Ridge long enough to know there are plenty of women who smoke pipes, Abby," he said. "Or chew, like Miss Cornwell."

She shook her head decisively. "No. No, this is definitely a male presence. It's the way he does things. The way he tries to communicate with me."

Jack leaned back on his hands, raising his face toward the sun. "What do you mean, tries to communicate?"

"He's trying to tell me something. With the books. He's been leaving them out everywhere, dropping them off the shelves. I'm sure there's a pattern to it, but other than the fact that the word 'bell' is in all of the titles, I don't see any other common factor."

He sat up straight. "You really think he's trying to communicate with you?"

"I feel sure of it," she replied. Then, smiling, she continued, "Like the night he conked Leda on the head with a book titled *Witch*. No doubt of his opinion of her."

They both laughed, and Jack shuffled over on his hands and knees to sit close beside her. She snuggled in closer to him and laid her head on his shoulder. "This has been a such a nice day, Jack," she whispered.

Turning, he framed her face with his hands, searching her eyes again in that magical way, with an intensity that shot straight through to her soul. "For me too."

She blinked and found it hard to hold his gaze. This was new to her, filling her with wonder along with the need. Attention, affection, she needed as much as the air for her lungs. She couldn't deny her body craved him, like parched soil needs rain.

But this was a new kind of connection. No one had ever looked at her this way, and as his sage green eyes studied her, emotions warred inside her. She closed her eyes, surrendered to her physical desires, and melted into his embrace.

The joy bubbling inside Jack's chest hadn't been there in a long time. Surprised when Abby even consented to join him on this hike, he was shocked at her enthusiasm. Never would he have guessed how well the cloistered librarian would take to the wilderness.

And this was no easy trail. He'd miscalculated on his choice, confusing the Tanawha with another trail he'd done a few years back with almost the same name. But she was a trooper. She trudged along in front or beside him, chattering a good bit of the time about the beauty of forest and all its nuances—a scampering squirrel, the way the ferns nodded and swayed over the stream, discovery of a wild orchid. Never once had she complained about the steepness of the climb or the distance they'd traveled to get here.

Now, she was gazing into his eyes with such a look of wonder, it made his heart ache. Until now, she'd been fighting letting him in, and he always sensed she was hiding behind a wall. At first, he thought the barrier was built of fear because of what happened in her past. He was convinced now her barrier had more to do with innocence. Not of the physical affection, but of the emotions too often lacking from the act.

Her body might not be chaste, but her soul had no idea what love was. Today, he hoped to show her.

When he lowered his mouth to hers, she surrendered, the tension drifting from her like fog evaporating in the afternoon sunshine. He kissed her tentatively at first, soft and chaste. Her unique aroma filled his senses, making his heart thrum faster, and his man parts stir. When her lips parted, warm and willing, he groaned.

Her tongue quickly answered his with bolder strokes,

engaging in a sensuous dance. She tasted sweet, like the wine, and when she brought her fingers to comb into his hair, another thrill zinged through him.

I must take my time, he reminded himself. This isn't just another roll in the hay. I want to show her the difference between having sex and making love.

He lay beside her on the warm cloth and covered her delicate skin with kisses. Leaving her mouth, he began on her forehead, pressing his lips beside her eyes, on her temples, and brushing across the tip of her nose. After one kiss on the sensitive corner of her mouth, he moved on to her perfect, shell-pink ear.

Passion flared in his groin as his tongue traced the rim, the silver studs acting as sexy speed bumps. A shudder shook her shoulders, and he buried his face against her neck and held her close, breathing in her scent, struggling to gain control. At the base of her neck, the pulse beneath her delicate skin tapped a tempting rhythm against his cheek.

"You okay, pretty lady?" he rasped.

"Hmm." Her moan, like gasoline on a fire, shot straight down through his chest, and within seconds, he was rock hard. As if sensing his body's reaction, her nails scraped along his scalp, sending tingles down his neck. Trailing lower, her fingers worked their way under his collar, around to the front, where she tangled them into the hair on his chest.

"Lose this," she murmured, tugging at the placket.

Rising to sit, he pulled his shirt free and over his head, all the while watching her eyes roam over him. The corners of her lips drew up.

"You're one beautiful man, Professor Wood," she said, pulling him down beside her as her hands swept over his chest, his shoulders, then lightly raking his back with her nails. His breath came faster, and he took in a shuddering breath.

Drawing away, he used a finger to tip her chin so he

could see her eyes. "You make me feel like a god. But I'm still a man, with weaknesses, Abby."

She took that moment to challenge him by stroking her hands down over his throbbing crotch, causing him to gasp and growl, "I want you. That's pretty obvious."

"I want you too," she whispered, laying her cheek against his chest. "Take me, Jack."

Only then, with her clear permission, did he allow himself to explore the places he ached to touch. Pushing one side of her silky tank off her shoulder, he kissed, then licked, then plucked her skin gently with his teeth. She arched up, inviting him to go lower.

Working his way slowly from her shoulder to the swell of her breast, he used his lips and tongue to tease her, and thrilled at the shivers rippling through her body. An enticing aroma rose from her hot, damp skin, and the taste of her drove him higher and higher. Catching the neckline of her blouse between his teeth, he tugged and said, "Lose this."

She rose and lifted it, revealing a lacy white bra cupping plump, perfect breasts. Passion surged through him with such intensity, he felt dizzy. "My god, you are so beautiful."

When she reached out both arms toward him, he was certain he'd fallen into a fantasy world.

"Take me, Jack," she repeated.

He stroked her cheek with the back of his hand and sought her gaze, then held it as his fingers trailed over her jaw and down her neck to trace along her collarbone. She shuddered, and surprised him by grasping both his wrists.

Placing his hands over her breasts, she whispered, "Here. Touch me here."

Both of his thumbs teased through her bra, where peaked nipples strained against the rough lace. She closed her eyes and started to pant.

"You're so sensitive here," he purred.

"I could almost come from just having you play with them," she gasped. "That was never . . ." She stopped, her lids fluttering open. "Nobody's ever paid them this much attention."

The fleeting thought, *selfish bastard*, drifted somewhere in the back of Jack's mind, but he pushed it away and said, "But oh, there's so much more I can do for them."

With that, he unbuckled the undergarment with one hand and it fell away. Her arms came up across her chest, almost instinctively, and she stared at him, wide-eyed.

"Let me see you, Abby. Let me relish the beauty of all of you."

Blinking, she relaxed, revealing herself to him. He cupped the back of her head as he lowered her down to the blanket. The whole time, her gaze held his.

When he captured one pebbled nipple in his mouth, she cried out and arched up, her entire body writhing from his touch. With his tongue he traced wet circles around the firm peak, and used his hand to roll the other nipple between his fingers. Her moans grew louder, and her hips bucked against his thigh.

"If you keep that up, this will be over before we get started," he growled against her skin.

But she was already unzipping her shorts and wriggling them off over her hips. "Touch me, Jack. It's been so long. Please, make me come."

He drew back for just a moment to admire the gorgeous woman lying next to him. Her body was feminine perfection, with firm mounds topped with now bright rosy points. Her pale skin stretched over a flat stomach, with a tiny dimple of a navel, and the patch of dark hair between her legs glistened in the sunlight.

She was the most beautiful woman he'd ever laid eyes on.

"You're so wet." He sucked in a sharp breath as his fingers found her core, and her moans urged him onward.

He stroked her only once, then twice before she came apart in his arms, screaming out, her nails sinking into the bare skin of his back. Her heart thudded wildly under his ear where his head lay on her chest. He stayed with her as wave after wave of pleasure shook her body, biting down hard on his lower lip to keep from coming with her.

A veil of sweat glued his cheek to her chest, and he wasn't sure whether it was more hers or his own. As he lifted his head, he found her gazing at him with wide, wondrous eyes.

"Oh my god. You're amazing. It's never been like that for me before." Her voice was thick with emotion.

What he hoped was emotion, and not just the afterglow of a mind-blowing orgasm. "Really? Didn't he ever . . ."

She was shaking her head. "Sometimes, he'd ask me to do some of . . . that. While he watched," she tipped her head toward her crotch, "but only when it was taking him longer to get . . . you, know. Ready."

Selfish, *impotent* bastard. Jack lifted himself up on one elbow and swiped the sweat off his brow with the other arm. This was *so* not what he wanted her to be doing right now. Comparing him. Even thinking about the other man who'd taken her virginity.

He let out a shuddering breath, then wrapped his fingers around her wrist, bringing her hand down to press against his now painful bulge. "As you can see, I don't have any problem getting ready for you."

A small smile curled her lips as a mischievous twinkle lit up her eyes. "Well, what are you waiting for?" Just as quickly, her brows knitted and she moaned, "Oh, no. I'm not . . . on anything. No birth control. He was . . . neutered. I mean, had a vasectomy. You know what I mean."

Jack dropped his head back and laughed. "Neutered, huh? Sounds like they did a pretty good job." He struggled to sit up and reached to unbuckle his belt, then unsnapped a small pouch hanging from it, producing a small foil packet. "A good Boy Scout is always prepared."

They made love in the afternoon sunshine with the gurgle of the stream and the rustling breeze in the trees as their background music, and Abby felt reborn. Jack's gentle, attentive lovemaking was so unlike what she'd experienced before, she almost felt like a virgin again. If this what sex was supposed to feel like, then in many senses, she was.

Afterward, they lay spooned for a long while with the sun warming their bodies, drying the sweat off their skin. Only when the shadows grew long, teasing the edge of their blanket and sending a cool breeze to blow over them, did Jack clamber to his feet. He lifted one edge of the blanket to cover her. She rolled onto her back to watch him dress.

He was a beautiful man, lean and toned with sculpted abs and strong thighs and just the right amount of dark hair defining his body as purely virile, ultimately masculine. Set against the backdrop of the mountains, he couldn't have looked more at home. Just watching the flexing of his muscles as he lifted his arms to pull on his shirt renewed the throbbing between her legs. He was strong, and sexy, and had brought her to heights of pleasure she'd never known with Cameron.

"Enjoying the show?" he asked, smirking as he caught her watching him.

"Mmm. You're so gorgeous. I could do it all over again right now."

Dropping to his knees beside her, he stroked his fingers along her cheek. "I hope this meant for you what it did for me," he said, his eyes misty. "I hope you realize . . ." He faltered, his green eyes burning into hers. "I love you, Abby."

She blinked, then slid her gaze away.

Why does he look at me that way? What more does he want?

"It's not just about the sex," he continued. "I want you to believe my feelings for you run deeper than that."

Pulling the blanket tighter around her, she sat up and nuzzled his neck. "I hope I can learn to please you the way you did me today." Around a yawn, she said, "We'd better head back, Jack. I have to work early tomorrow."

Chapter 17

The next morning, despite the dreary weather, Abby bounced down the sidewalk toward the library on light feet. Fog had settled over the foothills, lending a spooky, haunted quality to downtown. She didn't notice. Her day with Jack had ignited her from within with a glow even the weather could not extinguish.

Complete again. She'd found another man who would love her, cherish their time together, and this time there was no reason for shame. He was old enough to be settled in his own lifestyle and shared with her the same interests, the same passions. History, old books, quiet dinners in his cabin, and fulfilling lovemaking.

Her joy distracted her from the turmoil of her present, more immediate dilemma—her job and the fate of the library. But as she turned to climb the steps, the shocking view brought reality crashing down.

The planting urns were smashed and shattered, and what remained of their lovely fluted edges littered the entryway in jagged concrete chunks. Soil spilled down the steps onto the sidewalk. Delicate flower blooms lay shredded and dying around the planters' clawed feet. The graceful forms had been splattered with something red she hoped was paint.

"Oh no." She fell to her knees. "Oh, no, no." Futilely, she groped through the pile of crushed petals on the steps.

The flowers hadn't simply been yanked out by the roots. They'd been ripped and torn, crushed as though under an angry heel. With tears streaming down her cheeks, she gathered three stems that had somehow escaped complete annihilation, though their blooms were bruised and dangling from their stems. Cradling them against her, she unlocked the door.

She rushed to the back office and dug on the shelf for the vase, the one she'd found in the aisle the day after they'd placed the urns. The one the spirit left for her. Vainly attempting to prop the wilting blooms against the lip of the vase, Abby carried the pathetic arrangement into the meeting room and set it the middle of the long table. She plopped down in the chair, buried her face in her arms, and sobbed.

When a hand touched her shoulder, she bolted upright, her head snapping around. "Elijah?"

It wasn't her ghost. She'd been so lost in her misery, she hadn't even heard the bells on the door.

The odd, pink-haired Miss Cornwell loomed over her. "We done saw what they did," she began, patting Abby's shoulder. "We wuz comin' down here, Willa 'n me, to ask if we could volunteer a few hours a week. Until they get this whole mess straightened out some."

She squeezed her shoulder, and Abby stood.

The older woman pulled her into a stiff, awkward hug. "Don't you worry nothin' about this now, Miss Abigail. Me 'n Jonathan will bring you more urns down later 'safternoon. They'll match t'other ones perfect. Don't be cryin'."

Before Miss Cornwell finished speaking, the door opened again and two more women entered. One Abby didn't know.

The other was Mamie, her most enthusiastic book club member. "That desperate bitch," she muttered.

More women streamed in behind them, and within minutes the lobby was filled with over a dozen sympathetic faces.

"We're all your friends," Mamie said. "We're not going to let Leda Ludwig run you out of here, Abigail."

Over the next few hours, twelve strong-willed women sat around the meeting table and devised a schedule. Each one committed to a four-hour slot, including book club nights and Saturdays for story hour.

Abby sat in stunned awe as these women negotiated, planned, and set down a firm plan with no quibbling, no hesitation. It was the manifestation of a miracle.

Halfway through their session the door opened again, and Dianne whisked in, her purple gauze skirts twirling around her as she nudged the door shut with one generously rounded hip. In her arms she hugged satchels Abby soon discovered held boxes of delicate French pastries, which she ceremoniously spread on platters down the center of the table.

Not two beats behind her, Uncle Armand lumbered in balancing a coffee urn. A bag containing cups and all the coffee fixings swung from one of his burly arms.

He patted Abby's shoulder before heading out. "Jonathan and I will be out front cleaning up the mess." He gestured toward the spread. "Eat something, my dear. You need your strength."

Armand wore the same shirt as the day she first met him. The button-front, light blue linen might once have been one of his finest, but no longer. The front was spattered with old grease spots and flecks of paint. One point of the collar curled up like a snail, and the sleeves had been ripped from the shoulder seams in ragged lines. It was, obviously, his work shirt—when work involved a paintbrush or a screwdriver instead of a sauté pan.

Uncle Armpit.

Anytime she thought of her uncle, all she envisioned was that obscene, mutilated shirt and his skanky, hairy armpits. The first time she'd laid eyes on the "wonderful, sophisticated man" who had stolen her aunt's heart, he'd been dressed like this.

First impressions, she decided then and there, shouldn't always be the memorable ones.

Dianne waited until everyone had chosen a pastry and filled their coffee cups before making her announcement. "Abby, this is my cohort, my network." She waved her arm over the group. "We represent your local Wiccan sector."

Abby swallowed. *Okay, I knew my aunt was into Wicca but—*

Dianne cleared her throat. "We have been accused of some rather distasteful practices over the years, the girls and I, mostly out of ignorant fear. I assure you, we mean no harm. There is only one woman in this town who fits the commonly accepted definition of witch and better than any of us here."

A rumble of murmurs passed through the group. Abby glanced around the table, then up at her aunt.

Di continued, "Leda Ludwig is a sick woman. No matter. We're not going to let her rob us of one of this town's historical icons."

Alarm rose in Abby's chest like bile. "No, Auntie. I told you, no witchcraft. If I can't win this battle on my own—"

"We're not that kind of witch, child. While we don't intend to allow Leda to get her way, we also want to help her." She then looked out over the gathering. "Not one sister shall be left behind."

A cheer went up around the table. She waited, then finished her speech. "Armand and I are sponsoring a fundraiser dinner to support our public library. I'm asking all of you to take a pack of tickets out into the community. With the proceeds from this dinner, we could well fund not only additional staff, but also a generous acquisition fund for modernizing the collection our library has to offer."

When the last of the Friends of the Library Committee, as Dianne officially named the group, filed out the front door, Abby was buzzing and numb. Never had she expected such community support. She always knew she had a cheering squad in her aunt. What she never realized was that her

Wiccan network, as well as her amazing husband, were such caring givers.

"I'm so sorry, Armand. I'll never call you Uncle Armpit again," she mumbled as she hugged her uncle at the door.

He pushed her away and smiled into her eyes. "What? You think I do not treasure a nickname so unique?"

Then they both laughed and hugged again.

He whispered in her ear, "If your aunt had her way, this shirt would disappear in the rag heap. I've lost count of the times I rescued it from that sad fate. Me? I love it."

Jack awoke that morning with a mixture of joy and foreboding clenched in his chest. Crossing that threshold with Abby, for him, had been a sacred moment. He'd known all along he was falling in love with her. With their consummation, he could no longer deny it. Thoughts of her filled his mind and his heart, and he couldn't wait to see her again, smell her unique scent, and hold her in his arms.

Why, oh why had he blurted out the "L" word so soon? She was young and still messed up from a disastrous beginning to her sex life. Should he be surprised she didn't jump to say, "I love you, too"?

It had been an eternity since he'd let his guard down, and he agonized now, realizing, again, he'd given away his heart. He prayed he hadn't made the same mistake again.

By noon he decided he couldn't stay away any longer. Dressed and ready for his one o'clock class, he jumped into his car. He hadn't even made it up to the speed limit on the highway before he pulled out his cell and dialed the library number.

"Hey. Happy Monday." He tried to keep his tone light, fully aware he was not succeeding. Even he could hear the tension in his voice.

"Good afternoon, Dr. Wood. How are you this fine Monday?" Abby replied.

He wasn't sure how to read her. Was she being distant and formal? Or just kidding? *Oh God, please don't let me screw this up now.*

"I had a great day yesterday, Abby. I wanted you to know. A special, wonderful time."

He was gushing. Of course he had a good time. He got laid, didn't he? Damn. Why couldn't he have come up with something more suave to say?

There was an unusually long pause on the other end of the line, and he started to sweat.

I've done it now. I've botched his whole thing. I—

"Thank you so much, Mrs. Beardsley. Yes, we're having book club on the fifteenth. Looking forward to seeing you then." A pause. Then Abby continued in a hushed whisper, "I'm sorry, Jack. We've been surprisingly busy today, from late morning on. Ever since the meeting."

"Meeting? What meeting?" he asked, relieved but confused.

"You wouldn't believe it. All the ladies, those friends of Aunt Dianne's. They all showed up this morning and held a meeting. Someone's signed up for a four-hour shift every day this month. They're volunteering to help me keep things going here."

He could almost hear her smile.

"It's a miracle. Especially after what I found this morning," she added. In the background, the bells jingled again. "Oh. Gotta go. There's a group of the college kids I promised to help start on their summer projects."

"Abby," he began. "I—"

"I'm closing at five today. Wanna come by and hang out?" she asked.

"Yeah. Sure. Be there at five."

"'Kay, bye." The call disconnected.

Instead of feeling better, he felt infinitely worse. She'd sounded so casual. They'd just made love, for God's sakes. Didn't it mean to her what it meant to him? Or was he still just somebody to "hang out" with?

Maybe this was what she was used to. Perhaps the sex had been all there really was between her and this Cameron guy. Yes, in fact, she'd told him that quite plainly.

Maybe casual sex, the old "friends with benefits" arrangement, is all Abigail Stryker was looking for.

As Jack pulled his car into the college parking lot and turned the key, he glanced over to see Leda stepping out of her vehicle right beside him. He swiped a hand down over his face.

Christ. Exactly what he didn't need right now was a face-to-face with Leda Ludwig.

She grinned with exaggerated enthusiasm in his direction. "Mornin', Professor. How are things?" she chirped.

She was much more casually attired than usual. But this was summer, after all. Summer class schedules were part-time at best, and most of the regular faculty wasn't even on campus in June and July.

Still, he hadn't remembered his boss dressing quite so laid back—ever. No dark, tailored business suit today. Her bright pink sundress flowed around her legs as she moved. Sparkly bobs swung from her earlobes. Even her sunglass frames were pink.

"You're looking summery today, Leda. How are you feeling?" he asked, then winced.

Damn, there he went again. He couldn't seem to keep his tongue from tangling up with his feet today.

Her smile flattened, though only briefly before blooming again.

"Better, much better, thanks, Jack," she replied. She tipped her chin up and regarded him with a look that made his skin crawl. "Thank you for asking."

They walked together into the office, and he was not only surprised but a little creeped out when she slid her arm through his. The look on Clara's face mirrored how he was feeling. Her eyes rounded as she peered over her half-glasses, and he couldn't tell whether it was a shock or disgust twisting the corners of her mouth.

"Hey, kids, how's it going?" she asked, her voice a note or two higher than usual.

He twisted free from Leda's hold and headed straight for the mailroom. Prickles stood on the back of his neck when he looked up from sifting through the paperwork to see her standing in the doorway.

"Jack," she began in a hoarse whisper. Her gaze darted back over her shoulder in Clara's direction. "Could I have a word with you please?"

"Sure," he shot back. "I'll come to your office in a few."

"No. I'll come to your classroom." She checked the diamond watch on her left wrist. "You've got at least, what, twenty minutes or so before your class, right?"

Uh-oh.

His mind raced as he climbed the stairs to the third floor. It was almost as though he could hear his thoughts echoing in the empty stairwell.

His classroom. Why not her office? She wanted him on his turf, not hers. *What in heaven's name is this woman planning to pull now?*

He'd barely emptied the day's handouts out of his briefcase before a soft knock sounded, preceding Leda's appearance in the doorway. She slipped in and pushed the door to click behind her.

"Jack, we need to talk," she said in a sultry tone that made his stomach queasy.

"About what?"

As she approached he made a deliberate effort to keep the

desk between them, feigning intense interest in organizing his class materials.

She sauntered up to the desk's edge and rested on one hand. The neckline of her silky dress dipped low, revealing the curves of breasts seemingly uninhibited by any undergarments. He cleared his throat and swallowed hard, not sure if the wave of nausea was from the view or his nerves.

For what seemed like an hour, she didn't say anything. He kept his attention on his class materials, sifting and re-sorting handouts already collated. Maybe they' started her on some new drug, and it was causing a personality change. Maybe Dennis finally walked out on her, and she needs a friend. Maybe it was a full moon and she was coming into heat . . .

His stomach lurched, and for an awful moment, he feared he'd lose his breakfast all over his desk.

Her gaze burned into the side of his face. Lifting one hip to perch on the edge of his desk, she angled herself so her chin rested on one shoulder, regarding him through sleepy, half-closed eyes. She'd bathed in some expensive perfume that was making his eyes water and sting.

"Dennis just doesn't understand me." She murmured the words with the plaintive purr of a lost kitten.

So this didn't have anything to do with work. An even bigger alarm went off in Jack's head, and he could clearly see where this was headed. Thinking fast, he held up one finger, then pointed to the breast pocket of his shirt where his cell phone was stashed.

"Got it on vibrate," he said apologetically. He pulled the phone out and mashed a button, holding it to his ear. "Hey, Abby, how are you doing today? Did you have fun yesterday?" He turned away and strode toward the windows, lowering his voice as though in conversation.

In reality, there was nothing but a dial tone.

He shivered, remembering the change in Leda's expression before he turned away. At the mention of Abby's name, Leda's face underwent a terrible metamorphosis. Her eyes narrowed to slits as her brow crinkled in an abnormal contortion.

He dragged his make-believe phone call out as long as he could, glancing at his watch repeatedly. Ten more minutes until class started. He made a silent vow that if just one of his students showed up early today they were getting an automatic A on the next test.

When he finally faced Leda, she'd pushed off the desk and stood glaring at him, her hands on her hips. He had never been close to a snake threatening to strike. Her stance was as coiled and cocked as any pissed off cobra, and the hair on the back of his neck rose.

He spoke again into the phone. "Look, hon, my class starts in ten. I'll be by at five to pick you up." He did his best to imagine Abby's voice on the other end, even as the dial tone switched to the recorded message.

Fearing Leda might hear what he was really listening to, he quickly added, "Love you too, babe. See you later." He touched the end button.

As he slipped the phone back into his pocket he grimaced in Leda's direction and offered an apology. "Sorry, Leda. Now, what was it you wanted to see me about?"

For a moment, he wasn't even sure it was Leda Ludwig standing before him. Her face had become distorted, twisted with some kind of hideous rage he neither understood nor felt equipped to handle. A full thirty seconds elapsed before she spoke. When she did, she sounded possessed.

"I can't believe you're actually fucking that bitch," she hissed. "Bitch. What am I saying? She a witch. She's a bona fide bride of the devil, just like her silver-haired whore of an aunt."

A frenzied laugh cackled out of Leda, and he staggered a few steps back. His hands gripped the edge of the ledge along the bottom of the blackboard.

"How does it feel to know Beelzebub has been poking around in the same slot where you are, Jack? Does it make you feel different? Is it a thrill or does it burn, like hellfire?"

His stomach clutched and turned over on itself. *She's gone completely mad.*

A cold sweat covered his entire body as his mind raced. She was a woman, but she could still become violent. What if she had a gun, or a knife? Even if she didn't, who would ever believe he was trying to defend himself if he left a bruise on her?

Holding her gaze was one of the most difficult tasks he'd ever faced, but he was afraid to turn his back on her. He reached into his pocket again, retrieving the phone. As he lifted it to his ear, he kept his tone even and calm.

"Leda, I'm going to call Dennis now. He'll come and take you home, and you can get some rest. You look awfully tired."

Before he could dial, the classroom door burst open, and three giggling girls shuffled through, too engrossed in their own conversation to sense the volatile scene they happened upon. Jack wasn't sure whether to heave a sigh of relief or tense further, fearing for the students' safety in addition to his own.

Fortunately, the spell had been broken. Without a word or another sound, Leda spun and bolted out of the room. He crumpled into a sodden mass in his chair, thinking he'd never before enjoyed so much the childish chatter of the students huddling in the back of his classroom.

By the time his class ended at four, he was exhausted. He had problems keeping his mind on teaching—unusual for him. Once he stood at the head of a classroom, he typically settled into a zone, and the rest of the world melted away.

After the encounter with Leda, and with the worry of Abby on his mind, his attention strayed.

He'd been tempted to end class early, but was too afraid Leda might use that against him. Not for the first time in his life, he found himself wedged between a sense of duty and what he really wanted to do. All he could think about as he descended the stairs that afternoon was how desperately he wanted to be holding Abby in his arms.

As he reached the office at the end of the hallway, he stopped and peered around the corner through the lobby windows, trying to see if Leda's Mercedes was still parked out front.

"She's been gone almost three hours," Clara said, startling him as she appeared from within the employee lounge. "Left in a big hurry. What was up with her today anyway?"

"I'm not sure, Clara. Sometimes I think Mrs. Ludwig . . ."

Be careful what you say. You never know who might sleep with the enemy.

"I think she has a lot on her mind lately," he finished.

Clara's eyebrows nearly disappeared on either side of her dark widow's peak. She chuckled low in her throat. "I wonder sometimes how much Leda's mind has to do with her actions."

Jack drove into Caldwell and parked a half-block away from the library. It was still thirty minutes until closing. He needed a few minutes to gather his thoughts so he opened his windows and cut the engine. Breathing deep and slumping back in his seat, he went over what happened within the last twenty-four hours.

A freaking roller-coaster ride, complete with all the same extremes of emotion. From overwhelming joy to brain-numbing terror.

He was still sitting there when the old blue pickup truck approached from the north side of town, pulled over to the curb and parked, facing in the wrong direction a few cars in front of his. When the driver emerged, he recognized Jonathan Cornwell. The big man wrestled something large and heavy out of the back of the truck. A planting urn like the ones Abby bought earlier this spring. Jack turned to look up at the library entrance.

What he saw brought added another emotion to the ride—rage. What was left of the original planters, smeared with dark red paint or blood, lay in a heap near the curb.

His instinct overrode logic. He lurched out of the car and met Jonathan at the base of the steps. The massive man stood, legs planted wide apart, hugging a new planter lightly against his chest as though it weighed less than an ounce. Jack was a tall man, over six feet, yet standing up close to this mammoth human he felt as if he'd been dropped into Lilliput.

"What's happened here?" he demanded. The words came out foreign, threatening, even to him. He cleared his throat, reassessing the size of the man before him. "The planters . . . what happened, Jonathan?"

"We figure she musta done it," Jonathan mumbled. "That Ludwig bitch. We're making it right."

Jack took the steps two at a time ahead of him and burst through the front door. The doorbells clanged insensitively into the silence.

Abby peeked around from behind a rear stack. She was alone. "Hey," she said in a hushed voice.

"Hey."

How did he handle this encounter. Casual? Loving? Concerned? Maniacal?

His brain may have had other plans. His gut went with maniacal. "What the fuck happened here today?"

Abby blinked, then smirked. "Why Professor Wood, I don't think I ever heard you drop the F-bomb."

He swiped a hand over his face and shook his head. "I'm sorry, Abby. It's been a hellish day." He moved toward her, one hand motioning back toward the entrance. "Who did this?"

"Not sure, but it's all good now. The Cornwells are coming with replacements. And I have volunteers."

"They're here," he replied. "Abby, are you okay?"

His question went far beyond the ruined planters, and when she raised her eyes to meet his, he could tell she understood that. Thank God.

"Jack," she said quietly.

He came forward and laid his hands on her shoulders. "Are you okay? I mean, really okay? Not just the planter thing, but—"

"I'm fine. I'm great. I'm wonderful." She pressed both hands against his chest and looked up into his eyes. "Now that you're here."

His heart did a triple back flip somersault as he gazed down into those dark, mysterious eyes. Here was a connection he'd never imagined. She must feel it too. That same irresistible pull ever since the first day he laid eyes on her.

As they stood there embracing in between the J to L stacks and the L to Q's, he was certain he'd crossed a crucial life threshold. As he held Abby, stroking her silky, crooked hair and breathing in a scent he was sure had an intoxicating effect on his logic, he murmured, "I love you, Abigail. I've loved you from the first day I laid eyes you."

The scent of pipe smoke settled like incense around them.

Chapter 18

The next morning at precisely nine o'clock, Dennis Ludwig clomped up the steps to the library. This was a conversation he had been dreading ever since the night of the council meeting. He had hired this nice young girl, for Christ's sakes. How could he face her now? What on earth was he going to say? He'd gotten her tangled up in this huge, complicated mess and hoped she could somehow find a way to sort it out.

Something he'd been unable to do. How could he expect someone else to save the library from the scathing, determined scythe of Leda's ambition? In essence, he'd brought in an innocent outsider to help him do battle against his own wife.

Pathetic. I'm simply pathetic.

When he crept through the door, Abby was busy at the reception desk, the glow of the computer monitor casting an odd blue cast over her face. As she looked up, her expression transformed into a smile. Relief washed over him like a warm wave.

Maybe she doesn't hate my guts yet. But she will. Very soon.

"Abby, good morning." He'd rehearsed what he planned to say. Now that he stood face to face with her, his mind went blank.

"Hey, Dennis. How are you feeling? I've been worried about you ever since the other night." She stood and came around the counter. "You didn't look well at all. And how's Leda feeling?"

"I'm okay, Abigail. I'm more worried about you. How you're handling all this," he said. He shoved his hands in his pockets and looked at the floor. "You never should have had to deal these issues."

She came to his side and placed a hand on his shoulder. "Dennis, I'm young and I'm strong. And more stubborn than you know. We'll get through this. As long as I have your support, how can I fail?"

When he looked up at her again, he felt a hundred years old. He heaved a sigh. "I'm going to do everything I can to save this place. It's a legacy in this town. It's our history," he said. "Leda, she doesn't understand that. At least, that's what I used to think. Now I think she doesn't give a damn. All she cares about are her own ambitions."

As though saying her name caused her to appear, the door burst open, and Leda stood in the entryway. She advanced halfway across the space between them, leaving the door standing open behind her.

"I should have known I'd find you here," she spat. "Here, in your alma mater, fraternizing with the enemy."

He took two steps toward her, and she shot one hand up in front of her like a shield.

"Don't, Dennis. I've no time for your excuses." Her voice was unnaturally high, tinny, as if she'd been sucking on a helium balloon. Her eyes were wild and glazed. "I realize what's been going on here. You're trading me in, aren't you? This pretty young thing is a lot younger than I am. Time for some fresher kill, is it?"

"Leda, you're being ridiculous. Let me take you home. We can call Dr. Fagerty. I think maybe he needs to adjust your medication."

"No!" Her scream echoed through the quiet emptiness of the building like a single gunshot. She stomped forward, swishing past him until she was toe-to-toe with Abby. "You're going down, bitch." She poked Abby in the chest with one blood-red manicured talon. "This whole fucking mausoleum is going down, in smoke if need be. I will not be beaten on this issue. If anyone should know how determined I am once I make up my mind, it should be Dennis."

The tension was thick in the air, and Abby became aware of an odor even more tangible. It filtered in quickly, as though someone had just lit a pipe and blown smoke directly into the midst of their confrontation.

Dennis stretched out to grab Leda's shoulder, but she twisted away. Then she turned on him. "You," she spat the words, "are a worm-spined, washed-up old man. You've gone senile on me, Dennis. The most pathetic case of Alzheimer's dementia I've ever seen. You're lucky I don't move you into a nursing home where they can keep an eye on you, keep you out of trouble. And keep you out of my way."

Abby winced as his form wilted like a withering flower.

What an insensitive, sadistic bitch. How can she treat this kind old man this way? Is she possessed?

At that moment something snapped in the air, like an electric spark from a shorted-out wire. The hairs on Abby's arms stood as though lightning struck close by. Dennis must have heard it too because he flinched, his panicked gaze flashing around the room.

The lights blinked, swelling from blindingly bright to darkness. A beeping noise emanated from the telephone on her desk as though she'd left the receiver off the hook, yet it still sat cradled on its base. Movement above the reception desk caught her attention.

She looked up and watched in disbelief as the hands on the large wall clock moved too fast, then faster—*in reverse*. More and more rapidly, the hands spun counterclockwise, a gray blur against the white of the face. The clock vibrated against the wall until she was sure it would fly off at any moment.

She turned toward Leda, whose mouth gaped as she started backing away. Behind her, the front door slammed shut, and the deadbolt struck home with a loud snap.

The bells hanging from the knob swung wildly, yet didn't make a sound.

Abby came forward and huddled against Dennis, who wrapped his arms around her. He was trembling almost as violently as she was. The pipe smoke was now visible, flowing around them in a kind of oscillating, ethereal fog.

The first book came all the way from the rear stacks, sailing past the reception desk and whizzing so close to her ear she heard the whoosh. Hurtling with incredible force and speed, the impact came so fast she didn't have time to react. The book struck Leda flat on the side of her head.

She staggered, a sound bursting from her that could have been horror, pain, or pure rage. She clutched the side of her face, her eyes owl-wide as she stared at Dennis first, then Abby. She glared down at the book lying at her feet, front cover up.

"*Witch.*" She hissed the title with so much hatred a chill slithered up Abby's spine.

Leda whirled toward them then, moving in until her face hovered only inches away from Abby's face. Dennis staggered back a step, dragging her with him. He held out his arm.

"Don't you come any closer, Leda. I don't want to have to hurt you," he said.

In truth, his words sounded more fearful than threatening. Abby could feel the shudders quaking his body.

Leda's features were distorted, twisted so she was almost unrecognizable. Her heavy makeup and bright lipstick gave her face the look of a demented clown. Abby's stomach lurched as the expensive perfume she'd bathed in mingled with the sourness of her hot breath.

"You evil witch," Leda rasped. "Do you think your little display of witchcraft is going to frighten me? Not so much, devil whore. Your black magic trickery doesn't scare me one bit."

Seconds later, the second book came whistling through the air from behind them. It whizzed over their heads and struck Leda flat against her chest. She staggered two steps backward before regaining her balance by grabbing the edge of a chair set against the meeting room table.

With the wind knocked out of her, she was wheezing and gasping for breath when the next book fell out of nowhere. The huge volume thudded squarely on top of her head. She crumpled to the ground in an unconscious heap.

Dennis stood holding Abby in disbelief and shock for a brief moment. But after his wife hit the floor, he broke free and rushed to kneel at Leda's side. He picked up her hand and rubbed it between his own, muttering to her in a gentle tone. Abby felt such pity for him tears stung her eyes.

"Leda, honey, are you okay? Come on, babe. It's all over now."

Abby ran to the desk and dialed 9-1-1, and within what seemed like seconds sirens resonated down Main Street and the flash of red lights pulsed through the front windows. Leda remained motionless on the floor. Abby stood huddled against the reception counter, trembling uncontrollably, hugging herself and chewing on one knuckle. Her legs grew rubbery, and she slid down the side of the counter to rest in a crouch on the floor.

When they burst through the door, one of the EMTs came to her and took one wrist in his hand.

"Are you okay? Are you hurt?" he asked as he felt for her pulse.

She shook her head and answered clearly. "I'm perfectly fine. I'm not hurt. Take care of them," she said, nodding in Dennis and Leda's direction.

As the EMT's strapped Leda's immobile form to the gurney, Jack rushed in. He looked from Leda's limp form to Dennis, who was bending over her, still crooning.

Jack stooped and wrapped an arm around Abby's waist, lifting her to her feet. "What happened?" he asked.

Her armor of strength shattered into pieces, and she sobbed into his shoulder.

As the ambulance pulled away, a small crowd gathered outside on the sidewalk. She clung to him in the doorway.

"It happened again, didn't it?" he asked.

She nodded. "Worse. Much worse this time. It was the strangest thing I've ever seen, Jack. The lights went crazy. Books came flying out of nowhere. And the clock . . ." She closed her eyes and shook her head slowly. "It was the most frightening thing I've ever seen."

He took hold of her shoulders. "Abby, do you know what a poltergeist is?"

She blinked, then cocked her head, thinking. "I saw the movie years ago, but—"

"No. I'm not talking Hollywood here." He searched her eyes. "Your Aunt Dianne. Do you think she would be able to tell us something more about poltergeist activity? How to stop it from happening?"

"Probably, but I can't leave. There's nobody else here to—"

"The last thing we need now is for somebody else to get hurt. Lock it up. Put a sign on the door that says 'Temporarily Closed Due to Emergency.' We've got to find out what's going on here."

By the time she and Jack got to the front door of Ancient Healings, the group from the library had reconvened there. They were spilling out the door and huddled on the front porch, chattering in hushed groups. Mamie Greer spotted Abby first, and when she said Abby's name, all talking ceased.

She climbed the steps in front of Jack. “Where’s Aunt Di? And what’s going on here?”

“Your aunt is inside on the phone with the hospital. What the fuck happened down there, Abby?” Mamie posed with her hands on her hips in that no-nonsense, don’t-you-dare-try-to-lie-to-me posture that must have been extremely effective when she was teaching fifth graders. “Dianne watched the EMTs take Leda away. Did that fucking bitch attack you?”

Abby shook her head, unable to suppress the slight smirk she felt guilty for wearing. “If she had, do you think she would have been the one leaving in an ambulance?” Then she sobered. “Verbally, yes. I guess I had some backup I hadn’t been aware of.”

All heads turned to glare at Jack. “You hit Leda?” Three of the now excited, high-pitched voices rang out in unison.

His eyes widened, and he backed down a step, holding both hands up. “I had nothing to do with it. They already had Leda strapped to a gurney when I came in.”

At that moment the generous form of Dianne pushed through the group clogging the entryway to her shop. She stopped inches away and grabbed Abby’s shoulders. “Are you okay?”

She nodded. “I’m fine. Leda’s not.”

“What happened?”

Abby sighed and massaged her temples. Jack came up behind her.

“Is there somewhere we can all sit down and discuss this?” he asked. He addressed Dianne, then glanced around at the group surrounding them. “I think we need all of your help.”

Since there was nowhere in Aunt Di’s shop big enough to accommodate a meeting of that many people, Mamie suggested they head back to the library.

Jack spoke up. “I don’t know, Mamie. Some pretty crazy stuff just happened in there. I don’t want anybody else to get hurt.”

Mamie scoffed and flipped her hand. “Believe me, Jack, the only one in the path of the wrath of that ghost just left here in an ambulance.”

Murmurs and nods rippled through the group. Dianne added, “If anybody can handle this spirit, Jack Wood, it’s this bunch right here. Who knows? Maybe we can even convince Elijah himself to somehow tell us what he really wants.”

They headed back down the block with Abby leading, Jack clutching her arm. Not sure what she would find inside, she unlocked the door and creaked it open. Surely, books would still be scattered all about, and she wondered if the hands of the clock would still be whirling in their crazed, backward spin. Reaching for Jack’s hand and pulling him close beside her, she took three steps into the lobby and froze, blinking.

The books that had somehow come free of their places to assault Leda were nowhere to be seen. Nothing seemed out of place, and the clock’s hands rested properly in position to indicate the correct time of half-past ten.

Once they were settled around the meeting room table, Dianne spoke. “Poltergeist means noisy or mischievous spirit. It sounds to me the spirit residing in this place has certainly earned that title.”

Jack, close beside Abby, said, “Dianne, I know Abby has made you promise not to interfere with any sort of spells. It’s clear now, though, that what’s going on here lies beyond the realm of our understanding.”

A stout woman wearing a wildly colorful floral shift cleared her throat and clasped her hands together on the table. She directed her gaze to Dianne. “There’s the cleansing ritual, Di. But that’s for negative spirits. It sounds to me that what we're dealing with isn't necessarily a negative force. At least, not all of the time."

"You're right, Wisteria. This spirit only acts like a poltergeist when he's unhappy," Dianne said, "with a person or a state of affairs."

"He only tossed a book at me once, on my first day," Abby said. "It didn't hit me, and I honestly think he was just trying to get my attention."

Mamie said, "Well he certainly got the attention of the two ladies who tried to take over for Dana when she left. And I think it's safe to say he's not so fond of Leda Ludwig."

"Leda's the one who seems to be the evil spirit in this whole scenario," another woman said, one who's name Abby couldn't remember.

"You're right," Abby said. "Leda certainly qualifies as Elijah's enemy. She's the one who wants this place shut down and all these precious antique books sold off or trashed."

During the entire discussion, nothing happened to indicate a supernatural presence. No pipe smoke. No books falling or whizzing through the air. The windows remained closed and latched.

He's not evil. Harry wants something, and badly. I think he wants me to help him.

Halfway through the discussion, she stood, silencing them with upraised hands.

"I don't think our spirit needs to be 'cleansed' out of here. I do think he's trying to protect the future of this library. He's also searching for something." She shook her head. "He leaves books out for me, sometimes open to a particular page." Her gaze traveled from one face to another. "I think he wants help. Maybe with something that doesn't have anything to do with Leda Ludwig at all."

"What books, Abby? Can you list the titles? The page numbers?" Mamie asked.

"Aside from the word 'bell' in the title, no, I've seen no pattern." She promised to record as many as she could remember, as well as any future ones.

"Maybe, if we have the list in front of us, we can brainstorm and figure out what it is this spirit wants," Dianne said as they all rose to leave. She squeezed Abby's hand, then pulled her in for a quick hug. "Don't worry, hon. We'll help you whatever way we can."

"I know you will," she said, reaching for Jack's hand as they walked the ladies to the door. As they filed out, each one bid her farewell with the customary Wiccan wish.

"Blessed Be."

January 14th, 1890

My Dearest Elijah,

Our trip to the city had not a happy ending. I am frightened. We have had so few years together. Now it seems I may lose you, or part of you, far before I am ready to let you go. I must be strong for both of us. I will not further burden your troubled mind with my feminine ramblings. Starting today, my fears bleed only in ink on paper. The words thus released from my heart will bring me comfort.

So soon, too soon. At first, small oversights. A window left open after you had your pipe, even in the dead of winter. A book you were enjoying, sharing with me in discussion, and suddenly you have no recollection. Our sweet old mare Sassy left in the traces all night, tied up outside the barn.

What pains me most is to see how your confusion frightens even you.

The ledgers are at odds with the bank. You have been precise, always. But the discrepancies hardly concern you. The facets of your mind, like the smoothed edges of a tumbled stone, wax dull.

Dr. Emerson called it "senile dementia." He claims the impairment strikes only a small percentage of the elderly, and there is no known way to stop the deterioration. Unfortunately, it appears you reside within that sad percentage. Such a shame, he said. For a man of your years, your body is strong and healthy. Only your mind's strength wanes.

There are considerable years between us, dear husband. I knew the day we were bound, your life might end much sooner than mine. Now it seems you may leave me alone even though you still sit close by me. You have given me ten years of unspeakable joy. No matter what lies ahead for you, for us, I will remain by your side,

Faithfully in love,
Isabelle

Chapter 19

Dianne and her friends hadn't been gone more than five minutes when Abby smelled the pipe smoke. She looked up at Jack.

He nodded. "I smell it too."

He followed her back to the reading corner where the window now stood open by several inches. The smoke was so thick it was visible, floating like fog. Three books were neatly stacked on the windowsill. Abby plopped down in the chair as he lifted the stack and read off the titles.

"*For Whom the Bell Tolls*, Ernest Hemingway. *The Bell Jar*, by Sylvia Plath. *The Bell Messenger*, Robert Cornuke." He turned toward her. "It's bells, all right, Abby. But what does he mean?"

She covered her face with her hands and moaned, "What are you trying to tell me, Elijah? I don't understand. So it's bells. What with the bells? What am I supposed to be looking for?"

"It's almost like it's some kind of code he's communicating in." Jack paced the aisle between the stacks. "Those bells on the door. Where did they come from?"

"Aunt Di says they've been here forever. Dana liked knowing when somebody came through the door, especially if she was alone."

"That can't be it." He scowled and raked a hand through his hair. "What about the bell mounted in the lobby?"

"That's from the school where Isabelle used to teach."

"Okay," he said. "Might be a clue."

"Do you suppose he called Isabelle *Belle*?"

He lifted his shoulders. “I suppose. But why is he still looking for her here? According to the records, she died years before he did.”

A long silence hung between them, pipe smoke scenting the air like incense.

Then Abby jumped up and grabbed his arm. “Jack, Elijah’s not buried with Isabelle. Didn’t you tell me that?”

He nodded. “Elijah is buried in Boston, where he was born and grew up. And no, Isabelle is not with him. There aren’t any records to show—”

“Didn’t Elena tell you there was a family cemetery for the Laramys? Somewhere here in Caldwell? Wouldn’t Martin Laramy know where that plot is?”

“Even if he did, Abby,” he said, scowling, “I doubt he’d share that information with us.”

She whispered, “I’ll bet Elena does.”

An hour later, Abby and Jack met his sister at the last gas station on the edge of town before the winding mountain highway began.

Elena hopped out of her car and trotted over to his open window. “What’s going on, Jack? What’s happened?”

“Some really weird stuff, sis,” he said. “The kind of stuff I swore I didn’t believe in.”

She raised a brow.

“Leda’s in the hospital again,” Abby said. “Elijah beat her up with a bunch of books.”

“What?” Elena chuckled. “Elijah? Elijah who?”

“The ghost,” Abby said.

Jack shrugged. “Listen, sis. Don’t ask me to explain it. We just need to see where this Laramy family cemetery is. Is it somewhere we can access without a four-wheeler? Without getting arrested for trespassing?”

She nodded. “It’s not far off the upper end of Hoods Creek Road. It borders on public land, I think. There’s even a parking area nearby.”

They followed Elena’s small red van northwest out of town on the narrow, winding Hoods Creek Road. Abby saw few homes along the rural, country lane. The occasional small farms dotting the lush valley grew scarcer with each mile until they started up the mountain in earnest, the road having been cut into the steep grade on the north side. She figured they’d driven about eight miles, and it was slow going. Elena’s van crept to a crawl before every blind curve.

Finally, after what seemed like hours, Elena slowed once again, this time with a left turn signal blinking. Ahead in a small clearing, a makeshift parking area was delineated with huge old railroad ties set around the perimeter. It was unpaved, but speckles of white gravel, rapidly being reclaimed by the forest floor, defined its purpose.

It was nearly noon now, and the late summer sun was doing its best to burn through the sheltering density of the branches overhead without much success. As Abby got out she smelled the dampness of deep forest. A deerfly buzzed around her head, and she swatted at it. Jack had gone around to the back of his car and was digging in the backpack he always carried.

“Better wipe down with some of this,” he said and produced a vial of yellowish oil.

Elena wrinkled her nose. “What is it? Another one of your homemade concoctions?”

“Cinnamon and citronella oil. It’ll keep those deerflies and mosquitoes from inviting you to lunch—as the main course. How far from here is this place, anyway?” he asked.

As they wiped the fragrant oil over their arms and on the backs of their necks, Elena pointed to a path leading off to one side of the makeshift parking lot. “Not far. There’s a clearing a few hundred yards down that way.”

"A graveyard? Back here in the middle of the woods?" Abby asked, scowling as she examined the oily residue on her hands. "How on earth did you know it was here?"

"One of my daycare moms grew up on the piece of land right next to the old Laramy homestead. She said when they were kids they used to come out here at night, sit around and tell ghost stories and scare the daylights out of each other."

Jack handed Abby a cloth to dry her hands. "I think just being out here after dark would scare the bejesus out of me," she said.

They followed the vaguely defined path, not nearly as well delineated as the hiking trail Jack had taken her on. He walked ahead of them, lifting hanging vines and swiping at spider webs with a stick he picked up at the start.

Elena was right. They'd been walking only minutes when Abby caught sight of a bright clearing up ahead.

A rusted, metal railing edged a patch of land barely twenty feet square, the vines and underbrush of the encroaching woods winding through it on all sides. Set amidst the wild entanglement of untamed forest, the plot seemed surreal. The iron fence was barely knee high and had no gate. Six arched headstones dotted the plot—two at the rear and four standing in a row before them. The rear stones appeared older and were tilted, sunken off-kilter into the damp moss surrounding them.

They all fell silent as they passed through the opening in the fence. Although the burial ground had obviously not been cared for in decades, the grasses growing over the graves were low and soft green, stunted by the lack of sunlight. The carving on the two rear stones was so worn Abby at first couldn't read them.

Jack stooped near one and ran his finger over the letters. "Joshua Laramy. The numbers are almost gone. It looks like the date of death might be . . . 1837? Or maybe that's a nine. 1839."

"Would that have been Isabelle's father?" Abby asked. "No, couldn't be. Must have been her grandfather, or maybe an uncle."

He nodded. "I can't read what's written on this one at all," he said, pointing to the other tilted stone beside it. "I'd guess it was his wife."

Elena was stooping near one of the four stones lined up in the center of the plot. "I can read these up here better. Jasper Laramy, born 1823, died 1888. And here's his wife, must be. Edna Laramy, born 1836, died 1865. Wow, she wasn't even thirty when she died."

"Medical care back then wasn't what it is now," Jack said. "There were all kinds of epidemics, especially right after the war ended. Typhus, cholera, smallpox. Besides," he added, "a lot of women, especially out in the country like this, died in childbirth. Or from complications afterward."

Abby listened half-heartedly to their conversation, scanning the two headstones Elena and Jack were examining before wandering on to the last two beside them. These were set closer together than the other stones, almost touching. One was half the size of the other.

She lowered to her knees before them as she read the inscriptions, and her heart clutched in her chest. "Here she is."

The carving had survived amazingly well, much in contrast to those around it. Plus, the stone itself appeared different than the other two, slicker and shinier, like polished granite. An elaborate etching of a vine trailed below the curved upper edge, hovering over engraving cut deep into the stone, still plainly legible.

"Isabelle Laramy, born March 22, 1862. Died September 16, 1892." Her throat felt tight as she read. She struggled to contain her emotion as she read the inscription on the small stone set beside Isabelle's.

Shaped identically to her mother's, the baby's marker also bore the ivy engraving above the name. On top, a stone sculpture of a lamb rested along the curved upper edge. Its features had been smoothed by time and weather.

"Baby Girl Laramy. Born and died September 16, 1892." Abby's voice broke as she shot a glance at Jack and Elena who stood behind her.

The smaller letters carved near the bottom of the tiny stone read: *Sweetest Angel, Rest Forever in Your Mother's Arms.*

As Jack drove them back to town, Abby remained quiet and pensive beside him. It was just as well. He wasn't in the mood to talk as he wrestled with newly exposed emotions. Today's discovery had rocked him.

He was glad they'd found Isabelle's resting place, though he didn't know how that knowledge would appease Elijah Harvey's unrest. How do you get a message to a ghost? Surely not as simple as sending a card or an email with someone's forwarding address.

What had upset him was finding the baby's grave. Nowhere, in any of his research, had there been mention of a child. Of course, that made sense—if the baby died the day it was born, or was stillborn, no birth certificate would have been filed.

Why, then, after his death, would Elijah have been hauled back to Boston instead of being buried with his wife and child? Surely, a man with his money and influence would have made a will, or some prior arrangements, for disposition of his remains. What happened here, all those years ago, to tear a family apart like that, literally? Jack's gut told him that fact alone was enough to keep a spirit trapped in between this world and the next.

He knew, all too well, the agony when not only the woman you love, but also your child, is snatched from your life.

Over the years, he had almost convinced himself he'd gotten over it. He'd managed to cover the scar and push the lingering ache down into the cellar of his soul, clamping a heavy steel barrier over the wound. Seeing the inscription on that tiny headstone cut the bolt and flung open the door. The memories sprang to life and sliced through his heart with as much raw agony as they had that horrible day so long ago.

Abby hadn't asked to be taken home, and he was glad. He needed to be with her, talk to her, especially now. He needed to share with her the dark secrets in his past, just as she'd done with him.

He took her back to his cabin and arm in arm, they walked around the side of the house to the patio. He settled her in the loveseat, then knelt on one knee to search her face.

She gazed off into the woods beyond the yard, avoiding his eyes. "I'm not sure why that affected me so. I figured we'd find Isabelle. It was such a shock to find . . . the baby too." She stared into his face. "No wonder Elijah is such a tormented soul. He lost them both at once, in one wonderful, horrible day. Is that why he still grieves so? Is that why he's trapped there in the library?"

Jack shook his head. "I don't know, Abby. I can't explain that. What I can understand is his grief. A man losing the woman he loves and his child, all at once." He blinked and looked away.

That's a pain he could empathize with.

He felt her studying him.

"You seem to know that pain, Jack. Too well. It's not only empathy I see in your eyes."

Could she read his mind?

Fighting his emotions, he ducked his chin to his chest and squeezed his eyes shut. His chest ached, as though shotgun pellets peppered his heart. The wound was raw again, broken open. He swore he'd never talk to anyone about it, but he had to tell Abby. He'd not found a woman he even considered opening his heart to before.

Now there was Abby. The woman he loved.

"Okay." He heaved a stuttered sigh. "There's something I have to tell you." He stood, reaching for her hand. "Come with me. It will be easier for me to talk while we walk in the woods."

Abby followed Jack down the dirt road, past his house to where it curved deeper into the forest. Although unpaved, the hard-packed clay strewn with gravel bore signs of travel, though infrequent. Down, down, down the grade they wound, ending in a place where the mountains on either side rose up beside them. Leafy vegetation almost obliterated the light. As they descended, cool air pressed close around them.

Towering pines interspersed with huge oaks covered the steep slopes on either side, the trunks so big she doubted she and Jack together could span their girths with hands joined. Even though it was late summer, a thick layer of dead leaves from countless winters past cloaked the forest floor. The crude road continued for at least a half-mile, but she could see no other houses on either side.

"Mine is the last house on this road," he explained, as though he'd read her mind. "At least for now. There's a dirt path beyond where the roadway ends. It's a beautiful place. It's a place I go often when I need to think."

"It's so incredibly quiet back here," she said. "As though the woods blot out everything else, even time. It's like magic."

"'*I went to the woods because I wished to live deliberately, to front only the essential facts of life, and see if I could not learn what it had to teach, and not, when I came to die, discover that I had not lived*'."

He finished the quotation, then turned toward her and smiled. "Thoreau. Sometimes, I feel as though I'm some strange reincarnation of his spirit."

"I know Thoreau. His work, I mean. Very well. You do him proud."

Even though it was a sunny, bright afternoon, the tangle of greenery over their heads them mimicked twilight. At what she guessed was the lowest point of a valley where two mountains met, the man-made roadway ended abruptly, continuing merely as parallel depressions in the dirt.

A small stream gurgled along beside them with an occasional fallen leaf spinning and whirling across the eddying surface. In the distance, the grade began its slow ascent again at the base of the next mountain rise. A hundred feet ahead, a huge downed oak trunk lay across the path, forming a natural barrier to prevent vehicles from traveling further.

When they reached the log, Jack kicked it. "I always thought it was such a shame they had to knock all these old trees down. I suppose a land developer doesn't see it that way." He turned to face her. "They don't care about history. Or nature. They're only concerned with how accessible they can make their valuable building lots. But . . ." He sighed. "I suppose that's how my house got where it is."

He shook his head, stooping to pick at a piece of loose bark on one mossy end of the massive fallen tree. "Termites are already setting up winter quarters here. Guess all living things make the best of a situation." He rose and gazed into her eyes. "If they get the chance."

She didn't understand the meaning of those ominous words, and her stomach twisted. His gaze flashed away, flitting nervously from one place to another, as though he couldn't hold her gaze.

"What is it, Jack? Tell me." She moved closer, laying one hand on his cheek.

He stared off past her, and the muscles of his jaw tensed.

"You look like you're in mourning," she whispered. "Is it because of what we found in the graveyard? Did it hit you hard, like it did me?"

He squeezed his eyes shut and pinched two fingers to the base of his nose. "I am grieving, Abby. Not for Isabelle Laramy and her child. I'm grieving because of a secret I've been carrying around for the past ten years."

He caught her hand and led her down to the still-solid end of the fallen tree, where the surface looked dryer and more substantial. "Sit with me," he said, patting the bark beside him as he took a seat.

"This all happened," he began, taking a deep breath as if to fortify him, "when I was in my last year of graduate school at Duke. I took a part-time student teaching position, assisting one of the history undergrad professors. A goofy, undisciplined roomful of freshman. But we did have one star student." He turned to face her. "Her name was Dawn."

He spilled the whole tale then, how he'd fallen hopelessly in love with the pretty undergrad who stood out from the crowd the minute he caught sight of her.

"Most of my buddies went for the skinny blondes with huge, fake boobs. The valley girls. Dawn wasn't like that. She was only nineteen but sported the body of a siren. Marilyn Monroe style." He chuckled sardonically and scrubbed a hand down over his face. "Way too sexy."

Abby scooted closer to Jack's side and laid one hand on his thigh. He wouldn't look at her.

"I should have realized my own weaknesses. I was a healthy, normal young man who'd always been too focused on my professional future to acknowledge the other," he added air quotes, "parts of me that needed attention.

"There was sort of an unwritten rule that student teachers shouldn't get involved with the students. I asked her out anyway. I knew she was only a kid, for Christ's sakes, and by that time I was in my late twenties. I was only a few weeks away from my teaching certificate, rarin' to get started on my career. I was feeling like the big, accomplished man.

"I took her to the Ackland Art museum on a Saturday before Spring Break. Then we went to dinner, then back to my apartment. I swear, sometimes I look back and think, where was my head? You've surely heard the pun about men thinking with their, um . . ." He pointed to his crotch. "Well, that was me that night. I hardly knew her. I didn't even own a condom. Never expected I'd need one, not that night. It was only our first date. I never imagined we'd end up in bed. She came down on me like an eagle on a mouse."

He fell silent for a long moment. "Or maybe my starving body finally overrode my brain. She said not to worry about protection. She had it covered. I assumed this meant she was on the pill. Stupid, right? I guess I should be grateful I didn't end up with an STD."

In that one second his eyes flashed to hers, she could see the torment in his eyes. He was struggling with this confession. She guessed she might be the first to ever hear it.

She spoke softly. "So, you had a fling with a student, Jack. I had one with my professor. What's the difference? Did she die on you too?"

He hesitated, turning to gaze intently into her eyes. "This wasn't a fling, Abby. I thought I was in love. I was sure I'd found my soul mate, my perfect match. She was exactly as I'd dreamed my future wife would be. Gorgeous, ambitious, common interests, intellectually compatible. And physically, well . . ." He paused again, lowering his head. "My body had never been happier, and my brain was already planning our future together. We'd get married, have a family, and teach together in some small college somewhere. A rural town, a nice place to raise kids."

Somewhere in the back of Abby's mind, a warning

flag went up. She sucked in a breath and straightened as he continued.

"I had no idea. I was as ignorant as a male virgin. I didn't know her at all. She was a city girl, born and raised in New York." That summer when classes ended, he explained, she'd gone back home for a few weeks, to visit family. At least, that's what she told him.

"I spent the rest of that summer, with her gone, feeling as though I had a limb amputated. I did a lot of fantasizing." He glanced up at her, smirking, then snatched his gaze away again. "Not like that. About what our future would be like. Together.

"I searched for a bigger, nicer apartment we could share until she graduated. I started applying for teaching positions all around the Triangle area. I even put a deposit on a ring. As soon as she got back, I was going to ask her to marry me.

"Dawn breezed in from her summer in New York about three weeks before fall classes started. She'd been kind of distant, elusive while she was away. Whenever I could get her on the phone, she cut our conversation short. I figured it was because she was busy, catching up with friends. Or assumed maybe her family was in the same room, and maybe she hadn't told them about 'us' yet. It should have been a red flag that she never called me once the whole summer. I always called her." He crossed his arms over his chest. "The day she got back, I found her packing her stuff into a rental car on the curb near her dorm. She was leaving. Transferred to NYU, she said. Her old man had her a job all lined up at the Met once she graduated."

Abby laid a hand on his shoulder. "Oh Jack, that must have been such a blow."

He lurched to his feet as though she'd slapped him. "A blow. A blow? You have no freaking idea, Abigail. That was only the beginning of the surprises Miss Killer Dawn had for me."

He'd pressured her, he said, asking what happened to their relationship, to what they'd shared. She acted as if he was a casual stranger, trying to brush the whole thing off as a misunderstanding.

"I guess she had to pull out the big guns," he said, his voice breaking, "to get rid of me. So I would stop," again, in air quotes, "*bothering* her. So she dropped the bombshell."

Dawn had turned on him, calling him the biggest mistake of her life. He almost cost her everything. Her career, her future—those were her priorities. He almost snagged her, she told him.

"Her words haunt me to this day. *You're the big, bad expert fisherman, Mr. Mountain Man. But you can't catch me. Although your bait was certainly tasty, this crafty carp just wiggled free.*

"She'd been carrying my baby, Abby. She realized she was pregnant when she got to New York. And oh, how understanding and supportive her sensible, totally modern mommy and daddy were. They made an appointment for her with the local butcher shop, and they paid to have my baby scraped out of her."

Abby blinked, unable to think of a single way she could comfort this man. As torn up as she'd been to discover the unfortunate death of an infant a hundred years ago, this was different. Part of her felt anger toward the insensitive Dawn. Yet though she hated to admit it, part of her understood the panic a woman might feel at being trapped by an unplanned pregnancy. It wasn't a decision she ever wanted to make and prayed she'd never have to.

Her shudder wasn't due to the chilling air.

He didn't return to her side, sinking to sit cross-legged on the thick carpet of fallen leaves. With elbows on his thighs, he cradled his face in his hands. Abby could sense he was drawing away from her, physically and emotionally.

She understood. This was his own personal struggle. Her comfort was meaningless.

After a long moment she rose from her seat on the log and knelt beside him, wrapping an arm around him. "You can't blame yourself, Jack. You shouldn't feel guilty for a decision made by someone else. It was her body. Her choice."

He winced and a look of pure torment twisted his features. "She murdered my baby, Abby. I know she was young. I know she and I were absolutely not right for each other. But how could she make that decision without consulting me? Every time," he said, his voice catching on a sob, "every single time I hold one of my sisters' babies in my arms, I wonder. I grieve for the one who never got a chance at life."

Chapter 20

They sat huddled close on the leaf-padded forest path, arms intertwined. In silence, Abby pondered the depths of a quiet man she'd come to know as strong and sure. Jack had opened his heart to her and revealed a part of him she was certain no one else had ever known. She wasn't sure if he would feel better or worse for it.

Scratch that. Now that she knew the whole of what this man was about, she felt infinitely worse.

It was crucial, she decided, that she make her intentions about their relationship crystal clear. Abby was not the wife-mother type. She had no experience, nor had even been close enough to this sort of relationship to have any idea how to handle it. Reading to the children at story hour was as close as she wanted to get to child rearing.

Sex was good. Condoms were essential. Forever? White gowns and promises and babies? Not so much.

Then why this twisting ache in her heart? What was she missing here? How could someone crave something they didn't understand?

The rumble of thunder brought her back around to the present, to his presence in her arms. She sat back and smiled into his eyes. He searched hers with anxious questioning as she pushed a silvery curl from his forehead.

"Jack, your premature gray," she murmured. "It's not a genetic thing, is it? Your father, even now, probably isn't even as gray as you are, is he?"

His reply was a scoffing chuckle as he raked a hand through his hair and shook his head. "Nope. I guess I probably have Miss Killer Dawn to thank for that as well. The first strands of silver peeked through shortly after she was gone."

"Have you been in touch with her since then? Sometimes it helps," she asked. "Closure and all that."

His lips twisted, and his nod was almost imperceptible. "She actually found me on Facebook and LinkedIn a few months ago. No word for all these years, then all of a sudden she won't leave me alone. I don't even sign onto those sites anymore because she stalks me." He paused. "She left her curator job at the Met. Now she works for Sotheby's."

Abby blinked. "Does Martin know her?"

"Probably. Should I care?" He shrugged.

Snuggling closer to him, Abby laid her head on his shoulder. She might not understand his pain completely, but she did know how to comfort him. At least, physically. On impulse, she hopped up on her knees, framed his face in her hands, and covered his mouth with hers.

Their kiss was long and sweet, and when parts of her inside began to buzz, she broke away. She tipped her chin down, peering up and twisting her face into a scowl. "Jack, my butt is wet."

He threw back his head and laughed. "Mine too. No doubt stained with moss and leaf mold too. The ground never completely dries back in here."

They walked back to his cabin holding hands in the false twilight created by the forest and thickening clouds. Rumbles of thunder sounded twice more, closer now. A typical summer afternoon storm was rolling in over the Blue Ridge Mountains.

They made love on his rustic log-framed bed while the wind blasted intermittent splatters of rain against the western window. Their joining was a slow, sensuous dance at first, as he explored her body with gentle caresses and soft kisses. He undressed her, peeling damp clothes off piece by piece, planting his lips on her bare skin as he uncovered each inch. When all that remained was her lacy undergarments, she trembled. He pulled the thick duvet over her.

He dropped his own clothing to the floor and slid between the pristine white sheets of his king-sized bed, gathering her to him. His skin felt almost hot to the touch, and she snuggled in close, losing herself in his scent. Their lips came together and parted, and he explored her mouth with his tongue. She answered him eagerly, her breath quickening with the urgency of his kiss.

All the while he ran his hands over her. He slid one finger under the strap of her bra, easing it off her shoulder. His tongue began a searing path, tracing the edge of her ear to that oh-so-sensitive spot just below the lobe, down her neck, and along her collarbone. She arched toward him as, with one hand, he unfastened her bra, setting her breasts free. As his mouth closed over one pebbled nipple, she almost came undone.

He was a generous lover, worshiping her with tongue and fingers, driving her higher and higher. As he suckled one nipple, he skimmed a warm palm over the other, and the pleasure nearly had her losing her mind. Then his fingers wandered down, slipping under the edge of her panties. She wiggled free of them. His groan as he explored her hot center drove her passion to a frenzied peak. She climaxed convulsively around his stroking, exploring fingers.

As the waves of pleasure melted to a warm simmer, it was her turn to enjoy his exquisite body. She buried her face in his furred chest, reveling in his scent, now musky with sweat and desire. Her fingers trailed down the lean, hard muscles of his torso, over his flat stomach, following the dark trail of hair to her destination. Her fingers closed around him, and he gasped. Her hips arched toward him instinctively.

His moan told her control was becoming a serious struggle.

"I'm sorry, Abby. I'm not sure I'll be able to hold back once I'm inside you," he whispered hoarsely as she clung to him. "I need to be inside you now."

She tensed until he rolled away from her, and she watched as he slipped the condom over his length, awed by the beauty of his body. When he moved back toward her, she spread her legs and welcomed him in. Poised over her, he held his weight off her with sculpted, corded arms. As he entered her, his eyes never left hers.

This was an experience she'd never imagined. She'd never made love with her eyes open.

With Jack, it was more than just physical coupling. As he slid into her body, he climbed into her soul. His rhythm quickened, and she saw more than primal need in his sage-green eyes, so intent on hers. It was almost more than she could endure. His sincerity clutched at her heart, testing her emotional limits.

But all defenses, all logical thought evaporated as her body betrayed her. She climaxed again, with him, around him, clutching at his back with her nails as the waves of pleasure washed over her. When his weight fell heavy against her and his musky aroma filled her senses, a hot tear slid down her cheek.

As though nature herself had aligned with their passion, the sounds of the storm outside faded afterward. They lay for a long time wrapped in each other's arms under the pristine white duvet. She reveled in the contrast, the cool crispness of the sheets and the burning warmth of his skin all along her body. She tucked her head under his chin, nuzzling the base of his throat.

"Abby," he growled, his voice husky. "I never thought I would be this happy again. In a place where the future is still a possibility."

Her eyes flew open wide, and she was glad he couldn't see her face. She lay still against him while he pressed kisses on top of her head. Screaming protest, her mind urged her to rebuild her protective wall. Yes, this was the right thing to do. She must be clear with him. He was too kind a man to lead on. This, what they'd shared in these past moments, was all she could ever give him.

"I figured it was all over for me. I mean, I'm closing in on forty. I had accepted the fact I would probably live out the rest of my life like a hermit, alone here in the woods. I can't tell you what you mean to me. Now, there's a chance. With you, I've found love again. And you're so like me. We love the same things. You're so good with kids. Maybe there's a chance we'll have some of our own."

Her heart clenched.

How could she have been so blind? She'd seen him as safe. A modern day Thoreau. Aloof, independent, in love with nature and knowledge far more than he could ever love another of his own kind. Although they'd developed a close friendship, and been lovers, she hoped he would never want more from their relationship than that.

Yet even after all he'd been through, this man still believed in a happy ever after. The evidence had been right there in her face, she realized, but she'd turned her head and heart away.

Like whenever he was surrounded by his sister's children. His eyes twinkled with more than mischief that first day he'd led his entourage of little ones into the library for story hour, like some heavenly antithesis of the Pied Piper. The reclusive mountain man, the loner who spent his days teaching history, roaming about in the past, dreamed for more. Impossibly, his tragic blow to the heart hadn't permanently jaded him.

Why hadn't she seen that?

Her own heart was still encased in a calloused shield of ice. True, he'd managed to melt away one small part, allowing him entry into her life as a friend and a lover. She did love him in her own way, but her concept of love was obviously quite different from his.

Forever?

She wanted to leap from his bed and run. Marriage is an arrangement—like her parents' loveless existence. They couldn't provide her with the affection she craved because they felt no affection for each other. How could she ever consider subjecting another child to the kind of life she'd known? One where love is some magical myth found only between the covers of a book?

What frightened her most were the uncomfortable embers his dreams stirred inside her from when she was a child and still believed in happy ever after. Long-abandoned glimmers from before, when she was too young to know the love she read about was a fantasy.

Taking a deep breath, she gathered her scattered emotions back to her center. She knew what she wanted for her own future—to forever live vicariously in books, the way she'd mostly experienced life since she was a child. That was safe. She couldn't get hurt that way.

Abby pushed away from his embrace and sat up, pulling the duvet around her. She was suddenly feeling very exposed.

"Jack, I think maybe we're moving too fast here." The silence settled around them, heavy under the weight of her words. "I mean, I do love being with you. Making love with you. I do . . . love you. In my way." The words sounded strange coming off her tongue. As if she were speaking in a foreign language.

His peaceful, contented expression twisted with tortured confusion, making her heart ache. But the panic in her chest escalated.

"What you're talking about is . . . permanent," she continued. "Setting up house together. And a family. My God, Jack, until a few months ago I couldn't even imagine being seen out in public with a man."

She took a deep breath and blew it out. Swinging her legs down, she perched on the edge of the bed, still clutching the quilt around her. The room felt strange, foreign, the planked floor hard and cold under her feet. "I'm not sure if I'm cut out to be a wife and a . . . a mother, Jack. I was raised in a library. All I know is books. All I've ever loved is books." She glanced back over her shoulder. "Until you. I'd hoped you were just like me. I'd hoped we could enjoy a life of companionship, with our love of history and old books. Companionship, and some great sex. That's all. I'd hoped that would be enough."

The quilt dropped away as she snatched her sweater off the bedside chair and wrapped it around her naked body. The wool was scratchy and harsh against her skin. Jack said nothing, and his lack of response escalated her emotions. She stood and paced, breathing deep against the panic. Trying not to hyperventilate.

"Please try to understand. I got involved once before, in over my heart and way over my head." She stopped, pleading with her eyes. "I told you all about what happened to me. It's the closest I've ever come to a real relationship. I've never been a bride. Yet somehow, I ended up a widow."

A half-hour later, Jack drove her back into town. Abby gazed out the window at the sliver of setting sun piercing the broken clouds on the crest of the mountain. She sat in his car on a triple folded old bath towel so her still-damp skirt didn't stain the upholstery. Although Jack was able to change into dry things before they left, he had nothing at all that would fit her save a long T-shirt.

"I do have a dryer, you know," he offered. "Let me dry your things—"

"Uh, no thanks," she'd replied with a frown. "Just take me home."

When he finally rolled up to the curb in front of her

apartment, she could feel his eyes on her.

"I don't know what to say, Abigail. I guess I assumed too much." His voice was rough and strained as he raked a hand through his hair. "Guess I'm pretty good at that. I'm sorry."

"No, Jack. I'm the one who's sorry. I never meant to mislead you. I tried to be honest from the start. About everything." She looked at him then, unable to stifle the tears. "The Harvey Library is the perfect place for me, isn't it? I've a ghost that haunts me too."

As the sound of his engine faded into the distance, she was sure her heart was chained to his bumper. Her whole body felt hollow, ripped open and bleeding. Numb, yet aching inside, she wanted to let it all out in great, quaking sobs, but couldn't.

After changing into dry clothes, she went to the window and stared up the street toward the Harvey. Her new beginning wasn't even months old, yet had come grinding to a halt, paralyzed in what seemed like a glitch in time. Abby was floating somewhere between the past and future.

The next day Abby stood at the front windows of the library gazing out onto quiet Main Street. The midsummer heat had all but dragged time into reverse. Even with the gigantic air conditioning unit toiling away noisily out back, the temperature inside the building barely held at seventy-five degrees.

She worried about the humidity that was at this moment creeping, like an insipid serpent, into the spaces between the books on the shelves. Nothing in the world was worse for books, especially old ones, than heat and humidity.

The chances of upgrading the decades old air conditioning unit were bleak. Hell, the chances of her even having to worry about it much longer were even more pitiful. Why, for all these past years, hadn't there been more damage in the hot summers to the precious antique books? Perhaps, she hoped, there was some way Elijah's spirit intervened on their behalf.

About to turn back to her struggle with the meager book budget, a movement across the street caught her eye. The door of Laramy's Antiques swung open and out stepped a woman, one she'd not seen around town before. She had to be an out-of-towner, because if she lived locally she was definitely not the kind of woman your eyes would pass over and not remember.

Already tall, her height was further enhanced by the three-inch needle heels she navigated in as though she wore comfortable, old sneakers. Her glossy, mahogany brown hair fell in thick, perfectly arranged waves to her shoulders, and she was slipping on a pair of shades with crystal accents that flashed as she stepped out into the sunlight.

Wearing a suit jacket over jeans, Martin Laramy followed right behind her. Abby noticed that today, though, his signature plaid bowtie was missing. His white shirt was unbuttoned at the throat. Apparently the summer heat had even gotten to him.

The woman obviously didn't worry about sweat. She was wearing a hot pink suit, probably silk from its rich sheen, which hugged her generous curves with pure passion. The pencil skirt, ending at least six inches above her knee, revealed a shapely set of legs that reminded Abby of an old Marilyn Monroe poster.

She blinked as the woman, who gestured emphatically with her hands as she spoke, scattered more glitter around on the sidewalk than a disco ball. Clusters of gemstones adorned almost every finger.

Martin wore a big, stupid grin that made him look even dorkier than he had when she first met him. With both hands shoved into his jeans pockets, he was laughing at something the woman said, nodding and scuffing the toe of his leather loafer along the curb. Then he looked up at her, nodded again, and reached out to shake her hand.

Abby had to smile when the woman took hold, shook it, then pulled, causing him to stagger almost into her. She planted a theatrical kiss on his cheek. Color, visible from across the street, rose into Martin's cheeks.

She was so engrossed in watching this rather unusual scene, she jumped when the door burst open and Mamie Greer popped her head in.

"Hello? Where the hell are you, Abby gal?

"In here, Mamie. Just doing a little daydreaming. Really slow today, and god, is it hot or what?" Abby pulled the scooped neckline of her black T-shirt in and out, fanning some air onto her face.

Mamie shut the door and hurried to her side, pointing out the window. "Look, look. Did you see that little soap opera scene across the street? Who the hell is that, anyway?"

"That's what I was wondering. She's certainly not one of the locals, that's for sure."

"No, ma'am. Looks like a big-city girl to me. She's gad up even sluttier than old Leda-bitch."

Abby chuckled. "Guess she had some business with Martin. He seemed pretty happy to be talking to her. I didn't even think his face had the muscles to form a real smile."

Mamie perched a fist on her hip and cocked her head. "I think there's some big antique thing going on in Charlotte this week. I'll bet she's here for that."

"But why here?" Abby asked. "Charlotte is at least, what, sixty miles or more from here?"

"These antiques dealers go all over the country, beating the bushes for the big find. Haven't you ever seen that show on the History Channel? There are these two guys who travel around in a van to the most remote places in the country, picking around in other peoples' barns and shit—"

Abby held up a hand. "First of all, I don't watch TV much. Second, this one in pink silk and stilettos doesn't seem the type to be poking around in a place where her needle heel might sink in the mud."

"True," Mamie said, folding her lower lip between two fingers. "Pretty hard to walk in FMP's, even on level concrete."

Abby blinked. "FM . . . what's?"

"Oh, please, Abby. Don't tell me you don't own a pair of FMP's. It's a fashion accessory every girl simply must have in her closet. For those special occasions." Mamie winked conspiratorially.

"What does it stand for?" She tried to hide her embarrassment within a chuckle.

"Really Abby gal." Mamie scowled and crossed her arms. "I taught grade-schoolers my whole life and even I own a pair of FMPs." She cupped her hand around one side of her mouth and winked, whispering, "Stands for Fuck Me Please. Mine are pretty-please purple."

She reeled as Mamie continued, "Hey, when you get to my age, honey, you ask real, real nice."

Before trudging up the stairs to her apartment that afternoon, Abby stopped in to see Dianne. She and Vera were deep in conversation near the doorway of the little room where Vera did Tarot readings.

"I'm getting a lot more calls for your services. I think you ought to try to schedule another day or two here," Dianne was saying.

As the door swung shut behind her, both women turned in greeting.

"Oh, Abby. Why so glum? You look tired, girl," Di said.

"I am," she said on a sigh. "Just didn't feel like sitting

alone in my room just yet."

Her aunt flicked a glance toward Vera, who took the hint. "I'll look at my schedule, Di, and get back to you. It's great there's more interest in Tarot, huh? Why do you suppose that is?"

"I'm getting more traffic too, and I can tell you part of it's due to what Abby's doing down the street. She's reviving interest in this old town. I'm real proud of her."

As Vera brushed past her, she squeezed Abby's arm. "Keep up the good work."

The compliment should have boosted her mood. Instead, all it did was make her ache and feel empty inside.

When they were alone, Abby came forward and thudded her elbows on the counter. Her aunt had fashioned a colorful display under the glass. Tiny, woodland fairies frolicked around a mirror pond, and miniature trees glittered with crystal earrings and pendants. A playful, happy scene—the sight of it should not have caused a lump to form in Abby's throat.

Dianne moved close beside her. "You gonna tell me what's wrong? Or do I have to resort to clairvoyance?"

That made Abby smile, even as the sparkling crystals in the case blurred behind unshed tears. She shook her head. "If I knew, I could tell you, Auntie. But it seems I'm not really sure myself."

"Something else happen with Leda?"

"No. That whole situation is in limbo until next month's meeting. I'm just tired, I guess."

Di whisked around the back of the counter and dipped her head to see Abby's face. "Why the tears then? I think this is all going to work out, hon. I've told you, we're not going to let Leda get her way."

The opening door interrupted them, and Abby turned to see Elena slip inside and flash them both a smile.

"Hi, ladies. I can't believe it. I actually score an afternoon to go shopping all by myself, then get lucky enough to meet up with both of you on my way home."

Dianne dipped her head back and forth. "I hardly recognize you without two munchkins on either side."

Elena breathed out a long sigh. "Me neither. I feel naked, or like I left part of me at home. But Ed said he thought I needed a break, so he's taking Lexi and Eddie for pizza, *then* bathing them, *then* putting them to bed. I can't believe it."

"Wow," Di said. "What kind of spell did you put on that man? If you let me bottle it, I'll cut you in, fifty percent." Both women laughed.

But Abby couldn't pretend amusement. Talk of Elena's family only reminded her of the reason she and Jack couldn't be together.

Their laughter died as Elena took a closer look at her. "Hey, what's wrong? You look like you've lost your best friend." She rubbed a hand up and down Abby's arm.

"I have." Abby blinked, and a tear slipped down her cheek. It took a minute before she found the strength to speak around the ball of pain in her throat. Swallowing hard, she looked into Elena's eyes. "I think you're the one I need to talk to. I need some advice."

Twenty minutes later, Abby and Elena waited while Dianne locked the shop for the evening. She came out of the back room with a bottle of wine and three plastic cups.

"Sorry, but this is the best I can do on short notice." She set the cups on the round table in Vera's room and filled them each half full. Settling herself in the remaining empty chair, she said, "I don't know what's got you so upset, Abigail, but something tells me chamomile tea just won't cut it tonight."

She chuckled and sniffed, blotting her cheeks with the tissues Di gave her. "No, this is a bigger problem than tea can fix." She sobered and turned to face Elena. "I'm not sure if it's fixable at all."

Her eyes narrowed, and she bent closer. "Does this have

to do with my brother? Has he done something to hurt you?"

"In a way." There was no use even trying to stop the tears at this point. Abby threw the wad of black-stained tissues on the table. "He said he loves me and wants to settle down and have babies with me," she choked out.

When she looked up, both women were staring at her with their mouths open. A long moment passed before Dianne sputtered, "And your problem is?"

A sob escaped Abby's throat. "Auntie, you know I'm not qualified for a role like that. You've seen my parents' relationship. You know how I grew up. How could I possibly even attempt to be like . . . like her?" She motioned toward Elena, who captured Abby's hand in her own.

"Abby, listen," Elena said, "this isn't about being qualified. It's about what you want. I'm not surprised Jack wants you as his wife. He's in love with you—that was plain as day the first time I saw you together. I know he wants a family." She squeezed Abby's hand and whispered, "It's how he was raised. It's all he knows. It's all he's ever wanted."

Dianne slumped back in her chair with the cup of wine balanced between her fingers. "That's the problem, Elena. The kind of life Jack knows, and wants, is as foreign to Abby as a rainbow trout is to a goldfish." Her aunt fixed her eyes on Abby's face. "She's right, Abigail. You have to decide what it is *you* want out of life."

The words bubbled out of her like seltzer from a shaken bottle. "I want a companion, and someone to talk to, and spend time with. And affection. Like I had . . . before."

"No." Dianne slammed her cup down on the table and rested her elbows on her knees. "No, you don't want the kind of relationship you had before. I don't know all the details, but I do know that arrangement could never have gone anywhere. Never had any kind of future."

She blinked. "Exactly. That's why it was so safe. I never had to commit my heart to somebody who might break it. I never had to—"

"Do you want to live the rest of your life alone, Abby?" Elena asked. "With just your career and your books? It doesn't sound like you come from a close family. Is living alone in an empty apartment going to be enough?" She tipped her chin toward the ceiling—toward Abby's apartment. "I think not. I've seen you with the kids at the library. I think you have the potential for a great deal more."

"I think it might be enough." Abby lowered her gaze. "That's why I thought Jack would be perfect for me. He seemed so settled in his bachelor's lifestyle. I hoped maybe we could be just . . . friends. With benefits." She winced. Even to her own ears, the claim made her sound cheap and shallow.

When she glanced up, Elena was shaking her head. "Jack isn't that kind of man. He's an old soul who wants the same kind of old-fashioned family we both grew up in." She frowned. "If that's the kind of relationship you're looking for, Jack's not the right man for you. He's had his dreams shattered once before. Please don't do that to him again."

With a deep sigh, she set down her cup and said, "Thanks for the wine, Di. But I really better head back up the mountain.

Dianne followed her to the door to let her out. Abby stayed behind, sipping her wine, each swallow stinging a heart that ached inside her chest even worse than before. Now she'd not only alienated Jack, but his sister, who'd been nothing but kind and generous to her since the day they'd met.

She started when her aunt's voice behind her barked, "My dear, you and I need to have a talk."

Dianne plopped herself back down in her chair and lifted her cup, draining it before grabbing the bottle to refill it. She leveled her gaze on Abby. "Why, exactly, are you so afraid of a long-term commitment with a man as wonderful as Jack Wood?"

Squirming inside, her empty stomach tossed the wine into a churning, burning storm. She shrugged. "I don't know anything about love, Auntie. It certainly can't be what my parents have. Theirs seems more like a business partnership than a romance."

"I can't disagree with you there. Just remember, just because your mother is my sister doesn't mean we're anything alike." Dianne sniffed.

"Duh. But even you and Armand—I don't understand your relationship either. I mean I can see you care about each other, but—"

"I waited a long time for the right man to come along. My knight in shining armor, you might say. The man who loved me for *me*, complete with all the good and the bad and the ugly. A man who worships me, yet doesn't put ties on me in any way."

Abby searched her aunt's face. "You never had kids. Why?"

Dianne's shoulders drooped, and her eyes grew misty. "We tried. But I was already in my late thirties, and . . . well, it just wasn't in the cards for us."

"I never knew that," Abby whispered. "I'm so sorry, Auntie."

Her aunt waved away her sympathy with a fluttering hand. "No matter. I have to admit, I had mixed emotions about the whole thing. I wasn't sure I would be a good mom, but I *did* know Armand would make the best daddy." She shrugged. "Like I said, he's my knight in shining armor."

Blinking, Abby said, "How do you learn to be a good mother? It's such a big responsibility. What if you fail?"

"Abigail, it's called instinct. If you have love in your heart for a man who's your hero, you become a team. The rest comes naturally. Just like that." She snapped her fingers. "Magic."

Chapter 21

Jack spent the next ten days in Heart Hell. Here it was the most beautiful time of year in the foothills, and again, he was completely alone.

They say lightning doesn't strike twice in the same place, but he was now sure the old cliché was a bold-faced lie. Again, he'd fallen in love with a woman too young, and too different. A woman who didn't share his life's vision. He'd handed his heart over to someone who was unable to do anything except break it.

Summer classes were over, and the fall schedule didn't begin for three weeks. Fishing this time of year sucked. The water was too warm, even under the cover of heavy forest in the foothills. It might have been better in the higher elevations, but he wasn't interested in traveling. The higher he climbed into the Blue Ridge, the closer he got to his family—his parents, his sisters with their fulfilled, happy lives. Those reminders, right now, were simply too painful.

His garden, having yielded its bounty of tomatoes and herbs, was fading, withering in the long days under a relentless August sun. Too early to pull up and plow under, and too late to bother with the few stubborn weeds that endured. The sad, dying state of his garden reflected how he felt inside.

His entire life had ground to a halt, though he struggled in vain to sustain his routine. He extended his daily run to five miles. In reality, he was trying to outrun his feelings.

And losing.

Not usually much of an Internet junkie, Jack found himself surfing for the most ridiculous reasons. Fishing lures on EBay. Rare books on Amazon. He ached to continue his research on the Harvey Library, yet anytime he approached that avenue his heart fell into the intersection in a heap of bloody pulp.

Damn Abigail Stryker. Damn women in general.

He was sitting at his kitchen counter, nursing a glass of blood red Merlot and squinting at the too small screen of his 13-inch MacBook when he heard the purr of an engine, an odd sound on his seldom traveled dead end road. Then it stopped. Pushing down the lid of the laptop he slid off the stool and peered through his front window. A sleek black Mercedes coupe was parked directly behind his SUV.

The driver was alone, a woman with fluffy dark hair wearing large sunglasses. She stepped out onto his driveway dressed in white from head to toe, with crisp tailored shorts and a sleeveless, collared blouse tied off at the waist. The only splash of color came from her bright pink stilettos.

Too casual, too provocative for Jehovah's Witness. Avon lady, maybe? Maybe she was lost. One thing he was sure of as this woman made her way up the walk to his front door—she wasn't anybody he knew.

He could ignore the doorbell, though with his windows thrown wide open and classical music filling the entire house, he hardly thought the snub would go unnoticed. He considered running down the hall and turning the shower on, leaving the water to splash noisily until this stranger gave up and went away. Nah. He just wasn't that kind of guy. Sighing, he drained his wineglass, wiped his mouth on the napkin the glass had been sitting on, and went to answer the door.

She stood on his doorstep with one hip cocked, a heavy, oversized leather bag slung over one shoulder. Her identity remained concealed behind dark shades. A James Bond movie castoff? Mr. Clean's younger sister?

“Hello there, Professor Wood.” Her voice was like hot fudge after ten seconds too long in the microwave.

Jack cleared his throat. “Can I help you, ma’am?”

“You’ve done it before. And so well. It’s a definite possibility you could help me again.”

The woman slid off the sunglasses, revealing her eyes. Those Elizabeth Taylor turquoise, almost-too-beautiful-to-be-real eyes. “Hey Jackie,” she purred, running those eyes down the length of his body like a medical device performing a full-body imaging.

He blinked, then tried to swallow without sacrificing his tongue. “Dawn,” he croaked.

“So who is she?” Mamie hissed to Sandi, Murphy’s breakfast shift waitress.

Mamie slouched in the corner booth, her mug of coffee long gone cold in front of her. She was halfheartedly hiding behind the diner’s copy of the *Hickory Herald.*

Sandi held her order pad up in front of her, pen poised, slanting a glance back over her shoulder none too subtly. She shrugged. “Never seen her before,” she muttered. “Came in with Martin Laramy earlier. Seemed like Jack might have been waiting for them.”

Mamie folded the paper and laid it down next to her mug, straightening a little in her seat. “I’ll take the special, Sandi. Eggs over easy. Rye toast. Skip the spuds.”

The threesome occupied a table three booths down. Martin had his back to her, and Jack and this bombshell of a stranger snuggled close on the opposite side. The woman was dressed more casually today than when Mamie first spied her slinking out of Laramy’s in her hot pink suit.

Today her generous cleavage bulged threateningly above the scooped neckline of an electric blue tank. Her voluminous dark hair was contained in a sort of oversized ponytail, making her look like a somewhat mature cheerleader. The same crystal-accented sunglasses Mamie noticed yesterday were perched on top of her head.

Of all days for the cook at Murphy's to have a speed bug up his ass, it was today. Her breakfast arrived before she could have even cracked an egg in a pan. She peeled back the foil from a rectangle of orange marmalade, taking extra care to spread the goo on her toast as if it were the most important act she'd perform today. She couldn't hear a word of what was being said at Jack's table, damning herself for putting off those hearing aids her doctor claimed Medicare would pay for. When Martin Laramy rose to leave, her fork clattered to her plate.

Now those two were alone. Jack and this woman, who looked like a cross between a royal heiress and a porn star. If she got any closer to him he wouldn't be able to free his elbow enough to lift his coffee cup.

Mamie couldn't decipher anything from his expression, since his eyes seemed permanently glued to the table. The woman, however, kept talking at a rate that would make most auctioneers jealous and punctuated every third or fourth sentence with some sort of physical caress of Jack's hand, or arm, or shoulder.

Sandi had come back four times attempting to fill Mamie's cup but she hadn't so much as taken a sip.

"Want me to get you a fresh cup?" Sandi asked, a bit of impatience lacing her words.

"Please," Mamie replied. "And see if you can find out what the bitch's name is."

Sandi delivered the tab to Jack's table on her way to bring fresh coffee. After an elaborate display of jewel-encrusted fingers, his companion snatched the bill from under his hand. She held it up like a flag pressed against a gold-toned credit card as Sandi passed through. The woman signed the check, slid the card and her receipt back into her purse, then caught his hand as they slid out of the booth. Together.

"What's her name?" Mamie hissed when Sandi returned with her tab.

The waitress rolled her eyes toward the ceiling. "I'm not supposed to tell stuff like that, Mamie."

Mamie's eyes narrowed, and she growled, "And how many times did I save your little Gary's ass from suspension for cheating on spelling tests?"

Sandi huffed and slanted her eyes away, defeated. "Dawn. Dawn something or other."

An entire week and two days passed without a single phone call, a single visit, a single word of any kind from Jack. Abby knew deep down there was no reason she should have expected any contact from him. Christ, she'd broken his heart—again. Another young, ambitious career-minded female had led this surprisingly romantic, sincere man into a treacherous web. At least she hadn't gotten pregnant and aborted his baby without telling him. A small consolation which didn't do much to ease her guilt.

Was it all guilt? Or was there something deeper, more profound stirring inside her? She flipped back through her memory, back to when she was an innocent, albeit sequestered woman-child who had totally bought into tales of the knight in shining armor—hook, line, and sinker.

But Abby had no idea what a hero looked like. Nor real love. She'd just never been given the chance to witness that particular miracle.

With each day that passed, every hour without a word from Jack, her tiny apartment transformed from a cozy hideaway into a solitary confinement cell. Usually she could at least go down and hang out with Dianne when the loneliness got the best of her. Drink a cup of chamomile tea, chat about the town's latest gossip.

Not possible now. Dianne and Armand left Thursday for a long weekend, driving down to their cottage at the Outer Banks. Vera kept the shop open, but talking to her was like flossing with metal wire. Even story hour was on hiatus since most families were out of town on vacation while school was out.

It didn't help when Mamie Greer came bursting through the door at noon on Saturday with her heart-wrenching news. "That woman," she began, breathlessly and without even so much as a hello, "that fancy city gal who was coming out of Laramy's the other day? Well, she was having breakfast down at Murphy's this morning. And guess who she was with?"

Abby sat behind the reception desk unmoving, almost numb. She pretty much knew what Mamie was going to say and wasn't completely sure if she wanted to know.

"She was sitting in the booth snuggled right up to Jack. Right up to him, Abby." Mamie's hands flailed in the air. "It was disgusting. Embarrassing even, the haughty slut. She couldn't keep her hands off him."

The words pierced Abby's heart like a shard of broken glass. She tried hard to keep her tone even. "Did you ever find out who she was?"

Mamie's slow grin was proud. "You know me, Abby gal. There's a lot of people owe me in this town." She grinned with an almost sickening self-satisfaction. "Sandi wouldn't tell me her last name. She's gotta watch out for her own ass too, keep that job ever since that cocksucker of a husband of hers flew the coop. But she did tell me the bitch's first name. Dawn."

After the rest of that endless Saturday followed by a dreary, rainy Sunday locked up in her apartment, Abby's loneliness grew malignant. She parked herself in front of her only window, gazing down on Main Street, mesmerized by the rhythmic changing of the traffic light from green, to yellow, to red and back again. She lost track of how long she'd actually been standing there.

It was the aching in her hands that brought her out of her reverie. She looked down at her numb fingers clutching on the window ledge so tightly her knuckles had gone white. Blinking back into the present, she suddenly knew what she had to do.

"I may not be able to exorcise my own ghost, but I'll be damned if I won't free the spirit of Elijah Harvey."

It was dusk by the time she climbed the library steps. Downtown Caldwell was deserted on this sleepy Sunday evening, peaceful in the aftermath of yet another drenching downpour. Murphy's Diner was the only business open, where one car huddled close to the sidewalk in front of its door. Aunt Di's shop was dark and empty, the red and white CLOSED sign hanging askew in the glass door. Time itself had ground to a halt in anxious expectation.

Abby flipped the switches, turning on every light in the place, the loud snapping sounds echoing in the emptiness. She paused near the rear stacks and sniffed the air. Nothing. She checked the reading corner and found the window closed.

"You're not here," she whispered. "You may have already gone. Maybe all you wanted was for us to find Isabelle's resting place after all."

A movement above her head caught Abby's eye—the hands of the wall clock. Staring, at first in disbelief, she watched the second hand tick, slowly and methodically.

In the wrong direction.

Her heart seized in her chest, but she wasn't really afraid. This spirit had done nothing to harm her. In fact, he'd proved to be one of her most loyal supporters through all of this.

"Okay, Elijah. I get the message. You want me to turn back time for you." She hugged herself and shivered. "I wish somebody could do the same for me."

There's only one piece of the puzzle missing. The key. *I've got to find out where it fits.*

After tucking the skeleton key into the pocket of her sweater, she began upstairs in the office she'd only visited twice since her arrival. She ran her hands along the built-in shelves, pressing on the seams between the wall paneling. Again she scoured the drawers of the old desk and the secretary, searching in vain for some kind of hidden compartment.

There was no lock on the desk drawer, and the key didn't fit the one on the secretary. She tried it anyway, finding the key too large. She even rolled back the tapestry-patterned area rug in the center of the wooden floor. The planking there was darker than the faded wood in the rest of the room, yet there was nothing to suggest a trapdoor of any kind.

Abby stopped at the window and looked out onto the massive elm behind the building. Darkness was falling on the town in earnest now, and streetlights twinkled through the leafy branches. Remembering the pen, she glanced down. The worn velvet box still lay up close to the window sash. She'd returned it to the same place she found it after showing it to Jack that day.

She crept back down the stairs holding the box in her hand. After sweeping around behind the reception counter, she flicked on the desk lamp next to the computer monitor.

"I'd better put this away before I lose it," she murmured, dropping the key back into her purse.

Plopping down in the chair, she flipped open the tiny box and lifted out the pen. Under the light, she studied the elaborately curled design etched into the pen's barrel.

It looked like a monogram, but she couldn't make out the letters.

She pulled out the lap drawer and dug through, hoping Monica left behind the set of magnifying readers she sometimes used to read fine print. When Abby's fingers closed on the familiar shape near the back of the drawer, she shouted, "Ah ha!"

Donning the readers, she said, "Okay, Elijah, no fair telling anyone I was wearing these things."

She lifted the pen closer, holding it under the golden cone of light. For a moment, she could decipher nothing, only swirled lines of etching. Holding the pen horizontally, she twisted it up and down. It was when she turned the delicate cylinder upright, holding it vertically, that a gasp escaped her.

"They're not squiggles," she whispered. "They're letters. *I.L.H.* Isabelle Laramy Harvey."

Abby heard what began as a faint rumble, like that of a train passing close by. Then pandemonium broke as the vibration intensified, as if an earthquake was rocking the building.

She leapt out of the chair, throwing herself against the wall. The pen slipped from her hand and rolled behind the monitor. Terrified, she gaped as the tall stacks of books in the back began to sway.

Books came down everywhere, hitting the floor with dull thumps, some singly, some in clustered groups. The huge shelves shuddered as books, flung from their snug nests on the shelves, tumbled to the floor. The lights dimmed and brightened with an irregular rhythm, as though they might flicker out completely at any moment.

She buried her face in her hands, waiting for the fury to pass. The motions gave her the impression of an invisible searcher scrambling through the shelves, looking for something. Yet not one book sailed across in her direction, like they had at Leda.

Abby looked at the wall clock. The hands moved faster now, sweeping around the numbered face backward.

She jumped and screamed as the window near the reading corner flew open, and the pungent aroma of pipe smoke filled the air. A blast of wind blew in, clear across the length of the building, scattering loose papers on the reception desk, sucking sheets out of the printer tray, and drawing them to dance in the air like oversized, alabaster butterflies.

As they fluttered to the floor, abruptly, the wind ceased.

A tiny sound right beside her drew her gaze to the desk. The pen reappeared from its hiding place behind the monitor, rolling as though the surface was tilted. It whirled to the edge and fell, landing on the wooden floor with a clink.

She bent, instinctively reaching to retrieve the delicate, antique treasure.

Before her fingers reached it, the pen came to life, spinning and twirling on the floor. Its barrel bumped into the toe of her sneaker, and she screeched and jumped aside. She watched in silent horror as it followed a helter-skelter path, this way and that, as though searching for something it couldn't see. When the pen made contact with the edge of a blank sheet of printer paper under the desk, it stopped.

Incredulous, Abby froze as the pen drew itself up to a writing angle and scratched a word across the page.

"There's no ink," she sobbed, terror now completely unraveling her. She huddled against the wall, trembling uncontrollably. "It's an old dip pen. It can't make a mark without ink."

But it did. With precision, as though it were a ballpoint or a cartridge pen, the metal tip flowed across the blank paper, forming two individual words in an elegant, oversized script.

Belle

Letters

When the last letter was formed, the pen clattered onto the paper, motionless. In the same moment, everything—all sound, all wind, all vibrations in the air ceased. The lights came back up to full strength and stabilized, although the fluorescent lamps in the main room remained out, plunging the rear stacks into darkness.

The knocking on the front door threw Abby into a fit of screaming. It took her a few seconds to realize there was someone standing outside, pounding on the glass. With relief, she recognized Jack.

Chapter 22

Abby ran to the door and threw open the bolt. She reached for him as he stepped over the threshold, but Jack took a step aside, away from her. He kept his hands stuffed stiffly in his pockets.

"What happening here, Abby? What's going on?" His voice was tense, empty, and cold.

She blinked in shock and staggered back a step, feeling more alone than she'd ever felt in her life.

He cleared his throat and stared at her. "I stopped at Murphy's for a sandwich and saw the lights were on. You're usually closed Sundays. Thought I better stop by and make sure you were okay."

The formality of his tone washed over her like ice water. She covered her face with her hands and turned away. "Not exactly." She struggled to control the quaver in her voice. "But I'm fine, Jack. Thank you for checking in on me."

"If everything is all right, why did you start screeching when I knocked on the door?"

She tugged at one earlobe, then crossed her arms. "You startled me, is all."

"Has the spirit tried to make contact again?" He glanced around the reception area where printer paper was still scattered on the desk and floor. "Or was this just a printer malfunction?"

"Don't make fun of me," she snapped, bristling. "And don't don your grand professor stance with me. Not now." Straightening, she jutted her chin forward and drew back her elbows. "Yes. Elijah did contact me, as a matter of fact. Just minutes ago."

Storming behind the desk, she swept the ink-scribbled page off the floor. With the other hand she lifted Isabelle's pen. "He wrote me a note." She thrust the page toward him over the counter. Holding up the pen, she continued, "Using Isabelle's pen," laying the pen down beside the paper.

Jack's eyes widened as he lifted the page. He stared at Abby, down at the inked letters, then at the pen. "That's impossible. It's a dip pen."

Her frustration reached a boiling point. She slapped both hands on the desk and glared at him, shouting, "Don't you think I know that? This is a ghost we're talking about here, Jack. A paranormal entity. He doesn't have to follow the rules."

He blinked back at her, then at the page again. "So he did call her Belle. It's her letters he's after."

"God, you're a fucking genius!" She threw up her hands and whirled away from him. Clasping them behind her back, she paced behind the counter. "I'm so very glad you showed up to help me figure this out tonight, Professor Wood. What*ever* would I have done without you? I'm kind of surprised you took time away from your precious Dawn to even bother. Killer Dawn. Isn't that what you call her?"

His head snapped back as though she'd struck him. He cleared his throat and laid the paper down on the counter. "Look Abby, it's plain we're not even going to be able to . . . remain friends. Or to work together anymore on this . . . this problem. I'm sorry I bothered you tonight. You're obviously busy, tied up in your research." He swept his hand toward the stacks, where books lay scattered on the floor. "As long as you're not hurt, or in any danger, I'll be going."

He turned to leave but as he reached for the handle, the half-open door swung out of his reach and slammed shut. Abby jumped. The deadbolt locked, echoing in the silence.

He staggered back as the bells swung widely from the knob and the jangling echoed through the building with peals so piercing, she covered her ears.

He glanced back toward her, rubbing his hands together as though he'd suffered a powerful electric shock. "Okay, then," he said, twisting his shoulders. "I guess he doesn't want me to leave. So what is it you suppose he wants me to do?"

"Duh," she spat. "*Belle. Letters*. I suppose he wants you to help me find Belle's letters."

The lights dimmed again then, and a sound came from behind her. Jack eyes widened, causing her to spin around.

Her oversized, leather satchel purse came to life on the desk, and its pliable surface convulsed, writhing as though possessed. Abby's constitution faltered. She hugged herself, backed away into the corner, and covered her face with her hands. Her knees buckled, and she slid down the wall into a ball on the floor.

Instinct overrode Jack's fear and anger. He rushed toward the desk in time to see the cinched upper edge of Abby's bag pulled jerkily open by invisible fingers. The contents—cell, wallet, a tube of black eyeliner, inhaler—flew through the opening one at a time. Each item hung in the air for a second before clattering down.

A deep, metallic clank sounded as the last item hit the surface, echoing as loudly as the clanging of a great bell.

All movement, all sound ceased, and the room was again shrouded in eerie silence. The skeleton key lay glinting on the surface of the desk.

Jack came around behind the counter and dropped to one knee in front of Abby, whose trembling shook her body in great waves. "Abby." When he touched her arm, she screamed and scooted away.

She lowered her hands from her face and stared at him, her eyes glazed.

She's going into shock. "It's okay, it's just me, Abby." He held out his hand, and her gaze wandered over him, as though she didn't know who he was.

He waited, allowing the tension to spin down for a moment. "Come on, Abby. It's okay. It's me. Jack."

Finally, she put her hand into his. "I'll help you." He lifted her to her feet, then reached over with one hand and snatched several tissues from the box on the desk.

"Here," he said, handing them to her with a half-smile. "You're the scary looking one right now. Are you okay? Can you do this?"

She said nothing at first, only nodding as she swiped streaks of eyeliner off her cheeks. After a moment she sniffed, then straightened her shoulders. "I'm okay now," she said, and yanked her hand free.

Fully half of the books in the library had already fallen off the shelves, and the rear stacks remained in darkness. He flicked the switches on and off. The lights over them were dead.

"Do you have a flashlight in here?" He scanned the room, which suddenly seemed twice its size. "I don't have a clue where to even start," he muttered. "Those letters could be tucked into any of these books, hidden between the pages."

She shook her head. "No. They're locked up somewhere. In a box, or a safe, or some hidden compartment. A place that opens with that key. It's somewhere Elijah apparently, even with all his supernatural powers, cannot access."

Jack took a step toward the stacks. A thump sounded behind them, and they both jumped.

"The reference room," she whispered, her eyes wide.

As she rounded the corner Abby wailed, "No, no, no. These books are so old, so delicate. Elijah, please, don't toss these on the floor."

When Jack followed her through the doorway, the lights began their strange dance again. They dimmed, though only slightly, then brightened, exactly three times. She turned and met his gaze.

"I guess we're getting warmer," he said.

She scanned the three walls of the reference room lined with shelves. The book that had fallen, a census record from the late 1800s, came from the top shelf on the southern wall, the one on her left as she entered the room.

"Let's start here." She gingerly removed the ancient volumes from the upper shelf and handed them to Jack, who stacked them with care on the table. They worked in awkward silence, strangers joined on a project against their will.

He did at least share her respect, even affection, for these old, rare books.

He took each volume from her hands with careful precision, cradling each one as though it were . . .

A child. A pang shot through Abby's heart, and she swallowed hard.

I can't think about that right now. I have to stay focused.

She moved to the middle shelf. The third book was large and heavy, but as her fingers touched the binding it slipped toward her, falling out into her hands as if on its own. It was an old volume, bound in soft-cover leather that must have once been bright red. The letters etched in gold on its surface had survived amazingly well. This was not a book often sought by patrons.

"*To the Harness Fraternity: the Art of Making Harness Successfully.*" She read the title aloud, but when she looked back over her shoulder at Jack, he was looking past her and staring at the place in the wall hidden behind the book she just removed.

"There it is," he murmured.

She turned and saw the tarnished brass keyhole set into the paneling of the wall above the shelf. Laying the book down with care on the table, Abby helped Jack slide the adjacent texts free. A small, square panel in the original oak was clearly visible, hinged at one end up tight against the wall, the locking mechanism set into the panel's right lower corner.

"Get the key, Abby," he urged.

She scurried out the door and swiped the key off the desk where it had fallen minutes before.

The key slid easily into its rightful place. He jiggled it, feeling along the edge of the opening with his free hand. Within seconds the lock clicked as though the tumblers had been freshly oiled. A square panel of wood swung open revealing a secret chamber.

The stale air drifting from the space made her think of old attics and musty trunks. The cubicle was barely a foot square, lined with the same dark wood paneling as the rest of the reference room. In its center lay a black box. Jack slid the box toward the edge, dust and grains of sawdust sprinkling out over the lip of the opening onto the shelf below. Lifting it, he turned and handed the box to her.

It was rectangular, roughly eight by twelve inches, and made of wood or pressed paper covered with old embossed fabric. An ornate golden clasp, one that could be opened with a simple flip of the finger, held it closed at one end.

On the lid, the same elaborate scrollwork that appeared on Isabelle's pen covered the upper and lower corners. The pattern appeared to have been embossed directly into the fabric, the tangle of vines and leaves raised from the surface. Intertwined with the floral pattern, almost hidden in its intricacy, she made out the same initials, in the same style as on Isabelle's pen:

I. L. H.

Abby set the box down on the reference room table and looked up. “I guess we found it,” she whispered.

Jack pulled out her chair, then sat beside her, the box on the table between them.

She stared at it for a minute, then blew out a breath. “You want me to open it?”

He nodded. “I think that since it’s been you who Elijah has been trying so hard to communicate with, you should be the one who unveils the secrets that have been hiding in that chamber for almost a hundred and fifty years.”

She locked her gaze with Jack’s for a long moment before she turned and opened the box. The top sheet of folded paper was thick vellum. The rough-textured leaf, bearing the same decorative pattern as the box, was yellowed along its edges. Saying nothing, she pointed to the insignia in the upper left-hand corner of the page where the letters *I L H* appeared, tangled within the leafy vines.

Jack murmured, “Elijah must have had all these things—the box, the pen, the stationary—made especially for Isabelle and brought them to her from Boston or New York. I don’t ever remember seeing anything this fancy that originated from this rural area.” His tone was soft, almost reverent.

She arranged the documents by date. Four letters, the first of which was enclosed in a yellowed envelope, was addressed to Mr. Jasper Laramy from Elijah Harvey and dated June 16, 1881. The other three, on velvety, elegant stationary, were tri-folded underneath.

Abby took a deep breath for courage, then cleared her throat and began to read.

Chapter 23

Abby and Jack sat in the reference room as night fell over the town and darkness draped the library in a silent shroud. The readings didn't take long, but may have been one of the most difficult tasks she had ever faced. The letters told the gripping, tragic love story of Isabelle Laramy and Elijah Harvey. By the time she finished reading the last letter, her throat was thick and her heart ached.

Now she knew why the spirit of Elijah remained trapped within these walls.

September 2, 1892

My Beloved Elijah,

Sadly, your illness has progressed far beyond the stage where my words have meaning to your ears. I record these words on paper in the hopes that somehow, by some divine intervention, my intentions will make their way decipherable into your befuddled brain, whether in this life or the next.

The days grow near that the child you and I have created will make his or her way into our world. I wonder how you will react to this new addition. Will you be happy or angry? Feel love for the seed of your loins? Or be smitten with hatred and jealousy of another living creature that will surely demand more of my attention?

My body is heavy with your child, and caring for you has become more difficult in my condition. In truth, the task is nearly impossible for me to shoulder alone. I have called upon your sister, Deirdre, to come here to Caldwell from your family home in Boston. I have asked her to assist me, at least for a short while after the birth of our child. I grieve at this, my failure, Elijah, for surely you would consider my weakness a shortcoming of perseverance. I hope that if you ever read the words I've written here, you will try to understand.

I record these words to no one and for no other reason than to have them waiting should you ever awaken from your blissful—and sometimes not so blissful—ignorance of reality as we know it, to read and understand what resides in my heart.

I hope to give you a son, Elijah. I hope to provide an heir to carry on the name of your family, to rise up strong and smart and willing to take your place in the great and complex family you will leave behind, though I never got to know any of them, nor them me. Regardless, I hope to deliver into our lives a healthy child as living proof of the everlasting love we share.

At your advanced age, I'm sure no one ever expected you would beget an heir. It is our sacred secret, defying your illness, defying time. Yet now, I realize that due to your condition and my undeniable fruitfulness, I will be scrutinized and questioned as to my faithfulness. Please know that my heart and body and soul have been none but yours since the day we first met. Your mind, your memories are gone. Your body, as though acting in ignorance of your brain, continues to seek me still in the darkness of the pre-dawn. How could I ever deny you?

I love you, Elijah, with every fiber of my being.

I pray God will grant me the strength to bear your child with noble courage, raise him or her with solemn purpose and in proper dignity suiting your name and your family, in a manner that would make you proud. Even though in my heart I now face the sorrowful truth that you may never recognize the child I will bear is, truly, your own.

Forever Yours,

Belle

Swiping at tears now flowing freely down her cheeks, Abby whispered, “Elijah doesn’t know she’s dead, does he?”

Jack sighed. “Until now, I don’t think he did. They hadn’t named it Alzheimer’s yet, but the doctors knew the prognosis. They called it senile dementia. Apparently it came down pretty fast on Elijah.”

“I wonder if she told him she was carrying his child.”

Jack shook his head. “It sounds from her letters that his mind was too far gone for him to understand. It must have been terrible for her, facing it all alone, taking care of him, the library, planning for their baby.”

“She must have been lonely, or she wouldn’t have written those letters to no one. Her only way to vent,” Abby said. She stared down at the letters before her and cocked her head. “Why do you think Elijah couldn’t get to these before? He can open windows and toss books all about, even screw with the lights and the clock. Why didn’t he know where the letter box was?”

Jack’s gaze slid to the key lying on the table beside the letters. “I guess he didn’t have the key.”

“Do you think he knows now?” she asked.

“I guess we’ll see.”

The next morning, Jack wasn’t sure if it was his intrigue with the mystery of Elijah Harvey or his refusal to give up on Abby that drew him into town. She told him she would be going in early to clean up the mess, assess the damage, and re-shelve the books. He sensed at the time she wanted him to say he’d be there to help her. Still, he held back.

That last night at his cabin, she made her intentions perfectly clear. If he continued offering his heart to Abigail Stryker, he was likely bound for the same, if not worse heartbreak than he'd suffered with Dawn.

I'm a historian, he kept telling himself as he drove. These findings, the letters from Isabelle, and the story of a 19th century case of what had since been identified as Alzheimer's disease, were too important to shun. *Even to protect my ego, my pride. My once again shattered dreams.*

He tried not to admit it to himself. But even if their relationship could never be more than friendship, he couldn't bear the thought of letting go of Abby completely.

When he reached the city limits, he tried to call Dennis on his cell. No answer. How badly had Leda been hurt by the battering she suffered that night? And why she was the one who incited such rage in the ghost?

The ghost had been capable of messing with the lights, opening a locked window, and wafting pipe smoke about at will. He'd also tossed a book now and then at the two librarians Dennis tried to hire before Abby. Even once at her in the beginning. Nothing as physically harmful as the vicious attack they witnessed on Leda. It didn't seem to make any sense. As he drove, Jack started flipping through the events of the past six months in his mind, trying to decipher the facts into some logical sequence.

Dana Laramy had run the place for almost thirty years, and there had been no hint of unusual occurrences. The library had been just another boring, outdated local icon, fading gradually into the same aging monotone as the personality of Ms. Laramy herself. It was Dana's brother, Jasper, who ran the antique shop across the street right up until the day he died. Martin took over the shop back in the early spring—part of the spoils from his late father's will.

The whole town had been shocked since Martin hadn't been back to Caldwell in years. He'd been living in

Manhattan in some fancy high-rise apartment, hired on by Sotheby's when he was eighteen. No one could understand why he would give up his lucrative life in the big city to come to sleepy Caldwell. He had to be at least ten or more years away from retirement.

Everyone assumed, therefore, that the will must have included a healthy sum of money.

Dana announced her retirement soon after Jasper's death. She was already well into her sixties. A spinster, she was a strange, quiet woman about whom the locals knew little, even though she'd lived in Caldwell all her life.

Had she been involved with Dianne's Wiccan group somehow, wielding their help to keep the feisty ghost under control all those years? Jack dismissed the notion as he made the last turn onto Main Street. Dianne would surely have mentioned that when they had their big pow-wow last week.

And he knew his boss pretty well. Leda had always been an ambitious woman, yet had never shown the radical signs of hatefulness or instability she had in the past six months or so. That had started right around the time Dana announced her retirement. Right about the same time Martin came to town. Right around the time he inherited the antique shop along with a healthy sum of money on which to retire, apparently quite comfortably.

Not many people were aware Leda and Martin were siblings. It was one of Caldwell's best-kept secrets. The only reason Jack knew was because he'd dug around in so much local history over the years.

When Jack parked in front of the library, Abby was standing on the steps, deep in conversation with Dennis Ludwig. Her features were twisted with extreme emotion.

Oh God. I hope Leda hasn't taken a turn for the worse.

Jack hurried up the steps, trying to decipher information from the expression on Abby's face.

She smiled, though weakly, when she saw him. “Hey Jack. Leda’s okay, I guess. They’ve transferred her to Charlotte. She’s going to get some help.”

Dennis offered his hand to Jack. “Jack, I don’t know what to say to you except thank you, and I’m sorry.”

He looked ten years older than the last time Jack had seen him. His pallor was gray, glowing paler still against the whiteness of his hair. There were purplish half-moons under his eyes as though someone had double slugged him with a pair of brass knuckles. When Jack grasped his hand, it was eerily cold.

“Why are you sorry, Dennis? I just wish there was more we could have done to prevent this whole thing from happening.”

Dennis held up his hand. “I can’t explain what’s going on inside this building. It frightens me. I was about to tell Abby I’ve made a decision. Nobody else is getting hurt here.” He turned toward her, his frown drooping even lower. “I’m shutting the building down, hon. I called an emergency telephone conference with the board, and they’ve approved paying you six weeks severance. I’m sorry I dragged you here for an ill-fated pipe dream. I’m afraid trying to keep this place open after Dana retired was a bad idea. My bad idea. I’m sorry, Abby. I’ll need your key.”

Her face contorted further, transforming rapidly from an expression of disbelief to anguish to one of pleading hope. “Dennis, no, you don’t have to do that. Jack and I figured it out. Last night. He and I found the letters Elijah’s been looking for all along.”

The commissioner was shaking his head, both hands stuffed into the pockets of his trousers, scuffing the toe of his shoe against the threshold. “Abby, you and Jack, and I guess your Aunt Dianne too—you all believe this ghost, or whatever you want to call it is the spirit of this library’s founder. This Elijah fellow. I’m not one to believe in ghosts. There’s got to be a logical explanation for all the strange things that have been going on since Dana retired. Call me closed-minded," he cocked an eyebrow, wearing an apologetic smirk, "but I honestly don't think there's any ghost."

Jack took hold of his arm. "I don't believe in ghosts either. At first I thought Abby was out of her mind. Or a witch, maybe." His eyes shifted to hers with wariness. When he saw no flash of anger, he continued, "I honestly think we've figured this thing out. Please, come inside and let us show you what we discovered last night."

"The place is still a holy mess," Abby said, digging in her bag for the key, "but you won't believe what we found."

As the library door swung open, beams of golden, morning light flooded the entryway. Jack followed a step behind Abby, who led Dennis gently by the arm as though he were blind or scared to death of stepping inside.

For a brief moment, Jack felt blind too. The brilliance of the sun outside shadowed the interior of the building into hazy darkness. And he smelled the pipe smoke the minute he stepped over the threshold.

As she reached to snap on the overhead lights, he heard her gasp.

Not one book lay on the floor, from the reception area clear back to the rear wall. As though some miraculous maintenance crew had busied themselves through the night, the library was neat and orderly, as tidy and proper as after any final walk-through Abby had ever made. His eyes flashed to the clock. Its hands lay peacefully in the proper alignment, indicating the correct time of 9:02 a.m. Yet when his gaze passed the desk to the reading corner, he noted the window stood open a full twelve inches.

She turned in wonder to him. "Did you come back here last night? Did you clean all this up for me?"

He started shaking his head before she could finish the

question. "How could I, Abby? We left here less than eight hours ago. I don't have a key."

Dennis raised his head and sniffed. "There's that smell again." He started backing up toward the door. "I think we all need to get out of here, Abby. I can't afford for anyone else to get hurt."

"No, Dennis. Nobody else is going to get hurt. Here," she said, motioning to the reference room. The letters still lay scattered across the polished table surface. She took a step toward the doorway. "Let us show you what we found. Isabelle's letters."

It took some coaxing, but Dennis eventually consented to take a seat at the table beside them. She showed him the ornate black box and pointed up at the place in the wall where they found it.

"It was right behind this old book on harness making," she said.

Dennis nodded, heaving out a sigh. "That's probably not a coincidence. The old antique shop across the street used to be a harness shop, back in the 1800s. The Laramys were evidently pretty famous harness makers."

"The old skeleton key we bought from Martin Laramy opened the lock on the hidden safe, Dennis," Jack said. "That's where we found the box of letters."

He listened as Abby explained their tale to Dennis, who remained silent. The look on his face told Jack he thought they were both crazy, though he listened patiently, his tired eyes intent on hers.

"Thirty-five years? There were thirty-five years between them?" He swiped his hand down over his face. "Christ, I hope Elijah had a better handle on his wife's ambitions than I have on mine."

Jack's gaze slid to hers briefly, then quickly away.

"He must have, Dennis." Her tone was soft. "She took care of him even after he couldn't remember who she was."

Dennis dropped his head back, studying the tin ceiling. "A ghost. You two young folks are trying to convince me there's actually a ghost haunting this library."

Abby nodded and glanced at Jack. In her eyes, he read her plea for support.

"There's no other explanation for it, Dennis," he said. "If you read these letters, it makes perfect sense. Elijah may have been thirty-five years older than Isabelle, yet he actually outlived her by ten years. She died in childbirth. When she died, his mind was so far gone with Alzheimer's, he didn't even know who she was. He passed ten years later, unaware his beloved wife had gone before him."

Abby grasped Dennis' hand. "Elijah has been waiting here for Isabelle all this time."

Dennis stared at her, shaking his head. Then his gaze shifted from Abby to Jack. "Professor Jack Wood, I have a lot of respect for you. For your education and your integrity. So I'm gonna play along here for a minute or two. This ghost, this Elijah. Why do you think he hates my Leda so much?"

Jack clasped his hands on the table. "Dennis, isn't Leda a Laramy?"

Dennis hesitated, looking down into his lap. Then he sighed as he replied. "Yes. Yes, she is. Martin—you know the guy who runs the antique shop across the street? Well, that's her brother." He spoke the words so quietly Jack almost couldn't hear him. As though he were ashamed to admit what he was saying.

He cleared his throat, sensing Dennis' embarrassment. "It seems there were no reports of anything unusual in the library until after Dana Laramy retired. Dana is, what, Leda's aunt?"

The other man nodded. "She was old man Laramy's sister. When Jasper passed on last year, that's when Dana started talking about retiring. And that was after the reading of the will."

A silence settled over them in the still air of the small room. Jack could see how uncomfortable Dennis was talking about this. He glanced sidelong at Abby, who sat silent and wide-eyed.

"Dennis, we only want to help here," he said. "Of course, it's important for Abby to keep her job. But there's more to it than that, and you know it. I'm all about preserving local history. This place is a wellspring. If we lose the library, Caldwell will lose a big chunk of its heritage."

The commissioner thudded both elbows on the table. He sighed and dropped his head into his hands. "I know, I know. That's why I've been pushing so hard to keep it going myself. Something . . . happened, to Leda. After they read that will."

Abby touched his sleeve. "What was in the will, Dennis? What about it upset Leda so much?"

The moment stretched out so long and silent Jack wondered if Dennis was going to answer Abby. Finally, he spoke.

"Right after old man Laramy's funeral, they called a meeting. It was Leda and me and Dana, and Martin flew in from New York. We all met with the family attorney, down in Hickory. There was a million and a half in trust money. The will clearly stated it was to be split three ways—one-third to Dana, the other two-thirds between Jasper's children, Leda and Martin.

"The stipulations were concise. In order to get the money, Martin had to take over the antique shop and run it for at least five years. Leda had to work at the library for the same time period." He looked up at Jack, his brow folding into tense lines. "I guess it was a pretty strict family tradition. Ever since Elijah Harvey built the library for his wife over a hundred and fifty years ago, it's been run by the Laramy women."

Jack cocked an eyebrow and tilted his head. "I'm assuming Leda wasn't happy about that stipulation?"

A peal of laughter burst from Dennis as he sat back and lifted his chin. "Oh no, there was no way Leda Ludwig was going to run any run-down, outdated, useless old library. She'd just gotten the dean's chair at the college, and the new library there was about ready to open."

Abby asked, "So, what happened to her share of the inheritance money? Did she lose it?"

He shook his head, pinching the bridge of his nose between two fingers. "Not exactly. Her third is floating in limbo. She's got one of the best attorneys in Charlotte working on overturning the will. Apparently there is some fine print clause in it that says if the Harvey Library is no longer operational, the remaining trust money will be applied to the nearest functioning library. That, of course, would be the one at the college.

"But ever since then, since the reading of that will, Leda . . . my Leda . . ." He shook his head sadly. "She's been . . . changing, getting more aggressive and less rational day by day. At first I tried to ignore it. I wrote it off as frustration and disappointment about the inheritance. Then her behavior deteriorated, developed into something way bigger. Leda has become nothing short of obsessed with seeing this library fail and close down."

Sudden understanding lit up Abby's face. "That's why Elijah hates Leda so much. That's why he's spooked every new librarian who's come in here."

Dennis locked eyes with her. "That seems to be true. Why then . . ." He paused, raising his brows. "Why has he taken such a shine to you?"

Blinking, she sat back. She swallowed, and Jack could tell she was fighting back tears.

He answered for her. "I think Elijah Harvey believes two important facts about Abigail Stryker. First, how much she loves and appreciates this place, the building, and all the precious old volumes in it. And second," he squeezed Abby's hand, "Elijah knows Abby and I were determined to find out why his spirit is still imprisoned within these walls. Maybe we can find a way to free him."

They walked Dennis to the door, and he shook both their hands as he said, "I'm going to give you both one more shot at this thing. I don't understand it. I'm not sure I believe in it. But if you think you can free Elijah's spirit and make this library a safe place for the public to visit again, I'm willing to let you try."

Chapter 24

The door clicked shut, and Jack studied Abby's face.

She crossed her arms and asked, "What now? We've got the letters. We think Elijah has been waiting here, looking for Isabelle. Do you think he knows now she's not here? That she's gone ahead of him?"

Jack took a step forward, wanting so badly to hold her. But seeing Dawn again reopened his wound, reminding him of how much he stood to lose. He steeled himself, willing his arms to drop to his sides.

Abby had made herself perfectly clear. He could not, would not, allow himself to fall into that emotional mire again. With Dawn, he had an excuse. He'd been young, inexperienced, and distracted. None of those excuses applied anymore.

"I don't know, Abby. The letters have been out in the open all night. Yet we all smelled pipe smoke when we came in. And he opened the window. At least as of early this morning, we have to assume Elijah Harvey's spirit is still here."

They stood for a long, awkward moment in the doorway of the reference room. She twisted her shoulders as if working out a kink, but avoided his gaze.

He waited, but for what he wasn't sure. Stay focused on the task at hand, he chastised himself. *Keep this strictly professional*.

"I guess all we can do now is to wait. Is there anything else you'd like me to do before I leave?" He tried hard to sound casual, nonchalant, when the whole time his heart was writhing inside his chest. How could this not be right, he wondered? *How could I have fallen so hard, so wrong again*?

She turned her head away, her arms wrapped tightly around her. Her body language spoke more clearly than he wanted to believe. Sadly, the truth was plainly evident.

Abigail Stryker was a closed book. As many books as he'd opened in his life, he'd never wanted so badly to open one. With her, that power was beyond his control.

"No. Thank you for staying with me, Jack. Thank you for helping me find the letters." Her words were soft, spoken with a kind of neutrality she might have paid to any casual acquaintance. An interchange at the market. A chance meeting with someone new at the book club.

Her indifference sliced through his heart.

"I hear you're back with Dawn," she said, her voice so small he almost didn't hear her.

"What? Who the hell told you that?" he barked.

Small towns. You almost can't go to the bathroom without someone reminding you the paper roll was low.

"It's all right, Jack. I understand. She's a lot more mature than I am, probably ready to settle down now." Abby turned and met his gaze. The tears glistening in her eyes made his gut wrench.

"Abby, Killer Dawn may be a few years older than you, but more mature? Really? Worldly is the word I'd use. And certainly not in a good way." He shook his head, his mouth tasting sour. "Do you honestly think I could forgive what that woman did? Do you think I could ever trust her again?" He shoved his hands in his pockets and paced.

"It *was* her, though, wasn't it? What's she doing here?"

He snorted. "She's already gone. Just a convenient stop on a business trip. She left the Metropolitan Museum. Works for Sotheby's now. Not enough excitement as a museum curator, I guess. She's hit the road for her own personal Antiques Road Show." He paused and heaved a deep sigh. "She's been stalking me for about six months. Online, anyway. Guess she's decided her ovaries are about ready to dry up and thought maybe I'd be willing to act as sperm donor again."

Abby glared at him over her shoulder. "Did she actually ask you that?"

"No." He stopped pacing and let out a long breath. "She was casting though. Made it pretty clear she's had enough of playing single girl in the city and wants to try something new. Maybe the life of wife and mommy doesn't look so bad to her now after all. She figured I might be up for another go-round." His chuckle was dark. "Fat chance."

"Jack?" She had turned to face him head on with a penetrating gaze that made his chest tighten. "Do you still love her?"

How could she honestly wonder that?

He erased the distance between them with two long strides, then stopped short, less than an arm's reach away. He wanted so badly to embrace her, whisper words of love into her hair. Yet she was standing so rigidly, never making eye contact for less than a millisecond at a time. He couldn't bear to open his heart again and have her slam the door in his face.

But she dropped her arms to her sides. No longer clenched around her. Perhaps not a completely closed book.

"Abby, I'm not sure I ever loved her. I had no concept of what love was then." He lifted a hand toward her, and she didn't back away. He laid his fingers on her arm, trailing them along her skin. "I do now."

She blinked, and a fat tear slid down her cheek. He caught her chin in his hand and brushed the tear away with his thumb. "Don't do that, Abby. You melt when you cry."

His throat tightened, his next words thick and gruff. "And it melts me too."

Tentatively, Abby met Jack's gaze. His sage green eyes climbed into hers, offering without words a vow more precious than breath. An electric shock zinged through her.

Never had any man—any*one*—looked at her this way. It took her breath away, scrambling her thoughts and tilting the very ground on which she stood.

In that instant, a flash of light slashed the air above them, like headlights through a dark window. But it was broad daylight. And the spark was more brilliant, as if a sunray splintered through a crystal. They both jumped, and Abby shrank closer to him.

"What was that?" she whispered.

He didn't have time to reply.

A second later, wind blasted through the building with such intensity she let out a screech. Whining gusts tore through the lobby. With the whirling strength of a tornado, energy swirled around them, pushing them together with such force, his arms instinctively closed around her. She buried her face against his shoulder.

"What's happening?" she wailed, her words swept away the moment they left her lips.

"Look," he said against her ear, pointing toward the reference room. "Belle's letters."

Whipping through the air in a confused frenzy, Isabelle's letters took flight. They rose into the small space like a flock of panicked white pigeons. Frozen with fear and filled with disbelief, Abby clung to Jack as the pages came to life. Mimicking paper soldiers, they arranged themselves into a line.

The floating letters began a single-file journey out of the room in a path toward the rear window. He ducked as one sheet passed so close by his head, she feared it might catch in his hair. As he raised his hand against it, the paper dissolved in a wisp of smoke.

Within seconds, the letters congregated in the rear corner, fluttering over the reading nook. Then, as suddenly as it had begun, the wind tunnel around them died, although the letters continued to float gently in a circle above the chair.

Afraid to move, she clung to Jack, and he tightened his grip around her.

Between one blink and the next, the figures appeared, dreamlike and semi-translucent. Seated in the reading chair, a beautiful woman flickered into view. She was dressed in brilliant blue, a Victorian style gown made of something shiny, satin or silk, and lavishly adorned with white lace. Her dark hair wound around her crown in a labyrinth of curls. She gazed down at a pink-swaddled bundle in her arms, and she was smiling.

Abby was sure she'd lost her mind.

Until Jack murmured into her ear, "It's Isabelle."

So he can see her too.

Her chest aching, Abby watched as the woman crooned to the infant with words she could not hear. A powerful emotion washed over her, bringing fresh tears, but this time not from fear or sorrow. The glow surrounding Isabelle infused the air with blinding beauty, a sort she'd never imagined.

Something inside Abby's chest shifted and moved. The ice binding her heart shattered, crumbling and melting away. She blinked and sucked in a deep breath at the sudden, almost painful sensation.

So this is love.

In the next blink, another figure entered the scene—a broad-shouldered man in a pinstriped suit. In one hand, he held a pipe, but with his back to her, she couldn't see his face. Still, she knew.

Elijah.

He crossed the few feet from where he'd manifested to where Isabelle sat, and she lifted her face to gaze at him. Tears streamed down Isabelle's cheeks.

Do ghosts cry too?

He dropped to one knee before his wife, capturing her free hand in his and bringing it to his lips. With a tentative finger, he stroked the infant's cheek. Time stood still for a long moment as a silent bond was somehow restored.

Abby realized this man was seeing, for the first time, their newborn daughter.

"Oh my god," she whispered, choking back a sob. "He finally found them."

Gradually, the scene faded, like a dream into a foggy haze. Just before the wind recommenced.

Isabelle's letters paled into translucence. One by one, they fluttered out the open window, dissolving as they passed through what Abby guessed was a portal to another dimension.

When the last one disappeared, all was still. Then the smoke drifted in, aromatic with the cherry undertones she recalled so distinctly. It swirled all around them in a cloud, thick and visible. Then, just as quickly it, too, faded.

A sharp sound broke the silence and they both jumped. Squealing on its sash, the open window crept down.

"They're leaving," she whispered. "Finally, they're together again."

Slithering in jerky spurts, the window dropped lower, inch-by-inch until the frame slid home with a squeak. The brass latch clicked as it locked, all by itself.

They stood frozen in place for a long moment until Abby felt Jack's fingers under her chin. She turned to face him.

Her strong mountain man didn't look so strong at the moment, his face wet with tears, dark smudges under his eyes, and furrows etched deep between his brows. He looked human and weak and vulnerable. He looked like a man who'd been broken.

How could I have done this to him?

In a strangled voice, he choked out, "Theirs was a love that stood the test of time. Against the most impossible odds. Thanks to you, Abigail, they're together again. Forever."

She shook her head. "Not without you, Jack. I could never have fit all the pieces of the puzzle together without you. We did this together."

His eyes had gone dark, and she held his gaze with her own. She felt strong and steady and open for the first time. The connection between them was undeniable and more powerful than any she'd ever imagined.

There it was, right in front of her. It had been there all along. How could she have been so blind?

This was love, speaking to her in a silent language she finally understood. Her heart swelled with the sensation, one so strange and so new, she was dizzy and giddy. Laying one hand on his heart, she smiled.

"Elijah—and Belle—gave me a priceless gift of thanks. They've shown me what love is. And given my heart the courage to embrace it, return it. Your love." She tangled her fingers into his curls. "I love you, Jack. I hope I'm not too late."

His lids fluttered for a heartbeat, and he tipped back his head as if in silent prayer. When he opened them again, he tucked one strand of hair behind her ear before folding her into his arms. "Not too late, my love. Never too late."

He brushed his mouth over hers, and her lips sought his in a soulful kiss. Joy rose up inside her and spilled over.

Their kiss was sensual, yes, but tender too. Finally, and for the first time, more than just Abby's body reacted to Jack's touch.

The spirit of Harvey Library's ghost was free. And so was she.

They stood wrapped in each other's embrace for what seemed like eternity, yet when they finally broke apart, she noticed how the clock on the wall ticked on, methodically, at the right speed and in the right direction. Time was moving forward, and she wasn't about to waste another minute alone or afraid, or without the man she loved in her life.

She grabbed his hand and tugged him toward the door. "Take me home, Jack. Make wild, passionate love to me, then let's start making plans for our future. Together."

Epilogue

One Year Later

Dianne sat, comfy in her rocker on the front porch of Ancient Healings, flipping through the latest edition of *Sage Woman* magazine. A bead of perspiration tickled her cheek as it slithered southward.

Awfully warm for the middle of June. Thank heavens for this breeze.

The echoes of children's voices from up the street drew her attention.

Story hour must be over. And today must be treat day.

A stream of children, ranging from staggering toddlers to giggling first graders, spilled down the steps of the Harvey and formed a colorful brigade as they traipsed around toward the rear of the building. At last month's council meeting, Di proposed the city provide the library with picnic tables. Two weeks later, four new pine tables surrounded the shady base of the old tree flanking its northeast corner.

When she saw Jack's SUV pull over to the curb, she figured he could probably use a hand.

"Vera, watch the store for a few, will you?" she called through the screen.

"Got it covered, Di. My next client isn't due for a half-hour."

Business had been good since the library's revival. There were so many requests for Tarot readings, Vera came in three days a week now. Even old Laramy's Antiques was thriving. Martin cleaned the place up, clearing a space big enough in the back for several rows of folding chairs. He held auctions on alternate Friday nights.

By the time Dianne reached Jack's car, he'd already delivered one platter of cookies and was headed back. She grabbed the two gallons of milk, balanced one in the crook of her arm, then reached for the sweet tea.

"Hey, Di. Gee, thanks. If things keep up like this I'm gonna have to rent a van one day a month." He grinned and bent to kiss her cheek.

"Those smell divine," she said as he lifted the remaining platter.

They carried the treats to the picnic tables. She spotted Abby chatting with Elena, who struggled to balance her wriggling son on her hip. Lexi broke free from the group and ran toward her uncle.

"What kind did you make us this time, Uncle Jack? Chocolate chip? Pleeeeze say chocolate chip." She bounced around his knee like a rambunctious puppy.

He shook his head. "Oatmeal raisin this time. Aunt Abby had a powerful craving for oatmeal raisin."

Dianne caught his glance and wink. She set the drinks on the table and went over to give Abby a hug.

What a different girl than the one who moved in over my shop just a year ago.

Her niece no longer wore black. Today, her purple and white floral sundress billowed around her in the breeze. Her hair was growing out, and she no longer dyed it. Sunlight picked glints of gold and red out of her natural mahogany. And the cut was no longer crooked. Her bob curved evenly under her chin in a satiny sheet.

"Hey, Auntie. What'd you do, smell the oatmeal from all the way up the street?"

Dianne bobbed her head. "You betcha. I'd walk a lot further than half a block for just one of Jack's homemade oatmeal raisin cookies." She snagged one off the heaping platter, then snatched another. "Maybe two." She grinned and took a bite.

Her niece had moved out of the tiny efficiency apartment last fall, about two months before her and Jack's Christmas wedding. Abby wanted to keep the event small, but considering the size of Jack's family, along with Di's Wiccan network, that had been virtually impossible. The entire dining room of Le Petit Mon couldn't accommodate the guest list. So for their wedding gift, she and Armand rented the Evergreen Room at the Chetola Resort in Blowing Rock.

Whenever Di remembered that night, she got teary eyed. Abby and Jack said their vows under an arbor covered with holly boughs and poinsettia blooms with a crackling fire roaring in the stone hearth in the background. The bride wore a simple, white satin gown banded around her tiny waist with a red satin sash.

Abby had teased Jack that she would keep looking until she found a tweed tuxedo, but he looked equally handsome in forest green with a red tie and cummerbund.

Dianne blubbered through the entire ceremony.

Monica wanted badly to be there, but sent her regrets from Aspen, where she and Davin had taken his son on a skiing trip for the holidays. Miss Cornwell, her spiky pink hair topped with a delicate silver wreath, arrived on the arm of her son, Jonathan. Where they'd gotten a suit to fit the man, no one was quite sure. Sitting right beside them was Martin Laramy, decked out in his finest white shirt and tartan plaid tie.

Even Leda and Dennis Ludwig were there.

After months of counseling, Leda returned to her dean's chair, but left her position on the council. Instead, she worked two nights a week at the Harvey Library. She'd actually volunteered to take over while Abby was on maternity leave.

Of course, that was enough to ensure her stake in the family trust fund, but Leda really had changed. Di wasn't sure what kind of medication she was on, or whether they'd performed a lobotomy, but the evil side of woman had disappeared. Exorcised. Gone as dramatically and completely as the library's ghost. And Dennis looked younger and happier than he had in years.

While Dianne filled paper cups for the children, Jack settled next to Abby at the adjacent table. When she heard her niece squeak from behind her, milk sloshed everywhere. She spun around.

"What is it, dear? Are you okay?"

Abby's one hand lay protectively over her rounded tummy, her other fingers touching her open lips. Her wide eyes glistened.

Jack had jolted to his feet and was bending over his wife. "What's wrong, hon?" Worry bunched his brows.

She smiled up at him and whispered, "Either I swallowed a giant butterfly, or our baby just moved."

He closed his eyes and brought her hand to his heart. Then he kissed her cheek, knelt beside her on the grass, and rested his forehead against her belly.

Di blinked and fought to swallow the huge lump in her throat. "The little one is as excited about her daddy's oatmeal cookies as I am," she sputtered. She grabbed a napkin off the table and blotted her eyes.

Here I go again. Just like at the wedding.

CPSIA information can be obtained at www.ICGtesting.com
Printed in the USA
BVOW06s2132310716

457482BV00021B/138/P